LEGACY OF HATE

Anne Hampson

PIP
POLLINGER IN PRINT

Pollinger Limited
9 Staple Inn
Holborn
LONDON
WC1V 7QH

www.pollingerltd.com

First published by Minerva Press 1999
This edition published by Pollinger in Print 2007

The moral right of the author has been asserted

A CIP catalogue record is available from the British Library

ISBN 978-1-905665-62-4

LEGACY OF HATE

Author's Note

This work of fiction, based on fact, provides a picture of what life was like in the Isle of Man in the seventeenth century, but its main theme is that of the bitter feud which existed between the powerful Clan Christian of Milntowne and the two Stanleys, seventh and eighth Earls of Derby, ruling Lords of Man. It is the saga of an heroic struggle for freedom from tyranny, with one side seeking only justice and liberty, and the other imperiously refusing even to compromise.

When embarking on the production of a novel with an historical background I naturally expected to be involved in much in-depth research; what I had not reckoned on was the frustration caused by the inaccuracies, omissions and ambiguity of many historians, and also their seeming reluctance to write anything derogatory about the noble House of Stanley. So many questions for which I could find no answers, so many conflicting reports, so many discrepancies of dates. And perhaps more important, the paucity of information on the characters who were to predominate in my story. Such situation necessitated inventions and conjecture in excess of my original intention. However, I wish to stress that facts have been strictly adhered to as I found them in my research; there certainly has been no 'playing ball with facts and dates' as came from the unforgivable pen of Sir Walter Scott who, in Peveril of the Peak, not only muddled up the characters and their actions, but branded the Manx National Hero and other dedicated patriots as 'ruffians of a family called Christian who behaved in a barbarous manner to the noble House of Stanley'. The travesty created through this lack of research was deeply resented by the outraged descendants of the heroes, and in fact by the entire Manx nation. Nor did it help when, on being chastised by John Christian a few years after the publication of the book, Scott said he found the complaints 'fantastic' and added that it was his right to alter the truth.

A Manxophile since I first visited the isle when I was sixteen, I have always been interested in its early Viking history, so if was only when I bought a house which I discovered had been part of the vast Milntowne estate of the Christian family, that I went into the history of that family in some depth. The main characters that emerged were Edward and William, cousins of Deemster Ewan Christian X of Milntowne, and another William (Illiam Dhône who became the Manx National Hero) the Deemster's youngest son, all of whom were staunch patriots, undaunted by persecution, dedicated to relieving the wretchedness of the poor, fighting against the arbitrary imposition of taxes by the Lord and the Clergy. Two of these patriots suffered long terms of imprisonment at the hands of the seventh Earl, and the other death at the hands of the eighth Earl.

The victims of incessant raids by Scots, Irish and others who came by sea to plunder: their little island frequently tossed from one indifferent English Monarch to his current favourite, the Manx of the lower classes had deteriorated into a submissive, sullenly dispirited race, so perhaps there could be a modicum of truth in the assertions of some historians that their lot was improved by the coming of John Stanley to whom the island was given by King Henry IV early in the fifteenth century. Certainly some kind of defence was established, because raids became less frequent, although they did not cease altogether.

Throughout the fifteenth and sixteenth centuries the Stanleys were too occupied with accumulating great wealth – gifts from kings whose favourites they had become, usually through guile and craft but sometimes by threats – to give much thought to their little sea-girt kingdom, except, of course, as a source of revenue with which to keep the Stanley coffers overflowing.

This amassing of wealth in the form of manors in Lancashire and Cheshire, and vast tracts of land in Ireland, laid the foundation of one of the most important families in England.

But in the midst of this prosperity came the circumstance which was to change the history of the Isle of Man and cause much hardship to its people. The fourth Earl's death was followed only a few months later by that of his son and heir, Ferdinando, leaving a younger son, William, to inherit the title but no great wealth to go with it, as Ferdinando left three infant daughters, and although William engaged himself in a prolonged lawsuit, Alice of Althorp, Ferdinando's widow, achieved success over William's claim in her fight for her children's rights. William, therefore inherited an impoverished Earldom, with the Isle of Man eventually being settled on him. The lavish lifestyle indulged in by all the former Stanleys was no longer possible.

It was William's son, Lord Strange and later the seventh Earl, who, crossing to the isle when he was a mere youth of nineteen, announced drastic changes in the land tenures. He maintained that all land belonged to him as Lord of Man. These lands had been held by the Christians for hundreds of years, passing in a direct line from father to son, and held by the ancient Tenure of the Straw.

This tenure would be replaced by a lease for three lives, decided Strange. Any man who refused to sign this lease would be instantly evicted. Some of the smaller landowners signed, in a panic, but the Christians and others refused and the feud that had begun as a mere flicker generations before, was fanned into a flame that was to bring many years of strife to the island.

Alongside the land question ran the other major issue: the despotism of the Lord in his dealings with the poor which produced the three Christians mentioned who championed the cause of the ordinary Manx people, whose misery was increased by the intolerable oppression of the Church and about which the Lord did nothing because many of the benefices came directly to him.

Although it was Illiam Dhône who was to become the National Hero – because he died for the cause – it is Edward Christian who emerges as the most outstanding Manxman of his time. Daring pirate, Merchant Adventurer, Captain in the Royal Navy, Governor of the island then Commander of the Insular Militia, reformer, patriot and rebel. Like the more wily and subtle Deemster Ewan, his cousin, he was ever a thorn in the side of James, seventh Earl of Derby, whose stretching of feudal authority gave rise to increased unrest all over the island. But Derby had other problems. His help to Charles I in the form of five thousand soldiers and forty thousand pounds led to his being proclaimed a traitor by Parliament and what properties he did still own in Lancashire and Cheshire were sequestered. 'Groups assembling in a tumultuous manner' sent him back to the island with troops to quell the riot. He charged the Commander of the Militia with treason and Edward was sentenced to imprisonment for life in Peel Castle. And undoubtedly he would have served that sentence but for the invasion, eight years later, of Cromwell's forces which occupied the island until the return of the Monarchy. He was freed the same year as his hated enemy was beheaded as a traitor in the open square at Bolton. Ten years later Illiam Dhône was not so fortunate as his kinsman. Victim of the vicious desire for revenge on the part of the eighth Earl, he was illegally shot on Hango Hill within sight of his beloved Ronaldsway, once home of King Orry. Derby was severely punished by King Charles II for this murder.

Deemster Ewan was the only one who could stay the Stanleys' hand. What his hold over them was I have been unable to discover, but it an undisputed fact that but for his intervention Edward Christian would have been executed on the orders of James, the seventh Earl, of whom it has been written: 'He left a legacy of hate.'

While the Christians of Milntowne were the champions of the poor, rebels against the often irrational demands of the Lord, fighters for freedom by which they have come down in history as the staunchest patriots the island has ever known, they were by no means saints. I found Edward to have had a distinct dual personality, for while on the one hand he could fight against the tyranny of the supreme overlord, he in his role of minor overlord knew how to punish. Ears were cut off; floggings inflicted for small offences, and I found two occasions when, lusting after the wife of one of his labourers, he sent the husband to prison to get him out of the way. He trucked with pirates; he was into smuggling as were many of the islanders, and of course his plundering and pillaging exploits on the high seas in his youth, and his amassing a fortune at the expense of his employers, the East India Company, did take place.

But then, these Christians were direct descendants of Godred Crovan and his fierce Viking followers who had invaded and conquered the island several centuries before.

With the seventh Earl dying on the block, and his son dying relatively young from a long and painful illness, it would seem that the feud might end, but persecution of the Christians continued throughout the reign of the ninth Earl, resulting in many of them leaving to settle in Ireland or America. But the sufferings had not been in vain for in 1704 Deemster Ewan XIII of Milntowne and Unerigg, and two of his kin, negotiated the Act of Settlement – the Manx Magna Carta – which confirmed to the Manx: 'Their ancient customary estates of Inheritance in their respective Tenements, descendable from Ancestor to Heir according to the Laws and Customs of the Isle'. The Act, passed by the Keys was promulgated on the ancient Hill of Tynwald.

Up till now Fletcher has been the most famous of the Christians, but for me the most outstanding figure is Edward who was too popular a Governor, too powerful for the Earl's schemes, and even eight years in the formidable fortress of Peel Castle did not break his spirit.

All three were instrumental in bringing about the liberty, prosperity and peace which the Act of Settlement gave to the Isle of Man.

Son troo, farg as eulys ver mow dooinney erbee; As dty vasse, Illiam Dhône, te brishey nyn gree!

(For envy hate and malice will destroy any man; And thy murder brown-haired William wring our hearts!)

A refrain from one of the many Manx ballads written to the memory of William Christian of Milntowne, the Manx National Hero.

Anne Hampson
Poyll Dhouie Manor
Milntowne
Isle of Man

Chapter One

Don Felipe Ramires looked round the deck of the *Maria Pedrosa* and knew he had blundered when he threw down the gauntlet in a fit of hate and impetuosity.

Chaos everywhere: blood and bodies, sagging sail and rigging in holes. That cursed Manxman with Crovan's blood in his veins and the devil to protect him! The captain's fists clenched and his black eyes smouldered. Let the English ship come! His one obsession was still to capture the elusive Edward Christian and have him dangling at the end of a rope.

Groans behind him rose to screams of agony as he stood there, desperately trying to crush the pestilent insistence of his mind that he should surrender. He ought to have considered his noble passenger, she who, with her maid, the insignificant little English wench, was below, obeying his order to stay in the splendid stateroom. He shook his head. No, he would not surrender! And yet... Useless to deny they were in grave danger – the ship, the crew and the lovely Doña Clara, daughter of the illustrious Sanches Goncalo Adelina who had entrusted her into his care and to hand her over to the English duke to whom she was betrothed. Yes, he ought to have practised caution when the *Falcon* hove into sight. But he had not stopped to think, to remember that the accursed sea rover was notorious for his treatment of any woman he might capture. God, if he were to ravish the Spanish girl then he, Don Felipe, might as well throw himself overboard since he would never dare face her father.

If he surrendered, it could be on the condition that his charge be unmolested. Christian could take the English wench. Again Don Felipe shook his head. Even if his enemy made the promise there was no guarantee that he would keep it.

*

Through the scudding foam the *Falcon* plunged and ploughed, heading straight for the Spanish galleon, its captain's thick hair scuffed by the wind which was billowing the sails of the proud English vessel.

Edward Christian, ever aware of the Viking blood in his veins, had also the salt of the sea in his heart and at only fifteen he had been at the helm of a small ship heading out of the Port of Ramsey in the Isle of Mann. And now, at twenty-four he had had three years with the East India Company and was an expert at harassing the Spanish and Portuguese traders and plundering their ships.

After shouting an order he laughed as his guns began to belch, discharging their fire while the *Falcon* seemed to remain as serenely unscathed as its captain by the return fire from the defending Spanish vessel.

The *Falcon* came closer and Don Felipe bellowed out an order only to realise there was scarcely a man able to obey it. Cursing and shaking his fists, his bearded face twisted with fury and hate, he could only stand there in helpless frustration as, into the lull, came the mighty roar preceding the rush of flame and black smoke of the *Falcon*'s twenty-five guns whose target was the waist of the crippled ship. Then through the haze he could make out men armed with swords and boarding axes, eagerly awaiting an order from their master. And the cub would know exactly when to give that order! Don Felipe gritted his teeth as he heard a loud laugh, and he roared out another useless order. Blast his men for going down so easily! Let them writhe; it was only what they deserved.

Coming alongside, the *Falcon* raked the enemy ship with ruthless persistence which only ceased when at last the *Maria Pedrosa* was riddled, and bending under the strain. Exultation brought more laughter from the young captain whose raised hand was the signal for his men to board and within minutes they were swarming up the sides, using their axes as scaling ladders as they had done so many times before.

Despite his throbbing nerves and great fear for the safety of his charge, Don Felipe's eyes filled with contempt. What scurvy mongrels they were! Ruffians all, knives between their teeth, daggers and swords in their hands, faces greased with sweat and grime. They hadn't washed for weeks!

Standing at the head of the companion, sword at the ready, he searched for the hated Crovan's Cub, his obsession still that of seeing him dead. Don Felipe did not know how or when he had come to label him thus. Godred Crovan, mighty Norseman conqueror of the Isle of Mann just eleven years after William of Normandy had conquered England, had been dead and gone centuries ago – although his line had ruled in Mann for over three hundred years. And from that line had come the Christians, most powerful landowners on the island, and always bitter enemies of the Stanleys, Lords of Mann. It was a pity, mused Don Felipe, if in effect these Stanleys were kings of the island, that one of them had not ordered the confiscation of the lands which had for so long been a bone of contention between the two families.

Edward's men were still swarming up the sides while others had already sprung on to the *Maria Pedrosa*'s deck and were viciously attacking both the able-bodied of the Spanish sailors and the maimed. Havoc was wrought; the deck became a battleground of dead and dying as the Spaniards went down under the might of experienced, well-trained men under the command of an expert at the game.

Suddenly Don Felipe saw the man, separating himself from the melee down there. The tall, flaxen-haired Manxman had gained the companion and was gazing up at his adversary, blue eyes laughing, white teeth gleaming above the pointed beard, and the voice was loud and clear, the language Spanish as Edward Christian spoke.

"Do you fight, señor, or shall you offer surrender and save the lives of," he swung a hand to make a comprehensive gesture, "some of your men?"

But Don Felipe, protected by steel breastplate and morion, said he would fight.

"Folly, my friend," warned the Manxman, "but have it how you will."

"We shall soon see!"

Don Felipe supposed he had the advantage but had reckoned without the incredible speed of his opponent as, taking a leap which easily covered the first steps, he parried to thrust aside the Spaniard's sword, giving himself time to gain the quarterdeck. Blades clashed, but Don Felipe's failure to curb his fury at the Manxman's clever manoeuvre proved to be his downfall. He slashed out wildly even while being forced to retreat from the more controlled onslaught which very soon had him beaten. One of his men sprang at Edward, who might have been taken unawares but his own lieutenant, seeing the danger, thrust his dagger into the other man's raised arm.

Edward regarded Don Felipe for a long moment before saying, in English this time,

"Delaney will attend to that wound, señor. It is not serious – a mere scratch, in fact. Then you will be locked in your quarters."

He paused as the Spaniard's mouth tightened, and waited for what he had to say. But whatever it was, Don Felipe changed his mind and Edward added, "You are my prisoner, though what I am to do with you I cannot think. Perhaps I should have cut off your head and thrown you and it to the sharks."

"You pirate!" snarled Don Felipe, removing his morion. "I shall live to see you hanged yet!"

"Perhaps I shall not let you live. I believe I have a mind to curtail these aggressive activities once and for all." A small sigh escaped him. "What in the devil's name made you attack? Did not the name of Edward Christian put fear into you? It would seem that anticipation of my death overrode your caution."

Don Felipe's teeth snapped together.

"I am told you are a parson's son. How do you reconcile your sacking and plundering, your raping and roistering all over the seas with that? It can not last, dog! You will be caught and hanged!"

"You should have killed him," from Joseph Delaney and then, eagerly, "Shall I do it, sir?" The cutlass in his hand was already poised.

Edward hesitated and Don Felipe felt the hairs rise on his forearms. Perspiration oozed from his forehead as he waited, fully aware that his life hung in the balance. Just what was going on in the head of this fiend?

"Undoubtedly you are right," the Captain observed at last. "However, killing in fair combat and slaying in cold blood are very different. Do as I say and attend to his wound."

And as he caught sight of Don Felipe's changed expression he gave a gust of laughter. "You are surprised, señor? Given a change of position I fear I would not be so fortunate!"

Without pause the other man said, "Expect no mercy from me, sir, when eventually I have you as my prisoner."

"You should have killed him," said Delaney again. "He has just admitted he would kill you if he had the chance."

"Delaney," returned Edward in a very soft tone, "do you obey my order or do I have you put in irons... God's glory! What have we here?"

Edward stared, as if mesmerised by the vision of beauty which had suddenly appeared before him.

"A wench!" Tito, one of his men who had followed Delaney up to the quarterdeck, made a lunge and before Doña Clara knew what was happening she was grabbed around the waist and a stinking breath assailed her nostrils. "Let me be the first to kiss you, sweeting!"

But before he could carry out his intention he was taken by the scruff of the neck and hurled upon the deck. Christian turned to the three others of his men who had raced up to the quarterdeck.

"The next one to touch this woman," he said in a dangerously quiet voice, "will lose his ears." They knew he meant it, too, since there were several among them whose ears had gone overboard. "This is a noble lady..." Don Felipe turned on her wrathfully. "I told you to remain in your stateroom and lock the door!"

"Remain down there when all this was going on?" The fine dark eyes looked haughtily at him before sweeping over the man who had saved her from humiliation. "Don Felipe, I would have expected you could have defended your ship better than this." She motioned to indicate the writhing mass of humanity on the lower deck. "You, sir," to Edward, "by what right do you attack the *Maria Pedrosa*?"

Christian's mouth compressed.

"Be careful, señorita," he advised. "You are my prisoner and a rare beauty." His eyes took in the flawless skin, the high cheekbones contributing to the fine structure of her face. Arched brows were delicate and dark above eyes framed by thick curling lashes. Her raven hair was arranged in a full style of curls, and he frowned in puzzlement. How had she managed to do that herself? "I have been at sea for some months with no chance of bedding a female and you, wench, are exceptionally tempting." A faint smile hovered on sensual lips as he added, "So it behoves you to have a care. I am used to respect."

Her proud chin lifted but before she could speak Don Felipe intervened hastily, "This lady is on her way to England, to marry the Duke of Courtland. Should any harm come to her..."

"No harm, I assure you. I am not an ungentle lover."

Doña Clara coloured up but her dignity remained. The chilling retort she had ready was once again prevented from being uttered as Don Felipe repeated that she was a noble lady, and that she would expect to be treated as one.

"Surely even you would not harm a gentlewoman who is betrothed to one of your countrymen?"

"I take umbrage at the 'even you', but I make excuses for your fear – and your present humiliation. I would remind you, though, that my countrymen are Manx."

"But you are basically English?"

"I am basically a Northman. Our name comes from the Viking Gillocrist who was the kinsman of Godred the Third..." Edward stopped, to give an impatient intake of breath. "All this is of no matter. You, señorita, what is your name?"

She told him, adding that she came from a most illustrious family. to which he responded with a touch of humour,

"As I do, señorita." His eyes went to her hair again. "Allow me to congratulate you on the charming style of your hair. How can you do that yourself?"

"Doña Clara naturally has a maid with her," icily from the *Maria Pedrosa*'s captain. "It would hardly be fitting for a Spanish lady of quality to be travelling without one."

"Another female... !" began Tito before he was quelled by an ice blue stare.

"I would have expected the lady to be accompanied also by her dueña?"

The implied question was answered by Don Felipe's saying that this woman had taken ill at the last moment and it had been impossible to find anyone else. And he added without thinking,

"Doña Clara's father entrusted her protection to me. She is quite safe."

"Is she?" with an amused smile and a lift of those straight flaxen eyebrows. "Do not be too sure, my friend." But he was thinking of the other wench who was on this ship. A maid, a servant...

He glanced down. The pandemonium had settled and some of his men were already going through the pockets of the dead. He called out an order. "Attend to some of the injured – Spaniards as well. And throw the dead overboard before we have an unholy stench in our nostrils."

Then, turning again to Doña Clara, "Where is this maid of yours? Fetch her to me."

It was a curtly spoken command which once again brought her proud head up. Regarding him straightly with a glint in her eye she told him the girl was in the stateroom and he could fetch her himself.

Don Felipe sent her a warning glance, furious with her for the icy chill affecting his spine. Did the fool not know of the danger she was in?

"I said, fetch this maid to me." Christian's voice was low and almost gentle but the threat it carried was not lost on Don Felipe who said he would go and fetch the wench up. "Stay where you are." The voice was still low but there was an edge to it now as he repeated, "Fetch your maid up here."

Doña Clara still hesitated, though she did not much like either the Manxman's tone of voice or his expression.

"It would be wise, señorita." Don Felipe's words were a plea for he was terrified now, terrified that the savage Viking cub would ravish her over and over again... and then? It was not beyond the bounds of imagination that she could be tossed over the side of the ship.

For another long moment Doña Clara's defiant eyes challenged, then as Edward made a move towards her she finally obeyed his command.

"My maid is English," she was saying a few minutes later. She gave the trembling girl a shove which brought her close to Edward. "If you must have a bedmate, take her. I give her to you in exchange for my safety." The tone was one of confidence as she added with a sneer, "She is an orphan so there is no one you will have to answer to. Eleanor, curtsy to this – er – gentleman." She had previously used only pure Castilian but now she spoke English, though broken.

"An orphan." Edward looked her over, seeing an immature figure with slender waist and delicately sloping shoulders. Violet-blue eyes were wide with fear and the full, rosy lips quivered uncontrollably. Her graceful movements as she put some distance between them appealed to him in a way he did not understand.

"A pretty wench," he decided at last. "As fair as you are dark, señorita. Come back here, child."

The spot indicated by a flick of his finger was closer than she had been before and it was with a fast-beating heart that she advanced, dragging her feet. She stopped and stared up at him, suddenly affected in some strange way for there had arisen within her a sense of excitement, of expectation. She took note of the aristocratic bone structure of his face, the vivid blue eyes with the faintest hint of mockery in their depths as, for a second, they met those of Doña Clara. She noticed the bronzed tightness of his skin, the neat, pointed beard which, she felt sure, hid a firm determined chin. It seemed a shade darker than the flaxen hair curling, disarrayed, over his head.

With a careless movement he took her little pointed chin in his hand, but his eyes were on her hair – what hair! It was severely fastened back, on an order from her mistress, he surmised, and yet its wealth of colour, the golden glory so in contrast to the sable catching his eye as Doña Clara swung her head at the sound of a death scream from the deck below, could not be disguised by the lack of style. One hand still held her chin while the other came up from its rest upon his sword hilt to jerk away the tightly knotted braid so that her hair fell free and beautiful on to her shoulders. Ignoring the angry exclamation from her mistress he kept his attention with Eleanor. Clear, peach-bloom skin contoured over almost classical bone formation; a wide, intelligent forehead, creased now as anxiety held her in its grip. He saw the delicately marked brows curving above eyes wide apart and faintly almond-shaped. The full rosy mouth quivered as, under this examination, her fear mounted, yet to her captor it invited a kiss. The swift and arrogant action taking her by complete surprise, Eleanor responded with a kick on his shins and she was gratified to see him wince.

"A shrew!" Roughly he caught her to him, crushing her immature frame and curves against his iron-hard body. Struggling fiercely, Eleanor cried out to her mistress and to Don Felipe but no help came from either. More of the *Falcon*'s men were gathering, eager spectators, and with a dread that threatened to rob her of her senses she wondered if it were his intention to deflower her here, before their interested eyes. Her mouth was captured again, this time in a merciless kiss that left her lips swollen and bruised. She was conscious of ribald remarks and laughter. Bawdy jokes, then more coarse laughter, and all the while she was being subjected to a passion that seemed surely to get out of control any moment now.

"Let me go, please let me go!" she begged when at last she was free to speak. But even as she cried out the words she had no confidence in their effect, so it was with both surprise and relief that she found herself freed from that hawser-like embrace. She stepped back, staring up into his face. He was taking in her attire – the dull grey gown which hung loosely below the sash girdling her waist, its hem brought up in the style of a serving wench, or that worn by milkmaids on one of his cousin's farms, a style insisted on by Deemster Ewan, who, it was said, had sired more bastards than any other man on the island, and who liked to feast his eyes on dainty ankles, as Edward was doing now. He frowned without knowing why, at the low-heeled shoes that were plainly far too large for her. His perceptive eyes moved to the woman for whom this female worked. She was scowling and it was not difficult to read her thoughts, to assume that her intention was to cuff the girl once she had her alone. He found himself comparing the attire of Doña Clara with that of her maid. The Spanish girl wore a dress of violet taffeta, open-fronted to reveal an elaborately embroidered petticoat edged at the hem with exquisite and delicate lace. The white starched ruff which came to her chin was also of the finest lace. Her jewellery had the glitter of various gemstones including diamond earrings and matching pendant, a ruby bracelet and several rings to adorn the long slender fingers. A jewelled pomander hung from her waist.

Edward's expression was one of contempt and a sneer curled his fine lips. It was a pity he dared not ravish her; she needed a lesson to humble her, but she was betrothed to Courtland, who was a friend of the King, though Edward had never met him. A smile replaced the sneer as his thoughts took a backswitch and he was merrymaking with his sovereign in the company of others including John Beecham, who was a close friend of both... but John was far closer to King James than he, Edward, would ever be, because he preferred a *wench* anytime. James had dropped more than one hint, and doubtless the reward would be a title. Those situations were tricky, and so Edward tried never to be alone with the King, as he had no intention of incurring his disfavour and perhaps losing his head. His thoughts were returned to the present by the quivering yet musical tenor of the English girl's voice.

"Thank you, sir – oh, thank you very much!" She noticed his puzzlement and added in a steadier tone, "For not harming me, sir. You were aware of my fear."

"Not so confident, child," he broke in with some amusement. "How old are you?" he inquired as the thought occurred to him.

"Fifteen, sir."

"Nice and ripe," from Tito with a saucy grin which did not take long to fade under the sudden glint in the eye of his master. Eleanor looked at the man. Dirty and uncouth with hoops in his ears and bloodstains on his faded leather jerkin. A leather flask and a cutlass hung from his belt. Despite all this, and the lewd manner of speech which he used, Eleanor felt he was not nearly as wicked as he had appeared to her at first. He was full of bravado and yet he very plainly went in great fear of his captain.

"I believe I gave orders for aid to be given to the wounded." Edward's voice was like a rasp and the blue eyes glittered like chipped ice. "In five minutes' time you could have no use for those hoops of which you are so proud."

It was more than enough to make the man scuttle away, and despite the position she was in Eleanor could not stem the laughter which came to her lips. It caught Edward's attention and as she saw his lips quiver she knew that sensation of excitement again. She was just assuring herself that he would not molest her when she heard him say, "I have been at sea many months and now I have the good fortune to have as my captives two delectable maids here for my pleasure, so I repeat: not so confident, my child."

He stopped quite abruptly on seeing the arrogant expression in Doña Clara's eyes. His own eyes glinted. He dared not molest her but he would certainly put fear into the self-confident Spanish wench. "Yes," he went on presently, "two desirable females – an unexpected gift which no Christian worth his salt would decline to accept."

His mocking glance embraced them both. Eleanor trembled visibly but her mistress stared arrogantly back at Edward and coldly reminded him that she had offered her maid for his pleasure.

"So you did, madam," he returned in English. "However, I shall toss a coin to decide my choice for tonight."

"A – a c-coin, sir...?" Tears gathered in Eleanor's eyes. But she had not been robbed of all her spirit by her employer and she found herself mustering up enough courage to say, "Neither of us has done you any harm, so it would be unmannerly in you to take advantage of us..."

"He will never dare take advantage of me!" declared her mistress. And to Edward, "I repeat: you can take Eleanor."

"I shall toss a coin."

What Edward would really like to do was take a whip to her; he would enjoy hearing her scream for mercy.

"Sir!" intervened Don Felipe, his face twisted with anger. "You will not molest my charge! You would not dare. You might be a Manx savage boastful of your Viking ancestry, but your King is James nevertheless and, for one thing, he has abolished all forms of privateering. These murderous searoving escapades sanctioned by Queen Elizabeth are nothing more than legalised piracy which King James has banned, so you commit an offence against the Crown when you plunder and ravish and kill! Believe me, sir, I shall make it known to your King if one hair of Doña Clara's head is harmed!"

"An excellent speech," applauded Christian with a gust of laughter. "It was a pity, my friend, that you did not stop to consider the danger to this vision of beauty when you attacked my ship. For your information I had no thought of attacking you. I was after a more profitable catch in the form of the *Rosa Mendonca*, a Portuguese ship carrying gold. So you see, your witless act has upset the plans of us both."

"I agree it was a mistake," came the unexpected admission.

"The King of England is well aware of what goes on. Privateering can not be stamped out in one stroke. No doubt the new law will eventually prove effective, but we followers of Hawkins and Drake are not out of business yet."

"Brave words, Captain," sneered Don Felipe, "but of little use if you should find yourself lying with your Viking head on the block."

True, mused Edward. But if he should ever find himself faced with decapitation it would not be for privateering. He was thinking again of James, and his preference for men. It was perhaps prudent to keep away from Court for a while in case the King's appetite did not remain satisfied with his present favourite, the Scotsman, Robert Carr, who had risen to power a year ago.

Of course, there could be other catamites already in favour, lesser ones than the prime favourite. Nevertheless, it would be wise to avoid the King for a time. No sense in taking risks, putting himself in the position of being asked outright to become a sodomite's minion. Asked...? Kings *ordered*. Edward decided that when this voyage was over he would return to the Isle of Mann and his estate at Lezayre. There was Lough Mollo, too. He was his uncle's heir and he suspected it would not be too long before this second estate came into his possession. Yes, he would return to the island and settle down. Had any of his men known of this decision they would have laughed and told him he did not know himself. A searover of his calibre does not retire to the tame life at only twenty-four.

"Your thoughts, sir," said Doña Clara, "appear to be both far away and distasteful, judging by your expression."

He laughed and replied, "Yes, most of them were so distasteful that, should I reveal them, my lady would blush to the roots of her hair."

Which of course did cause her to blush and, glowering at him, she flounced away, saying she was going to her stateroom.

"Come, you!" she commanded her maid, but Edward Christian was not finished with Eleanor yet, and ordered her to stay. Then he ordered the Spanish girl to go below.

"Only when my maid is free to come as well," she retorted without pause.

The vivid blue eyes narrowed; she saw the accompanying compression of his mouth and thought that Don Felipe had not branded him a savage for nothing. She was moving even before he spoke.

"Señorita, you will obey my orders immediately they are given... or find yourself in irons. I make no distinction when it comes to punishment of those who forget I am master, so be warned – and you, too, my friend," he added to Don Felipe. "Go to your quarters and have that wound dressed." He glanced at Eleanor and added, almost to himself, "I want to be alone with this wench."

Don Felipe opened his mouth, then closed it again. Best to remain safe for as long as possible as any argument could result in his being driven to the side by some of these ruffians and thrown overboard on the order of their captain.

Edward gave Eleanor a smile as, taking her arm, he led her away from the gory scene on which she had shudderingly turned her back. He was about to speak when she said with a temerity which amazed her as much as it amazed him, "Is it not time you put a stop to this carnage, sir? Some of the men are still fighting. Surely enough blood has been shed. The wounded need attention and I do not see much being given, in spite of your orders." She was of the sudden opinion that if she could show courage to this man he would respect her for it.

"It was of course just a suggestion," she hurried on as his face hardened. "But surely a sensible one?"

His stare was so disconcerting that she hung her head, avoiding that piercing regard. Her hair fell in glorious abandon to cloak her shoulders and face. And she heard his intake of breath, then his quiet laugh as he lifted her head and gently smoothed back the golden curls, so as to see her face again.

"I like you, wench," he told her, all anger dissolved. "And so if it pleases you I shall give another order—" He swung around and bellowed, "Finish! This is the last time I shall tell you to see to the injured. But first, get rid of the bodies, or we shall have them a putrid mass that will turn our entrails green. And no looting! I shall flog any man who pillages before this mess is all cleared up."

"Thank you, sir," from Eleanor as she looked up at him with her wide violet-blue eyes. "But can I help with the injured? And do you not think the dead should be given a burial service?"

At this there was a loud burst of coarse laughter from several men close by. Delaney had gone with Don Felipe but Tito was there, and Carson and Master Williams and three others.

"A burial service," scoffed Tito, spitting on to the deck for no apparent reason. "With all this lot? No time, little sweeting..."

A fist shot out and he went reeling.

"What makes you take so many risks, man! Get down there before I run my sword through you!"

Eleanor shivered. Did he mean it? That blow was vicious... administered because Tito had called her sweeting... How very odd that the Captain should be so angry about it. After all, he and his men had little respect for women. That much had registered from the beginning.

He seemed to be of a dual personality, for was not his hand gentle just now as he smoothed the hair from her forehead? Heartened because she felt sure he was not all Viking savagery, she asked again if she could attend to some of the wounded.

"I know a little about..."

"My men are capable," he cut in abruptly. "I want to talk to you." He glanced around and then, "There must be a cabin vacant. Show me one."

"A – a cabin," her face turned ashen, "for – for y–you and me?"

The blue eyes lit with amusement.

"To talk – for the present," he laughed. "Child, I like you not when your face is white. Relax and let the colour return. It may help if I tell you I am not at this time in the mood for bedding a wench. Show me this place where we can talk in private and without all this infernal noise and skirmish."

But the hand-to-hand fighting had ceased and already bodies were being hauled over the side. Eleanor closed her eyes and her slender body shook visibly. What a waste of life – all those mothers' sons gone, and for what? She said feebly at last,

"There is no vacant cabin that I know of, sir."

"No?" with lifted eyebrows. "Where do you sleep?" He imagined it was a dark hole somewhere in the bowels of the ship and that was why he had not suggested they go there.

"On a pallet in a corner of Doña Clara's stateroom."

"I see..." A moment of indecision was dispelled as he added firmly, "We shall go aboard the *Falcon*..."

"No!" She shook her head vigorously, her face draining of colour again. "I am not going aboard that pirate ship! You have no right to take me away from my mistress."

"You would prefer to go down and have your ears boxed?"

"It would be far preferable to – to what you might have in mind."

She spoke in fierce and desperate accents, terror and defiance mingling as the two emotions struggled for supremacy, for still strong was the idea that if she showed courage he would admire her, but signs of real fear would make him despise her. Automatically she put a hand to her heart, which was beating so fast that it frightened her. But she lifted her head and hoped it was courage he saw in her manner and not fear. "I shall not be parted from my mistress, sir. As I have already said, we are both innocent in this quarrel you have with Don Felipe; we had no knowledge that he was intending to attack your ship."

She was looking up into his face, tilting her head in order to do so. And for a diverting moment she became absorbed in a thorough examination of his features. That he was handsome in a bold and very masculine sort of way she had already noticed. But now she was seeing more – the sharply etched contours accentuating the firm line of the mouth and arrogant set of the chin. His hair, not quite totally flaxen as there were darker streaks here and there, was cut close to his head at the front but longer at the sides and back. The wiry quality of the curls could, she felt sure, be associated with his ancient forebears. Suddenly aware of the deep silence between them she tilted her head in an interrogating gesture which he ignored, merely looking into her upturned face, saying nothing, giving away naught of his thoughts or intentions. Squaring her shoulders she spoke firmly, asking if he did not see how impossible it was for him to take her from her mistress. "For one thing," she added as the thought occurred to her, "she needs me, because she is unable to dress her own hair or press her clothes."

It was so innocently spoken, so matter-of-fact, that his eyes twinkled and a gust of laughter caught the attention of his lieutenant and he said with some amusement,

"You heard, Mister Crosby? You heard that a lady can not fix her own hair or smooth out her clothes?"

"Incredible," agreed Ted Crosby with a grin. But that was all; he turned again to the supervision of the gruesome work being carried out, with some speed now as when it was done the looting would be allowed.

Edward spoke to Eleanor at last.

"Undoubtedly you have a strong objection to being taken aboard the *Falcon*. However, it is my wish to speak with you, since you puzzle me in many ways. Your speech and manner..." He could have added more, her carriage for example, and the almost classical quality of her features. "I have many questions to ask... and to have answered," he added as if in warning. "I shall have to carry you because I am doubtful of your being able to get aboard the *Falcon* without this help."

He stopped as her head went up and a sparkle of defiance lit the lovely eyes. His voice was dangerously quiet when presently he said, "I advise you to submit quietly, since if you struggle and cause laughter among my men, I shall knock you out." So calm the tone but Eleanor could not possibly miss the threat, and after only a few seconds' debate she made no move of defiance when he lifted her in his arms and carried her down the companion to where, in the waist, a few of his men were already delving into chests of treasure. Uttering a curse he set down his burden, not too gently, and roared out an order. "Get out of here! I said no looting until that mess was cleared! Wright, what are you trying to do with that bar of gold – stuff it into your breeches?"

He was white with rage and Eleanor shrank away from him, wondering if she dare make a run for it and try to reach her mistress's stateroom.

"No – sir..." The man's face had gone pink beneath the grime. "I was not trying to steal it, sir."

"As for all the mess," interposed Thomas Winter who had an air about him and Eleanor wondered if he were more important than many of the rest, "this is not our ship and so why should we clean it up? As for the smell – of the dead bodies – we shall not be here long enough to be troubled by it."

His captain spoke softly, but in a tone that made Winter wish he had guarded his tongue.

"Winter, because you happen to be my personal servant it does not give you the right of familiarity. I warn you to take care. If you lose your ears you will be an offence to my eyesight and I shall be forced to replace you."

His severity was instantly vanquished by amusement as Thomas's hand came gingerly up to an ear in the way one would fondle a precious, much-loved object.

"I beg pardon, master," he apologised meekly. "I will go and help with the mess..." His eyes wandered to the treasures – gold and silver, spices and silks. "It will take some time." He was now looking at Eleanor and wondering if the Captain really was taking her on to the *Falcon*, and how long he would be away.

"Watch yourself," warned Edward perceptively. "You can pack this stuff only when there is nothing else to do up there."

He swung Eleanor up into his arms again; she felt herself to be as light as a doll. She was vitally aware of his heart beating, of the easy way he trod the ship's groaning timbers. She wondered how many helpless females he had treated thus, this roistering swashbuckling daredevil, a brigand with the air of an aristocrat.

Five minutes later he was telling her to sit down, having conveyed her to his quarters on the *Falcon* where her eyes widened at the elegance which surpassed even that of her mistress's stateroom. She took the high-backed chair which he indicated. Through the porthole the sun could be seen dying, painting the calm sea with saffron and crimson and a touch of gold. Edward Christian sat down at the oak table and stretched his long legs beneath it, his body in a slouched position against the back of the chair.

"And now for some questions," he began without preamble. "Why are you employed by a foreigner?"

"Doña Clara?" Eleanor smiled at him but there was no response. His eyes were coolly appraising. "I am an orphan as she said. My father died and a distant relative of his, living in Spain, offered to give my mother and me employment in her home. But on the way my mother died on the ship..." Her voice faltered as the rising lump in her throat prevented speech. Christian said soothingly,

"Take your time, child. There is no hurry."

He was surprising himself, for this girl was as tempting as any he had met, and God knows, he thought, I have the need! Why this delay? Why had he not flung her down on that bed over there and deflowered her? Yes, she was a virgin, and he had taken many a virgin before. So why...? But this one intrigued him... She was different.

"Thank you, sir." Again a smile broke and this time his response was swift. Eleanor knew a rising warmth within her, an emotion as pleasant as it was baffling. "I arrived there and this relative took over the burial of my mother..."

"She wasn't buried at sea, then?"

Eleanor shook her head.

"We were only a day away..." Again her voice failed but recovery was soon made and she went on to explain that the relative did not want her without her mother, who was to have been a sort of housekeeper, while Eleanor was to have been a housemaid.

"So you found yourself alone in a strange country?" Edward frowned and added in disbelief, "This relative did not just turn you adrift?"

"Oh, no! She found me the situation with Doña Clara who wanted to learn the English language so she was eager to have me as her maid."

Christian was nodding thoughtfully but the frown still lay on his brow.

"She has not proved to be a kind employer." It was a statement and Eleanor began to say that Doña Clara was not actually unkind; it was just that the Spanish were different from the English in the treatment of their servants.

"You must remember," she added finally, "that she gave me a home and employment when I was desperate, and I do not know what I would have done without her help."

He could have mentioned the only option open to her but he spared her blushes and instead asked if she had no other relatives in England.

"No. This lady in Spain was the only one."

"And how long have you been with Doña Clara?"

"Nearly a year."

"How do you come to speak so – er – nicely?"

"Nicely?" She appeared puzzled, saying her mother spoke in the same way.

"Tell me about your parents." Why all this interest? He was fast becoming impatient with himself. It could have been all over and done with by now and he could have been more profitably employed in seeing to the gathering of the harvest. In fact, there might still be time to engage the Portuguese galleon... but no! He might as well resign himself to his missed chance. "What did your father do for a living?"

"He was a tailor, sir."

"And your mother – what was her background?"

"She was of yeoman stock. Her father had some land..." She broke off and shrugged. "Is it important? My mother did not speak much of her parents and I believe they cut her off because she married my father."

"Not an unusual story."

What next? he wondered. She was ripe, as Tito had said... and he was hungry. He asked presently, "Where did you live before going to Spain?"

"Near Chester – about a mile away."

"You were born there?"

"Yes." Her manner became animated. "We used to ride into Chester. I love the river and the Roman walls – you can walk along them and see the town beneath. I was sorry to leave that lovely place."

Deva... and the River Dee. He had almost bought a house on the banks of the river, a stately home whose gardens ran right down to the clear sparkling water. An idyllic spot. He supposed the thing that deterred him was the fact that the sea's call was stronger. Maybe one day, when he was old, he would have a second home. The Lord of Mann, Stanley, owned much property in those parts – eleven manors in Lancashire and Cheshire, bestowed on him by a king who had never owned them in the first place.

"Do you know Chester, sir?"

With every moment that passed she was becoming more at ease with him. Her fear, though, for her chastity, was still a source of anxiety for this was a lusty fellow with a strong athletic frame and of course, there was the fact that, as he had said, he had been many months at sea ... She would have liked to know his age. He seemed so young, yet there was an undeniable maturity about him and in addition, he had been buccaneering for some time, that was evident. He was also Captain of a ship and master of tough sailors whose manner suggested they had been with him for a number of years. "Have you ever been to Chester?" she inquired more to break the silence than anything else. He nodded his head.

"Several times. I very much like the town and its very beautiful surroundings."

"If I had one wish," murmured Eleanor almost to herself, "it would be that I could return. I would like to live there forever - I mean," she amended, twinkling, "until I die." Unconsciously she threw out on impulse a hand and he caught it. Her heart missed a beat as a strange little thrill passed through her body. He scanned the lines on her hand for a long, studied moment before he stated, lifting his eyes to her face,

"You are going to live a long time - a very long time."

She blinked in surprise.

"I would not have thought anyone like you would know about such things. It is called witchcraft by some people."

He merely laughed and released her hand.

"Nothing sinister..." His attention was caught by the way she was gently caressing the hand he had held. "Your lifeline is extraordinarily long."

"You believe that it has real meaning?"

Christian merely nodded and she went on, "I do not think I want to be very old. I would be infirm with no one to look after me."

"You will marry and have children. They will look after you."

"Marry..." A dreamy expression entered her eyes; she looked across at him shyly, pausing for a moment, weighing her next words. "You, sir, are you married already?"

"Not yet." Amusement brought a quiver to his lips. "Why are you so interested, wench?"

She blushed and was silent. He laughed then, enchanted by her naivety, and her innocence. He asked himself again why he was spending time in talk when it could be passed far more pleasurably. His thoughts switched to the other one. A little more plump and perhaps more beautiful – it was hard to tell, as they were so different in colouring. Pity the arrogant Spanish wench was betrothed to a friend of the King. Had it been otherwise he'd have taken her by now, and it would have been as much to teach her a lesson as to satisfying the desire he had been forced to control for so long.

This one, though, this little innocent maid... not for her a swift and lustful cockerel-in-the farmyard act which would leave her deflowered and weeping. A sigh escaped him at the idea that he was becoming soft. That he desired this delectable wench could not be denied. Already the close proximity, and the hint of musk perfume assailing his nostrils, was causing heat to generate in his loins and he shifted his position. Eleanor was staring at him through those violet-blue eyes, now a little clouded. What was she expecting from him? He said curiously,

"Is Doña Clara planning to keep you with her when she is married to her duke?"

"I do not know, but I hope so. I pray every night that she will not decide to choose someone else and cast me aside in London."

"You will soon find another place even if she does." A rough note had edged his voice. Why should he care what happened to her after she arrived in London? "I had better take you back," he decided, rising from the chair. A swift smile was his reward.

"You are very kind, sir. But I knew you would not harm me."

He had to laugh. "What a little innocent you are, child. And how little you know me. I can not recall ever having been described as kind before."

Eleanor was rising from her chair; he held out a hand and she placed hers in it.

"I shall have to carry you again..."

He stopped, listening. Shouts and warnings, pandemonium the like of which could only be described as hell let loose. Leaving her, he shot through the door.

"Stay where you are," he flung over his shoulder but she knew she could not obey him, for she had heard the cries, too, and taken in the content of the words.

Chapter Two

She stood by the rail watching it all, hearing the Captain of the *Falcon* shouting out sharp, precise commands to his infamous crew.

"Leave everything! Come aboard – I shall flog any one of you who delays any longer. Any loot you already have can be brought aboard, but otherwise..." His voice was cut by the scream of a man falling overboard from the other vessel.

"Sinking..." breathed Eleanor, every nerve in her body rioting. "Doña Clara!" she screamed. "My mistress..."

"I ordered you to stay in my cabin..."

"My mistress – save my mistress!"

She clung to his sleeve and was sent sprawling on to the deck when at last he managed to free himself from the frenzied grip. Fury whitened his face.

"Get back down there..."

"No! My mistress – she will be drowned... Oh, God... save her..."

But the *Maria Pedrosa* was sinking fast now and Eleanor covered her face with her hands.

"She is probably in that boat – look." Christian pointed to where, in the misted distance, a small boat was precariously ploughing through a roughening sea.

"Bring her back!" cried Eleanor. "Bring her here, on to this ship!"

Christian's lips compressed. Without more ado he swung her up and carried her to his quarters and after giving her a hurtful slap, he locked her in.

She sat down and wept. Had her mistress escaped? And all those injured men on the *Maria Pedrosa*? All would die, for the Captain of the *Falcon*'s only concern was to get his own men back, off the doomed Spanish galleon. She had seen them swarming aboard, many carrying treasure stolen from the other ship. And some, fools that they were, had actually risked their lives in order to search for more loot.

She had seen another man fall overboard, seen a few of the *Falcon*'s men swimming strongly, then being hauled aboard by their comrades.

She was sobbing bitterly when at last she heard the key turning in the lock. Edward Christian, dishevelled but calm, stood there in the doorway, a look of stern censure on his handsome face.

"From now on, wench," he said severely, "you will learn to obey me. When I give an order it is obeyed immediately, understand?"

"My mistress..."

"Have you been listening to me?" The taut lines of his face, the compression of his mouth and the warning glint in his eyes... all these compounded to send shivers running along her spine.

"Yes, sir," she returned meekly. "I – I will do as I am told. But... Sir, Doña Clara – will she be rescued? The sea is becoming so rough—" She burst into tears, her face creasing like that of a small child. "Why was I not with her?"

He paused a moment and then, his eyes on her bent head,

"You should thank God that you were not with her—"

She glanced up, terror behind the tears.

"She... the boat...?"

"Went down," was his brief rejoinder. "Had she and the Captain remained on board I might have been able to save them, but my men tell me that they and one or two others took to the boat in a great hurry, without a care for the seamen."

His voice was a rasp; she knew instinctively that Edward Christian would never be the first to leave his ship. No, he would be the last.

"Are – are any of the *Maria Pedrosa*'s men saved?" she managed to inquire after a small silence. Edward nodded his head.

"A few. They will be put ashore somewhere on our way back to England."

England! This naturally flashed into her distraught mind the awful insecurity of her own future.

"What am I going to do?" she cried, glancing wildly around as if the answer lay somewhere in the stateroom. "Where – where are you going to leave me?"

He looked at her frowningly. What a damnable mess! Spaniards aboard he had to get rid of, and this homeless wench on his hands. Silently he cursed the man who had perished for his folly. Then he cursed himself for bringing this girl on to his ship. Had he left her on the galleon... His frown deepened. He would not have wanted the lass to die, even though it would no doubt have been best all round if she had, since he could see only one way she could earn a living. And if that was what fate had in store for her, then no harm would be done if *he* took her...

"I will think about that later," he answered at last. "Meanwhile we have to find somewhere for you to sleep."

*

It was six weeks later that the *Falcon* sighted the English coast. Christian, coming into his stateroom where Eleanor was seated on a padded bench, her face pale, her fingers entwined as they rested on her knees, stood appraising her for a long time in silence. She wore a full-length, loose-fitting gown of crimson brocade, with a linen jacket embellished to match the blackwork embroidery of the petticoat. Her mistress's clothes, carried aboard by Tito, in a chest which also contained a casket of jewellery. At first Eleanor had refused to wear any of the lovely clothes that had belonged to Doña Clara, but this dominating sea robber who had soon become her lover, had – in some exasperation – finally threatened to take a whip to her, and although she suspected he did not mean it, she prudently obeyed, but she drew the line at wearing the jewels. He had shrugged then, satisfied that she looked very lovely in the clothes which both fitted and suited her.

Slowly he came forward.

"You will soon be settled in a situation." He had promised to see her settled and he had in mind two titled ladies who could be approached.

Eleanor's face paled even more. How was she to tell him? Say it was not possible now for her to take a situation – not a permanent one, that was. Her mouth felt parched but her forehead was damp, her hands clammy. He said, puzzled, "You are not at all happy at the prospect of a new life. Is aught amiss?"

At first she shook her head, a mechanical gesture. But then she coughed nervously and managed to utter in half-strangled tones, "There is – is something, yes!" Into the colourless cheeks two bright spots of crimson appeared. "I – you – I can not take a situation, Edward. I am – am..." Her voice failed and she put her hands to her face and started to cry.

"You... ! God's glory, do not say you are—" He cut off, gritting his teeth. Another Christian bastard on the way. He ought to have left her on that ship to die! What now? Turn her adrift? He was resolved to go back to the island, thus avoiding the company of his King. It was imperative that he put some distance between James and himself – instinct warned him of this continually. Later, of course he would return to Court, before going off again to sea, joining Thomas Best with whom he had sailed several times already. Rollicking good sport they had had, and at the same time overloading their own coffers at the expense of their employers, the East India Company. Yes, they had both become rich during the past two years.

"Edward..."

The gentle voice broke into his thoughts and he looked down to scowl at her. Tears came faster and a sigh of asperity escaped him. He began to pace the floor then stopped. No use blaming everyone but himself for this damned coil he was in. This child had never had a chance, for although he had not used any kind of coercion, he had made it plain that what he wanted he would have. And so she had submitted, preferring to give herself willingly, while at the same time knowing that resistance, in the circumstances, could only be temporary anyway. A sensible way of looking at it, he mused. But then he had found her to be sensible, and logical; she possessed a quick, alert brain and the kind of intelligence that appealed to him. Assuredly she was different from the other females he had bedded. Had he been ready for marriage, and had she boasted any kind of background... but she was just a serving wench; her father had been a tailor. She spoke again and this time he regarded her with a softer expression. "Are you going to help me...?" She shook her head in a gesture of despair. "I have no one but you, Edward, no one in the whole world."

His frown reappeared but he turned so that she would not see it. Strange how he felt about this one. He had never been concerned over any of the others. He said eventually, "Let me think on it. You are right, of course, in saying that you can not take a situation." Impulsively he patted her shoulder. "Do not cry any more, child. Something will come to me..."

"You will take me with you to the island?" she broke in eagerly, since this way of helping her was the only one she could imagine. She noticed the start he gave and added hastily, "I do not ask to be your wife, Edward. I am fully conscious of the fact that you are high above my station." She lifted wide appealing eyes to his. "If you would find me some place to live – or perhaps I could be a kitchen-maid... or... or something," she added vaguely. "In your house?"

He shook his head. "No, that would not serve. But I have just had another idea."

Her eyes brightened. "What is it, Edward? Tell me – please tell me at once." She marvelled at herself, at her ability to conceal from him the fact of her love. He must never know; it was her own precious secret, to be kept within her heart. She would love him till she died.

"Tell me what you have in mind?" she added, wondering at his silence. He remained thoughtful, while she waited anxiously for him to reveal what his thoughts were. From his expression they were not altogether pleasant and a sudden access of foreboding robbed her eyes of the sparkle that had come to them. Undoubtedly he was reluctant to speak, and when at length he did she knew instinctively that the words were not a reflection of his thoughts.

"I am considering finding you a situation – do not interrupt, Eleanor. It is a situation different from that of servant..." He broke off and she knew a painful tightness in her throat. Something was wrong; she felt his conscience was troubling him. What, then, was this situation that was different? Tremblingly she asked,

"Shall I not be comfortable in this – er – situation? You look as if you are in doubt about my liking it."

He began to pace the floor again. Never in his wenching exploits had he felt like this. It was damned uncomfortable and he had the urge to relieve his feelings by giving her a sound box on the ears – which was so illogical that, seeing the humour in it all, he found himself laughing softly. And in response to her interrogating glance he told her again not to worry. He had it all worked out but would not tell her until another time.

"But, Edward—"

"Later," he put in tautly. "When I am ready and not before."

*

Eleanor looked at the man sprawled on the pallet, and closed her eyes. She could scarcely believe she was married to this filthy, drunken specimen of humanity.

"God," she prayed, tears gushing to her eyes. "Please God deliver me from this hell! Why did you let Edward do this to me?"

Her body was heavy, her mind filled with despair. Was this to be her lot? This hovel with its dirt floor and its walls of bare stone?

How well she remembered what had led up to this. Her swift perception which warned her that what Edward had in mind for her would be something she would not like. His words, devastating in their effect; she had been forced to race away and vomit. Her inside churned, almost as if the baby was moving already.

"Marriage..." She came back to him in his stateroom and had stood in the doorway, small and white and helpless. "Marriage to someone I have never even met?"

He glanced away, wondering again why he had these damned uncomfortable pangs of conscience. Nevertheless, she was just another wench he had bedded; he owed her nothing.

"On the island I and my family all have estates and vassals. You shall be comfortably settled with one of my labourers—"

"And have a baby every year?" she cried. "Never! I want something more! This is not to be my life. Edward..." Her small hands clenched till the knuckle bones showed white. "I want a better life than that. If you must find me a husband, then please let him be a yeoman, or anything better than a mere labourer." She spread her hands in a pleading gesture. "A tradesman – I used to attend to customers in my father's shop..." She tailed off as he shook his head.

"You ask too much! My servants obey my orders but others would not. No, child, it has to be as I say – you should be grateful that I am concerning myself with you at all!" Impatience edged his voice and a heavy frown had settled on his brow. Eleanor studied him intently through eyes misted with tears. It was strange that her deep love for him had no effect, that he was blind to it. And yet, she would not have it otherwise, simply because there was no possibility of his ever marrying her. She whispered at last,

"I could kill myself – that would be the better way."

She swayed in the doorway as an excruciating pain shot through her head. He rose swiftly and caught her in his arms. She closed her eyes, and relaxed in this moment of blissful nearness to him. Her hand came up to his shoulder and her eyes held a wistful expression as she murmured, unable to stem words which she knew would anger him, "These nights on the ship, Edward, do they really mean nothing to you? Will you forget them... or will they remain in your memory for always?"

"You *have* been thinking of marriage," he snapped. "Even while you knew, and admitted, it was impossible. Be satisfied that you will not be alone, that you will have a husband—"

"I have said I want no husband!" she cried fiercely. "Those nights were beautiful, Edward. How can you give me to another man!"

He thrust her away from him. "God's mercy! Why am I plagued like this? I have a mind to set you ashore in Portsmouth and let you fend for yourself."

She flinched. He was crucifying her; her brain was becoming numbed, she had no power to think - not of the present or the future. How cruel was fate, not only in having separated her from her mistress, but in having given her into this man's power, a plaything for his lust. And now... what had unmerciful fate in store for her future? She touched her stomach automatically, saw him frown darkly at the action.

"I shall have you a husband as soon as possible after we land on the Isle of Mann," he told her roughly, at the same time taking possession of the chair he had vacated a moment ago. He looked at her, his mouth tightly compressed. "Why cannot you get it into your head that you are fortunate? I am not casting you out into a cruel world. And it may interest you to know that you are the first wench that I have troubled myself about like this."

It was useless, she had told herself, as she stared across at him through her tears. His face was hard and set, without any sign of emotion. In fact, he seemed suddenly overcome with boredom as he lifted a lean brown hand to stifle a yawn. She had turned then, and left him, resigned to marriage with a stranger.

*

The man on the pallet stirred and yawned, revealing several gaps in blackened teeth. She shuddered and went outside, away from the noisome odour of gin and bad breath. It was the money from Edward that enabled Samuel Garrett to indulge so often. Five months she had been here, on this fair island with its hills and glens and its remoteness from the land of her birth. She had learned many things since coming here, about the way of life, how there was such a vast distinction between the wealthy landowners and their serfs. She had made friends with Alicia Quaile, daughter of a Quaile bastard, who was employed as lady's maid for Susanna, wife of William Christian, Edward's brother. Susanna was a kind mistress, a dainty charming lady with ringlets falling to her shoulders, with large dark eyes and a full, compassionate mouth. She had a son, James, and was breeding again. Eleanor had met her several times, and been treated most kindly, welcomed, in fact, as a friend of Alicia. Susanna gave them sweetmeats of marchpane, or had Kathleen, the scullery maid, bring them tea in the garden. This was at first quite unbelievable to Eleanor who had always been kept in her place as a servant.

Eleanor often wondered if William, lord of a vast estate and Member of the House of Keys, was aware that his lovely wife was not strong. Eleanor had sensed this at the very first meeting and mentioned it to Alicia.

"I feel it, too," agreed the girl. "She seems all right, but at times I hear her breathing heavily, or even gasping for breath. I hope she does not die, Eleanor," went on Alicia with tears in her eyes. "What would I do? Where would I go?"

"You have no parents living?"

"Mother left the island one dark night –you know of course that no one is allowed to leave here without the permission of either the Lord or his Governor. And they do not often give it. My mother was unhappy with my stepfather so she went off – I think with a man." She went on to say that she was fourteen at the time and had been with Mistress Christian for just a month. "I think my mother would never have gone unless she was sure I was settled," added Alicia finally.

Eleanor swallowed. Having had a loving mother she knew an almost physical pain in her sympathy for her friend.

"Your stepfather? Where...?"

"He died, in Peel Castle."

Eleanor frowned.

"He was in prison?"

"For stealing. He had ten lashes as well... There is no need to shudder, Eleanor, wrongdoers deserve punishment. My stepfather was a bad man and I am glad he is dead." The lovely eyes had suddenly darkened with an expression Eleanor disliked very much to see. "I believe in punishments being severe, and if I were offended against I would demand satisfaction." Her voice held an implacable note and Eleanor changed the subject.

*

It was only natural that Alicia should evince curiosity regarding her friend's marriage because, she said, Eleanor was far above 'that horrid drunken Sam Garrett.'

The time was right. Eleanor was in a confiding mood and soon she was hearing Alicia say, with an angry light in her eye, "I am so sorry for you, Eleanor. But the Christians are always thinking they have the right to take us if they wish."

"You, Alicia – are you sometimes afraid of your master?"

"I was at first, but the lady Susanna will always protect me."

"Is William very much in love with her?"

"I am sure of it." Alicia paused in thought. "He is not like the others – at least, not in that way. But he is very much like all the - in his hatred for the Lord of our island. You see, for many, many years the whole family has been engaged in bitter conflict with the Stanleys, and it is all because of the rights of our nation. The Earl of Derby not only wants to take all the lands away from their rightful owners, but he oppresses the poor."

All this Eleanor learned during the first month on the island, for she had come to know Alicia during the first week, when they had met on coming out of church. Alicia had smiled and asked if Eleanor was the girl who had wed Samuel Garrett. The chance encounter had developed rapidly into a sincere friendship, a circumstance which undoubtedly made Eleanor's unhappy lot a little more bearable. Another thing that made it bearable was that Sam had been forbidden by his master, Edward Christian, to touch her in any way whatsoever.

The marriage ceremony was conducted in Maughold Church by Edward's father, John McChristian, first Protestant vicar of the church, and Edward had been present. Eleanor, her eyes swollen and red from hours of weeping which had seemed to tear her to shreds, was as profoundly aware of him as she was of the life within her and of the long dark road she was to travel before death claimed her, merciful death, she thought, perhaps it would come soon... perhaps she would die in childbirth – ah, God, be kind to me and call me soon.

It was less than an hour after she and her husband had reached the hovel that Edward appeared, entering unceremoniously, his tall, aristocratic figure dominating the room. He was pale, noticed Eleanor, and he avoided her gaze. Why had he come here, to this mean and filthy dwelling to which he had condemned her and in which his child of noble line would be born and live, and probably die?

Sam, her new husband, already filled with ale, his leering, bloodshot eyes on her belly, found himself taken by the scruff of the neck and flung against the wall.

"I have decided that you give to Eleanor your name only – nothing more, understand?" The voice was like a rasp, the blue eyes stern and cold. He still avoided Eleanor's gaze as he continued, "You will give her the bedroom and you will sleep here, on this pallet."

Sam's protuberant eyes took on a challenging expression; the bridegroom had gained courage from the drink.

"She is my wife, sir! I shall bed her when I like – and it will be often," he leered, again fixing his gaze on her stomach. "She is a beauty and ripe and strong for many more—"

His words became a roar of pain as he was jerked back by his hair. Eleanor gasped, and felt sick. The long hair had been grown to hide the mutilation of his ears.

"Oh, God…" She lifted her stricken eyes to Edward's face. "What have you done to me? What is this – this *thing* to whom you have married me?"

"Eleanor—" He stopped and she noticed the spasmodic twitching of a muscle in his cheek. That he was deeply affected in some way was obvious to her and there came a moment of hope. Perhaps he would rescue her. But the hope soon died as she heard him say to her husband, "I shall watch you closely while I am on the island, and if you value your hide you will give me no cause for complaint. Should I find you have disobeyed my order I shall strip it off you with this whip!" He paused a moment as if to emphasise his next words, spoken slowly and very softly, "Inch by inch, Sam Garrett. I shall flay you inch by inch."

Sam Garrett's eyes blazed. He muttered to himself, "She is my wife. She should be with child as soon as feeding one bairn is finished." He looked almost defiantly at his master. "It is the lot of all women, even in your station, sir."

He stopped abruptly and stepped back, aware he had gone too far. Edward's riding whip was raised in a vicious sweep, catching Sam on the arm and bringing a roar of pain from his lips.

"You have heard what is my will! One more word of defiance from you, man, and I shall have you flogged."

Sam licked his lips, which seemed to have lost as much of their colour as his face. Eleanor looked from one man to the other, from her husband to the father of her child, one cringing, the other standing legs slightly apart, his arrogant self-confidence portrayed even in the way he held his proud head on broad, well-set shoulders. Her lips trembled as she met his gaze, seeing him through eyes dark with pain. He turned away abruptly, but not before he had read her expression. She did not trust her husband to leave her alone. And in fact, Edward himself had his doubts for after all, Eleanor was beautiful, tempting surely to a man who was her lawful husband, a man who, when in drink, gained courage and so was liable to take chances, as was adequately proved by his conduct just now. It had to be admitted, too, that this cringing meekness sat uneasily on his broad, weather-beaten face. Edward's eyes moved to the man's thatch of greying, straw-like hair reaching his neck. Those ears had gone one at a time, since losing the first one had not proved effective in curing the man of stealing his master's chickens. No, he was not to be trusted to leave Eleanor alone and Edward pondered for a while before telling Sam he would be compensated for his enforced repression. At which the man looked uncomprehending so Edward explained, "You will be paid for leaving Eleanor alone. She will be your wife only in name and, therefore, never in the same bed, so there will be no more children after this one."

He stopped abruptly to fix Sam intently with a warning stare. "I have promised you will be paid... but remember this, Sam Garrett, I know how to punish – yes," he added drily as the man stroked where an ear ought to have been – "you have proof that I know how to punish. So take care, man, for I meant it when I threatened to flay you inch by inch."

He looked every bit the ruthless Viking, thought Eleanor even while remembering his gentleness during those nights of love. She had learned then that there was a softness at the core of his being. She had seen, too, the refinement, the often impeccable manners which reflected his background, belonging as he did to the principal branch of the family, the Christians of Milntowne whose possession of most of the land, especially in the north of the island, afforded them the power to defy the Lord of Mann himself, to treat with arrogant disdain the Stanleys' repeated and obsessive attempts to appropriate the lands they had held for many generations.

There was a movement from Sam whose sallow face wore a sullen expression but Eleanor was relieved to see the resignation there as well, and when in answer to Edward's inquiry as to whether he understood, he mumbled, "Aye, sir," she was fully satisfied. Edward also appeared to be satisfied for, with a nod to Eleanor, he went out to where his horse was tethered to a tree. Her eyes followed the majestic figure and filled with tears which she tried valiantly to suppress.

These reflections were cut abruptly by the voice of her husband, his complaint harsh and loud.

"Is there aught to eat, girl? Hunger is tearing at my belly!"

Turning reluctantly, she went back into the cottage. Sam was supporting himself on one elbow, groaning loudly, his bleary eyes attempting to focus, and make shape of, the girl standing in the low doorway, the sunlight behind her, lighting her hair so that it gleamed like pure gold and he caught his breath. For five months he had lusted after her, and she was his lawful wife! True, there were whores for the taking, and he had money to pay them, but this maid with the swollen breasts and belly – he wanted to put his weight on her, to crush what the seed of his hated master had put there. An ugly twist to his mouth and the leering expression brought forth a warning reminder from his wife, and not for the first time she was saying, in quiet but strongly accented tones, "Forget not Master Christian's order, Sam Garrett. He is still on the island, as you very well know."

But away soon! She did not know, but Edward Christian was preparing to go to sea... and then...?

"I asked if there was anything to eat!" he growled, rising awkwardly from the pallet.

"There is naught till Davis brings the herrings."

"Have you been to the harbour?"

She nodded her head. "The sea was rough and so the catch is late."

"You could have made some oatcakes." His tone, coarse and belligerent, made her wince. "You are an idle bitch!"

"I get tired. The baby – it will come soon."

"Hmm..."

He managed to get on to his feet. His fat body stank of urine and stale sweat, his breath made foul by food rotting in the black teeth. "Then maybe I shall put another there."

Although she shuddered at his coarseness she was unafraid. Sam would never dare molest her after the threats Edward had made. Especially when he was still on the island, looking after his estate, and probably seeing Sam every day, as he worked on the land, as payment for the cottage and the piece of land surrounding it, and which he was supposed to cultivate. Others like him, more industrious, made good use of their land, growing oats and vegetables, and keeping a few fowls for the table, and for the provision of eggs. Sam's neglect made it necessary for Eleanor to go to the harbour every day, as they lived on herrings and oat cakes. Ale was cheap and Sam drank gallons of it, but Eleanor drank water, mainly, except when she visited Alicia. At those times she would have delicious cakes and, if she wished, warm sweet milk to drink. It was always a banquet, reminding her of the meals she had shared with Edward on board the *Falcon*.

"Drink plenty," she would be advised either by Susanna Christian or Betsy, the buxom serving-maid who seemed, in fact, not like a servant at all, so familiar was she with her mistress. Everyone adored Susanna... and everyone was anxious about her health. "Yes, lass, drink much milk, for that bairn must be strong and healthy, a credit to its father."

Eleanor no longer blushed at this kind of talk. It had not taken her long to realise that it was well-known that she carried a Christian's child. It was not frowned upon, either. Here on the island bastards were so commonplace that they never even carried an inferior status. Usually they bore the name of the father, different from England where they took the mother's name. On the island it was said of the Christians that they brought about an increase in their numbers – which also meant their strength – by deliberately producing bastards. At the mansion of Milntowne two milkmaids were at present breeding. Deemster Ewan was living up to his reputation.

Chapter Three

Eleanor entered the dim hovel and tended the fire, tossing turf and gorse on to the dying embers.

"Burn," she commanded, "do not let him come in and find there is no fire."

She had stayed longer than she should at Susanna's beautiful home, but Susanna had been so eager that she should see all over the mansion. It had been a matter of much puzzlement that the noble lady should take such an interest in her until one day she had said, her big brown eyes a little sad,

"You know, Eleanor, you could so easily have been my sister—"

"Your sister, Mistress Christian?"

No soon had she spoken than Eleanor grasped the real meaning of Susanna's words. She shook her head and added in a breaking voice, "No, madam, Edward Christian is far above me – we both knew it." She paused to swallow the painful little lump that had risen in her throat. "I feel you are blaming Edward, but no one was to blame. We were brought together in the kind of circumstances that were bound to have these results. I gave myself willingly—"

"Only because you knew he would take you by force," broke in Susanna and it was the first time Eleanor had seen this gentle lady show anger. "You are no ordinary serving-maid; you have breeding and he should have married you!"

"I have no breeding," returned Eleanor. "My mother taught me good manners, and as her way of speech was – well – above the ordinary for her station. I did tell you my father was a tailor – I too speak in this way, and for that I am thankful," she added with a sudden smile that lighted up her face.

Susanna was silent. She and Eleanor were in the lovely garden where flowers bloomed in profusion and birds' avian bustle was the only sound disturbing the silence. Alicia had been allowed to invite her friend to tea, as it was her nineteenth birthday. Susanna invited herself and seemed better in health, with rosy lips and a little colour in her cheeks, too. Eleanor was fast awakening to the realisation that Susanna was far different from the arrogant Christians into whose clan she had married. Her values were different; she never looked down on any other human being. Her priorities were also right; she loved nature and beauty, abhorred the cruelty of punishments inflicted on underlings for what was often a very minor misdemeanour. Wondering that her husband did not object to her treating as friends both her tirewoman and the girl who was pregnant by his brother, and now married to one of the lowest menials on his brother's manorial estate, Eleanor could not forbear to ask, which was in itself a sign of the familiarity which had sprung up between Mistress Christian and herself.

"William knows of course," was the reply from Susanna, "but he loves me and wants me to be happy." She looked at Eleanor with a smile. "It will surprise you to learn that William was not pleased to know that your child's name will not be Christian. In fact, he has told Edward that it should be, and that Edward should attend to the matter once the baby is born."

Eleanor's eyes had widened at this, even though she knew of the Christians' desire that their numbers should keep on increasing.

"And... Edward? What was his reaction?"

"He went quiet, as he always does whenever your name is mentioned."

"My name?" in a puzzled tone. "My name is mentioned? I had assumed that Edward would rather have forgotten I ever existed, were that possible."

Susanna was shaking her head. She looked at Eleanor with a curious expression.

"My husband and I have agreed that you mean something to Edward – that he regards you in a very different light from that of other women he has bedded. But the trouble with him, and indeed all the Christians, is that they consider themselves far superior to other people. They are the privileged aristocracy with roots back to Gillocrist and further to Godred Crovan himself. It was Gillocrist who gave them the name of which they are so proud. With Edward, it is the call of the sea, too, that prevents him from settling down. He is a swashbuckling freebooter whose life at sea has been a story of uninterrupted success and he has become very rich through plundering and the booty he collects by it." Susanna had paused then, for a long moment of thought. "One day, though, he will go too far, and then his exploits at sea will come to an end." Again she stopped, to regard Eleanor with a curious expression. "Perhaps then, he will awake to the fact that he is... dearly loved."

Colour rushed into Eleanor's face. She had not thought that anyone could have guessed her precious secret. She nodded soon and murmured,

"Yes, it is true that I love him. But, Mistress Christian, I know he can never marry me. As you implied just now when speaking of the pride of the Christians, they have to marry a kind like themselves."

Eleanor spoke with conviction. It was not her fate ever to have Edward Christian as her husband.

*

A sigh escaped her as she saw that the fire had gone out. The turf was damp, and perhaps the gorse too.

"What in hell's name have you been doing, wife!" The bellowing voice caused her to jump and the life within her began to thrust about. "This place is cold!"

"It will not take long," she began, thinking again of the lovely home from which she had come only an hour ago. "There should be some dry wood in the back—"

"Then fetch it, woman. What have you been doing?"

"I have been to see Alicia," she replied unhesitatingly. "I stayed a bit too long, but the meal will be ready within the hour." She looked at him in the eye, her lips pursed. "When are you going to tend the land here? Perhaps you would employ yourself usefully out there while I cook the herrings."

The bloodshot, protuberant eyes blazed. He had had enough of this damned whore! Breeding by his hated master, the man who had ordered the cutting off of his ears. And all because he had taken food when he was hungry. Then this female thrust on him! He had not wanted her - at least, not on these conditions. He spat into the flame which was now rising in the chimney.

"The land can rot!" he growled. "I work hard enough up there at the manor. When this bastard you are carrying comes, it is you who will be tending the land. I see you are growing flowers very well, so you can bend your back to something we can eat!"

Rising from her knees after making sure the fire would go, she looked from the window to the four rose trees she had put in, given to her by Susanna along with some sweet-smelling carnation plants and a dozen or so violets. Naturally her thoughts flitted to her friend's gardens, a magnificent setting for a lovely lady. How was Susanna? Today she had appeared to be in the very flush of health, but...

"Dear God, please do not let me lose my friend..." she prayed.

Within the hour she and Sam were sitting down at the rickety table eating a meal of herrings and barleycakes. He drank ale from a cup while she drank milk and water. He eyed her cup and asked where she had come by the milk.

"Mistress Christian gave it to me. I carried it home in a can."

"I do not understand why she has you there—" He spoke with a full mouth and Eleanor shuddered as the crumbly mixture of herring and barleycake spattered on to her own plate. Nauseated, she pushed it away and leant back in the chair. "I am telling you not to go there again."

He drew the back of a filthy hand across his nose then slid it along the side of his breeches. Above him two pictures with broken frames hung at a crazy angle, made that way when, in the early hours, he would come in and stagger about, touching the wall for support. Every day she would straighten the pictures, just as she would beat the threadbare hand-woven rug and sweep the floor. Was this to be her lot? she would ask herself while tears would firmly be repressed. "Did you hear me, wench? I said you are not to go to that house again."

"I shall go whenever I like."

Rising from the table she picked up her milk and went outside. The sun had come from behind a black and ominous cloud and its warmth on this October day was a welcome change from the week of chilly weather which she had feared would kill her flowers. But they had survived and were bright in the sunshine.

The baby began to kick and she marvelled as she watched the movement of her belly. Her baby... and Edward's. At first it had been a hated bulk growing in spite of her willing it to die within her. If she did not have it she could run away – oh, yes, she would defeat the law which prevented anyone from leaving the island. There were means, as Alicia's mother had proved. She had her mother's pendant, which no one knew about, hidden in a box which she had buried near the cypress tree by the gate. She could have given it to pay a boatman to take her over the water to England and her beloved Chester where flowed the shining river with its banks dotted with stately mansions behind which sprawled the ancient town named Deva by the Romans who once had a garrison there. Now there were narrow streets and alleys, and many taverns where men from the topsy-turvy half-timbered houses made merry of an evening. She recalled with sad and poignant intensity the tiny shop set snugly between two far more fashionable and elegant bow-fronted establishments on the Rows and over which was the gold and black sign her father had so cleverly painted himself: Joseph Challenor, Tailor. The pretty cottage with its well-established garden followed swiftly into her vision, the wattle and daub dwelling with its view to the river where the swans glided in the sunshine, their fluffy brown cygnets nervously keeping close. The strolls by the river or walks along the sandstone Roman Wall... So much had been hers in childhood, and could have remained had her father not died. But death was something over which man had no control, for had not she willed her bastard baby to die – ah, yes, over and over again. But now...? When it was moving so strongly as if fighting for the light it was almost ready to see? Now... She wanted her child, the seed of her dear love, for it was no bastard, but a Christian, and in this moment Eleanor swore that she would make him great. Him? A lovely smile broke. It would be a male child who would grow to a fine man with his father's good looks and physique... but a better man than Edward, a man with values such as those of Susanna, a good man and kind, certainly not the sort of man who would plunder and rob and cut off people's ears. A sigh escaped her; remembering the softness that lurked within that cruel and arrogant exterior she wondered if anything would happen that would bring that softness to the fore, if it were possible that Edward Christian could change.

*

Susanna, dainty in a stiff crimson brocade gown with an informal overjacket worn effectively to conceal her condition, stood on tiptoe to kiss her husband who had just ridden back from his weekly visit to his brother who had recently acquired the valuable estate of Poyll Dhouie in addition to the manor he already owned and farmed so profitably.

"Have you had a good day?" Susanna was feeling, and looking, exceedingly well today, a circumstance that cheered her husband since he had recently become troubled about her health.

"A most pleasant occasion, as usual."

"And," returned his wife perceptively, "you spent the time deploring the way the island is being run and devising ways of bringing about improvements."

"As a matter of fact, we were discussing the increasing power of the clergy. Mistress Callin has complained that she has had practically nothing under her late husband's Will."

"Well, I have to agree that this power of making Wills should be taken from the clergy. They frighten the poor people into leaving most of their property to the Church."

"To save themselves from damnation." Anger glinted in his eyes. "Derby should put a stop to it!"

Susanna changed the subject abruptly, asking about Poyll Dhouie.

"Edward is very pleased with his purchase. It is an elegant mansion as you know, and the surroundings are so beautiful."

"The woodlands? Yes, indeed. It must have one of the finest settings in the whole of Lezayre."

It was her husband's turn to change the subject, saying that despite his satisfaction with his two estates Edward was talking of going back to sea.

"He is? But what about these estates? Will he employ stewards to manage them?"

William shrugged his shoulders.

"He would have to find stewards, yes. But he might change his mind. It is time he settled down – found him a wife and gave up all thoughts of those mad exploits, for I am sure there was much danger involved."

She nodded. She admired bravery and daring but she was certainly not in favour of Edward's going back to sea. She had no idea what she wanted for her dear Eleanor, whom she had come to love as a sister; all she did know was that it had been a heartless act of her brother-in-law when he married her to that oaf, thereby condemning the lovely child to a life of drudgery and frustration. Sam Garrett was drinking heavily; perhaps he would drink himself to an early death.

"I hope he does have second thoughts—"

The words were out before she realised they must surely surprise her husband. He looked down into her face searchingly as he said with an odd expression,

"Why should you care whether or not Edward goes back to sea?"

She laughed and, tilting her head coquettishly,

"What are you thinking, William? He is very handsome and has a particular charm that neither you nor John possess—"

"Brother John is a clergyman like our father," he snapped. "They are not expected to charm the ladies... but Edward, yes he does have charm, and you, wife—"

"Am not in love with him," she cut in with a saucy chuckle. "I am glad you can be jealous, my love. It means you care. Mostly you Christians are wenchers and it is us, the wives, who are jealous."

"What a tease you are!" He bent to kiss her tenderly. "How have you been today?"

"I feel fine."

Which was true, although she still suffered some slight sickness in the morning, but she would be all right in a week or two when the sickness stopped altogether. Child carrying was distasteful to her but yet she was looking forward to giving William another child, and James a brother or sister.

He sat down on a settle by the crackling fire and stretched out his long legs. He held out a hand and eagerly she ran forward to put hers into it. She sank down at his feet and rested her head against his knee. He said tenderly,

"I love you, my Susanna. What a lucky man I am."

She sighed contentedly, so very thankful that he was not like his brother – heartless and haughty, or like Ewan who was always so aware of his power, his superiority. The Reverend John, her father-in-law, was a gentle kind man and William, to a great extent, took after him. And John, his father's curate, was also gentle and kind. It was Edward who was the odd one out...

Feeling her husband's lips on her hair, she looked up and smiled.

"Tell me what you have been doing today?" He kissed her forehead then leant away. "You have had that Garrett wench up here again?"

"She came to see Alicia – and me of course," she added on a challenging note.

"Why do you like her so much? You seem to forget she is far beneath you."

Susanna shook her head in swift protest. He sighed, fully aware of what to expect next.

"God made us all equal," she murmured. "I like not the ways of this island. There is too much difference between the rich and the poor."

"It is not only here, Susanna," he returned patiently. "In fact, it is probably worse across there." He looked at her and shook his head. "You could never make us all equal, my dear. Your little Eleanor could never even mix with us; she would be out of place, feel awkward. She would blush and stammer—"

"Nonsense!" she broke in angrily. "Eleanor does not blush and stammer with me! We are friends—"

"No, not friends. I forbid it!"

Something in the words and the manner of their delivery brought a puzzled frown to her brow.

"What—? Oh, good God!" She burst out laughing and to his annoyance it was some moments before she recovered. "William, it becomes you ill to hold such evil thoughts! You have been talking to Edward, who has told you about the King—"

"Susanna!"

"You will not adopt that horrified mien with me," she said, pretending arrogance. "I am not a child, William. Everyone talks about the King and his pretty boys – but I and dear Eleanor – I am ashamed of you!"

"Rubbish! I was not thinking such evil—"

"No? Then why did you forbid me to have her for my friend?"

"Because she is so very much your inferior!"

"Tell me, husband, by what sort of measurement do you assess a person's worth or status? Is there some right invested in you by which you are empowered to regard your fellow men as untouchables?"

A sigh of asperity escaped him.

"Do not exaggerate," he said wrathfully. "I have never regarded anyone as untouchable!"

She had been thoughtfully silent for a few moments when at last she queried, watching his expression closely,

"Are you willing to have a wager with me?"

"A...? What is this wager?"

"Ewan has asked us to dine with him on Thursday, as you know."
He merely gave an impatient nod of the head and she went on, "I
would like to take both Eleanor and Alicia—"

"You?" He stared in astounded disbelief. "You what?"

Susanna had the greatest difficulty in maintaining a sober
expression, so comical did he appear to her.

"As you know, I have for some months been teaching the two girls
in speech and manners – although Eleanor spoke prettily enough
already. Alicia has improved in the most incredible way. She can read
and write – Eleanor could do those because her mother taught her, but
I have lent her books and encouraged her to write short essays which I
have corrected for her. She is a bright child, William, most
intelligent; she learns quickly – they both do. I have been bored as you
know, since you brought me over here, away from my relatives and
friends – Oh, yes, I wanted to marry you, William," she added swiftly
as he was about to interrupt. "I am not making a complaint, merely
reminding you that I was bored. But after Alicia made friends with
Eleanor and brought her here, I thought it would be a good thing both
for them and me if I spent my time teaching them manners and – well,
seeing what the result would be. I am now of the belief that all the
poor need is educating."

"The idealist." He sighed again. "You are not serious, though, my
dear – about taking them with us? They have not been invited, so we
could not even if we wanted to."

"That is of no matter," she returned airily. "I am not very well so
I take my tirewoman with me – it is no unusual thing—"

"You only take your tirewoman when you are staying," he
interrupted, fast losing every shred of patience now. "We will be
there for a few hours only."

"I have said, I am not very well. At least, on Thursday I shall not
be feeling well so I want Alicia. And as she would feel lonely so I
agreed that she bring her friend. Ewan knows who Eleanor is."

"Of course. Edward's whore."

Susanna rose abruptly and put some distance between them, her
eyes sparkling with wrath.

"You have never listened to what I have told you about Eleanor!
The circumstances by which they were thrown together. She was a
virgin, a delicately brought up girl who met with misfortune. I hate
you to think of her as – as..."

He went to her and took her in his arms.

"I am sorry dearest. I know how you feel about her, how you always felt about Alicia. But, Susanna, they are *not* your equals and no amount of learning can make them so. They have no background, no ancestry of note—"

"And your ancestry?" She regarded him with a wide, challenging gaze. "Ferocious Vikings, plunderers and murderers whose other pastime was ravishing innocent females. And what now, even today? Deemster Ewan has ordered one of his labourers to be flogged for some petty theft. Is that human, something to be proud of? No, William; you Christians – and of course others who have power here and wealth – have much to learn about goodness and compassion, about tolerance and understanding."

"You can not have your men stealing from you," he protested, fully aware that he had been fighting a losing battle from the start. Susanna would take her two protégées to the dinner party whether he was happy about it or not.

"When people are hungry they will steal – any of us would."

"Ewan's vassals never go hungry."

"Perhaps not desperately hungry, but the flesh of a fowl makes a very desirable change from eating fish every day for years."

"You would agree that they steal?"

"Were I in charge there would be no need to steal. I would give them a fowl now and then."

"My dear..." He kissed her tenderly then held her away. "You have these strange ideas but they are good ones in many ways." He held her close, thinking of Master MacWalter who was defying him by refusing to grind his own grown corn at his mill. It was compulsory to use the master's mill! MacWalter's wife was grinding it at home in a machine they had devised. "Why do I hesitate in punishing him...?" He had spoken his thoughts aloud and now his wife was looking interrogatingly at him. He told her of his steward's defiance, and of his reluctance to punish him. "He is such a good and honest man," he ended as if self-defence was required.

Susanna smiled a wise little smile and murmured, her lips touching his cheek, "You have a kindness, William, and I have a premonition that one day you will champion the poor of this island, the oppressed – but have a care, my love, because the Stanleys are powerful, and they *are* the Kings of Mann, remember."

He stared down at her in some puzzlement.

"A premonition, Susanna? Truly?"

"The Stanleys have always bled the people of Mann—"

"But this present one," he broke in abruptly, "Earl William – and his wife, Elizabeth, who rule conjointly – trouble us little, merely collecting the revenue. They have not visited the isle yet and it would seem that the Earl has too many commitments in Lancashire and Cheshire – no, dearest, I feel you are wrong to say Lord Derby and his lady Countess are to be feared."

"The Stanleys have always taken too much from the Manx people, and they are still taking too much."

He smiled then and patted her cheek.

"What does my little love know about it? Tease not your lovely head with such things. Lord Derby is content to collect his rents and leave us alone."

After a pause during which she made no further comment he reverted back to the question of taking the two women to Ewan's home. "How are you to excuse such conduct, Susanna? Taking your tirewoman might be countenanced but why her friend, this very pregnant wench deflowered by my brother?"

"I have said, Alicia would be lonely on her own, with no one to talk to." She was rather afraid herself but nothing would have induced her to give that away to her husband. She was eager to carry out an experiment which would further dispel the boredom of being the idle wife of a rich man. It would be most gratifying if the experiment were successful, if the two girls' behaviour in the home of the noble Deemster proved that education was all that was needed to lift many of the downtrodden 'lower classes' out of a rut into which they had fallen. True, Eleanor had a yeoman grandfather, and a mother who cared, but Alicia had no such background. Deserted by her mother, and with a stepfather in prison, she would have had small chance of uplifting herself had it not been for her entering into the service of a kind and caring mistress. Susanna did consider herself to be kind and caring, and whenever possible she would treat her servants with the utmost consideration. She never forgot to say thank you, or to give presents at Michaelmas and on birthdays. She abhorred cruelty of any kind – and there was much cruelty meted out both by the manorial lords and the clergy. Injustice was rife, too. She had heard only yesterday that several parishioners of Lonon were sent to

St Germain's prison by the Vicars-General for one Sunday's absence from church. And that poor man who had been sent to prison for nothing more serious than leaning against the Communion table? To be poor in these times carried the very real risk of persecution.

*

Eleanor watched the approach of her friend as Alicia swung energetically along the lane, a pretty figure in her grey homespun gown girded tightly around the waist. Eleanor decided that the lace-edged cap and pretty shawl were gifts from her sweet-natured mistress. The girl's dark eyes held a mingling of excitement and anxiety which made Eleanor ask swiftly,

"Is anything wrong—?"

"Eleanor, my friend!" She had been hurrying and was a trifle breathless. "Nothing is really the matter, so do not look so troubled."

"Susanna...?" The girls always referred to her as Susanna when she was not present.

"It does concern her, yes, but it is nothing serious. She says she is a little out of sorts – Eleanor, do not, I pray you, look so distressed! My mistress is not going to die—"

"That word! Why have you said it?" Fear held her in its icy grip. She had found such a loving friend, but Eleanor had suffered so many disasters in her short life that she mistrusted fate's present kindness to her. If she should lose Susanna..."Just how ill is she, Alicia? Tell me; I must know at once!"

Alicia moved to sit down on a rickety three-legged stool and, in her well-mannered way, refrained from glancing around the grim hovel, aware as she was that such an action would cause her friend the deepest mortification.

"She is not ill, Eleanor – not any more than any woman is in her condition. But she and my master are invited to dine with the Deemster and as she is just a small bit afraid she might be sick and need attention, she is taking me with her." She stopped, her eyes sparkling. Eleanor waited for her to continue. "You know how thoughtful Susanna is for those who work for her. Well, she starts thinking to herself that I shall be lonely, all by myself in a room somewhere, then she hit on the idea of taking you as well, to keep me company. I am so excited, Eleanor! Milntowne! Such a great and noble mansion – and you and I are going to see inside it! We shall have a lovely meal served to us and we can chat over it and then perhaps we can saunter in the gardens – it will be dark but the moon is full so it will be romantic—"

"Alicia, I have to stop you. I am sorry but I could not possibly go with you, and indeed I am surprised at the suggestion. Surely Susanna knows it would not be a very comfortable situation for me to be in—" Elanor patted her belly automatically, and shook her head. "I am glad for you, dear Alicia, but sorry to have to refuse what Susanna unthinkingly considered would be a treat for me. She is aware that I am alone here every night so she thought it would be a pleasant change."

Alone every night… While Sam Garrett was drinking and whoring and bawling out to all and sundry that he objected to giving his name to his master's bastard. Alicia wondered if her friend was aware of all this talk among what her master's steward, MacWalter, contemptuously called the scum of Lezayre.

Alicia said persuasively at last,

"It is foolish in you to be troubled about your condition, Eleanor. Susanna is also breeding, remember."

"She has five months to go. I have only one month at most…" She tailed off, recalling that she was not at all sure if she did have a month, since her calculations had been vague in the beginning. "I look awful."

"You will look beautiful in the gown Susanna is lending you. It is one she herself wore when she was very big with James. She would have sent it with me today but she is trimming the cuffs with pretty white lace."

Excitement again brought a shine to her dark eyes and a frown to Eleanor's brow. How disappointed Alicia would be, for despite what she, Eleanor had said, it was clear that Alicia was taking her ultimate agreement for granted. Eleanor bit her lip, ready to voice another objection but Alicia was before her. "Susanna might think it is a slight – your refusal, I mean. So of course you have to come. And who is going to see you anyway? A footman will let us in and we shall immediately be taken by a serving-maid to the room where our meal is to be served."

"Has Susanna told you all this?" queried Eleanor watching her keenly.

"Not exactly," she admitted, "but it is what will happen—" She broke off and laughed. "For we can not dine with the aristocracy, not people of our station."

Eleanor nodded thoughtfully.

"I suppose you are right, it is what will happen."

It took her a full thirty seconds to steel herself to say yes, she would go with her friend, to keep her company.

*

The imposing mansion of Milntowne, turreted and sturdy, had been the seat of the Milntowne Christians since the mid-fourteenth century, having passed in an unbroken line from father to son; all except two had held the office of Deemster. Ewan was the tenth Deemster of the northern part of the island, a vast proportion of which - by judicious purchases and marriage portions - had come into the possession of the Christians, to make them the most powerful of all the landowners and a hindrance to the Lords of Mann in their attempts to appropriate these lands, a situation which had created the bitter feud existing between these two illustrious families.

Deemster Ewan had made many improvements to the dwelling which must have been owned originally by one of the first Viking settlers who named it Alptadair, meaning Swan's Glen.

Ewan had enlarged the house, installed the raised plaster ceilings of the era, and linenfold panelling to many of the walls. He had purchased from England carved oak tables and chests, exquisite tapestries and paintings, all of which were brought over in one of his ships. He had made a library fitted out with bog oak, and he had beautified the grounds out of all recognition. A man of great wealth and influence, he was also a man of exceptional intellect who never let an opportunity slip by. The most powerful man after the Lord himself, he possessed all the arrogant self-confidence of his forebears. At the age of thirty-five he had been Deemster for nine years, gaining a shrewdness that served him well both in his private and public capacity. Dark-haired and of an arresting mien, he was ever conscious of his own importance, and of all the great Christian family who between them owned a third of all productive land, all the best houses, the mills and many fishing rights. And like many others on the island they were involved in that highly lucrative business, smuggling. To his pretty cousin-in-law he was an enigma, a man of dual personality, for although he was often brutal in his punishment of wrongdoers, he was basically the champion of the poor, having spoken out against the oppression and injustice based on privilege and class or, quite often, the unscrupulous demands of a corrupt clergy. For they still demanded much, in spite of the unexpected intervention of the third Earl who abolished the practice of having to give marriage presents to the clergy, also death dues. But the clergy still held the right to make all wills and Susanna knew that the Deemster was working for this right to be taken away but as yet success was not in sight.

The sun was fading as the party entered the lofty hall after being admitted by a footman in immaculate attire. Eleanor, feeling far more relaxed and comfortable than she would have imagined – for the dress lent her was so cleverly designed that it hid a great deal – stood mesmerised by the splendour of Gobelin tapestries and carved oak, of silver sconces and candelabra. In the massive fireplace crackling flames gave added glow and colour to the brass firedogs. Alicia gave a little gasp while Eleanor, her composure recaptured, decided to be casual about it all, just as if such splendour was not exactly new to her. Susanna's eyes took on a very satisfied expression as she watched the girl discard her cape and hand it to the lackey. Ewan came from the drawing room and naturally expressed some surprise on seeing the two young girls. William looked at his wife as if to say that the explaining was hers alone. He handed his cape and gloves to the man and turned away.

Susanna said lightly, "Good evening to you, Cousin Ewan. I hope you do not mind that I have brought Alicia, my tirewoman, and her friend."

"Not at all," came the immediate response, with admirable aplomb. "I am sure you have a good reason?"

A tinkling laugh, a coquettish laugh which brought a frown to her husband's brow, rang through the hall.

"I feared I might be unwell, on account of bouts of sickness I have suffered recently, and so I wish Alicia to be on hand."

"Er – of course." Ewan, splendid in blue velvet and silk, cast a glance in Eleanor's direction. He knew her by sight; his eyes roved her figure before settling on her face. Her beauty had registered with him the first time he saw her, standing at the door of Sam Garrett's cottage. He knew she carried his cousin's child and, like William, he would rather have had its name to be Christian. He returned his attention to Susanna. "May I remark, cousin, that you have never looked less like being unwell. You are glowing."

The hint of dry sarcasm merely set Susanna's eyes alight again.

"Flatterer! I must admit I feel quite well at the moment." Her glance went to her protégées; they were still maintaining their respectful distance. "I can not lie to you," she twinkled, "as you know, I never have—"

"I do not know," he interrupted sardonically. "You are quite graceless, Susanna; and I would like to hear the real reason for the presence in my house of these two persons."

She shrugged her elegant shoulders.

"Of course. I was about to confess the whole when you interrupted me." She peeped up at him coquettishly, saw his glance slide to where William was studiously examining a painting which hung over the high mantel. She knew Ewan would like to have kissed her. What outrageous wenchers these Christians were! No wonder their clan multiplied quicker than any other on the island. "The truth is, my dear cousin, I have been relieving my boredom by giving lessons to those two."

"Ah! William did mention this nonsensical new pastime of yours. It appears you have strange ideas that our lackeys could become our equals with a few lessons on how to go on in polite society?"

He was laughing at her and although she blushed her regard was direct and challenging.

"You exaggerate but that is of no matter. I want you to have these two young ladies—" She stopped as he cocked an eyebrow. "Yes, Ewan, *young ladies*! I would have you invite them to sup with us."

"My dear Susanna, you can not be serious? They can go into the summer parlour and eat there, but certainly not at my table."

She bit her lip. She had been prepared for this, had admitted that her request was, to say the least, presumptuous, but she was set on proving the success of her experiment so she had no intention of giving up without a further attempt. And she used all her wiles, taking advantage of the knowledge that she had always been a favourite with the Deemster.

"I rarely ask you favours, Ewan. I can assure you that they do know how to go on – And they are very pretty, you must admit."

He looked at them, standing at the far end of the hall, both attired in gowns he recognised as belonging to Susanna. Silly little lass with her experiments... but he did have a soft spot for her... He said as the thought struck him,

"Do they know of your little scheme?" He slid a glance in their direction again. "I think not, since they are so at ease."

"That is just it! I have taught them to be at ease—"

"They have no knowledge of your experiment," he stated. "They are expecting to be sent to another room and that is why they are so calm. But," he wagged a knowing finger close to her face, "you shall witness their discomfiture once they know they are to sup with us."

"They are? Ewan, my very favourite cousin, I love you!"

He laughed at that and seeing William turn, he told him to take the scowl off his face.

"We all know that you are the only important man in Susanna's life." He stopped abruptly on hearing the heavy iron door knocker being lifted then dropped. "MacKewn—" He flicked a hand and the footman went to open the door. "Cousin Edward!" It was only natural that Ewan should send a swift glance towards Eleanor – in fact, they all did. "You sent word that you were not coming."

"Had a change of mind."

He was already handing his cape to the lackey and it was obvious that he had not yet noticed the two girls standing at the far end of the great hall. He took off his wide gauntlet gloves and proceeded to shake out the white lace cuffs that matched the ruff at his throat. His dark red doublet was slashed and paned, as were the sleeves, to reveal embroidered linen beneath. He wore full breeches and rosettes on his shoes. His stiletto beard was rather darker than the short, upward-brushed hair which was now the fashion and perhaps more suited to the London scene than that of a small, backward little island where fashion was usually somewhat out of date. To Eleanor, who had turned to face him, her cheeks drained of colour, her glorious hair falling in untamed abandon on to her shoulders, Edward was even more handsome than she remembered him. His tall figure had come into her vision at times, of course, because Sam's cottage was on the edge of his estate. But there had never been a face-to-face encounter as there now was – not since her wedding day when Edward had come to the cottage to pass his warning to her husband. Her mouth was dry, the palms of her hands damp. She wanted to turn and run, to be anywhere but here, in the presence of the father of her child. Her discomfiture was apparent to all and she knew that if Edward spoke to her she would reply in stammering accents. But suddenly she caught a sign from Susanna, almost imperceptible, the movement of her lips, but on the instant she knew that to lose her self-control would somehow reflect on this dear friend whose eyes were dark with anxiety. Knowing nothing of Susanna's "experiment" she yet was profoundly alert to the fact that, by losing her composure, she would in some incomprehensible way be letting Susanna down. And with this conviction came a new strength, a firm resolve to hold on to her dignity, to remember it was a Christian she carried, a Christian from a long and noble line.

She moved slowly, her head held high. But before she came anywhere near to Edward, Susanna, a sigh of relief having escaped her, was saying brightly, "How very nice to have another of the family for supper! Edward, you will be wondering why Eleanor is here. She came to be with Alicia, who is my maid as you know."

He nodded, smiling, his eyes fixed to those of the girl who, to him, had been very different from all the rest. God's glory, that hair! It was still the same, still shining with cleanliness and health. How did she come to be here? Came with Susanna's tirewoman? What was his cousin-in-law talking about? And what of Ewan – was he really having these two wenches to supper? He shrugged away these unanswerable questions and, coming forward, held out his hands to the one girl he had never quite managed – try as he would – to put along with all the rest whom he had bedded. Heavy with child as she was, he still found her beautiful... and affecting him in some strange way. She placed her hands in his, a smile quivering on her lips.

"How are you faring, Edward?" Was it a trite question, she wondered with a fearful glance at Susanna. Her nerves were rioting but her resolve to appear composed and dignified was still strong. "You look very grand in these clothes. I have seen you only in seaman's dress, you know."

He laughed, easing any slight strain there was. Ewan, eyes sardonically drawn to Susanna's satisfied countenance, decided there was certainly something in her experiment for no lady of quality could have dealt more serenely with a situation such as this. His admiration for Eleanor's beauty spread to something deeper and he thought it a great pity that she had no background and was, therefore, totally unsuitable as a wife for his cousin.

"A pirate's dress, you mean," he said in some amusement, indicating at the same time that they should all move into the room where supper was laid out on a wide oak table. With an almost imperceptible lift of a finger Ewan had a lackey by his side and was softly giving him instructions. The man looked covertly at the two girls then went away to enlighten the menials in the kitchen that the Deemster was entertaining a whore and a serving wench to supper.

"And there is Master Edward," he added as an afterthought. "So three more places are wanted."

"What has the master in mind?" in a puzzled voice from Jamie the footboy. "He can hardly bed them while his cousins are here."

"He would have difficulty with one of them," grinned the flunkey who had brought the news. "She is Sam Garrett's wife and looks ready to drop the bairn at any minute now."

And Tom MacAlister had no idea, at that time, just how close he was to the truth. For less than an hour later Eleanor was writhing in the agonies of labour, having been carried by Edward, moaning with pain, up to a bedchamber; and old Mother Corlett, the midwife, was already on her way, in the cart which Ewan had sent in all haste only moments after Susanna had cried, on seeing the sudden contortions of Eleanor's face,

"Her time is here. Oh, God, how could I know this might happen!"

But the three men were calm, Ewan and Edward acting swiftly. William, distressed by the moans of agony, was merely a bystander while Alicia followed Edward Christian up the wide, balustraded staircase and now she was seated by the bed, holding her friend's hand. She was fascinated by the expression on Master Edward's face, she afterwards told her mistress.

"Does he love her, do you think?"

"Perhaps. At any rate, she loves him."

"Poor, dear Eleanor..." She was thinking of Sam, who openly said he was not having another man's bastard in his house.

Susanna, sitting on the other side of the big bed, was holding a cool towel to Eleanor's forehead, aware of what the girl was going through, since she had been through it once herself. Woman's lot was a sorry one, she decided, dreading the day when her own time would come again. How many children would she have? Her fortune had been told last year, when she had been on a visit to her parents. She had been told by the gypsy that she would have three boys and two girls. Perhaps. Susanna felt wonderfully fit just now... but there were times when she believed she would die young.

"She is a sturdy lass," Mother Corlett was saying of Eleanor two hours later. "I expect no problems."

And only another hour passed before she was sending Alicia down to tell the men that a baby boy had been born.

"He is beautiful!" exclaimed Susanna. "Fair and strong and... dear Eleanor, so like his father."

"Of course." Eleanor, relaxed in that wonderful state of achievement and the absence of pain, smiled serenely and added, "I knew he would be like Edward. I wanted him to be." But better, she added silently. Like my dear love in looks but honest and kind, not the cruel pirate – no, never that.

"What shall you call him?" Susanna was asking gently as she pulled the covers up a little higher. "But perhaps so important a matter needs thinking about?"

Eleanor shook her head, then turned it to gaze lovingly at the miniature that lay in the crook of her arm.

"Edward Christian Garrett. That is to be his name."

'And one day he will drop the Garrett,' she thought, the merest of frowns touching her brow. She disliked intensely the idea of Edward's son having to take the name of another man, but it had to be... or so she supposed at this time.

Chapter Four

Two months had passed since the night he had held his son in his arms... A brooding expression so different from that of the swashbuckling searover caused Edward Christian's uncle to observe dryly,

"The time is nigh when you will be leaving us. I shall miss you, my nephew, for you have often kept me pleasant company. But a restless buccaneer is before me now who hath the seafever upon him again." The old man, sparse of frame and with a pale, aquiline face and exceptionally thin nostrils, stared through hooded blue eyes at the man sprawled in the gilded leather chair, his fingers tapping the arm, an indication of the tumult within him. "What makes you so unsettled? You have riches enough for any man; you have Lough Mollo – ah, I know it is not in your complete ownership just yet, but I am old and of late a pain in my chest has become troublesome..."

"I am not desirous of inheriting this estate, Uncle. Yes, I am afflicted with the seafever again. In fact, I was never really free from it, but there were reasons why I felt it safer to be here than to be spending time at Court while waiting for a ship."

"One reason," the old man said. "But the King now has Villiers as his favourite so you could safely go to Court. Do that, then come back here and resume the duties you have so efficiently been carrying out."

A sigh escaped his nephew. Yes, the King did have another favourite, and it might be safe to have a sojourn in London. But Edward was well aware that his decision to go to sea was now influenced by something altogether different from the fear of clashing with his sovereign and, most probably, ending up in the Tower. No... it was that bonny bairn, that and his beautiful mother... He had seen her only yesterday, carrying the precious bundle as she trudged the several miles to his brother's house where she would stay all day with Susanna and the pretty maid, Alicia. Eleanor had failed to notice him, riding the small nag along the lane leading to the Deemster's home where he was to join Ewan and others who were meeting to discuss some way of reducing the power of the clergy. Edward frowned. So many of his kin were now concerning themselves with the plight of the poor and perhaps he should be working with them. But how could he keep seeing his son and not hold him again? He would grow each week and month... he would have his first birthday... his second... In the hovel to which he, the child's father, had condemned him.

"I have to go!" he exclaimed, rising from the chair in a swift, restless movement that took him close to the window, out of which he stared for a long moment before adding, in a quieter tone, "There is more than you know, Uncle." He turned back into the cosiness of the room with its pine logs and peat crackling in the massive grate and its carved oak gleaming with the patina of age and the energy of parlourmaids and scullions. "I am aware that one day I must settle down but that day is not yet. Thomas Best—"

"Ah, him!" A bony finger was wagged and in the dull blue eyes there was a warning. "That man will lead you into trouble, for he takes too many risks."

"Thomas Best is merely a partner, so to speak. He does not control any actions of mine." Edward's voice and manner had undergone a dramatic change. He was again the arrogant, self-assured privateer, the daredevil feared by Spanish and Portuguese captains alike. "He has asked me to join him again, and the East India Company want me." He shrugged his broad shoulders. "I must go, Uncle. I have to."

The old man regarded him speculatively.

"It is that bastard of yours," he stated. "He troubles you mightily. You have mentioned him many times; he is on your mind, Edward. I cannot think, though, that your desire to leave the island has its roots in a fear that you might impulsively decide to make the child legitimate."

"Marry his mother? She is already married."

"That!" scoffed his uncle. "The marriage can easily be annulled, because it has never been consummated."

"How the devil do you know that?" demanded Edward wrathfully.

"Because Sam Garrett, when he is sodden with ale – bought no doubt with the allowance you have made him – bellows it out all over the village. Everyone knows the condition you laid down, just as they know the bastard child is yours."

"The... swine! I shall have him flogged – no, he shall lose his tongue—!"

"Not so hasty, my nephew. The damage is already done so you gain nothing by such a barbaric act."

"Barbaric?" with a lift of the straight thick brows. "Since when have you allowed pity into your heart?"

His uncle smiled faintly.

"Times change, boy. We Christians, and the Quailes and Curpheys, are concerning ourselves with the poor of this island. There is far too much misery and we could have a rebellion on our hands. Ewan and others, as you very well know without my telling you, are deeply troubled that Derby's subjects will rise up and fight against oppression."

"I am well aware of what Ewan and others are about," almost snapped Edward impatiently. "Yes, misery could animate discontent, but we were talking about Sam Garrett! Something has to be done with him."

"What?" shrugged his uncle. "If you continue to bribe him he will continue to drink, and a man filled with ale is a man with false courage. Sam Garrett might be afraid of you when he is sober but not otherwise. Forget it, Edward. As I say, the damage is done..." He broke off and paused a moment, thoughtfully. "What puzzles your family is why in God's name did you bring back one of the wenches you had bedded. She was breeding, yes, but others ravished by you must have been carrying bastards. Why this one? And why so anxious that she should be found a husband?"

Yes, why? Edward went over to the window again, the brooding expression returning to his face. He had been wenching since he was sixteen and had enough Viking blood in his veins to be able to forget a maid ten minutes after he had ravished her. But not this one... This child who into his power fate had thrown her... offered to him in exchange for the safety of her mistress. And he was remembering his inexplicable reluctance to violate her. But then the drowning of her mistress had thrown Eleanor and him together and the outcome was inevitable. She was far too tempting, and he had been a long time without the comfort of a bedmate.

Movements in the fields caught his attention; a labourer that reminded him of Sam Garrett. He was pulling potatoes with one hand while the other slid across his nose then down the side of his breeches.

Nauseated, Edward turned away. But his thoughts plagued him for he saw his son having such a man as a foster father, his son who was of the noble Christian blood. As if driven by some force beyond his control he looked from the window again, but this time it was a woman whose bulky form came to his vision, a hag shuffling along with a bundle of clothes she intended washing in the river. Would Eleanor become like that? Those people over there were what Deemster Ewan and many of his kin were fighting for – the Manx nation, they said, as if it did not mean people at all; just a nebulous mass of humanity referred to as a nation. Frowning heavily, he swung round to face the room again, an elegant room with fine carved furniture. His uncle was dozing, affected by the warmth of the fire. Not so old, but not well either. Yet he was by no means at death's door and Edward had no wish for him to be.

"Ah, you are waking up?" he observed with a smile not untinged with affection. Why had his uncle not made sure of having a son of his own to inherit the estate? Edward thought of Poyll Dhouie, an estate with productive spreading fields stretching far to join the extensive demesne lands of the Milntowne estate beyond which stretched for many a mile those parts of the estate held by the Deemster's numerous tenant farmers. Edward felt he would be quite satisfied with Poyll Dhouie – once he did decide to settle down – without bothering about Lough Mollo. But inherit it he would, because his uncle had willed it to him.

"Sorry. It was bad mannered in me to go to sleep while you are here." He lifted a hand to pull a bell rope. "It goes dark. I mislike that time between the dying of the sun and darkness. It depresses me. One feels sort of – in limbo."

A low laugh was Edward's response but when the lackey came in he immediately ordered him to light the candles. They were soon flickering and the old man ordered the curtains to be drawn.

"And we shall partake of some wine," he added. "Bring both the Rhenish and the Burgundy – Damme, man, move yourself!" The irascible tone made the man jump. Edward found himself saying, "Crenlit does not walk very well today. He suffers pain in his legs." And to himself, "Am I really becoming soft? Crenlit is paid well; he should move more quickly…"

"Ah, you did not say, Crenlit. I am sorry. Take a rest – but bring the wine first. I hope you will feel better tomorrow."

"We are both becoming soft," decided Edward but he spoke to himself. Aloud he said that, if his uncle wished it, he would make sure a conscientious man would be found to take over the stewardship of the Lough Mollo estate. He had already established a steward in residence at Poyll Dhouie.

"So you are definitely going?" Resignation in the tone but regret too as the old man added, "I am sorry at your decision but I have known for a while that you were becoming restless." A small pause when the wine was brought on a heavy silver salver on which also were the cups. "So you are content to leave the other situation as it is?"

"Other situation?" Edward watched Crenlit limp towards the door and then go through it. "What do you mean?"

"You know very well! You are content that your son shall be brought up by Sam Garrett?"

"He will be brought up by his mother." He reached for a cup and, filling it with the Rhenish, handed it to his uncle.

"If she should die…"

"She will not die. Her lifeline is extraordinarily long."

His uncle looked up at him in some amusement, the cup of wine held close to his mouth.

"It is the first time I have known you be interested in witchcraft…"

Ignoring that, Edward poured his own wine and sat down on the opposite side of the fire. His thoughts troubled him; he could envisage no way of regaining his carefree existence except by going to sea.

But he would have to see his son once more before he went…

*

The sun was dying below a sultry horizon as Edward Christian rode the lane leading to the cottage. Trees were bare, and the River Sulby seemed sullen and darker than usual in that melancholy half glow that heralds the onset of night. He had come at this time in order to see Samuel Garrett and make sure he put enough fear into the man to ensure the continued safety of Eleanor. He could have sent for the fellow but the work of getting up the potatoes was too important to take any man off the task.

He did not know just what to expect from Eleanor but was not surprised to see her face colour up when on coming to the door, she found herself face to face with him. They both remembered that night at Milntowne when, apart from the midwife, he was the first to hold his son but on that occasion Eleanor was scarcely conscious so perhaps she did not remember.

"How are you, my dear?" His voice was gentle and there was affection in his eyes. His glance went beyond her. "Is Sam in?"

She shook her head.

"He does not come for his meal any more but goes somewhere else for it." She stood aside and added curiously, "Why are you here, Edward?" There was little or no embarrassment now, and the blush had receded from her cheeks. "I heard it said that you were going to sea again." She took another step backwards and he entered the squalid dwelling and tried to close his mind to what he had done. But Eleanor was there, fragile and beautiful even in the well-worn homespun gown, the very young mother of the one son he really knew he had. His feelings were stranger than any he had known before; his thoughts flitted about to bring pictures of the *Falcon* and of his carrying Eleanor aboard, of the night his son was born, of the meeting with Ewan and the others who seemed dedicated to effecting changes in the laws, reducing the stranglehold the Church had on the people; young William, the dark one, second cousin to him, saying, at only ten years of age, "Why are so many Manx people poor? Why do we let them be poor? We could give them some of the good things we have ourselves." And the boy's father replying, "It is Stanley who is the culprit. He bleeds us all; he allows the Church to use intolerable powers to oppress the poor."

"Edward..." The voice came softly to interrupt his reverie and he looked at her. "Why are you here?"

"It is true that I go to sea soon, but I wanted to see little Edward, my son, just once before I go because it could be several years before I return."

"Your son? Is it so important that you see him?"

"I have this desire—" He stopped and listened. "He is crying?"

"No, just cooing to himself." The tenderness of maternal love shone in the big blue eyes. "Come, he is in my room. It is cleaner and I have some rather nice furniture which your sister-in-law gave to me."

"Susanna?" He was suddenly angry and humiliated and resentful all at once. "I could have sent you some furniture!"

"But you failed to do so," she returned gently. "Susanna and I are very good friends as you know." She moved to the doorway between the two small rooms which was all the cottage boasted. "She is kindness itself to me and I love her dearly. Alicia is my friend also. I have been very fortunate even though, sometimes, I know I am an exile and I yearn for my lovely Chester. One day I know I shall go back." She was beside the wooden cot where her baby lay looking at his fingers and making small noises. Edward moved, to stand above the cot.

"He looks very healthy."

"I manage to feed him. There is plenty of milk."

He glanced at the full breasts and nodded slowly. His mind was in disorder; he could not have said what he wanted as all was chaos within him. If only the wench had been his equal...but no, he was a long way from being ready for marriage. There was the sea... calling him, the adventure and the challenge, the booty... He said turning away, "I am satisfied now that I have seen him again." He looked down into her face and saw there was a rigid whiteness about it, a strained expression in her eyes. Her breasts were heaving, as if driven by a thudding heart. A tenseness gripped him... and a sudden desperation. He had to get away! Yes, before this disturbing and damnable emotion drove him to some folly he would be bound to regret sometime in his life. His manner changed and he became brisk. "You say Sam does not come home when he has finished work? Where does he go, then?"

"I have no knowledge of his activities – except of course that he sups more ale than is good for him."

"But he never tries to molest you?"

"Up till now he has not, but—" She broke off abruptly and shook her head.

"But, what?" The grim tone and the compressed lips were no reassurance to her simply because Edward was going away.

"He has threatened, but only in a – a kind of weak way. I believe I can look after myself should he forget your threat."

Edward said perceptively,

"You are afraid that once I am off the island he will attempt to assert his rights as your husband?"

It was more of a statement than a question and before she had realised it she had nodded her head. The fair tresses caught the sun's last rays and Edward drew a breath. God's glory, but she was beautiful!

"He might try. You see, he feels cheated—"

"He is well paid for his loss." The fine mouth tightened. "Are you sure you have no knowledge of where he might be at this moment? I want to see him."

"It is rumoured that he is working with smugglers."

"Smugglers, eh?" Edward became thoughtful. If he could catch the rogue and send him to Peel Castle... "From where does he operate?"

"I know not. Smuggling goes on everywhere. The shelter of Maughold Head is mentioned but the creek at Laxey, too. He could be anywhere, but I would say it was Maughold Head, as it is much closer."

Maughold Head. There was a boat of his own lying in that shelter, laden with wine. Best leave well alone.

"It would be difficult to prove anything against him; it always is."

"I know. As I said, smuggling is rife on this island. The English government must be at a great loss by it."

She drew up the white coverlet which the baby had kicked away. Then she looked up, her next words startling him. "Are you involved in smuggling, Edward?"

"Good God, why do you ask that?"

"You sound shocked, but you avoid my eyes."

"If I were a smuggler, would I be likely to tell you?"

She shrugged her shoulders. "Why not? I know you for a pirate, a searobber—"

"A privateer, that is what I am! A merchant adventurer!"

Eleanor smiled then and said with a hint of amusement,

"You like to draw a fine line, Edward, but no line exists. You plunder and rob on the high seas just as Hawkins and Drake did, with the full approval of the Queen, that was. You do not have the approval of King James because he has forbidden all forms of privateering. I think you are smuggling because the risks and excitement would appeal to your sense of adventure..." She looked down at her now sleeping child. "My little Edward will never rob or do anything dishonest. I shall teach him the difference between good and evil – and I mean him to be a great man one day."

There was sudden fire in her words, determination in her eyes. "Dear Susanna has promised that when he is old enough he can join James with his lessons. Of course, James is too young yet but when he is ready your brother is to fetch a governess from England."

"You have been very fortunate in having my sister-in-law for a friend." He looked sullen and she said without thinking,

"Would you not wish to settle down, like your two brothers?"

"Settle into a dull life?" He shook his head emphatically. "Perhaps one day, but I am unlike them in many ways. John, so content to be my father's curate. And William..."

He tailed off to become thoughtful. William who doted on Susanna. True, she was a pretty little piece, and devoted to him and her little son... but what a dull existence. He recalled the rumours he had heard that William had been given the opportunity of becoming Receiver-General, so it would appear that he was at present in Stanley's favour. Should he accept the office he would at least have other interests, which would take him away from home.

"William is a very happy man, Edward." Eleanor's gentle voice intruded and his thoughts switched. "And so is your brother John. He is so proud of little William, and no wonder for he is an adorable child."

He laughed.

"They are all adorable at that age." He paused a moment. "I ought to see Sam, just to make sure he will never be so foolish as to forget my warning."

Eleanor said curiously,

"Why are you so determined to keep him away from me?"

A strange silence ensued before he answered her.

"Because I might want you myself again—"

"Want m–me?" Her heart leapt and the blue eyes shone. "You – you might want me – sometime?"

He nodded his head.

"You are still the most beautiful wench I have ever seen. Yes, my dear, I could want you, sometime in the future."

But not to be his wife. She read that in his expression. Yet there must be something he felt for her which was special... and she was content.

*

"So your mind is firmly made up?" Deemster Ewan, in a close-fitting doublet and bulky paned trunkhose, was in the garden when his cousin had ridden up the long, tree-lined drive. But now they were before a glowing fire, drinking wine from Moorish-style cups – part of booty taken from a Portuguese vessel after a glorious fight revelled in both by Edward Christian and his villainous crew alike. "It is time, lad, that you forsook all this roistering and robbing and settled down."

Edward, sprawled in a chair with his long legs stretched out, laughed and lifted his cup, turning it idly in his hand.

"I would not be the only loser, cousin."

"Agreed. Nevertheless, we all have work to do – I suppose you know that your brother is to be given the office of Receiver-General?"

"It is settled? I had heard but I have not seen William for several days. I have been busy finding a suitable steward for Lough Mollo. I had already found one for Poyll Dhouie."

A slight frown settled on the Deemster's forehead. He sipped his Rhenish thoughtfully, his dark eyes staring fixedly into the flames.

"Why did you buy Poyll Dhouie if you were thinking of going to sea again?"

Edward shrugged.

"It was too close to the Milntowne estate, and I doubt not that you also would desire it to be kept in the family?"

"I had a mind to buy it myself," Ewan mused, turning his cup to admire its shape. Poyll Dhouie had for many generations been in the possession of Christians, but owing to an inheritance it had passed to the Curpheys fifteen years previously. The owner who had recently died had lived there alone for twelve years and on her death her nephew had decided to sell, having become rich on marriage to an heiress from Cumberland. "Well, though it is expedient to have the property back into the estates of the Christians, it is not good to leave a steward in charge for too long. And about Lough Mollo—" He broke off, looking stern, and they were both profoundly aware of the eleven years' difference in age. Ewan at thirty-five was even more mature than his years, the result of his many commitments since as well as his office of Deemster – which was hereditary – he was Deputy-Lieutenant of Peel Castle. "Lough Mollo, though not large according to our standards, is a valuable property, most productive. It will be yours, Edward, and it is that circumstance which you should be considering. This handing its running over to a steward can be a great folly."

"The two men are trustworthy. I am sure of it."

"Ah, well, be it on your own head." Ewan glanced at Edward, the handsome, buccaneering adventurer whose Viking blood took him ever roving the high seas. Two years with Thomas Best and the East India Company, along with all the years before, should have sufficed to cure the rogue of his fever. But the Company wanted him, and what they would pay him was only a minor part of the draw; there was the promise of exciting combat, with prizes of which a goodly portion would find itself in the pockets of the two men. Without thinking Ewan spoke his thoughts aloud. "One day, my lad, the East India Company are going to discover what you are about."

A slow smile spread over his cousin's face. He said carelessly,

"They would never be able to prove anything."

"Edward, you are a very rich man already. Why want more?"

"We all want more," Edward was swift to remind his cousin. "Look at the vast amounts of land you have added to the Milntowne estate during the last three years. It could be said you needed no more—" He spread a lace-cuffed hand. "All this, and the holdings you have in and around Maughold and Ballure. Between us we own half the island, or thereabouts."

"It is true we own a fair share, but whether we shall continue to hold it is a debatable point."

"Nonsense!" Edward had to laugh. "We have not held out against the Stanleys all this time only to let them win a victory over us now."

"Perhaps you are right. But we would be unwise to underrate the power of the Stanleys."

By tradition they had become so strong as to consider themselves invincible. Even their own kinsmen went in awe of them. Perhaps it had not been such a good move after all when John McCrysten, and his son, William, had put their names to a formal Declaration against Sir Stephen Scrope's claim to what was then the Crown of Mann. John had signed as the Deemster and his son as one of the Keys. Their weight and importance on the island had influenced King Henry IV to throw out the Scrope family's claim and allow the two Stanley brothers to continue to hold the island for the Crown of England.

This meant that Henry could give the island away, which he soon did, and from then on it was owned and ruled by the Stanleys.

Edward, showing no sign of anxiety over his cousin's words merely shrugged and reminded him that the present Lord of Mann showed no interest in his kingdom, so why worry?

"His lady is very astute," returned the Deemster. "She makes arbitrary laws; she has done nothing about reducing the power of the Church. It still makes all Wills, as you very well know. This allows it to arrogate considerable wealth to the clergy."

This specious enrichment of the priesthood was always overlooked by the Stanleys who also turned a blind eye to a great many other impositions. The Church also demanded a tithe from any person who wore his deceased relative's clothes. And should they refuse to bring in these dues to the Church they were refused the sacrament at Easter. Ewan was frowning heavily at his thoughts. Whatever his own shortcomings he was a champion of the Manx people. Felons he hated and his punishments were harsh, and sometimes brutal, but as with Edward, there existed a core of softness within the shell of granite, which meant sympathy for the victims of the clergy's greed.

"I agree about the power of the Church," Edward was saying with a hint of anger. "It is outrageous – but of course you have to remember why it is overlooked by the Lord and his Countess. They are taking a large proportion of these tithes."

"Of course," with a sneer of contempt. "So we can see no ending to that power unless we fight."

"There is one thing: the question of the land tenures appears to be sleeping," observed Edward thoughtfully.

The Deemster's sneer became more pronounced. This tall and stately man with the arrogantly imposing mien spoke with a confidence oddly lacking a few moments ago.

"They fear the Christians. We have harassed them for generations and shall continue to do so..." He was speaking to himself all at once and Edward remained silent. But he too was thinking that this feud would continue while ever there were Stanleys who – as they had done from the beginning – swore that all land was theirs, because the island had been given to them. With the arrogance typical of their breed they condemned the fact that the lands had belonged to the Christians – and a few others on the island – for hundreds of years. Other lands had been added by marriages to wealthy heiresses, and some by judicious purchase. "As you say," went on the Deemster presently, "the Earl and Countess seem not to be interested in anything except the collection of revenues from the isle. However," Ewan paused to give effect to his next words, "they could take into their heads at any time to come over – perhaps the Countess on her own as she is the stronger one – and new and more severe laws could be made. We landowners, especially those of us in high office, should be here, in readiness, united against any despotic moves they might think to make."

"You are suggesting I stay and take some office?"

"No, Edward," with a sigh of resignation. "Why suggest what you refuse to heed? Go, get this restlessness out of your system. You will be older when you return, and maybe ready for responsibilities. What does your uncle say of your decision?"

"He is resigned, saying he will die before I return, but he is not old."

"Not old, but lacks fair health. He was down with the ague six months ago and last winter he was sickened of a fever."

"I know all this, Ewan, but as you say I am not ready yet to settle here. I would like to go to Court for a while – if I felt it was safe – and then go to sea again."

"Safe?" broke in his cousin with an interrogating stare.

"The King, and his catamites. I found myself greatly in favour and was glad that I was due to join Thomas again. Robert Carr – the Scotsman – seemed to be falling from favour and I perceived the risk should James' eyes fall on me. But Carr is in favour again and made Earl of Somerset. Also, George Villiers is rising in the King's esteem so I might be at Court for awhile..." He tailed off and a frown touched his brow. "It will be after I have had another year at sea," he suddenly decided, "for I forget not the way the King was with me."

"He is married. One wonders at the man and his desires for others of his own sex." He smiled faintly. "Give me a buxom wench all the time."

A loud laugh escaped his cousin.

"How many bastards to date – or have you lost count?"

"There are many, for sure," grinned the Deemster. "More Christians to fight, if ever it should come to it."

"In England a bastard has by law to take its mother's name."

"I know it. And am glad it is not so here. Which reminds me, Edward, I mislike your son taking the Garrett name. We must do something about it. Susanna tells me that Eleanor – whom I must say I favour as she is a pretty-mannered wench who is applying herself assiduously to her lessons – has given the child the name of Christian and has told Susanna that he will be able to drop the Garrett one day. But I wish that he will be known as Christian now."

"Impossible, with Garrett being his mother's husband."

"Pity you married her to that clod. What made you?"

Edward shook his head.

"At the time it seemed a good idea, the only solution because, you see, I had no guts to abandon her. She is so different from any others... well, you know she is. You and William appear to have accepted her almost as family."

"We have, almost. She is after all the mother of my cousin's son, who is the nephew of your brother. So she is being accepted as of our family."

"But she – she has no background. Her father was a tailor in Chester." Did he want her to be accepted as family?

"So she told me. I find nothing wrong with any man who will employ himself in honest work. Eleanor's mother was from yeoman stock and Eleanor has been taught by her. Eleanor is now intent on improving herself even more. She is fortunate in having a friend in Susanna. Eleanor will see that your son is educated, also. She tells me she is determined he shall be a great man."

Edward's mouth seemed to have gone dry. He took up his cup which the Deemster had refilled.

"I cannot ever marry her," he stated firmly. "Surely you know that?"

"Certainly; it would not do. Nevertheless, she is here, brought by you, Edward," Ewan said in a low and faintly warning tone, "and here to stay – a situation to be reckoned with should you marry and settle..."

"What else could I have done with her!" he snapped, feeling as if a net were entangling him. "She had nobody to go to—"

"It was unwise to take a girl like her. There are plenty of whores about, who could have been abandoned, but you had to take someone who was above what you could forget and below your station so there could be no thought of marriage – marriage to you, I mean."

Edward pursed his lips. He misliked this conversation. He had come to tell Ewan of his decision to go to sea, a courtesy to which as head of the family, he was entitled even though the information had already come to him from William.

"I have to be going." He half rose from the chair but the Deemster flicked a hand to indicate he should sit down again. The fire was a warm red glow now as the flames from the pine logs had died down and only the peat was left.

"This matter of your son's name, Edward. I cannot countenance a Christian with any other name than his own rightful one."

A helpless gesture and a shake of the head from his cousin, and then,

"I have already said it is impossible to change it now. His mother's name is Garrett. It is not any use; it has to stay as it is. I do myself dislike my son's having the name of another man—" He spread his hands in a gesture of impatience. "While ever he lives Garrett gives his name to his wife's child."

"While ever he lives..."

"What—?"

"Is there nothing we can do – legally, of course?"

"Whenever was murder legal?"

This brought a hint of amusement to his cousin's eyes.

"How many murders have you committed, lad?"

"If you are suggesting that one more would make no difference then you have no love for me. To kill in fair combat is different from killing in cold blood, a crime for which I would be hanged."

"If we could get him jailed... for a very long time?"

"A man cannot be jailed for drinking too much ale. That is his only crime, except for trucking with smugglers, that is."

"Smugglers?" The Deemster's eyes flickered with keen interest. "We can jail him for life for that."

"And ourselves at the same time."

Edward paused, thinking of the boat lying at anchor at this very moment, waiting to receive a signal, its contraband including wool, hides and tallow. It would carry these goods to a little cove in Cornwall where the merchant would take up, in exchange, wine, salt, pitch and iron and bring them back to the island.

"Davies will be getting impatient to be off, but the English Customs are becoming more watchful and I am wondering if we should stay our activities for a while?"

"Perhaps. However, for this time – Davies will be patient, as he has so much to gain. If he had to unload the legal way he would be a great deal lighter in the pockets."

"Our own involvement prevents our taking any action against Sam Garrett—" Edward pursed his lips. "Because he is no fool, that one. Never goes about with his eyes shut."

"One never knows what might happen," said Ewan cryptically. He pulled a bellrope and when the lackey appeared he told him to bring in some coal.

"Yes, sir."

The man made a little obsequious bow of the head and went out. Edward asked in surprise,

"You have coal?"

"A little. That is why I use it sparingly. Our William's lady countess favours us; she sent coal to the Christians."

"She has some motive. Take care, cousin."

"I always take care," was his significant rejoinder. "It is some of you young ones who take the chances. Make no mistake, cousin, I am always on guard where the Stanleys are concerned. I forget not their speciousness down through the ages, nor that William's father came over here making laws which were to his benefit alone." He had cared nothing for the Manx nation and like his kin before him he came only when greed drove him. "His interference with the Keys only worsened this feud which lies smouldering between us."

"Pray it will continue only to smoulder, for our Lord's power has the King of England behind it."

The Deemster nodded his head. He was thinking of the hatred his father had felt against the fourth Earl, the present Lord's father. Deemster William Christian – the first to drop the prefix, Mac – had a deep admiration for Mary Queen of Scots and a bitter – perhaps unreasonable – hatred grew within him when Earl Henry consented to be one of the forty peers who sat on the trial of that unfortunate lady. It was known that Henry was a formidable enemy of the Queen and when she was condemned to die Deemster William told his son, "This dastard has driven in a wedge between the Stanleys and Christians that will rankle for many generations."

But it was not that which rankled. It was basically Derby's forging of the Keys, and the vexed matter of the land tenures.

Chapter Five

Little had changed in the squalid cottage that stood almost on the boundary between Poyll Dhouie and the vast Milntowne estate. Sam still spent his time away from home, drinking heavily and, he would say jeeringly to his wife,

"Whoring since I can get nothing out of you!"

Now and then, if he had taken more ale than he could handle, he would make advances but was always stopped by Eleanor's reminder of what would happen to him if he dared to disobey his master's order.

"Edward Christian will be back," she would say, while her heart thumped against her ribs, because despite the brave and defiant front, she was afraid of him. "And you do not want to hang, do you?"

"Ha," he laughed close to her face. "*That* will not affright me! They hang a man for rape, but for a man to take what is his right, from his own wife, that is not rape."

So true, and Eleanor was well aware of it. If only she could get away – but what chance was there without money? And where would she go?

She still went often to see Susanna, and now there was little Edward to take with her, a handsome sturdy boy of four years who was having lessons along with James, and William, who was coming up to three and a half. Elizabeth was the baby at only two, but Susanna was pregnant again and very near her time. Eleanor was also continuing with her learning, avidly taking in all that Susanna was willing to teach her. Edward Christian, after another year at sea with Thomas Best when further escapades had brought both men a goodly store of riches, was arraigned along with his friend and appeared before the Board accused of having illegally made large private fortunes. Edward's manner when answering the charge was said to be arrogantly that of the sea captain and he was never employed again by the East India Company. When news of all this reached the island

Eleanor was naturally saddened, and also a trifle anxious in case her son should inherit some of his father's wickedness. She watched him closely but as yet he showed no signs of anything that could cause her distress. He worked well with Susanna's boys, under the mature, grey-haired dame brought over from England by William. Eleanor was ever conscious of her good fortune in having Susanna for a friend. Alicia was still with her for although she often said she would like to marry and have children of her own to care for, she also declined any offers from men who were mere labourers.

"How can I face a life of poverty and drudgery after living here, in such luxury?" she would ask and sometimes Susanna would jokingly reply,

"The trouble is I have been too good to you, Alicia. You have the taste for the good life."

And I, too, mused Eleanor thinking of the splendour of Milntowne and of the charm and comfort of the vicar's home at Maughold. She had one day received the astonishing request from Edward's father to the effect that he had heard so much about his grandson from William and Ewan and others of the Christian Clan that he desired to see him. He had been as enchanted with Eleanor as with her son and so she had become a visitor to the vicar's home – though not a regular one since it was a long way to walk there from her cottage or even from the home of her friend.

Susanna was having a difficult pregnancy and her health was a source of anxiety to everyone around her for she was much loved both by her friends and servants alike.

At times, when she was alone in the cottage after putting her son to bed on the clean straw pallet in her room, Eleanor would dwell on that evening of her child's birth, and the deep and undisguised concern shown by the man who had sired him. Edward had come up to the bedchamber after it was all over and, taking the baby in his arms, had held it before him, gazing long and hard, shaking his head as if in wonderment at a miracle.

"My son," he had murmured almost to himself. Watching him, Eleanor rather thought he was thinking of all the other females he had made pregnant and realising that this child was the only one he had actually seen. Placing it in its mother's arms he had said gently, "He is a handsome boy, Eleanor; you have done a good job."

"He has your features," she pointed out.

"And your golden hair."

"It will darken as he grows up."

How much did he love his son? Enough to want him... and his mother? She would never be his wife. Yet lurking within her was ever the flickering hope that one day Edward would rescue her from the soul-destroying existence to which he had condemned her on that day when his father had married her to Samuel Garrett.

But four years had gone by and Edward was still away. He and Thomas Best had been given commissions in the Royal Navy and now he was at Court in the retinue of George Villiers who was rising rapidly in the King's esteem having superseded Robert Carr who had been out of favour for more than two years. This news came periodically from William who visited relatives in Cheshire, or Ewan who now and then had a sojourn at Warton Manor in Lancashire, the valuable property there being the moiety of his wife. But neither man had spoken with Edward, since he was in London enjoying the lavish parties and other entertainments given by a vain and indolent King whose contempt for women was known to all.

"I heard that Edward fell from his horse while stag-hunting." Ewan might say to Eleanor if he should visit William's home. Or "I smell trouble smouldering over there, though it might not flare while this present King is on the throne."

About a year later Eleanor met Edward's uncle for the first time. William and Susanna had been invited to Lough Mollo and the old man desired they take the children with them. As Alicia was ill in bed Susanna asked Eleanor to go along so as to help with the four children, and of course her own son was with them too. Edward's uncle, though frail, was mentally alert and he showed Eleanor a letter he had received from his nephew and heir.

"It mentions you and this little one," he said in answer to her glance of surprised inquiry as he handed the letter to her. "Perhaps you would like to put a missive in when I answer it?"

She nodded automatically, her eyes on the firm, rather untidy writing. Edward had asked about his uncle's health, also about the steward who was managing the estate. And then,

"Do you ever see Eleanor, who is friendly with Susanna and William and who visits Ewan too on occasions? I would like news of my son as he will be five years old now, a clever and happy fellow, I hope."

Happy... For the first time Eleanor knew bitterness against the man she still loved. How did he expect anyone to be happy, living in such squalid surroundings? Edward's wealth was known to all on the island; he could have afforded to take his son out of the squalor if he was so concerned about him. Yes, she would write a short note for the old man to enclose when he answered his nephew's letter!

She wrote to say she was very surprised that he should find the time to inquire about his son, and she would remind him that little Edward knew only Sam Garrett as his father. That, decided Eleanor, would certainly infuriate him and, she hoped, hurt him as well.

What the result was she never knew. Edward made no further inquiries about his son – or if he did, his uncle made no effort to enlighten her of it.

The boy was going to be clever, prophesied Susanna who was yet again with child, her fifth, and she was having another difficult pregnancy. Watching her sometimes, Eleanor would know a dreadful fear that her friend, whom she now called by her given name, was not now long for this world. Alicia felt the same and although like Eleanor her first anxiety was for the lovely delicate Susanna, she asked one day, looking at her friend through her tears,

"If my mistress dies, what will become of me?"

Or me and my child...? Eleanor firmly put away those thoughts because the close friendship which had developed between Susanna and herself was so precious that its loss would be so devastating as to swamp all else.

"She is not going to die, Alicia. We must will her to live."

"Will?"

"Think positively. Say she will *not* die and leave us!"

"She is so ill, Eleanor. I pray for her every night but she is no better. Look how many days she takes to her bed – All of yesterday and the day before."

"She is up today, though, and looking well, with colour in her cheeks – you must be thinking she is better?"

Alicia said nothing. Her heart was heavy and at times she could not think clearly and then the future would seem like a long misty road along which she was floundering without a friend in the whole world.

"But I have Eleanor... oh, God, already I am thinking that lovely Susanna is gone!"

The baby was born healthy and they called him Ewan after his father's cousin. This pleased the Deemster so much that he had a large party at Milntowne for the christening which of course took place at Maughold Church and was performed by William's father. Eleanor was invited and, looking around the gathering of Christians from many parts of the island, she knew a sudden access of real pride that her son was one of them. He was admired and petted but the one he wanted to be with was William, Ewan's youngest son who was now fourteen years old, a fine boy with thick dark hair neatly brushed back, and strong features, faintly aquiline, and eyes frank and large but yet a little too close to afford him that handsome quality which generous Nature had given to so many of this noble clan, the most powerful clan on the island.

The Christians... people of their own class admired them; the lower classes feared them. And the Lord of Mann, uncrowned king though he was, treated them with both caution and respect. Viking blood was strong blood, and none knew it better than the Stanleys who had always found them a curse, a hindrance to their aspirations.

Eleanor also pondered on the fact that Edward's father was of the Church. How could that gentle vicar with the compassionate eyes and kindly smile have sired anyone so wicked as Edward?

"Mother, can I go into the garden with William?" Edward's blue eyes, lifted to those of his mother, were wide and frank, his mouth rosy and half open in a smile. He had the strong bone structure of his father, the firm chin, already slightly outthrust, the rather proud set of the head upon shoulders that promised to be wide. "He wishes to show me the babies that Susie has had."

"Of course you can go," she smiled, aware that Ewan was interested that his youngest son should want to be with a boy so much younger than himself. William, 'the dark one,' had always taken to Edward even when he was a baby. "But, darling," went on Eleanor, "you do know it is not possible for you to have one of the little dogs?"

"Yes – *he* would kick it, just like he kicked that stray I brought in. He gave it gallstones and it died." He was turning as he spoke and so Ewan heard what he was saying. Then he sped away to join his friend and together they went out to the garden where, in a small shed, the spaniel was nursing four week-old pups.

Ewan watched them go, his eyes kindling. He was cruel himself at times, but any harshness was always directed at rogues and felons who stole or were guilty of other misdemeanours. He could never ill-treat an animal. Turning from the window, he espied the boy's young mother talking to Edmond Christian, owner of eight holdings at Bride and three in Andreas. He was a prominent member of the Christian Clan and an avid supporter of its ideas for bringing about some kind of reform for the island. Edmond was laughing and chatting with Eleanor, but nevertheless there was a certain reserve behind the façade and it was obvious to Ewan that he was all the time conscious of his superiority, that as Eleanor was a guest like himself it was incumbent on him to extend friendliness while at the same time keeping in mind that she was married to a serf and lived in a hovel.

Ewan's teeth snapped together, his admiration for the girl mingling with his anger against his cousin. True, marriage was out of the question, owing to the vast difference in status between Edward Christian and Eleanor. But he had had no need to marry her off to that oaf. If he was so concerned about her, seeing that he found her different from all the rest – why had he not set her up in a decent home? It obviously could not have been on the island, because Edward would marry one day. But he could have set the girl up in England, from where she had come originally.

It was too late now; she was married. And her husband, despite his excessive drinking, appeared to be in the best of health.

The smuggling...? Ewan had considered this many times, had debated on whether or not to pursue the man in his activities as undoubtedly he could catch him. But not only was there the risk of the man's divulging what he knew about others who were smugglers, there was also the fact that even if he did go to prison it would not free Eleanor; she would still be married to him and it would be expected of her that she be there when eventually he was released.

With a resigned sigh he approached the girl who had been in his thoughts. She glanced up and a ready smile transformed the seriousness of her expression.

"Ah, Eleanor, lass. You look delightful in this gown!"

"On loan from my dear friend," she said. "Are you sitting down for a moment?"

She had always admired the Deemster for his hard work, his assiduous attendance to his various public duties, the way he ran his estates... and she knew a deep gratitude towards him for the way he treated her – almost as an equal. She had gained in confidence by these visits to the great house where she mixed with the elite of the island. Because of Susanna and her lessons Eleanor was more than capable of holding her own in any conversation with the result that she had gained much respect. Nevertheless, she was under no illusions, cherished no false hopes. Her station was inferior, and beneath the friendliness of many of the Christians she perceived a certain reserve and, in some cases, she guessed they would prefer not having to talk with her at all. The Deemster was different; he admired her in every way – her looks, her manners and her wish to better herself. William, too, was fond of her as was John, his elder brother. Eleanor smiled as Ewan sat down next to her on the padded oak settle. "This is a wonderful party," she remarked automatically spreading a hand. "Thank you, dear Ewan, for inviting me."

He gave a wry grimace at that and said,

"I would never dare invite Susanna without including you."

"But that was not the reason why you did invite me." She spoke with confidence after pausing to straighten a fold of her gown.

"No, my dear Eleanor," was the swift response from the Deemster. "I invited you as one of the family."

She warmed to him as never before.

"That is the nicest thing anyone ever said to me."

"Is it?" with a lift of an eyebrow. "Surely my cousin has said nicer things than that?"

She shrugged and shook her head. He noticed the glory of golden hair catching the sunlight as it filtered the room through the high window.

"Edward never professed to love me," she murmured at length, turning to smile rather wanly at him. "I was just another wench to be pleasuring with."

"No, you are wrong." He looked sideways at her. "There is something special between you and my cousin, and there always will be."

She was thinking of this later when walking home along the narrow, muddy lane on one side of which were the Milntowne lands and on the other the equally productive pastures of the Poyll Dhouie estate. She thought of the cottage, the squalid hovel from which escape seemed so far away. How sombre it would appear, rising from the mist when eventually she approached it. The sulky aspect of the River Sulby made things worse, that river which had so conveniently provided access to those Viking marauders and, later, to the mighty Godred Crovan who had made himself king of the isle.

Eleanor was holding her son's hand and her thoughts switched as she heard him say, as he trotted happily beside her,

"Do you know what we were talking about – me and Illiam?"

"What, my little love?"

"About the poor, and Illiam said when he grew up he was going to be like his father and fight those Derbys who want to take all the money from the Manx people."

She had to smile, so serious was his expression.

"Well, so long as you do not join in any fights I shall be happy. You are too young to know, my love, but I will tell you this: the Derbys are the Lords of Mann and, therefore, more powerful than any Manxman can ever be."

"Not more powerful than Deemster Ewan! Illiam says that Earl Derby is frightened of his father."

Eleanor frowned. While she admired the determination of the Deemster and others to bring about improvements in the lot of the Manx nation, she did not believe it to be a happy circumstance that Ewan should encourage William to take such a keen interest just yet. After all, the boy was only just fourteen years old. A fine boy, the youngest of the three legitimate sons of the Deemster, he was so much darker than the others that he was called Illiam Dhône – the Dark William.

They came to the big house, the manor house of Poyll Dhouie, which had fine gates and tall cypress trees bordering its long, curving drive. There were lights in several windows and a dog was barking a complaint from the restrictive walls of a tall barn. There was another mile to walk; she wondered why she had taken this way home instead of the shorter one which would not have brought the manor house into her vision. It would be dark by the time they arrived at the cottage. Edward tripped and would have fallen into the mud had she not closed her hand tightly over his.

Sometimes his father stayed at this property of his, so near... and yet so very far away. His son, this wondrous creation of their union, was passing his house and he did not know. Tears seldom were allowed to fall but they fell now, rolling down cheeks that had become pale. She had no desire to go home, to that hovel, but she must, because there was nowhere else she could go. A terrible feeling of helplessness and depression flooded over her; it was as if a smothering blanket enveloped her and she was fighting to escape. It was an uncanny, frightening sensation causing her breath to catch in her throat. Whatever was the matter with her? Letting go of her son's hand she pulled her shawl more closely around her, for a dreadful shivering brought with it a feeling of icicles invading her blood.

"Mother - what is wrong?" Little Edward gazed up anxiously into her pallid face. "Are you not feeling well? Oh!"

Again he slipped but this time fell face down into a pool of mud that also happened to have in it horse droppings. The little boy screamed and began to writhe about in an effort to get back on to his feet again. And it so happened that a small nag appeared from round the bend in the lane and within seconds Master Crellin, Edward Christian's steward, who was living at Poyll Dhouie, was picking the boy up, having pushed Eleanor out of the way.

"Thank you, Master Crellin," she cried. "I should not have let go of his hand. How awful!" She used her hands in a fruitless attempt to sweep away some of the evil-smelling mud. "We have a mile to go! He will contract a fever—"

"No, Mistress Garrett," broke in the good steward soothingly. "We shall have him inside and clean him up, then find him some clean attire. My son's clothes will be just about right."

"You are very kind."

The relief was so great that, feeling as she did, the tears came in a flood and she felt an arm about her shoulders.

"Calm yourself, lass. No real harm is done."

Which of course was correct. Young Edward was soon cleaned up by his mother, who was allowed to use the tub. Mary, the housemaid, brought clean clothes and when some marchpane was brought along with a cup of warm milk, it seemed that the lad was thoroughly enjoying himself. Eleanor had mud on her dress but this was not difficult to remove and soon she, too, was seated before the leaping flames of a wood fire.

Mistress Crellin came in from the yard carrying a basket of eggs. After the initial surprise she became brisk and decided they must stay for the meal which was almost ready. Eleanor protested, saying they had come from the Deemster's party.

"But you ate hours ago," from Mistress Crellin in the same brisk manner. "You must be getting hungry again by now. No, sit you down, lass, I want no help but Mary's."

"We are staying, Mother? I like it here." Edward spoke with his mouth full of marchpane and with another piece poised, ready to be eaten. "This is a very nice house. Not as big as the Deemster's but it is so warm and the chairs are soft to your back." He leant against the leather and added, this time a trifle anxiously, "We are staying, Mother?"

"I suppose so," she smiled.

"Mister Garrett will not be in for his supper so we can stay a long time." The rest of the marchpane disappeared and he began to lick his fingers clean.

Mister Garrett... Eleanor had never told him to call his fosterfather that, but as she herself always did so, it was inevitable that her son would do the same.

It began to rain as they ate their meal and within half an hour one of the howling gales which so often lashed the island was sweeping across the countryside. And it persisted until, at close to midnight, Mistress Crellin decided it was not possible for them to brave such a violent storm. They could be blown over and killed, she declared, and went off with Mary to prepare one of the spare bedchambers, taking with her a candle from one of the sconces on the wall.

Briefly Eleanor thought of Sam, coming home in the early hours. As he never came to her room he would have no knowledge of her absence until the morning, when he would find himself having to prepare his own breakfast.

*

Susanna had felt the pain in her chest when she was at the party. Now, at eight o'clock in the evening she was in agonising discomfiture and both her husband and Alicia were with her, their faces strained and pale.

"I had better fetch the doctor." William rose from his chair by the bed. "Do not leave her, Alicia, till I get back."

"No, sir, indeed I will not." Her heart was beating far too rapidly for comfort, and tears were difficult to hold in check. Her beloved mistress... was she dying? She was so white and her features were twisted with pain. Alicia held her hand, while at the same time holding a cool damp cloth to her brow. "Please God," she whispered through trembling lips, "do not let her die."

Suddenly her mistress gave a shriek and for a moment seemed to be in the throes of some kind of a spasm. She twisted on the bed, her fingers clutching the cover while moisture oozed from her forehead. A moment later she was still again, and a little calmer.

"Eleanor," she whispered. "I want my dear friend. Bring her quickly, Alicia, go fetch your little friend for she is my friend also and I want her – Do you hear me? I want Eleanor!"

Another scream rang through the chamber and tears streamed down Alicia's face.

"Mistress Susanna, I cannot leave you to fetch Eleanor. My master bade me stay with you till he came with the doctor—"

"I want Eleanor," moaned her mistress. "Will you not obey me?"

Alicia shook her head. "I will send Elizabeth—"

"Elizabeth is old and slow. You can run... Elizabeth does not know where Eleanor lives—"

"I can tell her," broke in Alicia rising from her chair. "I shall tell her to hurry."

"I want you to go! Elizabeth will not find the cottage in the dark."

Alicia passed a tongue over lips that had gone dry. She could not leave her mistress, no, not for anything. She said she would send a footman but again Susanna proved awkward and petulant. Nothing would satisfy her except that Alicia go to bring Eleanor.

"She will have to bring little Edward..." Alicia spoke to herself, praying desperately that her master would not be long.

"I can not leave you," she began again when suddenly Susanna's eyes blazed and she somehow gathered the strength to sit up.

"Alicia, you will obey me, your mistress!" She shot out an arm, indicating the door. "Go, I say, and bring Eleanor to me..." Her voice weakened again and she fell back on to the cushion. "Bring my little friend..." She burst into tears and turned her face to the wall. "I need her, to give me strength, and you defy me, the girl I have loved and helped—"

"I will go," broke in Alicia, resigned. "I will run all the way but I must send Elizabeth to you, dear mistress."

She sped along the lane as fast as her young legs would carry her. It was pitch black and pouring with rain; she realised that her mistress was right: Elizabeth would not have found the cottage in the dark. Trees caught by the wind groaned overhead as she turned into the narrow gateway. No light showing at either of the windows. Eleanor could not be in bed, surely, not at this time. But perhaps she was tired after the party and the long walk home. Alicia went to the back of the cottage but no light was discernible there either. So still... and lifeless. She shivered as a strange fear entered into her. But her mission was urgent and she hurried back to the front of the house. The door was half open; she had not noticed it before. She called out. No answer. Were Eleanor and little Edward fast asleep? It was not yet nine o' clock and Eleanor had told her often that her regular habit was to read for a long time after she had put her son to bed. It was for that purpose that Susanna had given her so many tallow candles.

Perhaps she was ill! Alicia went through the living-room and into the chamber which she knew was used by Eleanor. She called out again, and wondered why. She knew there was no one in the cottage. But where could they be? Sam of course was in the tavern, drinking ale – or perhaps he was in one of the Poyll Dhouie barns with one of the whores who gathered outside the alehouse.

"Eleanor," she whispered, "where can you be? Tonight of all nights to be away somewhere, when our dearest Susanna needs you—"

She stopped and swung around, relief flooding through her. But it was not Eleanor. The bulky figure in the doorway reeked of ale and stale urine... She was about to speak, to ask where his wife was, when he spoke first, plunging forward in a drunken frenzy and caught her about the waist.

"Ready, wife! Yes, I came home to have you! It was Ned, he made a wager with me. He said I dare not take my own wife!"

His foul-smelling mouth was on Alicia's before she could open it to speak. She struggled fiercely, speaking to him once her lips were freed but he seemed too filled with ale to comprehend. He grabbed her hair and at the same time punched her in the face. In the blackness of the room he was as unable to see her as she was to see him. She screamed as loudly as her terror-blocked throat would allow. She managed to tear herself away and screamed again, words this time to tell him she was not Eleanor, that she was Alicia who was tirewoman for Mistress Christian. But the man was maddened with rage and lust and he grabbed her again and flung her on to the filthy straw pallet. He fumbled in the dark, tearing at her clothes, cursing her for her struggles. He was atop her naked body and she uttered a moan, a prayer for the good God to help her...

*

It was the Deemster who was holding the court, which was in a room in Peel Castle. The prisoner had pleaded over and over that he believed it was his wife he was taking, but Ewan, sterner than Eleanor would have believed, refused to accept the excuse.

"You knew it was this innocent girl you were ravishing. You knew your – wife was not at home."

"No, sir..." Samuel Garrett was grovelling in his desperate bid for mercy. No fool, he was well aware that the Deemster wanted him out of the way. "How would I know, sir? This wench had no right to be in my house!"

He was at breaking point, ready to cry. Eleanor stepped forward and asked if she could speak to Ewan. He regarded her sternly as if angry at her intervention. But he drew her aside for all that.

"I believe he was so much under the influence of the ale that he really did believe it was me he was – was molesting."

Ewan shook his head, his eyes dark and hard as metal.

"I am surprised you plead for him, Eleanor. However, it is very clear to me that he knew what he was doing." He paused a moment and then, still in the low voice he had used so that others in the court would not hear, "You do realise what you have escaped?"

"At the expense of my friend." She felt she would never ever recover from the shock of knowing her dear friend had been raped instead of her. "Poor, poor Alicia, going on that errand of mercy..." Eleanor's voice broke. She was living again that terrible time when, going straight from Poyll Dhouie to take little Edward to his morning lessons, she had learned of the terrible fate that had befallen her friend. Susanna, miraculously recovered, was a different woman as, pale with anger, she was demanding of her husband that he bring a charge against Samuel Garrett immediately. Ewan was told and he came at once, to talk with Alicia who was distraught and weeping incessantly, sure she was with child.

"He was so – so savage and filthy..." The weeping was renewed and went on and on. There was no consoling her and both Eleanor and Susanna were in tears.

"Why was it not me!" cried Eleanor. "Dear God, why Alicia?"

"I blame myself," sobbed Susanna. "I insisted that she go to fetch you – I thought I was going to die and wanted you to be with me."

"The doctor found it to be only something that she had eaten at the party," explained William. "Something that obviously disagreed with her. She was in great pain."

"I do blame myself," Susanna had begun again when Ewan interrupted her.

"There is only one person to blame and that is the rapist himself. And he shall pay the full extreme penalty." Ewan spoke with more confidence than he felt.

Ewan had had Sam apprehended and thrown into prison in the dungeon at Peel Castle. And now he was on trial, with the Governor there but as a spectator, as the Deemster held his own court, which was similar to that of a manorial court in England. Sam was terrified but, like the Deemster, he was well aware that, because he was married, the situation which could mean the death penalty could not arise.

"You will be taken back to prison until I have further considered your crime." Ewan had been thoughtful throughout the hearing. He wanted the man's life... and he had to think of some way in which his objective could be achieved.

He went straight from the castle to his kinsman, Robert Christian of Ballastole who had graduated at Trinity College in Dublin and then entered at Gray's Inn. The barrister greeted his cousin with a cordial,

"Well met, Ewan. This is surely a pleasure. But you appear serious so it is nought of a purely friendly visit?"

"You are right." The dark eyes were cold and calculating. My cousin has some set purpose, decided Robert, offering him wine. "It is a complicated situation which I am sure you can straighten out." Ewan sat down to one side of the glowing fire, and took the cup of wine offered to him. He explained as briefly as he could and ended with, "I want his life, nothing less." He sent the barrister a challenging glance. "Now tell me, how can this be brought about?"

Robert was shaking his head.

"If the man is married—"

"He is. I have said so," broke in Ewan impatiently. "But there must be some way! I want Eleanor freed from this oaf!"

Robert eyed him with a curious expression.

"Is it that you are wishing to bed this wench?"

"Undoubtedly I would enjoy taking pleasure of her. But no, she is the mother of Edward Christian's son."

"Ah, I have heard of this story." Robert paused to sip his wine. He had been practising in England for several years and on his return he had heard some small gossip about this young woman who had been accepted by the Deemster and, in fact, by many of the clan Christian. "Now..." He became deep in thought. "This marriage, I believe, has never been consummated? That is, I heard a story that Edward had made Samuel Garrett marry the girl but had forbidden him to bed her. Not quite fair as I see it." Robert fingered his neat, pointed beard. "It is a strange condition for Edward to have made."

"He had his reasons. Moreover, he paid Sam well, so well that he could afford to fill himself with ale every night." Contempt vibrated in the Deemster's strong voice as he added, "The man is evil; he is dirty and lazy—"

"Then why did Edward marry off this girl to him?"

The Deemster shrugged his shoulders impatiently.

"I shall never quite know what was in the lad's mind. He said she was different from any other female he had bedded." Ewan explained how the two had come to meet and that when Eleanor became pregnant Edward could not desert her. "She is certainly different – you must meet her one day, Robert. She is a rare beauty, and she is highly intelligent—" He broke off and a heavy frown gave a glowering expression to his face. "Why this waste of time? I want you to think of a way by which I can hang the fellow."

"In the ordinary way, of course – I mean, if he had not been married—" Robert broke off as Ewan spread his hands in a gesture of asperity.

"I know it would be simple if he were a single man! The girl would be given the ring and the rope! And she would choose either marriage or that her attacker be hanged. In the present situation Alicia could not be given the choice of marriage, so all that could happen to her attacker was imprisonment. And that would not free Eleanor since she would still be married to him."

"I mentioned this non-consummation of the marriage." Robert spoke after some moments of thought, his long fingers again touching his beard. "Perhaps you have not realised that the marriage can be annulled?"

"Ah!" Ewan slapped his knee. "Why did that escape me! But it proves the value of a legal mind. Yes, you have hit on the solution. The marriage will be annulled so Sam will be single. Alicia will be given the choice... and she will choose that he be hanged!"

Robert looked at him curiously and murmured,

"What about Edward in all this? Is he not to be consulted?"

"Perhaps. I shall have to send my eldest boy to fetch him over. He is at Court at present, having been to sea for some years."

"I think he should be consulted." A slight pause and then, "You will be needing my services in this annulment?"

The Deemster smiled.

"I confidently leave the matter in your capable hands, Robert."

Chapter Six

A week later Edward was on the island, and rode straight to Milntowne. Ewan's son, John, had been sent post haste to London and as he remarked to his father afterwards, he had never seen such fury come to a man's face as when John spoke of Sam Garrett's intention of ravishing Eleanor, for a wager, and while possessed of a lust brought on by a surfeit of ale.

"I shall slit his throat!" he had snarled. "He was told to leave her alone!" He seemed, to John's way of thinking, more violently enraged over what had *not* happened than what *had*.

"Father has arranged for an annulment of the marriage," John had informed him, and so there was little more for Ewan to tell.

"The annulment can really take place?" Edward's relief could be felt by Ewan when he assured him that the annulment was in fact being put through at this very time.

"So this Alicia will be given the choice either of marriage to him, or..." Edward's teeth ground together. "I shall watch with pleasure the scoundrel dangling from the end of a rope."

Ewan had to laugh.

"What a bloodthirsty fire-eater you are!" And, after a pause, "The fate of the other wench seems not to trouble you in the least."

Edward shrugged his broad shoulders.

"I scarcely know her."

"She is a very close friend of your Eleanor, and still in a sorry state I am told. This business," Ewan went on grimly, "has caused more heartache than you imagine, lad. Susanna blames herself, while Eleanor wishes it had been she—"

"What!"

"God's glory, Edward, calm yourself! Eleanor, being the true friend that she is, feels that it should have been she who was seduced and not an innocent girl who was a virgin."

"I am mighty glad it was not she." The fervency in his voice brought an odd expression to his cousin's eyes.

"I could almost say you love this wench," he remarked slowly.

"My feelings for Eleanor have always been a mystery to me," admitted Edward on a sober note. "I can not say I love her, though."

"Nevertheless, there is something quite extraordinary between you. Of course, you are aware of her love for you?"

A frown crossed his cousin's brow at this.

"I would be happier were it not so."

"Guilty conscience, eh, lad?" The Deemster leant back against the soft leather of his chair. "Women are the strangest beings. Why should a girl like Eleanor love a man like you?"

Edward gave a gust of laughter and remarked that his cousin was not very flattering.

"Females always find me attractive," he added, thinking of the lovely titled lady-in-waiting to the Queen who had come so readily to his bed while her husband was away. Then there was the voluptuous Henrietta with the aged husband... "Court, my cousin, is a fine place for enjoyment."

"'Tis to be hoped you are allowed to keep to your preference for females."

"Ah, that?" An instant of frowning silence and then, "James' lust for his own sex is insatiable. Nay, as yet he has not spoken outright. And his hints I have been able to ignore."

"Not for ever. 'Tis time you came home and took over Lough Mollo from your uncle. He would like it."

Edward fell silent. He had no wish at present to settle on the island. Life was still too exciting. He had enjoyed his role of Vice Admiral, the favour bestowed on him by his friend, George Villiers, the King's number one favourite, having been made Lord High Admiral. He had been twice at Court, the first time for a year, and this time? Well, until it was no longer safe.

"You mislike the idea of taking over Lough Mollo?" Ewan's firm voice cut the silence and his cousin glanced up from his contemplation of the andirons supporting a massive log burning on the hearth.

"The time is not yet," he replied but added on the instant, "I shall stay a while, though, to see this business through and also to settle Eleanor and my son."

"Yes, they will have to be provided for." Ewan sent him a direct look. "At present they are with William and Susanna – but John will have told you? It was done for their protection."

"Yes. It might not have been safe to leave them in the cottage."

"Not with Sam Garrett's ale-drinking associates spitting out threats as they are doing."

"They...?" Edward's eyes kindled. "They have actually threatened her, knowing I would part their ears from their heads, yea, and have them flogged till they drop! Have they no fear of us any more?"

"A man filled with ale often has the courage of a lion."

"True," conceded Edward having calmed down. "This annulment – how long is it to take?"

"Not long at all; it is straightforward. Robert sent a messenger yesterday to say the marriage will be dissolved by the end of this week."

And Eleanor would be free...

"You puzzle me, Ewan," he said at length. "Why is it that you have always wanted Eleanor to be free of Sam Garrett?"

"Simply because she is too good for him. She ought never to have been married to him – but I have told you this before," Ewan supplemented on a note of impatience. Then he added with a sidelong glance at his cousin, "I suppose it has occurred to you that the annulment in itself will achieve what I – and you and many others who have come to love Eleanor – desire, which is to free the lass. So why, you are asking yourself, do I want his life?"

Edward gave a quick laugh.

"Faith, man, you take me for a fool. We both want Sam Garrett's life for the same reason: he knows too much of our activities."

The Deemster inclined his head.

"Just so, my cousin. But there is another reason why I believe he should die."

"Yes?"

"Imprisonment ends sometime. Were Sam Garrett released, be it in five or ten years' time, neither Eleanor nor her son would be safe. Surely that had occurred to you?"

"To tell truth, I have it in mind to take them off the island. Eleanor comes from Chester and she has often spoken of a desire to be back. I have the opportunity of a rather charming house on the banks of the Dee—" he broke off and gave a shrug. "It is only an idea at present."

"A good one, nevertheless. A new life for them both." Ewan glanced at his cousin perceptively. "A haven, somewhere to fly to if, when you marry – and it can not be long – life becomes tedious."

"I shall say naught of such an idea!"

"But it is there," retorted Ewan laughing. He tugged at a bell rope. "Let us drink to the success of our plans."

Edward had to laugh.

"Drink to a successful hanging?"

"Why not? It was a marvellously fortunate occurrence when Sam ravished that innocent maid, for now we can be free of him, of the danger of his learning even more about our smuggling activities and then," he wagged a finger on which a diamond solitaire gleamed in the firelight, "it would mean blackmail since he is that kind of man."

"I agree. There is much discomfort in an awareness that someone knows more than they should about you."

A lackey entered the elegant room and was told to bring the wine.

"Both Burgundy and Rhenish," added Ewan, "and something to eat."

"There is some of the green goose left, sir, if that will do?"

"It will. And some sweetmeats. Nothing else."

The lackey brought forward a drawtable and put on it slices of the goose and a basket of sweetmeats. The two bottles of wine were opened and the men served, all done in silence, as was the departure of the man.

They talked about the coming trial, then about Edward's life at Court.

"Is it not a life to tire you?" inquired Ewan taking in his cousin's fashionable attire – the high-waisted doublet of embroidered silk, the matching breeches, full and worn to just a little above the knee. The ruff was stiff and small – a mere cup of lace to frame the bronzed face. Shoe rosettes seemed designed to complement the spangled garters. "One continuous round of pleasure, with a goodly portion of wenching thrown in, I doubt not."

"Wenching? *You* talk of wenching." Edward's brows lifted and a hint of humour curved his lips. "How many bastards have you sired while I was away?"

"Now how would I know for sure?" returned the Deemster with some amusement. "However, make no mistake, Edward, they all come willingly. Force is one thing no lass can ever accuse me of." Ewan poured out more wine for them both. "Tell me, what else occupies your time besides all these frivolities?"

"Hunting, and hawking – but I expect you to regard them as frivolities also?"

"How old are you now, Edward?" He made a swift calculation and answered his own question. "Thirty. Time for settling down."

No, thought his cousin, not quite yet. He changed the subject to inquire about his brother.

"William? Now there is a hard worker. He manages his estate; he attends to his public duties most conscientiously. There is a man whose example you would do well to follow."

Edward grimaced. He was still profoundly aware of the eleven years difference in their ages, and also that Ewan was the head of the family.

"One day, perhaps," he conceded. "I wonder, though, am I cut out for all this patriotic activity with which so many of you have become obsessed?"

"You will join us eventually," stated Ewan with confidence. "Our aims are merely to obtain for our little nation what is fair and just, to free the Manx people from the persecution of the Derbys. In short, Edward, we are fighting for liberty from oppression." The strong voice vibrated and a glitter came to the Deemster's eyes. "There are some impatient ones who would bring more aggression to the fight but my way is more subtle. The Stanleys might bluster – they invariably have done so – but they know how far to go. The Christians have always held a power formidable to each generation as it comes along."

"But the Stanleys never seem to give up." Edward paused, expecting some comment, but Ewan was staring into his cup, a faraway look in his eyes. "Perhaps this one is desperate. As we have remarked before, he inherited little but the title and this island."

He thought of the vast estates owned by the present Lord's late father, so much wealth, gained mostly by gifts from sovereigns whose favourites they had become but many manors had come as dowrys on marriage to wealthy heiresses. But William was not his father's heir since he had an elder brother. Ferdinando, whose mysterious death only months after that of his father left the main wealth of the Stanleys to the heirs general – his three very young daughters whose mother had put up a fight for their rights. The King, seeing that the dispute would take several years to resolve, sent in Sir Thomas Gerard because the isle could not remain without a Captain in case of any sudden attempt at invasion by an enemy. Thirteen years elapsed before the island was restored to the Stanleys.

"Desperate?" Ewan spoke at last, coming from his reverie. "Greedy, Edward. William owns valuable properties in his own right. There are estates in England and Wales as well as here, remember." He shook his head. "No, it is the inherent greed of the Stanleys which impels them to attempt further taxation. But it is not the Earl so much as his lady. She resents not being able to live in the princely style of her father-in-law who had no less than two hundred and twenty servants in his household."

"She seems to forget their good fortune in inheriting the title and island at all. If Ferdinando had not died so very conveniently after enjoying his inheritance for a mere seven months they would have had to be content with what they already owned."

Ewan was nodding thoughtfully. His cousin watched him running a finger through his neatly trimmed spade beard and automatically touched his own chin. Always ready to follow the fashion set by London, he had dispensed with his own beard and was now clean-shaven.

"It would be interesting to know who was responsible for Ferdinando's untimely demise."

"'Twas said a servant did it – but was there any proof that he was poisoned?"

"No actual proof, but he had all the symptoms, and they had to bury him quickly because of the foul smell of his body."

"You are thinking that had he lived the rule might have improved?"

"In the long term it perhaps would have been possible. Yet we have to remember that he struck at the Tenure of the Straw. No, I can not believe that Ferdinando would have been sympathetic to our cause." Anger edged Ewan's voice and he reached out impatiently for the bottle of wine and refilled his cup. "What he ignored was that the Christians have held land on this island long before the Stanleys were thought of!"

Edward said nothing. Would the time come when he himself would be caught up in this feud between the Christians and the Stanleys? It was very possible, seeing that so many of his kin were involved, owning as they did one third of the entire island between them. Meanwhile, though, the vexed question merely smouldered, doing no real harm, since it seemed the Earl had little or no interest in his island kingdom, and although the Countess was a formidable faction to be considered she, too, was not at present making a nuisance of herself. And in the seven years since they had become the joint Sovereign Lords of the Isle of Mann they had not once taken the trouble to visit it. The revenue, paying for the upkeep of the castles and their garrisons, and also some of the expenses incurred in the management of the Earl's English estates, was a bonus for which the Stanleys had, for generations, done absolutely nothing for the island in return. The Manx people, warm and generous, would have forgiven and forgotten had their rulers come over and walked among them, lived in their midst for part of the time. As it was, they were regarded as oppressors of the poor and persecutors of the rich, wanting to rob them of lands which had been passed down through ten or more generations.

The Deemster was the one to break the long silence which had fallen between him and his cousin.

"They have sons, so there is a chance that the heir, when he does come into his inheritance, will be more reasonable towards our complaints."

"James?" Being at Court for the past year Edward was naturally in possession of all the current gossip. "It is said that for a twelve-year-old he has a remarkable maturity, and it is common knowledge that he takes an avid interest in the kingdom he will one day inherit. He and his mother are very close and it is said he gives her advice and they make decisions without even consulting the Earl."

The Deemster looked frowningly at him.

"So you fear he will eventually give us trouble?"

"That is hard to say. I would not proffer an opinion." Edward quaffed his wine and leant forward to put his cup on the table. He smiled. "Let us not tease ourselves, Ewan. The lad is only twelve years old. He is not likely to rule over us for a long time yet."

"One never knows..." The frown became more pronounced. "We shall just have to wait and see."

*

Eleanor was in the garden with her son when Edward arrived at his brother's house, and after a few words of greeting between the two he hurried outside where Eleanor and young Edward were seated beneath an apple tree. He stopped, an unwonted emotion filling his whole being. The sun on that glorious hair... the half smile on those rosy lips... the delicate lines of her profile... And his son... sturdy and laughing at something his mother had read to him from the book in her hand. Edward knew a dryness in his mouth, a strange inertness in his body. She glanced up and he moved then, to take the hand held out to him.

"Edward, you have come – oh! It has been dreadful..." She stopped, glancing at her son. "You will want to talk to little Edward for a while, and then I will send him away and I can tell you everything."

"I believe I know everything," was his grim rejoinder.

"Not all," she returned softly, and then, to the child, "This is your father, dearest. I told you he would be coming. Stand up, and say you are glad to see him."

She had coloured slightly on first perceiving Edward's tall straight figure striding across the lawn towards her, and her heart had given a lurch. But, managing to assume a calm exterior, she rose from the grass and straightened her gown. "I have tried to prepare him, but he might be shy at first."

It was with exceeding curiosity that she watched the two eyeing each other in silence for what seemed an eternity. Tall for his age, the child held his head proudly, a serious expression in the clear blue eyes. His father was shaking his head slowly from side to side, as if deeply affected by some kind of disbelief. At last he spoke, moving forward as he did so.

"What a fine lad he has become. Give me your hands, son – nay, let me hold you..."

His arms went about the boy and another silence ensued while he held him close. For Eleanor it was a moment of profound emotion which she felt she would remember forever, this meeting between the two she loved and who, she had fervently hoped, would love each other. There was no doubt about Edward's love, for it shone in his eyes... but what of the boy, held at arms' length now and looking uncertainly at the man who was yet a stranger to him?

Eleanor's cup was full when she heard him say, a slow smile dawning, "I like you, sir. I like you very much." The smile deepened. "Mother said I would like you, but I was not sure, but I am now. Shall you be staying with us for always, sir?"

"I..." Edward seemed lost for words; his glance went to Eleanor who was quick to come to his rescue.

"That is not possible, dearest. Your father is such a busy man and he does not live on the island, anyway." She stopped and it was her turn to appeal for help. There was the merest pause before Edward answered, his hands moving to take a gentle hold on his son's shoulders.

"It is true I can not stay for always, Edward, but I make you the promise that I shall come and see you regularly from now on." He stopped rather suddenly as Eleanor's little gasp caught his ears. He turned to look at her, with a sort of tender affection that made her heart turn over. "It is no idle pledge, my dear. I mean to watch my son grow up."

The next hour was spent in father and son getting to know a little about each other, and then the boy jumped up and said he must be going.

"My Latin lesson will be in five minutes', and Mistress Fisher does not like us being late."

He sped away, watched by his parents until he was out of sight. Eleanor, seated on the grass, her knees drawn up to her chin and wrapped around by her arms, looked up through her lashes at the handsome man who had been her lover for one brief period of bliss. He stared down at her for a space before squatting opposite on the turf.

"I would have had it a happier occasion that brought you at last to see your son," she murmured, her expression sober now, her big blue eyes shaded by distress.

"Is it not a happy occasion?" he queried in surprise. "I am here to share in the celebration of your freedom."

He seemed elated. Were he and the Deemster planning to imprison Sam Garrett for life?

"Sam Garrett truly believed it was I who was in the cottage – how would he know it was another woman? Tell me that, Edward?"

"Ewan told me that you are trying to defend him." His voice cooled as he added, "It is impossible that you do not desire your freedom?"

"So right," she agreed but went on to point out that the annulment would give her just that. "So why," she went on, observing him closely, "should he be given a long sentence?"

"You mean, you are against this trial? What about your friend, who is the victim?"

"Yes, I know Alicia wants him punished. I hate him, too, make no mistake about that, Edward. And I ought to hate you, too, for being the cause of the five years of my life spent with such a creature, a life of drudgery, in squalor I was never used to."

Her eyes were too bright, her lips quivering. He swallowed thickly and, rising, brought her up beside him. She looked down at the hand he held and felt her heart to be melting.

"I know now I did wrong in taking the simple way out. Believe me, there is naught I regret more than giving you to that man. But soon you will be free and I have plans for you and little Edward. I am buying you a house by the river... guess where?"

He was suddenly so much like a small excited boy that it was impossible to see him as the ruthless Captain of the *Falcon* who had looked so casually at men writhing in agony on the deck of the Spanish galleon.

"You... you are taking me back to... Chester?" Her breath caught and a trembling hand went to her breast. "Edward, is this what you are saying to me?"

He nodded his head.

"I should have done it in the first place, and the past can never be undone or forgotten. But mistakes can, in some measure, be rectified. Yes, my dear child, I am intending that your life and that of my son will be far more comfortable from now on."

She felt herself to be in a daze. Chester! Where she had spent so happy a childhood: the river, gleaming in the sunlight, the graceful swans, the fishing boats passing up river for their catch of eels. And the elegant houses – of course, it would be one of the smaller ones just back from the river that Edward would be buying for them. She felt his hand closing more tightly on hers, felt its strength and its warmth.

"Is it really true?" she breathed at last. "Oh, Edward, tell me I am not dreaming!"

"'Tis no dream, my little Eleanor. I have the chance of this house – perhaps you know it? It is called Deva Place..."

"Deva Place!" Dazedly she shook her head. "But that is one of the most imposing – you must be mistaken," she cried. "Deva Place can never be for me! No, never, for it would be too expensive to buy. You have not given it any thought, Edward. There are some small houses with gardens—"

"I certainly have given it thought," he broke in firmly. Which was untrue. He had merely taken a look at the house with the idea of buying it for an investment, but when he knew Eleanor was to be free he suddenly saw her in it, though it was not until now that his mind was finally made up. "I admit that at first a small home came to my mind, but now I desire that both you and Edward shall live in comfort."

It was some time before she could take it in and when finally her mind accepted and stored it, the important matter of her husband's forthcoming trial was instantly at the fore. She spoke again of her conviction that Sam had believed it was his wife whom he was molesting.

"In which case," she went on reasonably, "his guilt is not great enough for him to be imprisoned for life."

"For – life...?" So she had not yet grasped the real reason for the annulment. It were best he kept silent, decided Edward.

"Yes, for life. I am told that is the sentence for ravishing a virgin." She drew away from him, and for a brief space her attention was diverted by the avian bustle in a tall oak tree where a gathering of starlings darkened its top branches. "Sam should not receive a life sentence, Edward," she almost pleaded, aware that his influence could sway the Deemster's decision. "He was, in his ale-clouded mind, attacking me, his lawful wife—"

"God's glory, Eleanor," he broke in wrathfully, "I am almost led to believe you want the rogue to go free!"

"Not free, as that would never satisfy Alicia."

"And as Alicia is the injured party, it is she who must decide. She was an innocent virgin attacked and ravished and Ewan tells me she is distracted, certain she is with child. Would you have her attacker go free!"

"No, I have already said it would not be right to Alicia for him to go entirely unpunished. But my sense of justice tells me it is wrong for him to pay the same penalty he would do if he had known it was an innocent virgin he was attacking." She paused but he was too angry to speak. "It is such a dreadful business, and I am so confused as to what would be the correct punishment for Sam. After all, a husband is allowed his - er - rights..." She smiled faintly and added, "Were it you, Edward...?"

"That is different!"

"Ah, yes, it would be, would it not? You are of the superior Christian Clan and take what you like from whom you wish. But he is little more than a serf, one of your lowest labourers, so he has no rights. Tell me, just what are the Deemster and all the others fighting for? William informs me that their concern is for the poor."

"It is certainly not for rogues and rapists!" He glowered at her and she saw him again as the master who had threatened to cut the ears off the head of one of his seamen. Merciless, he seemed now, with ice glittering in the blue eyes and the mouth compressed into a thin cruel line. "Samuel Garrett will receive the fitting punishment or his crime—" He stopped to wag a warning finger close to her face, "and I do not want you, madam, jumping up in Court and pleading for him, do you understand?"

"Oh...! How can you call me madam in that tone of voice! I shall do as I think best - and that will be to plead that Sam be given the benefit of the doubt."

"There was no doubt! According to Ewan, Alicia told him over and over that she was not you but he was so deep in the throes of lust that there was no drawing back. Make no mistake, he knew what he was doing." His voice was quieter now and when she saw his expression she breathed again. For one fearful moment she had thought they were going to quarrel. "He did know, Eleanor," repeated Edward in the same quiet tone. "Leave this to the people who understand the mind of these scum we unfortunately have in our midst. They do nothing either for their country or themselves. No, they are not what Deemster Ewan and the rest are fighting for." He stopped and abruptly changed the subject. "You are different, Eleanor, from the lass I first knew. What has happened to you in the last five years?"

She smiled faintly, pausing for a moment to watch the play of light and shade as the sun began its slow descent to the line where sea and sky met. She would miss this enchanting little island with its hills and glens, its pristine beaches and its ancient burial sites where one could wander into the past and paint one's own pictures of how life was long, long ago. Did men fight then for their rights? Were there men like Sam Garrett and women like Susanna? A small cough reminded her of Edward's question and she turned to him again.

"Five years must change a person," she murmured. "I have grown up, matured. Susanna has changed my life, too. I have gained confidence as well as knowledge. And being a mother changes a woman, you know."

He nodded thoughtfully.

"I expect it does. Yes, you have matured and I do not know for sure if I am happy with the change."

"You have changed too," she reminded him. "You seem to care about your son and want to provide for him, so different from the time when you cared not how we fared." Her voice was soft and faintly tinged with regret. If he had not been a proud Christian, or she had been the possessor of a dowry... "This house," she mentioned, deciding it would be unwise to talk any more of Sam, "you are to visit us there? I mean, you told Edward that you intended seeing him regularly."

"Would you object to my visiting him regularly?"

She had to laugh at that.

"Edward, if you wish to see him you will do so – with or without my consent."

"Yes, I will. He is a son to be proud of and I do want to watch him grow into a fine man."

She looked down at her clasped hands, wondering what would be the outcome of these regular visits.

*

"Well, Eleanor, you are free, an unwed lass again."

Susanna lay on her bed. She had been reading but put the book away when Eleanor entered the room. "Does it make you happy?"

"I am happier, of course. But, Susanna, I am so sad for Alicia. She weeps all the time."

"Where is she now?"

The gentle voice was weaker than Eleanor had ever heard it; she saw that her friend had put a hand to her chest, as if to ease a pain there.

"I saw her as I came in just now. She was in the small closet by the front door, her head in her hands. I spoke to try to comfort her but she seemed not to like my being there. She was crying so, and it is all my fault!"

"Not so," argued Susanna angrily. "When will you stop blaming yourself? If anyone is to blame, other than the rascal who caused all this misery, it is Edward!"

"My Edward?"

"Certainly your Edward. He must have been of sick mind to marry you to Sam Garrett."

"He did not know me very well at that time, and he was thoughtful, in a way, because he could have deserted me, and what would I have done then?"

Susanna merely made an impatient sound with her tongue, then leant back against the cushion, and closed her eyes. Eleanor sat down by the big bed with its canopy of carved fruitwood supported by four pilasters, fluted and topped by the smiling heads of cherubs. The luxurious hangings of embroidered damask matched the coverlet and the padded board at Susanna's head. The seat of the thrownchair was cushioned with the same material. It stood to one side of the carved wooden chest on which stood a pewter basin and ewer and a large soap dish. Tapestries clothed all the walls except the one where the massive chimney piece reached right to the ceiling. For a moment Eleanor's thoughts went to Deva Place, which she had seen only from the outside, but she imagined its interior would be equally as splendid as this beautiful house in which she had been made to feel at home for almost as long as she had been on the island.

A strange disturbing sound issued from Susanna's throat, causing Eleanor to start with fear.

"Susanna, are you all right?" Her face had paled as anxiety flooded over her. "I will fetch William – he is somewhere around. I saw him riding towards the hillfield as I came by."

"No, dearest Eleanor, I am not so unwell that I need to take him from his work. Just bring me some water. My throat is so dry."

"And it hurts?"

"A little."

"I had such a sore throat once and Lizzie Curphey made me up a drink from herbs she grew in her garden. It proved to be an excellent remedy and I gave the rest to Alicia who had a sore throat later. I will see if she has any remaining."

Alicia was where she left her, in the small closet, weeping bitterly.

"Dear Alicia, please try to stop crying," begged Eleanor, taking the shaking body in her arms. "I know how you feel, and the suffering you have endured—"

"Do you!" she screamed, drawing away and standing up. Her eyes had a wild look and the once-lovely mouth was twisted into an ugly line. "Have you ever been ravished - stripped of all your clothes, even down to your shift! No, you have not, and yet you say you understand. That vile filthy man with breath fouled by ale and rotting teeth!"

"Alicia, stop!" Eleanor took a step towards her and held out her hands. "Dear Alicia, we all love you dearly and are only trying to comfort you. This conviction that you are with child - it is as yet only the result of fear. You can not know. It is quite impossible."

"What is to become of me? Where will I go?"

"Susanna will always look after you," returned her friend gently. "You know very well she will."

Alicia turned away and Eleanor saw her shoulders heave.

"Susanna is going to die."

"Alicia - no! How can you say so? She is ill at times, but always she recovers - Alicia!" Eleanor took her by the shoulders and swung her right around. "Why do you say this? Have you some knowledge?"

The girl nodded her head.

"The doctor told Master William. I heard him."

Eleanor sank down into the chair vacated by her friend. She had known, deep down... but yet she had never allowed her mind to accept it sufficiently for it to become a reality. It had been rather like a sort of dull ache which she had pretended was not there at all. But now... This was stark reality, the bald truth.

"Oh, God, why - why!" She buried her face in her hands and wept. "Why a wonderful lady like Susanna! Why her?"

"Yes, why her?" Bitterness mingled with anger when Alicia went on, "Good people! And fiends like Sam Garrett are given the health and strength to ruin a maid's whole life! Why," she cried vehemently, "if there is a God, does he let such things happen!"

"Alicia!" Eleanor, shocked by this blasphemy, forgot for the moment the sad news she had been given. "Do not speak so of the Almighty. He knows what is good for us all—"

"Oh, be quiet, Eleanor! You talk like a fool. How can it be good for me to have been deflowered by that – that pig! And is it good for me to be with child, and soon to be made homeless? Answer me that before you chide me, and take on that shocked expression! And if you are thinking the Church will throw me into prison for blasphemy, then I do not care!"

"No one is going to know what you said. And I agree that it is the most terrible distress that is upon you at present, but it was not God who did it, Alicia."

"Then why did it happen? And why is our beloved Susanna going to die? God has ordained it, no matter what you say." She had dried her tears but her cheeks were red and swollen and her body still shook with sobs. "It is said Sam Garrett will only go to prison, but I wish he could hang! I would watch them hang him, watch and laugh and wish it could take a month for him to die!"

The wild look had come into her eyes again and her voice was little less than a scream as she went on, a foam oozing from her mouth, "Why does not the victim have the right to say what the sentence shall be?"

"You would have the right, Alicia, if Sam were a single man, but as he is married to me..." Eleanor tailed off, her blue eyes widening to their fullest extent. "My God," she breathed at last, "so *that* is why they arranged the annulment..." Again her voice faltered to a stop as she saw the look of dawning perception in her friend's eyes.

"Of course! I can have him hanged!" Alicia began to dance around like someone possessed. "I can have him hanged – *hanged*! Eleanor, surely you are glad for me?" She stopped her pirouetting to stare inquiringly and to add, "You are no longer married to him so he is single... and I shall be given the choice..."

"You would choose to have him hanged?" Eleanor stopped. "But of course, since you could not possibly take the ring."

"I shall choose the rope, and seeing Sam Garrett at the end of it will at least be some compensation for the misery that lies so heavily upon me." Alicia wiped her mouth with her apron. "Will you stand beside me, Eleanor, and watch him die?" Her eyes glittered. "You must!"

Eleanor shook her head vigorously from side to side. She felt sick, for although she had a black hatred for Sam Garrett for what he had done to her friend, her sense of justice cried out in protest at the idea of the death sentence. Also, Sam had been plotted against, his sentence contrived. The Deemsters' Courts held the power to dispense with juries, which was in accordance with custom, or the traditional unwritten laws of the island. This omission of the formalities of civil law meant that the Deemster could summarily pass sentence without the culprit having been tried by a jury.

"No," she answered dully at last, "I shall not be witnessing the murder of Sam Garrett."

"Murder!" Alicia's eyes blazed. "It is plain that you do not want him to be hanged. But you would, if it had been you! I wish it had been you – oh, why were you away from home on that particular night when Susanna ordered me to go and fetch you? I hate you! I hate you for being away..." Her voice failed her on a choking sob and she put shaking hands to her face. "I am not in my right mind, Eleanor. Forgive me. I mean it not that I wish it had been you."

"It should never have been either of us," Eleanor returned, moving to take Alicia in her arms. "It was the unpredictable workings of fate, as is this which is happening to Susanna. We have to learn to bear it all, though it is hard." She paused, holding her friend close. Then she asked for the throat physic and they were soon entering Susanna's bedroom hand in hand.

*

It was all over. Samuel Garrett was dead. Eleanor had been forced to give evidence but the Deemster made his questions brief and to the point. Edward's sharp eyes never once wavered from her pale face as she spoke, merely telling of her absence from the cottage on the fateful night. Alicia's evidence took longer and she repeated that she had told Sam over and over again that she was not Eleanor and that she had been sent by her mistress to fetch her. She told of finding the cottage empty and was about to come away when she was attacked as if by some savage who had punched her in the face. Listening, Eleanor saw that her friend was determined to be revenged and she had to admit that there was some excuse. The tense moment came when Alicia had to make her choice and the rope and ring were produced. Without a second's pause she chose the rope, the only choice she could make.

Edward came to the cottage a week after the hanging and said he was going over to Chester to buy the house. Eleanor was there only because she wanted to collect some clothes, as she was still staying with Susanna, where her son was at present, taking his lessons.

"Susanna's time with us is short." Edward had been given the tragic news by his brother who was bearing up bravely, but it was plain to all who knew him that he was broken-hearted. "I suppose you will not want to make the move until – well, yet awhile?"

"No; I want to be with Susanna till the end." She was stuffing a grey homespun dress into a hand-woven bag. "Alicia thinks she will have to leave. She is Susanna's tirewoman so there will be no tasks for her to perform once... once her mistress is... is gone—" She caught the sob in her throat but sudden tears escaped. Edward took her in his arms; she felt the warmth and comfort of his strong frame, the gentle touch of his finger as he flicked away a tear from her cheek. "One thing is fortunate, though," she added when she had recovered, "Alicia is not pregnant."

"That will relieve her mind of something. And in time she will forget that unfortunate experience." He drew her even closer as he spoke and a shudder passed through him. In his relief at Eleanor's escape he cared little for the sufferings of her friend. "She is lucky that no real harm is done."

"Lucky! How like a man!" she said, looking up at him.

"The Deemster is satisfied with his day's work?"

"Sam Garrett? Justice was done; the punishment fitted the crime."

"I was bound to realise the real reason for the annulment."

"'Tis all best put behind us," he almost snapped, releasing her at the same time. He looked down at the bag, with the drab, well-worn gown peeping out. "Do you have to take a thing like that with you?"

"I need a change so I can wash this one. And that is all I have."

He frowned and turned, slapping his ridingwhip against his leg.

"Soon you will have fine clothes. I expect you will enjoy shopping at all the best establishments in Chester?" A smile curved his lips as he turned to face her again.

Her eyes lit up.

"Yes, indeed. I still have difficulty in believing we are to have such a beautiful home. Tell me I am not dreaming, Edward?"

The plea in her voice, the merest hint of anxiety in the big blue eyes... He caught her to him and his lips met hers in a long, lingering kiss.

"You are so lovely." His hand caressed her face, her throat, and came lower to find the small firm breast hidden beneath folds of dark blue fustian. "No, child, you are not dreaming."

She drew away, and again wondered what would happen once she was established in a home provided for her by the father of her son.

Susanna lingered for three more months, with both Eleanor and Alicia at her bedside, and William, trying to bear up but twice Eleanor found him in tears.

"My dearest husband..." Susanna often had difficulty in speaking but she had days when she was as articulate as any of them. "Dear William, hold me... hold me close..."

She tried to ease herself up. Eleanor and Alicia left the chamber silently as the grief-stricken husband slid an arm about Susanna's shoulders to help her.

"Why!" seethed Alicia, eyes blazing. "Why is God doing this to us!"

"Perhaps – perhaps..." Eleanor shook her head; she was in tears, and scarcely able to think. This tragedy brought back so vividly the last days of her mother's life – the hopelessness, the feeling of frustration, the straining against fate. "If it is God's will – if he wants Susanna—"

"Wants? He wants to rob those babes of their mother! William of his loved one! You and me of the best friend we ever had – or ever will have!"

"I have no answer at all," admitted Eleanor helplessly spreading her hands. "All I keep telling my–myself is th–that she will be at p–peace..." The tears she had been trying to suppress flowed on to her cheeks and her body began to shake with sobs. "Like you, Alicia, I ask why? She is so good and kind and selfless in all she does. She has always put others first." She stopped, the sobs rising in her throat to choke her. "How shall we get over this?"

"I shall never get over it! I want to remember her every day of my life."

So many people would remember Susanna...

The day came when they all knew she would never see another dawn. There had been no need for the doctor to tell them for Susanna was scarcely conscious. Her hands, so thin and white, had for days been clutching the coverlet but now they were relaxed, and on the waxen features a bloom had appeared. The cheeks were no longer sunken, the mouth no longer twisted in pain. Eleanor bent to kiss the still, cold lips and then went outside to join Alicia who had already made her own silent farewell. And now they had left their friend alone with her grief-stricken husband, so they could be together, just the two of them, at the end.

*

Susanna's death left a terrible void and Eleanor often wondered what she would have done without her dear Edward to comfort her. He wasted no time in getting her away, confident that the move to Chester and establishment in her lovely new home would go some way at least in diverting her thoughts from continually dwelling on her loss. Alicia was going with her as a sort of nanny for little Edward, a circumstance that greatly pleased his father because this, too, would help to make things easier for Eleanor – and for Alicia, he added to himself as an afterthought.

Chapter Seven

The delightful black and white Tudor mansion stood proudly on a slight eminence above a gentle curve of the river. Eleanor, enjoying the soft June evening with its scented breeze drifting across the flower-filled gardens, stood by the lovely statue of Ceres and let her eyes wander to the solidly built stone house on the opposite bank of the river. Sir John Kingsley, kinsman, though distant, of the Duke of Lennox, was the owner of the stately mansion, having inherited it five years previously on the eve of his nineteenth birthday. A handsome young man of quiet disposition, he had seemed inordinately shy and tongue-tied on that first day they had met.

Eleanor's lips curved at the memory, because it should have been she who was disconcerted, seeing that the seventeen-year-old son of the wealthy Sir Edward Kingsley was so far above her. But she had felt far from shy, or inadequate. For after only two years as Lady of the Manor, she had gained even more confidence than that which she had acquired as a result of her relationship with Susanna Christian. And of course, she mused, turning at last to walk slowly back to the house, it could have been the difference in ages which caused shyness in John, who was five years younger than she – which seemed quite a lot at that time. Now, however, when he was a more confident twenty-four and owner of a venerable estate, the difference seemed somehow to have diminished.

They had met on the stone bridge, he crossing one way and she towards the opposite bank. A smile, then a word of greeting and the next moment they were walking side by side, John having suddenly realised he had forgotten something.

"Oh, dear, I shall have to turn back..."

He had not meant to walk with her, she realised, but it just happened. And two years later, when he had inherited the title and estate, he asked her to marry him.

She had said,

"Have you not thought of my age? I did tell you how old I was."

Yes, she had merely mentioned the difference in their ages... and said nothing of her pregnancy...

She had naturally refused him and later had shocked him a little by saying,

"John, since we are good friends, I have something to tell you. I love someone dearly, and he visits me from time to time. I explained about Edward by saying I was a widow, which in one way is true. But my husband was not Edward's father – No, do not interrupt, John, or look so shocked. I will tell you all..."

"And now, if you no longer want us to be friends I will understand." Her voice had been low and, she afterwards realised, faintly pleading. John had said in a strangled voice,

"This man – is he married? But surely – I mean, Edward is eight years old. Was his father married at the time? And if not—?"

"His father comes from an aristocratic family and it would not have done for him to marry me. I never expected him to do so."

"I come from an aristocratic family, and I want – wanted to marry you!"

Eleanor was still reflecting on that rather dramatic scene as she entered the elegant drawing room with its tapestried walls, its carved tables and chairs, its linenfold panelling and its magnificent view across the river to the parklands which formed part of the Kingsley demesne. She sat down and took up the pretty tapestry she was at present working upon. But a moment later she was glancing up as the door opened and Alicia came in.

"I supposed you had gone to rest," commented Eleanor in some surprise. "You said you were tired."

"I could not settle. Oh, Eleanor, I am so excited! Am I really to be wed tomorrow, and to such a charming man!"

"It is no more than you deserve – but I shall miss you, oh, so very much."

"And I you, and the children – though Edward is now away at school. But darling little Susanna, growing up to be so like her namesake." She paused, thinking of her good fortune in being taken by Eleanor on the tragic death of her beloved mistress.

"If you come to my new house," Eleanor had said, "it will be as much as my companión and friend as to look after little Edward."

And for seven happy years they had been together, but now Alicia was to marry and would be living in the village of Plumbley, more than thirty miles distant.

"Yes," mused Alicia taking a seat opposite to her friend, "I shall miss my darling Susanna, and all of you, but, Eleanor, I can ride here to see you."

"Of course, but it is a long way and you have to think of the time when the bairns arrive."

A deep and soulful sigh issued from Alicia's lips.

"I shall be so happy to have many children – well," she amended with a grimace, "about three or four."

"Not fifteen like Margaret Quaile who will be your cousin-in-law. The Quailes do seem to breed abundantly."

"And I am marrying a Quaile." She paused. "Oh, well, it is in God's hands."

Eleanor smiled. It was a waste of time trying to convince Alicia that God did not have a hand in every little thing that happened. For herself, she believed that people were captains of their own souls, responsible for the most part for their own actions.

"I expect," she said musingly at last, "that Robert will have more sense than to have a large brood. Besides, he loves you too much to want to make you pregnant every year."

She thought of that young man, and his unconcealed adoration of Alicia. She had met him when he came over from the island with Edward Christian, who was visiting Eleanor and her children. Robert Quaile had inherited a small estate in Cheshire and Edward had suggested he stay overnight with Eleanor before riding on to Knutsford where the lawyer's office was situated. It was love at first sight for them both when Alicia and Robert met, and now they were to be wed.

Alicia became thoughtfully silent and Eleanor took up her embroidery again. She was missing her son, but on the other hand she agreed without hesitation when his father said it was time he went away to school. She had dainty little Susanna, golden-haired and with the sweetest disposition imaginable. Edward adored her, would toss her in the air knowing she would scream with delight, and he would tire before she did. For Eleanor it had been a happy time, and even the news that Edward was to marry gave her scant heartache, so resigned had she been right from the beginning, to the fact that he would never marry her. And Ewan, much as he admired her, would never have approved of so unsuitable an alliance. The girl whom Edward had married, almost a year ago, was the daughter of the wealthy Sir Cavalar Maycott, whom Edward had met the previous year when he was surveying the Castle of Dover, among others, which required fortifying, and he had advised his friend the Duke of Buckingham to do this.

The silence was broken at last by Alicia's saying, a little wistfully,

"Eleanor, do you never give a thought to Sir John - I mean, that he loves you is so very plain. Would you not consider marrying him?"

Eleanor laid down her embroidery on the cushion beside her. She smiled faintly.

"You cannot have forgotten that I love Edward - my very dearest Edward, the man who sired my two beautiful children?"

Her big blue eyes had lost none of their brightness, despite the fact that she was nearing thirty. Her figure was still trim, too, and made exceedingly attractive by the expensive gown she wore.

"But he is not *your* Edward," Alicia reminded her with a hint of asperity. "It is only Elizabeth Maycott who can say that. Now, if you married Sir John—"

"It will never be," interrupted Eleanor quietly. "Sir John knows it and is resigned."

"He does not look elsewhere."

"He is young yet. He will be looking elsewhere eventually."

"And then you will have missed your chance," returned Alicia with a frown. "Do you not want to be a married lady, not ever?" she added curiously.

The smile on her friend's lips deepened.

"As it was fated that I can never marry Edward Christian, then no, I have no desire to be a married lady, not ever."

"I wonder," mused Alicia almost to herself, "if Edward has ever paused to think on such wondrous love that is his - and which he has never deserved," supplemented Alicia as an afterthought.

"One day he will think on the love I give to him..." Despite the confident ring there was nevertheless a wistful little catch which could not go by unnoticed by her friend. "Yes, the day will come, and then, Alicia, I shall come into my own."

"You are not sure."

The statement merely brought a shrug and a little sigh as Eleanor rose from her chair and wandered over to the other side of the room and stood for a moment by the carved oak Jacobean chimney piece, at either side of which were gaps in the panelling where books were kept. On a table at one side stood a pewter vase filled with flowers and on another table daffodils and narcissi flaunted their golden glory from a priceless Ming vase.

"I believe I am sure." Her answer came softly, as if spoken to herself. "Edward must love me," she gestured with a comprehensive movement of a hand, "or he would not have given me all this. He brings something beautiful every time he visits me."

A wry grimace was Alicia's reaction to this but tact and love for her friend stemmed words that could give distress. But Eleanor could accurately guess at Alicia's thoughts. All was booty, confiscated after a battle on the high seas. Eleanor said dismissively,

"Edward is done with life at sea. He was done with buccaneering some years ago. He is settled now to married life and to the management of his two estates."

She went over to the window, wondering why she was restless and hoping her friend would not notice. The lily pond was looking well, with the flowers opening and the multicoloured plumage of the ducks catching sunbeams. The fine sloping shrubbery at the back flaunted many shades of green and gold, while behind it rose a line of elegant cedars of Lebanon. She loved her garden, though it was small in comparison to that across the river, the noble home of a friend whose respect she had retained in spite of her confessions. Did he still love her? Alicia seemed to be very sure that he did...

"I wish our dear Susanna could have been at my wedding." Alicia spoke into the silence, jerking Eleanor from her reverie. She shook her head.

"Even if she had been alive she would not have crossed the water. She became very timid of ships."

"I often think of her, and her great kindness to me. I was not happy that her husband took another wife. I would like to see this Mary Quaile, who, I suppose, is a relative of my Robert, though he has never mentioned her." There was a discordantly harsh note to her voice as she added, "I hope I shall not be expected to be civil to her, if ever we do meet, that is."

"She is not related to Robert. Her name is only Quaile because she was the widow of a Quaile – whose name was Robert, but I expect you know all this?"

"No, I knew it not. But all the same, I shall never be civil to her."

"My dearest Alicia," demurred Eleanor, "how can you blame this Mary? William wanted her for his wife, and she has married him. She has committed no sin."

"She has taken my dear Susanna's place!"

Eleanor said no more. It was plain that Alicia felt that William should have remained faithful to his wife's memory for the rest of his life.

A few hours later Alicia went to bed, and Eleanor was not long in following, but first she went softly into the dainty bedchamber of her daughter and, stooping low, she kissed the rosy cheek.

Presently Eleanor was in her own bedchamber, a large airy room furnished with a four-poster bed with curtains of blue velvet, several inlay chests and a washingstand with a pewter bowl and ewer. For some reason her heart had become heavy; she felt low in spirit, depressed without knowing why. Perhaps it was the prospect of losing Alicia – though she was inordinately happy that she was to wed a handsome, well-set-up young man. Poor Alicia had said over and over again that no man would want to marry her after Sam Garrett had ravished her, but Robert Quaile had not appeared to be troubled about it at all. He had known about it, of course, because he lived not too far away, and it transpired that he was one of the many who declared that Sam received his just deserts.

"I shall lie awake," she murmured, taking up a hairbrush and employing it with vigour. "What is the matter with me? It must be the thought of losing my dearest Alicia. It can not be anything else."

She laid down the brush and rose from the chair. The night was soft as silk and she went downstairs again and out into the mothy darkness. Across the river lights flickered in the windows of Kingsley Hall, and also in one or two of the cottages dotted about its rolling acres of pasturage, cottages in which lived his labouring men. Suddenly she knew that the way she felt had nothing at all to do with losing Alicia. No... she wanted Edward, wanted his arms about her, his lips on hers, his body close. She had told Alicia that she was not troubled about his marriage... but she was. The thought of his bedding another woman – oh, she had never been so naive as to suppose he had changed his ways. He was too lusty a fellow to live the celibate life for any time at all. She had heard about the Court ladies' escapades when their husbands were absent from home, sent away on some business for the King. But marriage was different, so permanent and final. It told her that any spark of hope that might have lingered was now crushed.

"But I am lucky," she told herself as she wandered across the wide expanse of well-manicured grass towards the rose garden where perfume filled the air and the statue of Minerva shone as the moon sailed from behind the scudding clouds. "I have so much – all this and two lovely children." She swung around to take in the moonlit gardens and pond, the fair house with its stables close by. Two ponies stood motionless in a small enclosure. "Yes, I have so much... but tonight I am filled with this desire for my lover."

What was he doing at this very moment? Was he abed with his wife, or drinking wine with the Deemster and some others of the clan Christian? Did he give a thought to her at any other times than those which he spent with her, here in this romantic and peaceful setting? That he had never known any depth of love for her she accepted, but often she recalled Ewan's statement that there was something special between Edward Christian and herself. Eleanor had long suspected that the Deemster's feelings for her went deeper than he would ever admit. She was confident that if ever she should want a friend, other than Edward, Ewan would be there with sympathy and help – sympathy? Why had that word come into her mind? Without sense or reason she found herself dwelling on it, and she became more and more depressed.

"Oh, but I must throw this off," she told herself impatiently. "I can not be dull and glum for Alicia's wedding."

*

Edward Christian sat in the drawing room at Milntowne, having come to discuss with his cousin the offer he had received from James, Lord Strange who had crossed to the island after the death of his mother, that capable lady who had managed the island's affairs for the past fifteen years, with the help of her son who was now assuming full authority on the island.

"He has come to take up the reins, and in all probability to look around and investigate how best he can draw more profit from our isle." Ewan's mouth went tight and there was a glitter in his eyes. "I trust him not. He is a typical Stanley in that any act will be for the further filling of the Derby coffers."

"Shall I accept this post?" asked Edward, reaching for the tongs to pick up a piece of coal that had fallen on to the hearth. "As you know, he has got rid of that inefficient fellow whom Lady Derby befriended, and so the office of Governor has been offered to me."

"I wonder why?" Ewan looked up. "As you know, it has been said of the Stanleys that every move they have ever made was done with strategy in mind."

Faintly his cousin smiled.

"Like you, I have no illusions about our friend Lord Strange. He is a clever, scheming devil who, no doubt, has some reason of his own for desiring that I shall assume the Governorship. What I am seeking from you is advice. Shall I accept?"

"I like not that wife of his either," mused the Deemster, for the moment ignoring his cousin's words. "Charlotte de la Tremouille has been used to extravagant living, so she will surely encourage Strange to impose more taxes."

"She brought her husband a massive dowry, so that should suffice for the rumoured royal state in which they live." Ewan stopped somewhat abruptly as his cousin shook his head.

"Only a moiety of that dowry was paid – and it does not appear that any more will be forthcoming. No, Strange will not gain more from that direction, so he will be looking to this island for the means to maintain this extravagant way of life." The Deemster's mouth compressed again in the thoughtful silence that followed. "As we Christians have always been a thorn in the side of the Stanleys, why should Strange ask you to be Governor? And what about the Earl – does he not have a say in all this?"

"Derby has always left everything to his wife to organise. Their son has taken over and I am sure it is with the approval of his father." Edward shifted impatiently in his chair. "You know all this, Ewan; you know that Strange is now in charge—" He broke off as the door opened and a footman announced, "Mister William, sir, the Receiver-General."

"What the devil is the matter with him?" were William's first words. "Since when do *I* have to be announced?"

"He is new," laughed Ewan, waving a hand as an invitation for his cousin to sit down. "He insists on being exact – he worked for Lord Morcambe who has a reputation for being a stickler for etiquette. Well, what brings you... your expression tells me you have news."

"Lord Derby has assigned all his property to Strange." William stopped there to await the effect of this unexpected intelligence.

"What! You mean – but when and how did you hear this? We have just been discussing Strange and his high-handedness in coming over here and taking complete charge."

"He had the authority." William sat down on the opposite side of the massive fireplace. "He is a sly one, that, deliberately keeping quiet about his father's abdication. I will wager he was waiting for someone to challenge his right, and then he would spring this upon us."

"Gloating, no doubt," observed Ewan tightly. "I sometimes wonder if that one is right in his mind."

"Perfectly right, but cunning as they come." William went on to explain that the dismissed Governor had called upon him earlier that morning and said that he had challenged Lord Strange's right to get rid of him in this summary manner. "Strange replied that he had every right, and that was the end of it. Then only two hours ago the *Maid of Mann* came in and Captain MacLucas gave me the news, which he had picked up in Liverpool just before he sailed. It seems to have come from one of the Earl's stewards – as we all know the Earl still owns manors in Lancashire and Cheshire – who had been talking in the inn there, on the quay. Had too much ale and mumbled on about a Deed which his master had signed, passing almost everything he owned to his son; this island was of course included, so now we have Strange as Lord of Mann."

Ewan was frowning heavily and as always when he was perturbed in mind he called for wine. Venetian glasses were brought and the wine poured into them.

"Did you know," said Ewan at length, "that the office of Governor has been offered to Edward?"

"No!" He stared in disbelief, then his eyes narrowed. "You as Governor, and I as Receiver-General... there must be some motive for favouring us Christians." He shot his brother a glance. "Have you accepted?"

"Not yet, but I feel I could do a deal of good."

Ewan nodded mechanically before sipping his wine.

"Accept, that is my advice, cousin. We might as well keep as many of us as we can on the Council. Yes, Edward, accept the office."

And at that very moment Lord Strange, drinking with the cronies who had accompanied him from England and who were staying at Castle Rushen as his guests, was saying with the hint of a sneer,

"Having shifted the one my mother appointed, I had discourse with Captain Christian with whom I was newly acquainted and I chanced to feel myself fortunate since this fellow, apart from being excellent good company, seemed to have abilities that would serve me well." He laughed loudly and quaffed half a tankard of ale. "He was amusing to me, being at one moment the rude sea-captain and the next the refined gentleman, having civilised himself by being at Court, friend, gentlemen, of none less than the late King himself—"

"James? Ho, ho! Another of his minions—"

"Not he. This Christian is as male as all the rest. We have a few of his bastards here to prove it." His loud laugh rang through the elegant apartment and was instantly joined by those of my Lords Brierly, Stonleigh and Horsley. Attired in the height of fashion, owners of large estates, they had welcomed this sojourn away from their spouses.

"Go on," urged Lord Stonleigh, "what else about this Captain Christian?"

"He hath made himself a goodly fortune by robbery on the high seas, and again that is to my advantage."

"It is?" from my Lord Horsley in a puzzled voice. "But how?" Lunging forward across one of his friends he took up a pewter tankard and quaffed a goodly amount of the ale it contained.

"Being rich, I bethought to myself that he would be content to hold the Staffe without pay…"

"Clever of you, James! Tell us, was he fool enough to accept?"

Lord Strange shook his head, but his next words rang with confidence.

"Not yet. They have to have their heads together, these Christians, and have a discussion. But he will accept, not aware that I intend to keep him only till I choose another."

Laughter again, and a few moments of jeering comments about the man whom James Stanley was intending to use for his own ends, then he would be treated as summarily as his predecessor.

"Perhaps," commented Lord Brierly, a more sober-minded man than his companions, "it will transpire that he will hold the Staffe for longer than you plan at present. After all, you are not intending to make your permanent home here, surely?"

"Good God, no, he can not!" in a horrified voice from Frederick Horsley. "Who in their right mind would want to reside on an out of the way little island such as this!"

Lord Strange gave no sign of his anger that his kingdom should be decried like that. But he made a mental note not to invite Lord Horsley ever again.

"And if you are to be back and forth from Court to your home at Lathom," continued Lord Brierly as if no interruption had occurred, "then it might be prudent to leave this Captain Christian in charge."

"It might," conceded Strange after a thoughtful pause. He was thinking about his wife of one year who was expecting their first child. He would wish to be with his family rather than creating an enforced separation that was unnecessary. He was compelled to be at Court since he had duties there, and he certainly had no wish to displease his King, Charles, who was having an anxious time at present, owing to his disagreements with the Commons and he needed support, so some absences from home were inevitable. "Yes, he said, glancing at Brierly, "you could be right. Perhaps the Captain will prove even more useful to me than I assumed."

Again he lapsed into silence and this time his thoughts were not with his wife, but with his sovereign. If only Charles had heeded the repeated warnings given him by his father who recognised the growing influence of the Commons. But Charles was headstrong; he believed in the divine right of kings, that he was the supreme ruler whose word must be obeyed to the letter. In this state of blind fantasy he failed to see that trouble could be the outcome of these strained relations which were begun in the reign of his father. Frowningly Lord Strange dismissed these dismal musings and once again he was wondering how he could institute policies on the Isle of Mann that could bring him in more revenue. He had to have more money somehow. If his wife's father had kept his promise of a large dowry none of this irksome scheming would be necessary. He dwelt with growing frustration on the stand being made over the land tenures. If he could only have his way by force...

No, he dared not use his militia to gain his own ends. If that had been an expedient way then his grandfather would have resorted to it.

His thoughts flitted about and he was thinking of his uncle Ferdinando. His untimely and inexplicable death could have proved most convenient had it not been that he had left offspring and a widow of particularly strong character who had been determined to fight for what she called their rights. But it was *Stanley* money! Stanley wealth gone along another line, that of Althorp, and then to become dowrys for the three daughters Ferdinando had left. Alice, his widow, had told James's father he should be thankful for what he did get, and said she regretted her agreeing to his having the Isle of Mann.

However, although she had eventually agreed upon this concession, it had not been entirely left to her, as King James had taken a hand while the negotiations were going on.

And now, mused Lord Strange grimly, he was the uncrowned King of Mann and he intended that these troublesome Christians should be constantly aware of it.

*

"So you have accepted." Ewan had come to Lough Mollo with the intelligence that he was crossing over to England and to ask if Edward had any message he might give to Eleanor.

"Yes, I have accepted it, though I have a suspicion that our wily friend has some plan to make use of me only until he chooses some favourite of his to take my place."

"I believed so at first," admitted the Deemster, sinking his body into a chair and stretching out a booted leg towards the fire. "But I rather think he will be far too busy to attend to aught but the collecting of revenues, which task now falls to you, cousin."

"Partly." The Water-Bailiff was also involved in collecting taxes for the Lord. "I wonder am I playing with fire by this acceptance."

The Deemster glanced at him and murmured wryly,

"It appears not to trouble you over much."

"What does trouble me is this unrest over in England, caused by the King's stupidity. It is to be hoped we on the island can avoid repercussions."

"Charles is dancing on the edge of a precipice, but he is blind to it. Yes, I dare say we shall manage to stay out of trouble. Right along the troubles over there have passed us by." Ewan walked over to the carved wooden cradle and stood looking down at the sleeping child. "A sturdy lad, but he will never be as handsome as his half-brother."

Edward sent him a sideways glance.

"I sometimes wonder if what you feel for Eleanor is deeper than you would have us believe."

"A lovely lass, with brains and resolve. I admire those with spirit."

"You mean, her resolve to make Edward a great man?"

Ewan nodded.

"And her daughter, she hopes for her eventually to marry into the English aristocracy."

"She aims high." A strange smile took the severity from Edward Christian's lips. "I guess that what Eleanor sets her heart on she will achieve."

"I wonder if she has ever set her heart on gaining your love."

"I do love her."

But his cousin was shaking his head.

"No, there is no deep love on your side... at present. But as I have said before, there is something exceedingly special between you two, something beyond comprehension."

Beyond comprehension...? Edward had felt it to be just that, and had wondered how it differed from love. He made love to her with a tenderness not shown to his wife; he could almost say he cherished her. And after making the belated decision to provide for her, he desired for her more and more comfort; he bought beautiful things for the home, and jewellery and pretty clothes for her. His wish was for Eleanor to have everything she could desire.

Could it be love after all? But no, because there was no all-consuming passion, no desire to make her his wife.

But that young puppy opposite... The heavy frown that darkened his brow naturally brought a question from his cousin and he laughed then and said it was nothing, nothing at all. Yes, that young titled youth with so much to offer. Eleanor had scoffed when he had said,

"He is in love with you; it is perfectly plain."

A laugh and a toss of the golden curls, a touch of his lips with hers and a final,

"Do not be silly, Edward. He is a mere child, while I am a matron with two growing children and my first grey hair has made its appearance."

"I really came to ask if you have a message for Eleanor." Ewan spoke into the deep silence and his cousin glanced up. "I am going over to England and shall be calling on her and if she will have me I shall stay overnight, and then ride on to Kirkham."

"Kirkham? Something wrong?"

"Not that I know of," he answered lightly. "But it is wise when one owns a property to visit it at intervals just to see it is being taken good care of."

Edward nodded his head. The Kirkham property was part of the Deemster dowry of Jane Skillicorne who married Deemster John McCrysten who had died almost a hundred years ago. The property, Prees Hall with its farms and rich pastures, had come down through five generations and was now owned by Ewan, although some of its acreage had been sold off. John McCrysten had been an astute man of business, buying land all around the house now called Milntowne, and had also improved the building itself, giving it the first tiled roof in the island, dismantling the fortifications erected by his forebears, and effecting interior improvements, some of which were retained when Ewan beautified the house some years ago. It was this John who decided that as there was the mill on the land, he would rename his house and since then it had been known as Milntowne.

"Well, do you have a message for Eleanor?" repeated Ewan, frowning at these silences. "You appear to be meditating?"

His cousin laughed.

"Your mention of the Kirkham property set off a thought chain – er – yes, of course I shall send a letter to Eleanor."

"Have you been over this year? No, I do not recollect your going."

"Time, cousin, time. Lough Mollo was neglected after I left as my uncle lost interest. I have a difficult task before me before it begins to make a profit, but I shall be in Chester quite soon."

"Never mind. We have the overseas trading."

He grinned at this but was sober immediately. It was not often that the Deemster let go of his dignity.

"Smuggling. Yes, I have been thinking, though, that now I am Governor I ought to become a respectable member of society."

"Really?" with a lift of his brows. "The day when you become a respectable member of society will be when you are too old for any kind of sport!" He paused a moment. "Perhaps you should give it up. After all, you amassed a fortune while at sea."

"The happy life!" exclaimed Edward nostalgically. "Excitement, danger, wenching – it was so good to be young, and single."

"You are still young, but more mature. The sea would not afford you the same satisfaction now as it did then."

"No... I am nearing forty – but that is not old and who knows, I might have an urge to sail the high seas again."

Ewan merely shrugged. Edward would never go to sea again. He had come home with a wife, had taken over his inheritance and now he was Governor of the island, which meant he was in charge during the absence of the Lord. He had too many responsibilities for it ever to be possible for him to leave the island for any length of time.

*

Sir John Kingsley rode across the stone bridge and within a few minutes he was lifting the heavy iron knocker on Eleanor's front door. A manservant opened it, smiled a welcome and, because his mistress was expecting the visitor, he showed him straight into the drawing room after taking his cape.

Eleanor's eyes brightened and she gave him her hand to kiss. His serious grey eyes beheld the ringless fingers and a small sigh escaped him. If only she would let him put a ring there...

"John, I am so happy to see you!" exclaimed Eleanor, taking in the velvet and silk of his attire, the high-waisted doublet slashed and paned with a shoulder cape falling over one arm. The neat starched ruff of fine linen was edged with lace. His hair was brushed back at the sides and upwards at the front. Only the spade beard betrayed him to be not quite up to the height of fashion. But it suited him, she thought, recalling that Edward, having spent some time at Court, had followed fashion and was now clean-shaven. "For some reason I am in the depths of depression. I think I am missing my son too much, but it will pass. Do sit down. You would like some ale?"

"Why did you send for me?"

His bronzed face with its fine noble lines and firm mouth, carried a serious expression and the grey eyes beneath their straight dark brows were regarding her with a sort of expectancy in their depths. "I am here at your bidding... and always will be," he added so softly that she scarce heard the words at all. But she had, and a hint of colour rose in her cheeks.

Was it fair, to use him like this? It had become a regular occurrence since Alicia left Deva Place to get married.

"I have to be honest," she answered decisively. "I want company, John, someone to talk to. The days seem so long since Alicia went away and with Susanna going to school each day..." She gave a shrug of her shoulders. "I should not have been so selfish as to ask you to come. Were you busy? Have I taken you away from your work?"

"No, dear, I have such an excellent steward that any work I do consists merely of riding round the estate." He looked directly at her, forcing her to meet his gaze. "You are well aware that it is always a pleasure for me to be here, with you. So keep on sending for me; promise, Eleanor?"

Her mouth suddenly felt dry. This constant hoping on his part, the pleasure-pain which she could fully understand, and perhaps a terrible feeling of defeat when, alone at home, his thoughts would turn to her.

"I – I..." She caught her underlip between her teeth. "It is so unfair of me, John, because I can never love you." The big blue eyes she lifted to his face were bright with tears unshed. "I can never love you," she repeated, "never."

"But will you marry me?"

She was too full to speak and a long moment of silence went by. She thought of all that he was offering her – the beautiful home, an Elizabethan mansion constructed of stone mainly but embellished with dark red brick quoins. Ewan had described it as an architectural gem, and he had only seen it at a distance. There was an imposing gatehouse with four octagonal turrets, and over this dignified entrance were the arms of the Kingsleys, carved in stone. Inside it was a treasure house of Jacobean carving and beautiful furnishings. Its ceilings were plastered in delicate tracery of white and gold; and complementing the general air of magnificence was a treasury of rare tapestries and paintings. The ruins of a Norman manor at the back of the house marked the site of the original dwelling.

Eleanor sighed. Yes, all that John was willing to share with her... without ever having her love...

"I am honoured, John," she said chokingly. "You are too good to me always, so kind. But, my very dear friend, I can never marry you." She paused but he seemed to be swallowing a sudden blockage in his throat. "I have a birthday next month, John, and I shall be thirty."

"What of that?" His voice carried an access of harshness and there was now a cold challenge in his eyes. "Well, tell me!"

"You are only twenty-five."

"Five years' difference. Is that any reason for us to abandon the idea of marriage?"

He was fighting for what he desperately wanted and her gentle heart went out to him. If only she had never met Edward – But then she would never have met John at all. She would now be some lady's tirewoman.

"I could never marry without love," she murmured at last. "I dearly love the father of my children—"

"But he does not love you! How can you care so deeply for a man who never intended marriage? A man who has recently married someone else?" He paused a moment, and frowned. "I fail to understand you. A love like yours should have its true reward. Oh, that it were mine..."

He swallowed again and the firm lips trembled above his beard. He looked at her, sitting on the opposite side of the fireplace, her gown of lightly patterned material contrasting with the layered ruff and deep cuffs of embroidered linen. His eyes went to her hair, which was rarely confined within a cap and today it fell freely on to her shoulders in a cascade of gold tinted with sunlight slanting through the high wide windows. He caught his breath... and swore he would one day wed her. And all at once he was uplifted and, on an impulse he could not contain he said,

"I can wait! I have all the time in the world. One day, Eleanor, dear, you will be mine – I know it!" He lifted a hand imperiously to forbid the words she was about to utter. "Say nothing. We are friends and it must stay that way. I would not end our friendship even if you desired it so. And if you were to forbid me to visit here, I should still come! Our friendship will endure. Make me a solemn promise."

He knew what she had been about to say: that it were best the friendship end now, but his insistence bore fruit. She had not the heart to bring this lovely relationship to an end – nor did she want to do so. She had come to rely on these visits, look forward to them for, as she had said, hers was a lonely life now that her dear friend had gone and her son and daughter were at school.

"I shall not be the one to end it," she promised at last. But she did feel impelled to add, "However, John, you could meet a charming girl and fall in love. That beautiful house and the estate... an heir should come along; it is only right."

Her voice was gentle and tinged faintly with sadness. For this was a sad situation in spite of the pledged friendship. *She* loved Edward and John worshipped *her*...

"I love you," John replied, gazing steadfastly into her eyes. "I shall always love you, so there can be none other. My mind tells me I shall have to wait; my heart will be patient." Then suddenly he was brisk, as if aware that sentimentality should be brought to an end. "How about that ale you offered? So much talking brings on a thirst." Amusement tinged his features now and in seconds they were both laughing.

"It will be here directly," she promised and a few minutes later the footman who had admitted John was there with the beer on a silver salver.

"You are not going yet?" she was asking when his tankard was empty. "I wanted to show you my roses. They are still in full bloom although it is mid-September."

He rose and before she could do likewise he had reached for her hand and was gently bringing her to her feet. The action brought them close; he bent his head and she remained still. He had kissed her before, a mere touching of her cheek... but now...

It was the loneliness, she later excused herself. She had needed comfort and John was there to give it. His kiss had been full of tender love and respect, his hands so gentle on her hair. She had not reciprocated but neither had she repelled him by even the merest gesture. It was not a prolonged kiss, and afterwards they had each looked steadily into the other's eyes, a smile fluttering to Eleanor's lips.

And suddenly he was brisk again, though he still held on to her hand.

"Come, dear, and show me these very special roses of which you are so proud – but I must tell you that my roses are just as beautiful."

"How do you know when you have not seen mine?"

"Because I grow the finest roses in the county!"

"Pompous man! And you do not grow the roses; Stevens does. At least," she amended, "he is the overseer of all your gardeners."

John laughed. She thought: he is equally as handsome as my Edward, and just about as tall, but he is dark whereas Edward is fair, like his Viking ancestors.

"You are right about Stevens. He ordered the roses two years ago and had them planted in the sunken garden which you have not yet seen – although you have seen most of the grounds, those immediately surrounding the house, that is."

They were strolling along a pathway between two delightful shrubberies at the end of which was the lily pond where the brightly plumaged waterfowl were preening themselves in the warm sunshine. It was an idyllic afternoon, clear and bright with a sapphire sky tinged with wispy fair-weather cirrus clouds silvered by tints stolen from the sun. Birds sang in the trees and the hum of bees drifted to them, a whisper on the fragrant air. . John glanced down into her eyes, pure happiness in his own. Guilt overwhelmed her but she stifled it. Today was wonderful... a rare day the like of which might never come to her again. For this brief space she forgot Edward, Alicia, and even her children.

"I must admit," John was saying a short while later as he stood with her by the rose garden, "that they are as special as you said they were."

"I am hoping they will last because I want to send some to decorate the church on St Michaelmas Day."

"They should last even longer. I have had roses in November. The weather was particularly mild, though." He glanced around. "Shall we walk or would you rather go in?"

"We will walk. It is such a beautiful day!"

Enthusiasm such as this could scarcely pass unnoticed and she felt an added pressure as John's hand tightened over hers. She smiled happily up at him, forced to do a little skip now and then as, for some reason, his pace increased.

"It was wonderful," sighed Eleanor when after strolling in the gardens for over an hour, they were once again in the house. "You have certainly cheered me up."

"I am glad." He was by the window seat, staring out over the ground they had just covered. "This place is very beautiful."

"Yes, it is. I am exceedingly lucky. Edward has been good to me." She broke off rather abruptly as he swung around, his dark eyes narrowed. She had said the wrong thing. She should have known better than to praise Edward to the man who considered he had treated her badly to say the least. "I think we shall have some refreshment. Tea and some special biscuits made by Bessie. She is an excellent cook." Eleanor reached for the bellrope. "You will stay?"

"Of course, gladly."

He sat down on a gilded leather chair and soon the tea and biscuits were laid out on the table along with plates and cups.

"Have you not any desire to go to London?" asked Eleanor conversationally as she poured him tea. "All gentlemen seem to visit the capital periodically."

"I have no interests there. No, it is too comfortable here. I am fond of Chester, and the estate takes as much time as I want to give to it."

So easily satisfied, she mused, but thought he really should be thinking of marriage and children. His life should be fuller than it was. He should have someone to love him.

"There is some unrest, I have heard. The growing Puritan movement and the King's disagreements with the Commons."

"You seem to know a lot about such things," he observed with some amusement. "How comes this news to you?"

"I hear things when I go into town. Also, some of Edward's relatives visit me from time to time and they seem to know everything that goes on."

She passed him the biscuits, a question in her glance. He said yes, the biscuits were special; he had enjoyed the one he had just eaten, and he helped himself to another. "Deemster Ewan – I have told you about him – appears to be troubled that if something really drastic breaks out here then it will affect the island."

"Drastic? What does he mean by that?"

"Well – conflict, perhaps... But it is unthinkable! No, I have no idea what Ewan means."

"We have no need to worry," decided John lightly. "It will all be resolved – and quite amicably, I doubt not."

He helped himself to a third biscuit and told Eleanor that if ever she desired to get rid of her cook he would be more than happy to employ her. "I remember the excellent cakes she made, and which you served up the last time I was here."

"She is a gem. Edward found her for me."

"You are lucky in your servants. Alicia was another gem, since she seemed willing to turn her hand to anything."

"She was not a servant – I had had her for a friend since before Edward was born, as you already know."

He nodded mechanically and murmured,

"A long time, as your son is now thirteen – nearly fourteen."

"And very clever as you are aware, John." Her eyes came alive. "He was mastering Latin and Greek when he was very young. He has decided he wants to be a lawyer so we are hoping he will go to Trinity College in Dublin."

She was animated and the wish flashed through John's mind that had he been the boy's father – then he realised with a little shock that he was not old enough.

"He is a fine boy," he commented. presently. "I hope you realise all your ambitions for him."

"I am giving him what I did not have, a good education."

"It was unfortunate that your father died so young."

"Yes; it was dreadful. He was only thirty-three..." Her voice trailed as she became momentarily lost in thought. Fate was so strange for had her father lived then she would never have met Edward, or be living here, or chatting with Sir John Kingsley. "He was a good man, and I pray each night that my son will be like him."

Different from his father, mused John, wondering even yet again how Eleanor could love such a man – one who robbed and plundered just for the fun of it – no, not just for fun since he had amassed a fortune as a bonus. He had met Edward Christian and been prepared to dislike him on sight. Strangely, though, it had been impossible to dislike him. He had a certain air of affability about him, and he was good company. Nevertheless, John could never have made a friend of him, even had the circumstances been different from what they were.

It was dusk when he rose to leave.

"When shall I come again?" he asked, ready to mount his horse. Eleanor had come out with him to the yard, the shawl about her shoulder having been donned at his request.

"Tomorrow?"

"Same time."

"I had word from a seaman whose boat came over last week. Ewan is coming and he will be staying overnight. Perhaps you would like to come to sup with us? I expect him on Friday week."

"Ewan... From the way you have spoken about him he sounds to be an admirer of yours?"

The note of pique could not be missed but Eleanor pretended not to notice as she answered brightly,

"Not an admirer in the way you mean, John. He admires the way I do things."

He laughed then and pointed out that she had failed totally to explain.

"Or perhaps I am teasing," he smiled. "I do know what you mean dear. He admires your courage, which is what I admire also." He mounted the horse, a splendid creature so very different from the small, dark horses on the Isle of Mann. "Good night to you, my dear. Sleep well, and I shall be over tomorrow."

"And about Ewan's visit?"

"Oh, yes, I shall be interested to meet this very important gentleman."

He leant forward to pat the horse's neck, and then he was cantering away and she watched until he reached the bridge.

Chapter Eight

It was late afternoon when Ewan arrived at Deva Place, having ridden from Liverpool where he picked up a horse. After a warm greeting between him and Eleanor he explained that he had intended coming over a month earlier but was delayed, having matters of importance to attend to. A trial, he said, was one thing, and some business for Lord Derby.

"So you and he are friends?" she asked when he was seated with a cup of wine before him. His horse had been stabled by Eleanor's groom and the clothes he had brought in a bag were being pressed by the new maid, Charlotte.

"Not exactly, but we have never actually displayed open animosity towards one another."

He leant back in the chair of goffered leather and breathed a sigh of contentment. "I always find it so restful here..." He looked at her with affection. "You are a very restful person, Eleanor."

"Thank you, sir. But how dull that sounds." She picked up her glass and sipped her drink, regarding him over the rim. He was over fifty years old now and although his thick hair was greying and lines fanned out from the corners of his eyes, his figure was trim and his shoulders square, his back straight. "How is Edward?"

"Fine, in good health. I have a note for you in my bag. You shall have it just now."

"His little son...?"

"Is well, and growing. But I told Edward he will never be as handsome as young Edward."

She coloured but it was plain she was pleased.

"You always say the nicest things to me," she smiled. "I have always appreciated your accepting me, as after all, I was no different from the other wenches Edward had—"

"Be quiet! Certainly you were different. You have sterling qualities which I greatly admire... in fact, my dear, if Edward had not provided all this for you, it was my intention to do so."

"Ewan, what are you implying!"

"All that is dishonourable—"

"There should be none of such talk betwixt you and me. I love Edward and shall love him till I die. There will never be any other man for me." Her eyes wandered to the window; shadowy figures moved on the distant lawn in front of Kingsley Hall. "Tell me about everyone," she urged bringing her attention back to him. "How is the Receiver-General?"

"William is working too hard. And I perceived he seemed down, depressed."

"If only dear Susanna had lived."

"Yes. It was a sad business. Mary Lucas - or I should say, Quaile, is a charming enough lady but not right for him." He frowned and added, "Susanna was gentler, and she spoiled him."

"And Mary is - different?" Eleanor brushed fingers through her hair to take it from her face. "I feel sorry for her. It must be difficult being a second wife."

"She was happy enough to marry him. But never mind her. Let me tell you about Susanna's sons. James will be going to Oxford and William is to go to Dublin—"

"Oh, that is where I hope my Edward will go! I did tell you, the last time you came, that he is brilliant at Latin and Greek!"

"Yes," with a hint of amusement, "you did boast about his academic prowess."

She laughed and coloured enchantingly.

"I can not help being proud of my son. I made a resolve before he was born that he would be a great man. Well, he might not be great like the King is great, but he will be respected and looked up to. I mean that, Ewan."

"I doubt it not, my child. And as I was saying before you interrupted to appraise me of the superior intellect of your son, William, who is going to Trinity College, cherishes the ambition to become involved in government activities in England. He wants to be a parliamentary officer."

"And leave the island?" she said in some surprise.

"He is not the heir, remember. James will inherit Knockrushen."

"But that was Mary's dowry."

"Knockrushen is now William's property and he can leave it as he likes. His children by Susanna do have to be provided for."

"You know, Ewan," said Eleanor with a sudden frown, "it is most unfair, this thing about dowries. If I owned property and married I should be very angry at being obliged to give it away to my husband."

He laughed and she recalled that a goodly part of his vast wealth had been acquired through marriages of his ancestors – and of course his own wife's moiety was no mean amount, though less perhaps than that for which he had hoped.

"The solution, my dear, would be for you to remain a single lady."

"Yes," mournfully, "how right you are. Either give up one's property or remain single." She paused, watching him staring into his cup. "Tell me some more news," she pressed, changing the subject. "How is Edward managing to look after both Lough Mollo and Poyll Dhouie and attend to all the many duties attached to being Captain of the island?"

"Edward has more energy than all of the rest of us put together. He manages all right, so you may rest your head about him."

"And William – Illiam, the dark one of your brood? He is eighteen now and very clever – so Edward told me."

"He is doing very well, yes." He pondered for a moment. "I intend settling one of the estates on him later. I have enough to provide for all my children. John will eventually have Milntowne."

And be a Deemster like his father, she thought – number eleven.

"William often talked so seriously for a young boy. He told my little Edward that when he grew up he was going to be like you and fight the Derbys who took all the money from the people."

"He will be a patriot, yes. I only hope he will always practise my kind of diplomacy." His eyes narrowed and his mouth went tight. "It is the only way; I have learned how to handle these Stanleys. And I know just how far to go with safety." He looked directly at her. "It would be dangerous for anyone to forget that they are the Lords of the isle, the suzerains."

"But they are afraid of you – at least, James is."

A strange smile touched his lips.

"He is, that is correct, so I shall always be safe. But for others..." He cut his words and frowned. "The trouble is, Eleanor, there is so much hate and malice... and those can be a danger to any man." He looked up. "Do I talk in riddles, my dear? Let us forget the Derbys and talk of more pleasant things."

But after a while the conversation somehow drifted to the troubles besetting King Charles in his quarrel with the Commons. And Ewan said something which made Eleanor ask if it were possible there could be civil war.

"But no," she added shaking her head. "There would never be a civil war in our country."

"There have been civil wars before," he reminded her gravely. "King Charles is weak; he allowed himself to be led by Buckingham far too much. The Commons quite naturally became impatient with the influence the Duke had over him. It is my view that it will run out of patience altogether." He stared space for a long moment, and Eleanor thought he looked so grave, so anxious. "Buckingham was one of his father's favourites, one of his pretty boys, and Charles seems to have been almost totally under his influence. However, with Buckingham now dead things might improve."

"The Duke is dead?" Eleanor's eyes widened in disbelief. "What did he die of? He was so young."

"You have not heard? He was assassinated last month."

"Killed? He was a friend of Edward. He told me of the merry times they had at Court together – with their particular crowd, that was. How did Edward take it?"

"He was shocked, naturally. It is said a fanatic murdered him but he was so much distrusted by the Commons that it is my opinion that his death was a well-planned operation to rid the country of a pest."

"And now, will the King be more reasonable and try to work with the Commons instead of against them?"

"I have it on good authority that he threatens to rule without Parliament."

"Is that possible?" frowned Eleanor, having recently become a little more interested in politics – in so far as this were possible, with her being here, in this quiet rural place to which news of goings on in London came only spasmodically. She wondered if John Kingsley knew about the assassination of the Duke – but if he did he would not have considered it to be an important enough subject on which to converse. He had shown his disinterest in politics one day when he said that the country survived in spite of politics and not because of them.

"The King can dissolve Parliament again, yes," said Ewan in answer to her question. "He is obstinate enough to do so."

"It is all to do with money," sighed Eleanor shaking her head. "Everything in the world seems to do with money."

He smiled in some amusement as he replied,

"Not quite everything, my dear."

Passing that over she reverted to the conflict between King and Commons, declaring again that money was the chief bone of contention.

"It is known even up here that the King illegally collects Customs duties and that he forces the wealthy to make him loans which he knows he will never be able to pay back. He is offering titles, also, and fining those who refuse to accept them."

"All this and much more," returned the Deemster thoughtfully. "The religious disagreements must not be treated lightly for you have to remember disasters, right down through the ages, that have resulted from the often fanatical intolerance in matters of religion. Also," he added frowningly, "another expedient he has resorted to is the compulsory billeting of his soldiery, without payment. For me, it would be irksome enough having soldiers in my home without the added annoyance of doing it free of charge."

She had to smile. The Christians had never gained the reputation for giving anything away.

"Oh, well," she rejoined carelessly, "there will never be an occasion when your island is so affected, so brighten up that frowning countenance, Ewan, and have some more wine!" And without waiting for his yea or nay she leant forward and refilled his cup again. He was still frowning though he remained silent. Why trouble Eleanor with his gloomy predictions? Trouble could be a long way off – or perhaps not happen at all. But if there did happen to be serious trouble between King and Parliament, then how could the Isle of Mann remain serenely untouched? Already the unrest was beginning to surface, the result of what was happening here, in England. The Manx nation had suffered a long time... it only required a spark... Drat the King! Yet he was not wholly to blame for his belief in the divine right of kings. The bigotry had come down from his father who soon lost popularity by his attitude of arrogant intolerance towards Puritanism, and he had been the one attempting to get money by selling titles and monopolies. He too had been dominated by Buckingham and others of his minions, though never in such a strong degree as that of George Villiers, who rose rapidly in his sovereign's esteem. King James had also riled Parliament by making his addresses to it in a lofty manner, actually extolling the supremacy of kings, even comparing them to gods. It seemed as if his son was destined to follow on similar lines, indoctrinated as he was to his father's ideas of the patriarchal nature of sovereignty. It could be said that he was the victim of his predecessor's warped judgement and, therefore, was more to be pitied than blamed. Yet he should have the sense to realise the importance of the warning finally given to him by his father, that he should beware of the growing power of the Commons.

"You are so solemn and quiet," chided his companion, and a smile broke as he emerged from his reverie. "Why worry about the goings on here in England? The Isle of Mann is a kingdom quite separate."

"Not totally, my dear; it pays homage to the Crown of England."

"Oh, I understood it was not anything at all to do with England. After all," she added as the thought occurred to her, "the Lord of Mann is entitled to wear a crown, so I learned from Susanna. I wonder why he prefers just to be the Lord."

"Strategy. The Crown of Mann was dispensed with when Thomas, the second Earl, became wise to the ways of King Henry VIII who was so quick at chopping off heads. Thomas, with the cunning of his clan, decided it were more politic not to run the risk of ruffling a temper so unpredictable as that of his overlord."

A sneer rolled the Deemster's underlip – noticeable to Eleanor despite the beard, and in the grey eyes lay an expression of contempt. Clever of Thomas, he was thinking, but then it had always been so with the Stanleys, otherwise they would never have become possessed of so much wealth and had so many honours bestowed upon them. They always had the good fortune to be in the right place at the right time.

He was thinking of the sheer good luck of Lord Stanley when he found Richard's crown on the battlefield at Bosworth and was able to place it on the head of the victor, Henry VII the first Tudor king. If that was not being in the right place at the right time, he thought disgustedly, then nothing was.

"You are quiet again, Ewan." Eleanor's soft, musical voice once again intruded and he made a little gesture of apology. "But if I interrupt anything you wish to ruminate over?"

"Not at all, my dear Eleanor. I was just thinking about the Stanleys and their incredible good fortune which never seems to desert them. They have always been in some position where they could please the King – whichever King it was at the time – and so they had numerous valuable gifts showered upon them. It is quite amazing, when one examines it. There can be few others who have been so blessed by fate."

"But fortune did desert them once, Ewan. The Stanley wealth has gone along that other line."

"They still have plenty, but not sufficient for the life style they desire."

And so they are bleeding the inhabitants of the island, she mused, wondering why people should be so greedy.

She too was thinking of that Thomas Stanley who had been able to place the crown of England on the head of the victor of Bosworth Field. He had received gifts of manors and land, had been made Earl of Derby, made Constable of the king's household.

Ewan was fingering his empty cup and she offered him more wine but he instantly declined, rising from his chair.

"I will go and change," he told her, moving from the fire. "You shall have your letter directly!" He smiled down at her with affection. "You are very lovely, my dear. Have I ever mentioned it before?"

He made a sudden grimace even before she replied,

"Many times, Ewan, in fact, far more than is good for me."

"Just what is good for you... or should I say, good enough? Tell me about this friend you have invited to sup with us. His house is rather special. I have already remarked about it. Is he in love with you?" he asked bluntly and although a hint of colour rose in her cheeks she was able to answer coolly,

"We are friends; I told you. Just friends."

"Who find pleasure in each other's company."

"Yes, indeed. I am happy when he is around. It has been lonely since Alicia left and Edward went away to school."

"Where is the wee one?"

"She goes to a small select school every day – except for the weekend – and it is best as she has no playmates around here. You will be seeing her in half an hour, when Marie fetches her home from this school."

"Marie?" he echoed. "I have not met her. She must be new?"

"Her parents are very poor, her father being a cripple. I was told about her and so she is here – happy, I believe, and able to give her mother money for food."

"You are a lovely lass, Eleanor. I envy my cousin more every time I come here."

"Ewan, you are an outrageous flatterer. Do you suppose I am in ignorance of your reputation?"

"This is no subject for a female," he retorted with mock sternness. "I am away. Shall be with you for supper – No, before, as I want to see how much our little Susanna has grown."

Our little Susanna... Eleanor's eyes were misty as she watched him cross the room and disappear through the wide oaken door. She had come a long way from possibly becoming a tirewoman to being accepted by the noble Manx family of Christian.

*

It was the following afternoon and the Deemster had been gone since early morning. Marie, young and of a warm, friendly disposition, came out to her mistress in the garden. Eleanor had been cutting flowers for the house and, turning with a smile, she looked inquiringly at her maid, having swiftly taken in with approval the starched white apron worn over a dress of dark blue homespun. The cap confining her dark curls was as spotless as the apron.

"Madam, there is a gypsy at the gate..." She paused self-consciously for a moment. "I – we – my mother and I never turn a gypsy away, in case they put a curse on us."

Eleanor managed to suppress the smile that leapt to her lips and instead made the sober response,

"Bring her in – I expect it is a woman?"

"No, madam, it is a man – but he looks quite nice and – harmless," she hurried on to say.

"Very well, fetch him in, but first, Marie, tell Will to come at once to remove some weeds that are growing in the herbaceous border."

"Yes, madam…" The girl scanned the length of the border. "I do not see any – ah, yes, madam," she said with dawning perception, and sped away to the full-throated song of the thrush that appeared each morning in the tall ash tree and left only when dusk was falling.

The man, tall and lean, came across the lawn with Marie by his side. Eleanor's eyes slid momentarily to the gardener who was looking nonplussed at the border which he so meticulously kept free from weeds. But catching Eleanor's eye, and aware of the gypsy's presence, he immediately grasped the situation and bent over the patch of ground close to where he stood.

"Good day to you, lady." The voice was strong but quiet. "I pray pardon for this intrusion."

"There is something I can do for you?" Eleanor made a swift appraisal of his appearance. He wore clothes that were patched but clean, and heavy boots. His beard was neat and darker than his greying hair which was brushed severely back from his high, weather-beaten forehead, yet was incongruously long at the sides.

Long at the sides… A vision glided into her memory, that of Sam Garrett who had his ears cropped. She had felt physically sick on making the discovery, but this time she experienced no such abhorrence… and of course she was not sure if this man had lost his ears. He did not seem to be a man who would break the law.

"I am here only to beg," was the bald admission which naturally took her aback. She knew not what she had expected, but it was not this unhesitating admission. Beggars had come to her door many times, and invariably they hedged around before coming to the point of their visit. "I prefer to beg than steal, though neither is what I would desire, could things be different."

There was an element of pride about his manner which told her that it had been with the greatest difficulty that he had resorted to begging. She said curiously, her eyes again straying to the long hair at the sides of his head,

"What would you desire, stranger?"

"You sound kind, lady."

"I asked you a question." She turned without waiting for an answer and told Marie it was time she was going to call for Susanna. The girl obeyed, having made sure Will was still within calling distance of her mistress.

"I would desire work, lady. Employment is unfortunately denied me."

"Oh, why?" Eleanor stooped to put the flower-filled basket down at her feet. "You seem able to work."

He paused a moment, plainly having difficulty in how to begin. And when at last he did open his mouth it was clear that he was having the greatest difficulty in framing his words.

"I worked on a manor belonging to my Lord Derby and – well – there was a theft of some eggs and two chickens – I did not steal, lady! I was satisfied with my wages. I lived alone in one of the cottages and so I could manage very well. But I was blamed and..."

"Lost your ears?"

A hand went to the side of his head and for a moment his teeth snapped together. "I also was thrown off the estate, not even being allowed to collect my few belongings. And so now you see me, and know all." He looked down into her big, compassionate eyes and waited.

"Who did this horrific mutilation?" she demanded, anger she had never known welling up within her.

"It was at my Lord Derby's order, lady."

"But you protested your innocence?"

"I tried, and in fact managed to speak out but he gave me no attention or time. He told his steward to take me away and – and cut off my ears."

She winced as in imagination she was witnessing the savage act and wondering that any man could carry out such a barbaric order. Derby... The feudal lord, scion of the House of Stanley on whom so many natives of Lancashire and Cheshire still depended for a living. She said quietly,

"So no one else will give you employment?"

"That is right, lady." He glanced away but she was quick to read what came to the silently moving lips, "God, but I am mortal hungry!"

"Come into the house," she invited, "and my cook will give you something to eat." After calling to Will that he could go now and do something else, she led the way to the back door of the house. "Marie, my maid, took you for a gypsy," she said as they walked along, "but I saw at once that you were not one."

She asked him his name, which was Robert, but he was known as Rob, he added. No, he had no relatives at all, his father and brother both having died in the service of the Stanleys.

"And that is how I came to have the cottage to myself," he explained as at last they were nearing the door.

"A cottage? Or was it a hovel?"

She turned on reaching the door, to see what his reaction would be. A faint smile touched the firm lips and she thought: he would make a handsome young man, with a little care and some food inside him.

"How does one compare? I lived in some comfort. A straw pallet to sleep on and a table to eat off."

She closed her eyes. The awful poverty of the masses compared to the luxury and extravagance of the masters. She said as they waited for Bessie to come to the door,

"I suppose your father was alive when the previous Lord Derby had over two hundred servants in his house?"

"Yes, lady."

That was all before the door was opened and Bessie's inquiring eyes slid from her mistress to focus on the man standing beside her. Eleanor quickly explained and saw the man safely into the kitchen and seated at a well-scrubbed table not far from the stove on which hung a large iron pot of soup.

"His name is Rob," she was telling Bessie who had followed her to the door, obviously ready to voice a protest. But she was given no time for that as Eleanor added, "When he has eaten his fill – and give him some of your delicious cake after his soup – bring him to me. I shall be in the drawing room."

Back in the garden with the basket in her hand, Eleanor meandered slowly along a series of winding pathways, and now and then, through bushes or trees, the lovely manor house of Kingsley Hall came into view. She would have liked to give Rob some employment but firstly she would have to ask Edward for extra money, for his wages, and secondly, she had no cottage in which to house him. But John had...

*

The Deemster was away for two weeks and on his way back to catch the Isle of Mann boat he again stayed overnight with Eleanor. They had supped and as the evenings were closing in the candles were lighted in the sconces and on the table was a silver candelabrum. Ewan's face was a mask of inscrutability as he faced his hostess across the table. They had chatted over the meal and now he was drinking wine while she was eating marchpane. That he strongly disapproved of the employment of Rob was very much in evidence.

"But he wanted work, and also he had been ill-treated," was her protest when he said outright that she should have sent the man packing, and without food. "How could I refuse to help him?"

"'Tis far too soft you are," he retorted with a stern inflection. "There will be a swarm of others begging at your door from now on!"

"No such thing. He has been here for two weeks now and no one else has come to beg."

She had explained to Ewan that John had taken rather a lot of persuading, because he knew Lord Derby, and his father had been a regular visitor to Lathom House when the Countess was alive. But Eleanor had at last persuaded John to let Rob have the cottage which she knew was vacant on his estate, and as John could find only three days' work a week for him it was agreed by all that he would give Eleanor three days as well. She worked him only two but paid him for three, having drawn on some savings she had. The extra day gave Rob time for the cropping of the piece of land that went with the cottage, and also for the reading Eleanor encouraged him to do.

"I am surprised that John Kingsley would let himself be persuaded to take on a felon—"

"Rob is no felon!" interrupted Eleanor wrathfully. "I know an honest person when I see one and he is honest! I should have thought you would have been the first to condemn Derby for such barbaric treatment of a fellow human being – yet why should I?" she added inconsistently. "You do it yourself!"

"Derby was right to punish a thief – and you, my girl," he added pointing a finger at her, "had no right to listen to his pack of lies, much less take him in and give him work. If he steals your silver, Edward is not going to be pleased at having to replace it."

"Oh, you are stupid, Ewan." She was so angry she scarcely realised that she was forgetting the respect she always afforded him. He was so esteemed and feared on the island that even his own kin often cringed before him. "You refuse even to give Rob the hearing I have asked for. However," she added with less anger and more pique, "you can put in all the bad words you like about him but I shall be proved right. So go home and tell Edward what I have done. 'Tis quite uncaring that I am!"

He shook his head.

"We shall never change you, my dear cousin... and I guess that, deep down, we do not want to."

And after that they continued to chat until after midnight.

"As I mentioned, the boat sails in the afternoon so I shall not have to leave quite so early as usual." He bent to kiss her cheek as they both stood at the top of the wide, balustraded staircase. "Good night, little foolish lass. Sleep peacefully."

Once in his bedchamber Ewan gave a deep sigh and his face was grave. He had heard and seen much in London that disturbed him. And he had ridden to Windsor to visit a friend and heard of the goings on both there and Whitehall. The King seemed so naively blind to the increasing power of the Commons, and its animosity towards him. Even the assassination of his favourite had not pulled him up with the jerk one would have expected. He gave lavish parties and presents to his favourites; he had hunting parties in Windsor Forest and masques and balls at Court. Ewan was troubled, not for England but what a civil war could do to the island as regards repercussions. This short-sighted policy being adopted by Charles was so very reminiscent of that of his father that one wondered if what was so inherent in him could ever be rectified. This belief that a king was God's representative on earth and, therefore, responsible to Him alone seemed to run through everything he did, every action he made, and to Ewan with his astute and farseeing mind, there could be disaster ahead for this Stuart king who doggedly followed the path of his own beliefs.

Ewan poured water from the ewer into a basin and washed his face and hands. Then he took out some notes he had made and sat down in a chair by the window to look over what he had written. Charles was still ruling without Parliament, after having adjourned it earlier in the year. He had supporters, many of them, and therein lay the danger: he would feel safe should there be trouble.

Perhaps, decided Ewan as he presently closed the little book, he should send Edward to talk to the King. After all, he had been a friend of his father, and he was with Charles when his father sent him to Spain in search of a wife. Yes, perhaps someone from the little Kingdom of Mann could reason with the King.

*

The letter which Edward had sent to Eleanor and delivered by his cousin, was so affectionate that she felt warm and secure. But what made her really happy was the promise that he would be over for a visit before the end of the year. She told John she was expecting him sometime in November but what she did not know was of the decision of Ewan to send Edward to talk to the King.

So it transpired that he arrived unexpectedly one mild balmy evening in mid-October, when she had invited John to dine with her.

The two men greeted one another stiffly and then Edward, booted and spurred, went to his bedchamber to wash and change his clothes. John made a grimace and said perhaps he had better leave.

"No, certainly not, John. Edward knows of our friendship and you two have been in one another's company before."

John looked at her and gave a small sigh.

"'Twas not a comfortable situation though," he reminded her. "He is jealous, and yet he has never wanted to marry you. Surely, dear Eleanor—"

"I love him," she said simply but on a little sad note. "There are times when I almost wish I did not care like this, but I do and always will, so please, John, be content to be my very dear friend... until you meet the lucky woman who is destined to become your wife."

He was slowly shaking his head even while she spoke.

"You seem to overlook the fact that I love you just as strongly as you love him, and I shall always love you."

He rose from his chair, tall and straight and smart in a dark doublet and breeches, with his hair brushed back at the sides and up from his forehead at the front. The ruff of spotless white linen was edged with fine lace while the cuffs were made entirely of lace. His black shoes boasted no rosette embellishments, but were tied with the simplest of bows. He was not dressed in the very height of fashion but his attire had the mark of elegance and immaculate taste. Not for him the desire to shine at Court; he was a gentleman farmer, owner of a manor the income from which supplied his needs, for they were modest. Nevertheless, he was possessed of other valuable properties and for this reason Eleanor wished he would marry and have children. She told herself he would not always be in love with her, for anything unnourished must surely die. She hoped he would always be her friend, even when he did marry, because he did have a special place in her heart. He insisted on leaving and she walked to the gate with him, which was at the end of a long, tree-lined drive. On her return she met Edward striding towards her and she ran to him, eager for his arms around her.

"So your friend has gone," was his unnecessary observation. "Is he here often?"

"This is no greeting after months and months," she protested when he made no attempt to take her in his arms. "Tell me more about why you came so soon – I mean, sooner than I expected?"

"We shall talk about it later."

The eyes glittered with anger suppressed and she saw again the ruthless searover, the man who would have ravished her mistress had he dared. But no... She saw the grey in his hair, the fan lines at the corners of his eyes. He was older now, fifteen years older. He had mellowed, softened. This mood was merely jealous anger and she thought it a very strange paradox that he could know jealousy without loving her and she, who loved him, was not jealous of his wife. Resignation was the key... and Edward would have to become resigned to the fact of her friendship with John, just as she had resigned herself to his marriage to Elizabeth Maycott.

"Then come in and Bessie will feed you."

She slid her hand through his arm and smiled up at him. "But first, come upstairs and see your daughter. She grows more beautiful every day – and it is many days, and weeks and months since you have seen her."

His anger was dissolved by her charm and her smile and the tender pressure of her fingers curling around his arm.

"My precious girl!" He took her in his arms and kissed her over and over again. "Susanna will never be as beautiful as her mother!"

"What flatterers you Christians are!"

"Ewan? God's glory, wench, how many admirers have you!"

"'Tis three by my reckoning."

Her saucy response earned her a slap on the behind. "I shall have a word with Ewan," she warned, "and tell him you have used violence upon me."

"You are a wretch, Eleanor, but you have cast this spell over me from the moment I set eyes upon you, when you were just a child."

He slid an arm about her waist and they strolled, bodies close, towards the house. The moon was bright, and rising to outshine the stars; the river gleamed, serenely calm, the slopes running down to it dotted with trees and shrubs and bordered by thick briar hedges. "This is such a restful place," Edward murmured, bending his head to brush her cheek with his lips. "I shall come more often... yes, I must..."

Eleanor saw that his attention had strayed to the noble Tudor mansion across the water, where lights were beginning to flicker in the windows.

"Ewan tells me you have taken pity on one of Derby's serfs." The abrupt change of tone to roughness was startling. "And you and this John have made an agreement as to his employment."

"John had the cottage but not the work. I suspect he has made a job for Rob, but it is for three days a week only, so I employ him for the other two."

"Two," he frowned, stopping in the path to look interrogatingly at her.

"He is a free man," she informed him with a hint of defiance. "I am of the opinion that five days on the land is sufficient work for any man. He deserves two days to himself. I have lent him books and bought him a hornbook. He needs time for his learning."

"Good God, woman, this felon is not your concern!"

"He is no felon," she snapped drawing away from him. "Nor is he a serf. I employ him as a labourer in the grounds and John has him working in the fields or with the horses – whatever needs doing. He has his cottage and is settling in. Both John and I have found him some furniture and rugs, and he has a proper bed to lie on."

The defiant note was still there; it was also reflected in her eyes.

He said in a hard voice,

"You and this John appear to have much in common."

"In that we are both humane, yes, indeed, Edward. John is a kind man—"

"And I am not! Are you daring to compare us?"

She smiled wistfully.

"You know you have little kindness in you, Edward. Ewan let it slip that you had one of your men whipped and put in prison for stealing a hide, which he needed to make his children shoes for the protection of their feet. You have not changed, Edward, even though you are now the Governor of the island."

"Damn my cousin," he swore wrathfully. "What made him mention that?" He gave her no time to answer as he went on, "The man deserved it. Stealing is a crime which requires punishment!"

She would have walked on again but his hand shot out and she was swung roughly around to face him.

"Edward – you are hurting me!"

"This man – Sir John Kingsley – just how far has the affair gone?" Anger had brought threads of colour creeping along the sides of his mouth, which was itself tightly compressed. "Tell me, I say! I asked if he comes here often and noticed your evasion. Now, I demand an answer! Seems to me he is always here!"

Her blue eyes glinted. She had come a long way in the fifteen years she had known him; confidence, slow at first, had advanced dramatically under the sympathetic influence of her dearest Susanna, the lost friend who would never be forgotten. The fact that Sir John Kingsley both loved and respected her was a circumstance bound to enhance her stature and self-esteem; it could not possibly have been otherwise. A woman with two bastard children, the mistress of their father, and yet she had won the respect of a nobleman. She had only to say the word and she could become his wife... Lady Kingsley. She looked up at Edward and said coldly,

"John comes whenever I invite him, and it is often."

"Then it stops! He will not come into my house again!" Anger had him well within its grip and before she could manage to break free he had taken her by the shoulders and shaken her till her breath seemed to be leaving her body. Tears threatened but were determinedly suppressed. She escaped from the grip of cruel fingers and faced him defiantly, so small beside him, and recalling for one brief moment that fearsome mastery of the Captain of the *Falcon*.

"Your house?" she repeated. "I had believed you bought it for me."

He made no answer and now a sort of sulky silence had come over him. "However, should it be possible for you to take it from me, Edward, I would accept John's offer... of marriage."

"Marriage!" He stared disbelievingly. "Did you say – marriage?"

"John loves me..." She smiled and shook her fair head. "Is it not ironical, Edward, that a man I have no love for wants to marry me, while the man I love married another – Oh, yes, I was always resigned, ever aware that you were – are – far above me so marriage between us was impossible, an..."

"No, it was not!" he broke in a strangled voice. "God, why was I so filled with these beliefs of all the Christians, that we are superior? Yet what are we? Our ancestors robbed and raped and plundered; they tortured and murdered – all this before settling down and making laws and calling themselves kings – of royal blood – what in God's name does it mean? No, there was no reason at all for my not marrying you!"

"Except that you did not love me," was her gentle reminder at which he made an impatient gesture and said what did that signify since most marriages were those of convenience.

"It has always irked me that Edward was not legitimate, and then came my daughter. 'Tis a bane to me, knowing they are bastards." He was in the grip of some strong emotion and for one moment she thought he was going to cry. "I did not love you," he continued after a long while, "but now..." He looked at her, looked deeply into her eyes. "Now, I am not so sure."

"Not sure that – that – you love me?" Her gaze was fixed to his unblinkingly. Her whole body was trembling. Was she at last to hear words that would fill her cup to the brim? "Edward, what are you trying to say to me?"

"I do not know, Eleanor," he admitted in a low voice. "'Tis some thing inside me that is twisted and I feel confused." He took her hand and now his touch was gentle, and in his eyes affection such as she had never seen before. "Do not ask me, sweeting. Let it go on as before. Elizabeth has so recently had a child, and she loves me I think." He stopped and Eleanor wondered if it was guilt that she saw in his eyes now. "There are other circumstances causing anxiety – but you know of them. Ewan told me you and he were discussing the King."

"But why should you worry?" Her voice was low and the bitter disappointment she had just a moment ago known was cleverly concealed. But it hurt that he had been so close to telling her he loved her and then made the excuse that he was confused. "What happens in London is too far from the Isle of Mann for there to be any direct repercussions."

"We can only hope so. I am to speak with His Majesty and see if he will listen to reason. I recall that his father once told me he was beginning to recognise and fear the rising power of the Commons. But James was possessed of this unshakable belief that he was put on this earth as the advocate of the Almighty, and this he has passed on to his son."

Eleanor sighed impatiently and walked on towards the house.

"Have a look at your daughter," she advised. "That will dispel this mood you are in."

He smiled then and took her hand. Together they mounted the stairs to enter the pretty bedchamber wherein lay their six-year-old daughter, sleeping peacefully beneath the ornate canopy which hung atop the big bed with its fluted columns and its elaborate headboard.

"She looks so tiny." Edward stared with wonderment at the rosy cheeks, the golden curls, the long eyelashes and full red lips which were moving as if the child were having a dream. "A replica of her mother."

He straightened up. Eleanor was frowning slightly as she wondered if ever the time would come when the young were regarded as children in their own right and not as miniature adults wearing the same clothes and hair styles, beginning to follow adult pursuits much too soon. But all she said was,

"She is beautiful, is she not, Edward? I hope you will always be as proud of her as you are today."

"You have high hopes for her. Ewan was remarking on it."

"She will be a lady of quality," returned her mother with the light of determination in her eyes.

Edward went off early the following morning and for a few weeks Eleanor waited to see if she was pregnant again, just as she always had done after one of his visits. She was happy with her two children and hoped she would not have any more. But then at the end of November he was back at Deva Place and this time stayed for a month. For Eleanor it was an idyllic time because her lover was getting to know his children better than ever before, Susanna who was home each afternoon, and young Edward who came home on Saturday afternoons and stayed until early Monday morning when his father would ride with him to school. The arrangement whereby he could be home for the weekends was made specifically so that father and son could become more closely acquainted with one another; it had been thought of by Eleanor immediately she knew of Edward's intention of staying for a whole month. It was not normally allowed for boarders to do this but the head tutor was no match for Eleanor's smile and charm of manner and so an exception was made.

The four would ride every Sunday to church in Chester and afterwards ride along the river bank. But on the last Sunday snow fell quite heavily to dispel the unseasonably warm and sunny weather they had been enjoying. Sometimes Susanna would mention her "Uncle John" and her father would stiffen and go quiet, whereupon Eleanor would charm him out of it by quite simply reminding him of her love.

"You know, sweeting," he said one day, "I am beginning to feel exceeding sorry for Sir John Kingsley."

"I try often to persuade him to look about for a suitable woman so he can marry and have children. His possessions are substantial so he must have an heir."

"You will not mind when he marries?" Edward regarded her with an odd expression.

"I very much desire that he will marry – I have already said so. He is too good and kind to be wasted."

"Wasted," laughed Edward. "I expect you mean that if he remains unwed it will be some female's loss."

"That is it exactly, but..." She drew an impatient breath. "John listens and then immediately shakes his head and says he will never marry anyone but me."

She peeped up at him, saw his mouth tighten and his face muscles become taut. She wondered what he would say if she expanded on that, told him that John always insisted that one day he would have her.

"Well, since he can never marry you he is foolish to continue hoping."

"But you threatened to turn us out of Deva Place," she reminded him mischievously, "and so I shall have to marry John so we can be provided with a home."

"Eleanor," he gritted, "you do ask for trouble. What is the object of this teasing, might I ask?"

"Did you mean it?"

His blue eyes glinted. It was mid-morning and he and Eleanor, having returned from a brisk walk along frosty lanes, were in the drawing room drinking warm milk by the glowing coal fire.

"You know full well I never meant it!"

"Then why waste breath? You forbade me ever to have John here again."

"I am still not happy about this friendship."

A small pause before she remarked intrepidly,

"John is no Christian, you know."

He glowered at that and she knew that at one time had she made such a remark it would have been at her peril.

"We are not all like the Deemster!"

She said nothing. Word had come of the rumour that the Governor of the island had made advances to the wife of one of the soldiers in the garrison at Castle Rushen, but of course it could be untrue. Eleanor had an open mind. She had never been under any illusions regarding her lusty lover.

On the morning of Edward's departure it was snowing heavily, but he had a good reliable horse, and it was not too long a ride to Liverpool where he was to board one of the Deemster's boats. Eleanor wondered what kind of contraband was aboard the *Maid of Mann*.

It was a sad goodbye, as they had come closer than ever before during that month when they had done so much together. They had ridden into Chester several times. She had done some shopping, showed him her father's shop, and they had walked round the city on its high Roman walls. The weather had for the most part been kind to them and even when it had snowed they had enjoyed the views from the windows over the grounds of the house to the river and beyond to the more extensive lands forming the manor of Kingsley. John had been over to supper several times and Edward was forced to acknowledge his rival's good qualities and admit that Eleanor had spoken naught but the truth. The children liked him and he even went out to play in the snow on the Sunday it had kept Eleanor and Edward indoors. Edward did say, in a voice which was a mingling of envy and pique, "What it is to be young. The energy of the man!" He had glanced at Eleanor, standing at his side by the window. "You can see there could be nothing between you and him. The man is far too young for you."

She had to laugh, and could not help reminding him that he was nine years older than she.

"'Tis different. The man should be older."

"Have it how you will," was her obliging reply. "My life is far too full and happy for me to spoil anything by picking an argument with you, dearest. Kiss me, Edward, it is more than two hours since you did so."

He did as requested, and asked,

"Has it really been a happy time, my dear?"

"You must know it has. We have all been together, and I pray we shall be again, for you did say you would come more often?"

"I intend to..." The blue eyes wandered to the three playing outside. Eleanor perceived that he was still a little troubled about her friendship with the youthful Sir John. "Yes, I intend to be with you all again quite soon."

Before he left he and Eleanor had a long talk about the future education of their son and it was decided definitely to send him to Trinity College in Dublin. Already he had had some practice in fencing, running and dancing. He was a good horseman and his classical learning was considered excellent by his tutors.

"As long as this fatuous presumption by Charles of the Divine Right of Kings does not cause a war our son should have a happy, peaceful and long life."

Edward had not said much regarding his errand to the King and Eleanor had not pressed him for information. She had no interest in things so remote any longer; if men had nothing better to do than risk losing their heads by playing dangerous games then let them. She had important things to do, like bringing up her children and looking after her home. She had Edward's visits to look forward to. Life was pleasant and without complications. She had no thought that anything could change it, not drastically, that was. Sorrow she had known by the loss of her father and mother, then Susanna. She could not envisage any more and so she blithely went on her way, enjoying her friendship with John, her shopping trips into the city, and her garden with its myriads of flowers and trees, cared for with pride by Will and Rob who enjoyed each other's company when working side by side on some border or doing other jobs together. John had found Rob to be a trustworthy and conscientious worker, so much so that he had made a substantial increase in his wages.

Everyone was happy and content, with nothing to go wrong.

Chapter Nine

It was with a frowning countenance that Captain Edward Christian studied the communication that had been brought by messenger from Lord Strange. This was serious. A trumped up charge in the first place, made by Thomas James, Captain of HMS *Lion's Whelp*, that he, the Governor of the Isle of Mann, had been trucking with pirates.

Since his appointment five years ago he had carried out his arduous duties with efficiency and zeal, earning the esteem, and even the admiration of Lord Strange who, being seldom in his small kingdom, was obviously intending to keep him in office permanently. This suited Edward, since he had trustworthy stewards both at Lough Mollo and Poyll Dhouie. Life was running smoothly, with regular visits to Chester relieving the dull routine of home life and the frigidity of his wife. Eleanor was his angel and her home the heaven to which he would fly whenever the opportunity arose, which was not as often as he would have liked, owing to his duties as substitute for the Lord of Mann in his absence.

And now this. It could disrupt his life, could even mean that Strange would relieve him of his office.

Leaving the house, he rode to Milntowne and was glad to find the Deemster in.

"Read that," he said without preamble handing him the missive.

"But…" Frowning darkly Ewan read it again. "You answered the charge made by Captain James."

"Of course. The man who they say is a pirate showed me a Commission that appeared to be all in order – it *was* all in order – so I had no reason to detain him or impound his cargo."

"Thomas Wentworth," mused Ewan, tapping the paper. "He says your explanation does not satisfy him and he has informed Lord Strange that the matter is not ended." He looked up. "This Wentworth is one of King Charles' favourites entrusted to bring the north of England, and Ireland, to subjection. He is a meddler who will do anything, go to any lengths to curry more and more favour. He is after a title, and he will get one, mark my words!"

"I see..." Edward picked up the letter from the table on to which his cousin had dropped it. "Yes, it is all in here, is all explained. When I first read this I could not understand Wentworth's motive but it is clear now." He read again, this time with more perception. "Wentworth says in his letter to the Admiralty, 'Surely so long as these pirates make their return to Mann as to a market for the vending of their stolen goods they will hardly be beaten from their harassing and infecting channel and therefore I beseech your lordships that there be a severe hand held on him, and heavily feel his transgression both towards his Majesty's Government and...' This is the key! *His Majesty's Government*, meaning that Wentworth has been most alert in the interests of His Majesty who is being robbed by these pirates—"

"Who escape Customs duties with the help of Captain Edward Christian." Ewan's mouth was tight. "He intends making you the scapegoat. It could have been anyone but this false charge made by—" Stopping abruptly the Deemster slapped his hand on the table. "The whole thing from beginning to end is a setting up affair. If my guess is right this Captain James is in on it."

"What are we to do? As you see, Coke in his reply says he will instruct Wentworth as to what action shall be taken. He seems to have the impression that I invite rather than apprehend these pirates, and ends by saying it will not be endured."

"Yes, I read all that." The Deemster became thoughtful. At last he looked up. "Wentworth means trouble – in fact, everything he does creates trouble and although he will get his title, I would not give much for his chances of holding it for long. He is another who flaunts the power of the Commons and if he is not careful he could lose his head."

"You believe so?" Edward sent him a puzzled glance. "You mean, there is a possibility of his being impeached?"

"It is said the Commons like not the ruthless manner he adopts to subdue the people. And if he is impeached the King will find himself being forced to sign the death warrant. However, what eventually might happen to Wentworth is of no matter in this present situation. But as I said, he means trouble. If he can have you convicted it is another step to that title he is after. So we have to be one stride ahead."

"I fail to see what I can do other than wait to see when I have to appear before the Commissioners." Edward gritted his teeth. "To think, I finished with all that was illegal when I took office, and now I am wrongly accused."

"You could call it poetic justice," commented the Deemster in some amusement. But this mood was gone instantly as his brow puckered in concentration. "The only thing is to wait at present, but meanwhile I shall think of something to thwart these rogues."

It was a month later that a messenger from Lord Strange brought the news that 'Captain Christian fail not personally to attend us at the Council Chamber in Whitehall on Friday the fourteenth of February next.' The copy had been written out by Lord Strange himself and was from the Commissioners for the Admiralty.

"So have you thought of anything?" Edward was asking within a few hours of receiving the missive. Ewan nodded and said yes, he had thought of something.

"You must say you are too ill to attend."

Edward frowned.

"I should think we will need to give some better excuse than that."

"What could be better? If you are ill you are unable to travel."

A long silence ensued while his cousin pondered on this. "It would only be a temporary measure. They would send another summons later."

"Surely," agreed the Deemster, then added coolly, "And you are still unfit to travel – in fact, to travel any distance at all would cause imminent danger to your life."

"Can it possibly work?" frowned Edward. "They will send yet another summons."

"And who will tire first?" Ewan was smiling one of his cool sardonic smiles. So sure of himself, thought Edward. Nothing ruffled him for long simply because he believed he was a match for any man.

The message was duly delivered to Lord Strange at his residence, Lathom House. He scanned the brief note through sceptical eyes and asked the messenger if he had actually seen the Captain.

"Yes, my lord."

"In his bed?" Lord Strange, himself an expert at deceit, did not believe that the robust Captain Christian was so suddenly – and conveniently – ill.

"Yes, in bed, sir."

"He seemed unwell?"

"He was extremely ill, my lord. He looked to me as if he was nearing death."

Lord Strange smiled, much to the disgust of the messenger who told his wife later that he had always known the Stanley cub had no heart.

The report was duly dispatched to the Admiralty and it was another two months before the second summons arrived, again by messenger sent from Lord Strange who had been ordered by the Commissioners to see that his Captain obeyed the summons. But again the messenger saw Edward abed and the same report as before was sent to the Admiralty.

With the passing of a further three months it seemed that the matter had been dropped, and it was to transpire that it had. But Lord Strange decided to substitute the Deemster as governor and so Edward lost his position and for a time it rankled because of his innocence. The document in question was definitely genuine. However, it afforded him more time to himself and he went over on one of Ewan's boats and stayed for six weeks with Eleanor. Susanna, now thirteen years of age, had become a dainty golden-haired beauty who attracted admiring glances whenever she went out. Edward, her brother, was eighteen and at Dublin University and was reading law.

"You are happy that our children are all that you desired?"

Edward had told Eleanor of his dismissal, and the reason for it. She was saddened while at the same time glad to have him over for a full six weeks.

"Yes, I am very happy. But how is Susanna to meet the kind of gentleman I want for her? He must be wealthy and titled and good-living. He has to be kind and gentle and trustworthy. Faithful too. I do not want my darling with a husband who will even look at other women – Edward, what are you laughing at?"

"God's glory, lass, there is not such a paragon in the whole world!"

"Oh, yes, there is, but he is too old for her."

"Kingsley? Ah, yes, the perfect man."

"There is no need for sarcasm. As a matter of fact, he is the perfect man."

"Then he must be a bore!"

"Not so! You forget, Edward, that you are talking about a very dear friend of mine, and one of long standing."

He sighed but yet there was no fear within him these days. Eleanor's enduring love was all his until the end. He knew now that he had never deserved such devotion, that his initial treatment of her was something he fervently wished he could erase from his mind. He had tried to make it up to her in many ways even while knowing that expensive gifts were never of much importance to her. And now... he knew he loved her and he had told her so, had spoken the words which he had always known she wanted to hear.

"John Kingsley is a fool," he stated at last. "He knows he can never have you."

"I wish he would listen... well, he does listen but my advice never registers. He is determined to remain a bachelor."

Edward shook his head. She noticed the increase in the number of grey hairs, the added lines fanning out from his eyes, eyes that were once so bright and challenging, in those days of freebooting and plunder. Now they had a dullness about them, a tiredness which she did not like at all. But his health was excellent; he could take long walks with her, play tennis and ride long distances.

"The man is besotted, and I pity him." Edward looked at her, at the golden glory of her hair in which he saw no grey, although she declared she had some. "How old is he now?"

"Not quite thirty, so he still has time to meet a charming girl and marry. It is so much what I wish for him, to be as happy as I, and with children to love, to nurture and watch grow into the kind of people you want them to be."

Her eyes had become dreamy and Edward drew a deep breath, sadly aware of what he had missed in life by considering, in the beginning, that she was not good enough to marry a Christian. And yet Eleanor had told him, on the night, not so long ago, when he had held her in his arms and said he loved her, that she was happy not to be married to him because, she maintained, most of the married people she knew were at times quarrelsome with one another.

"It does seem that if you see too much of each other you become tired of your spouse, irritated by things they do, whereas, in the beginning when you are in love these things do not matter."

"You are saying that married people fall out of love?"

"Sadly it appears so."

"You are thinking of me – and Elizabeth, of course."

"You have not said anything much about your marriage, but if it was successful and you were perfectly happy with your wife, you would be with her, not me."

True, he mused. But he was not unhappy with Elizabeth. He had grown into the habit of living with her, and up till a short while ago his official duties had absorbed much of his time; it had also entailed a social life in which his wife could not participate. Nevertheless, there was no doubt in his mind as to where he would rather be. His gaze was tender as he said,

"Let us talk only about ourselves, sweeting. And as the sun is shining how about a long walk along the river?"

"Nothing will suit me better!" Rising from her chair she kissed him full on the lips. "Dearest Edward, I love you so much!"

"In spite of everything?" He grasped her hand as he rose to stand beside her. "I have not lived an exemplary life up till now, have I?"

"You are what you are," she returned seriously. "But although you have done many wicked things, I have always loved you... and I always will love you."

"You will see changes in me from now on."

The promise was spoken with his thoughts elsewhere. He was recollecting some of the "wicked things" Eleanor had mentioned but there were many others of which she was in ignorance – and of which he was now ashamed. His only excuse was that he had been younger then, and missing the buccaneering life at sea where morals and manners had no place. There had been the time when, lusting for the wife of one of his labourers, he had sent the man to prison in Castle Rushen on a minor charge just to get him out of the way. Then there was the illegal buying of cattle to sell again at a profit. The charge against him could never have succeeded as Ewan the Deemster presided over the Court, and Ewan was as involved in cattle dealing as was his cousin. What the accused had done, stated the Deemster, was to buy cattle for his own use, and no one could say this was contrary to the laws and customs of the Isle. Another charge, that of forestalling the market by engrossing corn with the intention of selling it again at "extensive rates to a foreign captain" was quashed within minutes, the Deemster himself having been engaged in this activity also. And as the Deemster had also received wines from "one

Cornelius, a pirate" that charge brought against Edward Christian came to nothing.

It had not been entirely for profit, mused Edward in fairness to himself. It was more for the excitement, the satisfaction he gained by the knowledge that he was doing something illegal, just as he had done so many times at sea.

"We shall now have to take more care, though," Ewan had warned his cousin with a wry grimace. "Let us cease these activities for a while."

"You," Edward said angrily, yet not without some degree of admiration, "manage so cleverly to escape detection. When shall we see *you* charged?"

The Deemster had laughed at the very idea. He was so cold and calculating, so astute, so prepared for any contingency. No one would ever catch him unawares; he left no loopholes by which he could be incriminated in anything unlawful. The only real danger he had been in, mused Edward as he walked beside Eleanor along the sunlit banks of the River Dee, was when Sam Garrett possessed too much knowledge of their smuggling activities. Ewan had dealt successfully with that problem, just as he would deal with any others that might occur.

The six weeks seemed to fly by for Eleanor but, strangely, there was no yearning for him to stay longer. She had of necessity seen very little of John for although she had insisted he sup with her and Edward on occasions, he always appeared uncomfortable and eager to be away to his own home. His loneliness troubled her and immediately she said goodbye to Edward she sent Will over to Kingsley Hall with a message. John came eagerly and they spent the rest of the day together. It was late summer and the flower borders had lost much of the colour that had been so much in evidence when Edward first arrived. But the sun was still warm, the swallows were still around and the swans on the river had not yet sent their cygnets away to fend for themselves, although they were now almost as large as their parents.

"I have missed you..." John's voice dropped to a whisper. "Say we shall have many days like this, my dear?" He had taken her hand in his and he gave it an affectionate little squeeze. "The crumbs have been few these last six weeks."

Crumbs... She flinched at the word and her compassionate heart went out to him, the friend who had become so dear to her, a faithful friend who still insisted he would have her in the end. No use telling him she would love Edward Christian till she died; nothing to be gained by pleading with him to look around for some suitable girl and marry her. At first Eleanor had been confident that his love for her would fade and that he would marry and have a family. She had even envisaged her making a friend of his wife and thought it would be nice for everyone concerned. She had pictured children playing on the lawns of the Hall and she could sit in her own garden and watch them. Her hopes proved only to be dreams, John was still young, though, she would tell herself, and one never could tell what might happen.

The following day they rode into Chester and Susanna came with them. She had her own ideas of what she would wear and as her father had given her a substantial sum of money she suggested she do her shopping alone.

"I take such a long time choosing," she laughed, "that you would both be bored."

"Very well," from Eleanor, thinking how pretty she looked in her riding clothes, and with her golden curls gleaming in the sun. "Where shall we meet, and at what time?"

"Oh, I will ride home on my own."

"Are you sure?" John looked anxiously at her. "We can wait, Susanna."

The girl shook her head.

"I should feel obliged to hurry. No, please let me come home in my own time, mama?"

"Of course, dearest, if that is really what you want."

"Then do not let it be dark." John spoke rather sternly without realising it. "We shall worry if you are alone in the dark with beggars and felons walking about looking for someone to rob."

"Yes, sir," returned Susanna pretending meekness. "I shall heed your warning and be home before dark."

Left alone, Eleanor and John soon found an urchin ready to hold their horses and they decided to walk along the walls above the city. John took her hand and a sigh of contentment issued from his lips. How long before he could woo her in earnest? he wondered. Edward Christian was nine years older than she... A heavy frown crossed his brow momentarily. It was wrong to wish a man dead. And how his beloved Eleanor would suffer if her lover did die before her.

"I must live every moment without thinking of the future," he said to himself. "This is my day, with another tomorrow if she is not busy – and I am sure she will not be."

They walked for over an hour then went into the park. Then they went to an inn for refreshments, walking again afterwards, this time on the river bank but an altogether different length from that which was close to their homes. Here the city was close, and the church with its Norman arches and its ancient history. Here one could board a pleasure boat and take a sail, or take tea at one of the little tearooms which were springing up along its banks.

"Oh, but it was a lovely day!" Tired but happy, Eleanor sank down into a cushioned chair immediately they reached home and looked up at John. "You will stay to supper of course?"

"I must go and change – but, yes, of course," he smiled. "I shall sup with you and Susanna."

"I forgot to tell you, she is to stay with Alicia for a while. Susanna and she have always agreed well together and Susanna is entranced with the twins. As you know, I allow her to ride that distance only with Rob as an escort."

"A good, trustworthy man. I can not say I fully approved at the time you befriended him, my father having been a friend of the Derbys, but your instinct proved correct, as it always does," he ended with a deepening of his smile.

"You see, John, I myself was befriended, by Susanna, as I have told you. I know what it feels like to find someone who cares how you fare, what becomes of you. I saw at once that Rob was genuinely ready to work, but with the Derbys' influence being so strong no one anywhere near to their estate would have dared to employ a man he had accused of stealing."

"Well, Rob has never disappointed either of us – in fact, he is the best man I have ever had."

"And he keeps his little cottage so charmingly neat. I noticed the garden; it is lovely, with the flowers and the briar hedges he has grown all around it. I noticed he keeps a few hens in a plot at the back."

John nodded his head.

"I let him have that bit of extra land because he seems so eager to supply himself with as much food as possible." Eleanor had noticed that Rob had one large plot at the back of his cottage put down to vegetables and, at one end, he had put in some fruit trees and bushes. "I wonder if he will ever find a nice, homely woman and get married."

John laughed.

"You are always wanting someone to marry."

"Not always. You and Rob ought to have children."

"Shall we change the subject? How long is Susanna to be with Alicia?"

"Oh, a few weeks. Susanna is always so eager to be with the twins." She paused but John remained silent and she added after a while, "I am most anxious for my daughter to make an important marriage, but how is she to meet a rich and titled gentleman?"

He thought: Susanna's name is Christian and she comes from a noble Manx line, but she is a bastard. And yet, he was soon thinking, I would marry her mother tomorrow if she would have me.

"It is difficult," he mused. "If you knew anyone in London to whom you could send her for a while, then she would have the opportunity of meeting noblemen."

"Yes," eagerly from Eleanor. "I know of no one, but Edward certainly does. I must talk about it with him the next time he is over. Susanna is young yet, of course, but I do want her to marry well."

John looked at her animated face and knew a little access of apprehension. Supposing Susanna, who had a rather strong personality, inherited from her father, no doubt, should meet and fall in love with a man totally different from what her mother desired for her? Eleanor would be devastated and he thought it a pity that she had set her heart on a splendid marriage for her daughter.

"She would have to go to someone who could make sure she entered the kind of society which produces the kind of man you want for her."

"Edward was at Court; he knows many people who would be willing to see that my daughter meets the right kind of gentlemen."

He rose to go. He was troubled still, because he believed Eleanor was aiming rather high for her daughter.

"I shall be back within the hour," he promised. "It does not take me long to change."

Chapter Ten

Sir John Kingsley stood with Rob and looked around him at the newly ploughed fields which lay ready for the spring sowing. The granary was still well-stocked as were his cellars. Meat that had been salted was plentiful and the ewes in the far pastures were showing swollen bellies – a healthy sign.

"It is a good feeling, sir, to see all this." Rob, tall and straight and clean-shaven with an Arab brown skin and deep-set eyes, spoke with pride which brought a smile to his master's face.

"So right you are, Rob. And now I feel it is time for me to say how glad I am that the lady across there decided to give you the benefit of the doubt – I am of course speaking about the accusation made against you by my Lord Derby."

"It is a long while past, sir, and time heals hearts as well as hurts. I believe I have forgiven the Earl."

"Mistress Eleanor has been teaching you charity and forgiveness. You do well to heed her, Rob, just as I often do."

But not always, mused his labourer, well aware of the fact that Mistress Eleanor would like her friend to marry and raise some sturdy children.

"She is the most gracious lady I have ever met." Rob's voice had an access of reverence about it as he added, "Her kindness, her understanding of people's problems – it is quite remarkable."

And quite remarkable, thought Sir John, how I can converse like this with an underling. Yes, Eleanor has taught us both much.

"Tell me, Rob, how is the learning coming along?"

"I can read any book you care to give me," was Rob's ready answer and his eyes had taken on a brighter look. "I write too, very well, or so my mistress assures me. It has opened so much for me, this learning. I am taking an interest in so many things now that I was ignorant of before."

"I saw you in the city the other day. Mistress Eleanor had given you leave apparently."

"I asked if I could change my day off from Saturday to Tuesday as there was a man coming to the church to talk about the architecture and I was interested to listen as I have been reading about buildings – the castles of the Normans, for instance, and our church in Chester is of that period."

"It is good to hear of this interest, Rob. Any other interests?"

"Well, I go into a tavern sometimes for a pint of ale and hear talk. The King seems to be acting most foolishly?"

It was a question which John felt it incumbent on him to answer.

"He is ruling without Parliament, which is a great mistake. You see, Rob, the Commons has been gaining in strength for some years. King James saw it and it is said he warned his son to take care."

"But I hear the King does not take care. There are some very well educated gentlemen who go into my tavern, who have been to London many times and they know all that is going on there."

"You sound so serious, Rob." John sent him a searching glance. "What else do these gentlemen talk about?"

"It is said, sir, that the quarrel is becoming so serious that there could be a war."

John began to shake his head, but stopped and frowned. Rob had heard only what was true. The situation between King and Commons was just about as serious as it could be, and it seemed hard to believe that the King in his blind folly could not see even a glimmer of the danger ahead if he did not heed the warning his father had given him.

"Did these gentlemen mention John Hampden?"

"Yes. He has been imprisoned for refusing to pay taxes which he considered unfair. He is a brave man, sir, to defy the King."

"Tell me, Rob, would you defy the King?"

"I would fight for what I believed was right," came the unhesitating reply and his master nodded his approval.

"We have to remember that this crisis concerns religious as well as political issues. The King is pro-Papist, but the Puritan power grows and he should practise tolerance."

"Perhaps he will," said Rob hopefully. "We do not want a civil war to happen with families divided and friends fighting against friends. I pray, each Sunday in church, that God will spare our fair country a war."

"You are a good man, Rob."

For the first time John would have liked to know more about the accusation which had resulted in the barbaric mutilation which would necessitate Rob wearing his hair long for the rest of his life. Was it Lord Derby, as Rob had said, or could it have been the son, Lord Strange who had issued the order? Strange seemed to have inherited his mother's ruthless disposition, judging by what was going on in the Isle of Mann, so it could have been he who was responsible for the order, even if he left it to his father actually to give it.

"Thank you, sir. I have always tried to do what is right. My parents were deeply religious and as a child I had to attend church. I like going to church; it makes me feel at peace, envying no man."

John glanced at the long hair, and suddenly felt humble. Perhaps he should have done more for Rob, who had been with him and Eleanor for almost five years now. The labourer excused himself and John's gaze thoughtfully followed the tall straight figure till it was lost to view in the little copse in which his cottage stood.

*

The frost was like a sea of diamonds glistening in the pale sunlight but there was a warmth within him as Sir John Kingsley walked briskly across the fields on his way to Deva Place. This glow was always with him, and this spring in his step, whenever he was on his way to the home of the woman he loved.

She greeted him with that familiar smile of welcome and her hands reached out for him to take. That there was a bond between them she had not denied and there were times when, watching her expression, his mind would tell him that she cared – Not with the depth of passion which characterised her feelings for Edward Christian, but with a gentler, more spiritual attachment which, he knew without any doubt at all, would, if broken, be as crucifying to her as it would be to him. Yes, there certainly was a bond, a bond so strong that it could only be broken by death.

"It is so cold," she was saying as she preceded him into the elegant yet cosy drawing room through whose window could be seen the river, the stone bridge and the lovely Tudor mansion that was Kingsley Hall. "Come and sit by the fire."

The flames gave off the only illumination for as yet there was no need to light the candles, but they were in their sconces, ready when required.

"May I say you look beautiful, as always?" The half-smile was reflected in his eyes as they wandered over her figure, still slender, still delectable to him as when, seventeen years ago, he had first met her, on the little stone bridge... and fallen in love with her on sight. "I have not seen this dress before?"

"I bought it in Chester only yesterday, and today I wear it in your honour." She pirouetted around for him, laughter in her eyes. "It comes from a shop newly opened and which sells the latest London fashions. You will note how low it is cut across my – here." She made a gesture indicating her bosom. "The elderly woman who owns the shop seems to know everything about materials, and she told me that the lavish use of this silk is meant to create a classical look, as also is the drapery of the sleeves. I am wearing it because it is your birthday, dearest John – and also Bessie has made a very delicious-looking cake, and of course some of your favourite biscuits."

"You spoil me, Eleanor, but I thank you for all the trouble—"

"Trouble? It is no trouble to dress myself up in this finery." She patted her hair. "Did you note the flowers? They have to be worn in order to enhance the dress."

"I shall begin to think you vain," he teased and before she knew it he had taken her gently in his arms and kissed her on the lips. "I did note the flowers and they do enhance the dress... and the charming wearer."

"Tell me what you have been doing," she urged, taking a seat on one side of the hearth while he sat down opposite to her. "How does it feel to be all of thirty-four years old?"

"The same as when I was thirty-three," he laughed, stretching his long legs out towards the fire. "Why should I feel any older?"

"No reason." She paused and then with a tiny sigh, "My next birthday will certainly make me feel older."

Another pause; she glanced across at him, taking in the youthful look brought about by a shorter, less full hairstyle that was now the fashion. The wide lace collar, too, seemed to make him look younger than when he wore the narrower ones which were going out of fashion. "I am forty next birthday."

"Which is almost a year away," he reminded her and then added quickly, "You do not look even thirty – and you are well aware of it."

"My son is twenty-three quite soon."

Only eleven years younger than John, she mused, her thoughts diverted for a moment. Edward was a real joy to her, having never given her a moment's anxiety. He was good-living without being a prude, ambitious without being greedy... in fact, he was all she wanted him to be – Her thoughts cut and a smile hovered on her lips. A great man, she had declared he would be, but there had come the time when she was asking herself what she had meant by 'great'? Edward was a *good* man and she was satisfied.

"How is he?" John was asking. "Has he written lately?"

"No, I would have mentioned it if he had, but he will write soon. He had at first wanted to work in London – and he did go with his father for an interview, but when he came back he said he preferred to be in Dublin."

"I recall that Edward took him to London." He looked at her and added, curiously, "Does Edward never hanker after having a sojourn in London? He was once a favourite at Court, you said."

"It was a long time ago when things were different. Both King James and the Duke of Buckingham were living then. And although there were disagreements between King and Commons they were not nearly so serious as they are now." She shook her head vigorously. "I would hate it if Edward desired to go to London for he would be sure to become involved in this quarrel."

"It is to be hoped his duties on the island will keep him there." He said this to reassure her, as he had no wish for her to begin fretting over the possibility of Edward's going off to London and, in all probability, running himself into danger. "You were saying that he has been reinstated?"

"Yes. Lord Strange appointed him Captain-General of the island."

"Then I can see he will have no inclination to leave and go to London."

"You are right, John," she returned with a sudden smile which took the rather troubled frown from her forehead. "Edward can never offer his services to the King's cause, not while he has all these obligations on the island."

"The King's cause?" repeated John with a curious inflection. "Is it the King he would be supporting – if he ever did decide to join in the fight, that is?"

"I have wondered which side he favours," admitted Eleanor, spreading her skirt to avoid its creasing. "Obviously it is the King who is in the wrong." She stopped rather abruptly, her eyes widening. "You mentioned 'fight'. It sounded so ominous. A – a war will not become inevitable, will it?"

His face was suddenly very grave.

"No one can foresee the future, Eleanor, but the news is that Charles commits one folly after another. He has now antagonised the Scots by encouraging Archbishop Laud in his attempts to impose his policy and the Covenanters are fiercely resisting it. Laud is persecuting the Puritans – he is as great a fool as his sovereign, and there are many who predict disaster."

"This sounds very serious." She looked at him. "How do you come by all this news, John?"

"Strangely, from Rob."

"Rob? But how could he receive news from London?"

John explained, adding that Rob was even more highly educated than he had at first thought possible.

"He has you to thank," he ended with a tender smile.

"I have always said that the poor should be educated, that they are only where they are because of a lack of education. I told you how it was with me, having the good fortune to find such a caring friend as Susanna Christian. And so I encouraged Rob to learn and you can see how improved he is."

"Yes, indeed." He stared for a moment into the leaping flames sent up when a pine log slipped in the grate. "Did I mention that Saunders is leaving me?"

"Your steward? No. What is the reason?"

John smiled faintly and said,

"He is getting old, my dear. I seem to remember your saying so yourself."

"I did, but where will he go – I mean, he has no home but the cottage you give him."

"He shall stay there, and I am giving him a pension so he and his wife will have no worries. Rob will take his place."

"Rob! As your steward? Oh, dear John, you are wonderful! This is such welcome news. Have you told Rob yet?"

"Not yet." He was smiling in some amusement. "You look so happy," he told her and went on to say that the troublous times about which they had just been talking appeared to have small significance beside this piece of local news. She laughed but was soon serious again, desirous of learning just what this persecution by the Archbishop could eventually mean.

"Well, the Scots certainly are not going to submit. They are prepared to go to war in order to retain their freedom of worship."

"War... But that would not be civil war," she pointed out almost with relief. "Charles fighting the Scots will not affect the whole of our country."

"You think not? We shall see."

And with that John was not intending to go further. He wanted to know how long he was to be kept waiting for Bessie's delicious biscuits, the cake, and the tea, a commodity so expensive that only the rich could afford it.

The meal was an intimate occasion, the table being laid close to the fire and on it warm bread straight from the oven, butter, fruit and the biscuits and a cake which was prettily decorated and which John had to cut. Candles had been lighted in the sconces and, added to the fireglow, gave the room a special cosiness and warmth in which its two occupants basked, happy in each other's company, and for this present time oblivious of the world outside and all the problems with which it might soon be faced.

*

In the year 1639 violent storms swept across the island and a vast amount of damage was done. Ewan lost two ships and Edward one. Several seamen lost their lives, a circumstance which greatly upset the Captain because two of them had sailed with him when he was Captain of the *Bonaventure* frigate, a command he had attained through the influence of his friend, the Duke of Buckingham.

Ewan, noticing uncharacteristic dejection, told him philosophically that no amount of regret could bring the men back and the sooner he accepted this the better.

"It is not that alone," he confessed. "This outbreak of war with the Scots – it could be the spark that ignites something that affects us all."

"I know," thoughtfully from his cousin. The Bishops' War, caused by Charles' support of Archbishop Laud's determination to enforce his High Church ritual throughout the whole of England and Scotland. "This war is going to be costly for Charles, and where is he to get the money to pay for it? I have it on good authority that Lord Strange has made loans to him and of course there are the enforced loans, but all is thrown into a seething pot of discontent."

"You must have noticed the growing unrest here." Edward, now devoted to his little country as he had never been before, could see grave trouble if the powers across the water continued to ignore the danger waiting at the end of the road they were following. "What happens over there must have repercussions here."

"Hmm..." The Deemster became lost in thought for a space, and then, "After all the early strife in its history, this island of ours has more recently remained untouched by the conflicts and altercations of the rest of the world. We have lived in our own little private sanctuary with nothing to worry us except the greed of the Derbys, but now..." Again he was lost in thought for a long moment, before saying, "If Strange has to raise an army in support of the King then he is going to pay for his soldiery by inflicting even higher taxes on this island."

The Captain nodded in agreement. He was thinking of the already deteriorating relationship between the Lord of Mann and himself. It was of course, mainly the matter of the land tenures but Edward had also expressed his objection to the continued power of the Church and the effect of that power on the poor of the island. The Church still maintained its absolute authority in several vital issues, all of which were calculated to increase its own wealth to the detriment of the common people. He had told Lord Strange in no uncertain terms that he would not cease to work for the attainment of democratic conditions for the Manx people, even though it meant resisting the will of his lordship. This had infuriated Strange and caused a rift which Edward knew would not easily heal, although he was not entirely without hope. If Strange would only cease to emulate his King in the manner of dealing with his subjects, then contentment for all concerned might be achieved.

But unfortunately neither the King nor Lord Strange seemed to have learned the meaning of the two words: tolerance and moderation.

The Manx people were not basically aggressive; they were always ready to acknowledge Lord Strange as their rightful king and the fact that he was uncrowned made no difference to the respect in which he was held. But for some considerable time they had been burdened beyond endurance and now there was often open defiance where the paying of taxes was concerned, and if pushed much further they would fight. But this kind of a situation was not what the Christians wanted to see. Ewan the Deemster and his sons and many others of high standing on the island desired only to bring about an improvement in conditions, and that it be an achievement effected by peaceful negotiations. But the proud Stanleys had always flaunted their superiority before the inhabitants of their little kingdom and the present Lord of Mann was certainly no exception. Unrest was simmering all the time and in view of events over the water Ewan, actually fearing a Manx uprising, suggested his cousin go across to talk with Lord Strange at Lathom House.

But instead of the visit having the desired result of persuading Strange to come over and attempt to right some of the wrongs, it brought to an end Edward's career as Captain-General of the island.

Strange received his lieutenant into the massive, fortified mansion of Lathom House cordially enough, offering him wine and other refreshment after having him shown into the luxurious withdrawing room overlooking magnificent water gardens and colourful borders and parterres.

"It is impossible for me to come over to the Isle of Mann," he began after hearing what the Captain had to say. "King Charles has summoned me to York, owing to this outbreak of the Scots rebellion. He needs much help. Another thing is that if, as you fear, an uprising could occur on the island, I am of the firm opinion, Edward, that you would be one of the ringleaders."

So quiet the tone, and so direct the look he sent the Captain. Edward's eyes never wavered. He said, in an equally quiet voice,

"From the day you appointed me to my present position I have worked in your interests, and shall continue to do so—"

"But with conditions," his lordship broke in rudely. "You make too many demands of me which I am not able to confer..." His voice trailed to silence and Edward noticed the sudden compression of his lips. "You look around you in disapproval," observed Lord Strange coldly at last.

"I see that you have a luxurious abode here. It seems to me that you could very well reduce the island's crippling taxes. Also," Edward continued without giving his lordship time to speak, "these impositions of the clergy, the subtle artifices by which they deceive the poor, their arrogations which delude – and prey on – superstitious minds, always to the detriment of these people and the result is that power and riches continue, in my opinion illegally, to fill the Church's coffers. I am speaking of the way the priesthood convince a superstitious people that to save their souls they must, when making a Will, leave much of their property to the church. It is time this encroachment by the specious faction of our society be brought to an end, and this you can do, James, by an act of Tynwald restraining the clergy from interference in temporal affairs." His voice retained its soft inflection but it was firm and to the point nevertheless, and a glint came into Lord Strange's dark eyes. "Some people are easily made to believe that the impositions are approved by Rome."

Lord Strange rose from his chair and, taking his glass of wine with him, strode over to the window and stood with his back to it. Edward noted the arrogant lift of the head, the narrowed eyes and wondered if the day would ever come when this arrogance would be subdued.

"So many complaints," snapped his lordship after sipping his wine in silence for a time. "If the Manx people are so gullible as to give away their possessions in order to ensure a passage to heaven then let them. I have no intention of interfering, especially now, when I am called to assist the King put down this rebellion."

"James, I do wish you would not treat your subjects as if they were about to be inmates of a house for the mentally deranged! Yes, they are gullible but the Church puts fear into them! Are you so lacking in interest in your possession that you have no care at all for what goes on?" Edward was furious with the man, who was as stubborn and short-sighted as his King. "So you are not doing anything?" he asked when his lordship did not speak.

"I have already said so," answered Strange curtly. "There are more important matters needing my attention."

He looked harassed, thought Edward, but there was no pity in his heart for him. "This rebellion must be put down before it gets out of hand and the war spreads."

"If the King would show a little common sense none of it would have happened."

"You would question the actions of His Majesty?"

"He is a fool! There seems to be no limit to the follies he commits. Not only does he presume to rule without Parliament but he is rash enough to raise an army for no other reason than to impose Laud's wishes on the Scottish kirk. Would any man with any sense at all bring about a war for such a flimsy reason? He knew that the lowlanders would uphold the National Covenant, and would fight for the right to worship as they chose. Where is he to find the money for this war?"

"I expect he will summon a new Parliament." Lord Strange was most unhappy at the turn of events and was much in agreement with his lieutenant, but he would never have told him so. And if he was to be away at the war, what could this Captain Christian get up to? He said slowly and deliberately, "These complaints you regularly present to me – they are concerning the common people, but the real issue is the land tenures, is it not?"

"It is there," assented the captain, "and always will be until an agreement is reached which is acceptable to all."

"No such agreement is possible. The Tenure of the Straw must be replaced by a lease for three lives. Some have already accepted – and you all will in the end."

"I believe not! The lands have been in our possession for too many generations for us to let them go without a fight."

"A fight?" repeated Strange swiftly.

"I am not referring to an armed combat. But make no mistake, James, we shall no more relinquish our lands than you yours. Think on it and for the sake of us all stop following blindly the steps being taken by the King, who is his own worst enemy."

"My family have always supported their sovereign, and always will do so."

"The cost could be great this time, James. Do you want to die in battle?"

"An honourable death," he answered casually. "Others of my family have given their lives for their King."

"Ancestors? Perhaps they have, but life is precious, James, so should be valued."

"If it is my fate to die in battle I shall go happy, if it is in the service of my king."

Edward drew an exasperated breath. Why argue with such a man?

If he did die in battle it might be a good thing for the island since his son might possibly have more sensible ideas than his father.

"I had best leave," decided Edward rising from his chair. "If I ride hard I can catch the *Maid of Mann* which sails at midnight."

"No, do not go yet." His lordship gestured and Edward sat down again. "We have things to discuss. Stay overnight and catch the Deemster's boat tomorrow evening."

Although Edward frowned impatiently he had no alternative but to obey an order from his lord. What was to come next? he wondered, fully aware that the atmosphere between them had never been more unfriendly than at present.

"This growing unrest in my kingdom," began Lord Strange, "it should have been your first concern to crush it. But instead, you have encouraged my people to resist paying some tithes. This is not showing loyalty to your overlord, is it?"

Edward regarded him across the wide room. He seemed darker than usual with the light behind him and the black jerkin which he was wearing over the dark grey doublet giving his face a sallow look. Overlord... He had been a mere twenty when he first came to the island bent on changing the land tenures, seventeen years younger then the man he chose to be the Captain of the island. Now at thirty-two, he still appeared young, whereas Edward at almost fifty had aged and he knew he looked older than his years. He said in answer to James' question,

"It is my belief, as you very well know, that the Manx people are being treated unfairly."

Again he glanced around at the luxury, the ostentatious use that had been made of money. It was true that much of the vast original Stanley wealth had gone along another channel, making it impossible for James and his wife Charlotte de la Tremouille to enjoy the same standard of living as his grandfather who had employed two hundred and twenty servants in his household, but Lord Strange was scarcely suffering hardship, because his father was wealthy in his own right. And he had been given the Isle of Mann as a bonus. "I feel I have commitments to my fellow men on the island," he continued firmly. "I deny ever having been disloyal to you, James, and I hope it will never be necessary for me to go against your wishes—"

"You already have gone against my wishes, man!" interrupted Lord Strange with a growing hint of anger. "You and I seem to have reached a point when we are weary of each other. You will be replaced, for I have conferred favours upon you and because of it you have become unbearably covetous of more. I find your many demands intolerable and wish no longer to have such troubles on my mind."

Edward was not too surprised, nor was he too upset. He had been in office for near on ten years altogether and many were the times when it had irked that his duties kept him away from Chester for weeks and sometimes months. This freedom would be welcome, and now that he was dismissed from his office he could say,

"You seem to forget, when you mention favours, that I have never been paid for my duties as Captain-General of the isle."

A flush spread over his lordship's face and anger darkened his eyes.

"The honour of the position should have been sufficient reward."

"If you say so," smiled Edward leaning forward to pick up his glass which a lackey had refilled for him. "I believe that you put the Christians in all the high offices in the hope that we would all feel so honoured that we would employ our energies in furthering your desires. I am not a fool, James. I know exactly why you remove me from my post. It is solely because I and all the insular landowners of our isle, hold views in complete opposition to those held by the Lord of Mann." He rose again from his chair. "I believe there is naught more to say to one another, so if it pleases you, James, I shall endeavour to catch the *Maid of Mann*."

As he rode away Edward glanced around him, at the massive six feet thick surrounding walls, at the many towers – nine on the outside alone. The moat was a full thirty yards wide. The place was like a fortress, he thought, as he rode through the gatehouse where sentries on guard saluted him then returned to their statue-like rigidity. Would this house ever have to withstand a siege? he wondered. There was a possibility – should the King provoke any further, and stronger unrest among his people

*

It was not without some excitement that Lord Strange met the King at York. So small, this man whose belief in the divine right of kings had brought him to this. But Strange, loyal as all his illustrious forebears had been, was ready for battle and the idea never entered his head that this man on the black shining horse could do aught but conquer the rebellious Scots and thereafter force them to adopt the episcopal policy laid down by his archbishop.

"I am glad to see you, Strange. How is your father?"

"Not in good health, sir. He desires only to live quietly in a house he bought near Chester."

"He is fortunate to be able to rest," commented the King with a hint of wistfulness in his voice. "Why am I plagued with those who defy my supreme authority?"

"'Tis foolish of them, sire. But we shall soon have them on the run."

The King nodded. He was magnificently attired in blue and gold, with a long cape of crimson from beneath which a silver cuirass shone in the sunlight. His spurs gleamed, his sword too, matching the splendid harness of his horse. In his hat the white feathers moved gently in the zephyr of a breeze which also parted his hair to reveal pearl studs in his ears.

The following day they rode together, two men whose object was victory and the glory of achievement.

*

Lord Strange tossed sleeplessly in the massive curtained bed, his mind unable to accept that his King had been forced to make peace and that Charles was contemplating a second attack.

Lady Strange entered the bedchamber silently and, bending, gently caressed her husband's forehead.

"Dearest," she murmured, her lips close to his cheek, "it has come, the despatch you were expecting from His Majesty."

James sat up on the instant.

"What does it say?"

"Exactly what you knew it would say. James, I like it not that you go to war again. If you were killed..."

He took her hand.

"Pine not, my love. I am not ready for death yet!"

"But do you really want to go? Perhaps I ought not to say what is in my thoughts, James, but I shall."

"Of course," he smiled, "you always do."

"It is no jocular matter. I feel the King is leading us all into danger. Why does he not pause to consider what could be the consequences of this attitude? After all, it is so trivial. What does anyone care about how the barbaric Scots worship?"

"I believe it is pride that makes our King persist. He truly believes he is being guided by God."

"Absurd! God has nothing to do with it!"

"Do not let our king hear such words, my love." He stepped down from the bed and she handed him his breeches. "That lovely head was never created for the block."

She shuddered.

"What a terrible death! To walk along that platform, to meet the executioner holding his axe—"

"Dearest, stop! I pray you! Nothing like that is ever going to happen to any of our family so why should we tease ourselves with such matters?" He took the buff-coloured doublet from her hand and kissed her at the same time. "We shall soon finish off those Scots," he promised cheerfully. "I shall be back with you all in no time at all!"

But as he rode away to join the King again the anxiety he had hidden from his wife returned. Undoubtedly Charles was running blindly into danger. In order to obtain funds for this second campaign he had been compelled to summon a new Parliament at Westminster. But the members refused any grant of money until he had listened to their grievances, and this infuriated the king who seemed to assume that, after having ruled alone for eleven years, he could just summon Parliament and immediately be granted money for what might yet be another abortive confrontation with the Scots.

James shook his head as he rode along, a thousand soldiers closely following, and his bodyguard even closer. Charles in his anger and frustration had dissolved the Parliament he had called a mere few weeks ago and, with support from loyal subjects like Strange, was able to launch the campaign which he maintained would be blessed by the Almighty so could not fail. The Lord had instructed him and the Lord had to be obeyed.

But again defeat was to be his and in November 1640 he had to throw himself on to the mercy of the English Parliament in order to obtain money for the two costly and disastrous enterprises.

Lord Strange rode home to his house at Lathom and hoped all that had happened to the King would have a sobering effect that would prevent once and for all his acting so foolishly again.

Charlotte, his wife, had some good news: she was pregnant again and that seemed far more important than anything that might be going on outside those fortified walls.

*

It was some time later that Charlotte learned of the dismissal of Captain Christian and the knowledge distressed her since she had liked the Manxman although they had met only three times, on those occasions when he had come over to see her husband about some matter concerning the administration of the island. She was seven years older than James in years, but far older than that in maturity and she felt the Captain was an excellent choice and although she had known that James had originally intended the post to be only a temporary one, she had assured him that he would do well to hold on to a good and loyal servant for as long as he could.

"Why did you decide to dismiss him, James?" she asked with a frown that deepened when he shrugged his shoulders.

"There were serious differences," was his non-committal reply. "The matter need not trouble you."

"But it does trouble me, James. Captain Christian was a good man to have and I consider it a great folly on your part to have replaced him with this man, Greenhalshe."

"Greenhalshe is a good man, with large estates and much prestige on the island. I have made a sensible move."

His manner of delivery was intended to tell her the matter was ended but Charlotte was not at all satisfied. She felt the Captain to have been trustworthy in spite of his objections to tithes and other impositions which were the lot of the Manx nation.

"You have so often remarked that the Captain pleased you very well, that he readily obeyed your every bidding and I seem also to remember your saying that if anything went wrong with any order you gave he would blame himself, but if it went right he gave you all the credit."

"I agree he served me well in the beginning, but he asked favours of me and the more I granted them the more he asked."

James flung away impatiently, loath to be angry with her when she was so near her time. He wanted the subject dropped.

"What were these favours?" she persisted.

"Oh – er – I fail to remember!"

She fell silent then but her thoughts were not happy. Although she loved her husband she was not blind to his many failings and disliked the prejudices which often led him suddenly to dislike someone. Also, he would make use of people who were his inferiors and when they had served his purpose he would rid himself of them, usually by inventing some vague and unimportant charge as an excuse for his action. Charlotte was curious to know the real reason why her husband had dismissed what she considered to be a loyal servant.

"It is very strange," she murmured presently, "that you can so easily forget, when I know your memory is extraordinarily good."

James swung around, dark eyes blazing.

"What is this cross-examination! Captain Christian and I fell out – when a prince hath given all and the favourite can devise no more, both grow weary of one another."

Charlotte looked at him with a frown between her eyes.

"What a strange thing to say, James. Were you quoting something?"

"I could have been – look here, Charlotte, will you please let this matter drop!"

"I am sorry that my questions anger you," she said coldly, "but you yourself said it is not good to anger these Christians who are so strong."

His eyes widened arrogantly.

"You appear to forget, madam, that almost every post of authority on the Isle of Mann is occupied either by a Christian or one of his near kin."

She made no comment on that but she was not ignorant of the fact that James believed it was in his own interests to keep on the right side of the powerful clan Christian, if that was at all possible.

"This feud that has existed so long between the Stanleys and the Christians," she began, "it is understandable that they refuse to hand over to us lands that they have held for so long."

He hesitated a moment and then,

"I have not told you before, but I have had men on the island searching for ancient documents. Some have come to light which prove that when lands were parcelled out after the Viking invasion those given to the Christians – and others – were not given as outright gifts but the holders of the lands were tenants-at-will to the King."

She sent him a puzzled glance.

"What difference does that make to us?"

"Do you not see? The King owned all lands... and I am king of the island so all land belongs to me."

Charlotte pondered on this for a long moment before saying as the thought occurred to her,

"These documents – how can they have survived since the year 1077 when Godred Crovan conquered the isle?

"Why not? Documents have survived much longer than that."

"They are genuine?"

"You sound as if you believe I would forge them."

"I do not know."

"What!"

"I was going to say that it is a strange coincidence that it is only recently that these documents have come to light. I should very much like to converse with those who so conveniently discovered them for you."

He was furious and it showed. She was far too astute, this wife of his, and too ready to question his actions. He said wrathfully,

"We need money, desperately. If I can take those lands I will then offer them back for them to buy. I can gain a fortune—"

"Oh, no, James! That is dishonest."

"What is dishonest in claiming what rightly belongs to me?"

A sigh escaped her. She was so tired; this swollen belly was such a weight to carry. Nevertheless, she had no wish to go to her chamber and be alone. She and James had been enjoying a happy few months together but recently he had seemed depressed and restless.

"I am sure, James," she said on another deep sigh, "that the matter of the land tenures will be settled eventually. It is impossible for you to take these lands. Their holders would enlist the help of the King."

"The King, my dear, has too much on his mind to trouble himself about an island he scarcely knows exists. And as for my just taking the lands, well, I am offering the holders a lease for three lives and they refuse, so they shall have the lands taken from them and to get them back they must buy them from me."

He was all arrogance, she thought with a faint smile to herself. All arrogance and no confidence. He knew without any doubt at all that he would cause a revolution on the island if he were to make one move to grab lands that had been in the Christians' possession for several hundred years before the island was even given to Sir John Stanley in the year 1405. But it did strike her that James must be in dire straits if he needed money so urgently. She asked what he had meant just now when he said money was needed desperately.

"We are comfortable," she added endeavouring to soothe him with a smile. "I never complain."

He knew what she meant.

"You were used to so much more before you wed me, Charlotte. Through your parents you are related to every royal house in Europe and you were brought up in the most extravagant luxury and if only my father had been the elder son I could have given you a life that was comparable—"

"I have said, dear James, that we are comfortable – more than comfortable, in spite of the loss of all our English possessions. We can still afford some luxuries..." Her voice trailed as she noticed his expression. "What do you mean by saying we need money desperately? We can not be *that* desperate."

"I lent the King a large amount. And it was a very costly business, going to war, not once but twice."

"Ah, yes, I see. But you need not have made a loan, surely?"

"Yes, I did need to. Charles was desperate for money and the Commons refused to give him any."

"What about this Ship Money and Tonnage and Poundage, and what about all the money he must have made by fining the gentry who refused to accept knighthoods?"

"All that went even before the two Bishops' Wars."

He shook his head as if he would clear from it some pressing and troublesome problem. "It is being rumoured that the Commons are fearing another hostile move by Charles."

"But if he is impoverished how can he begin fighting again?"

"You forget the army in the north. There is also the garrison of Ireland. Charles could use both those if he so wished."

"Good God, would he be so foolish?"

"There is no knowing what he will do next," returned James impatiently. He had been trying to be no more than an uneasy onlooker regarding the quarrel between King and Commons... until the summons came, calling him to take his garrison, and himself, to fight for his King. "Personally I feel sure he has no intentions of using those armies but, unfortunately, Parliament's fears are growing. They are sure the King will employ those armies to force his absolute will on them."

"The garrison in Ireland..." Her brow puckered in concentration. "It is under the command of the Earl of Strafford, is it not?"

"Yes, that is right." He looked interrogatingly at her. "Why do you ask?"

"The Earl was Thomas Wentworth, the same who brought false charges against Captain Christian?"

"He did not bring the charges," corrected her husband, "but he refused to accept Christian's explanation."

"So Wentworth – or Strafford as he is now – would support the King by bringing the Irish garrison over here." She was murmuring to herself. "Do you know, James," she said at last, "I would not like to stand in that man's shoes today."

"Whatever do you mean?" The frown on his brow betrayed his puzzlement. "Sometimes, Charlotte, you talk in riddles. Is it to prove that you are cleverer than I?

She smiled affectionately at him and denied that she ever had considered herself cleverer than he.

"No, what I fear for Strafford is that if Parliament takes it into its head it could be that they would destroy him, just to feel safer, since if he is not in charge of the garrison he can not use it against them."

"Another would soon be found to replace him."

"But perhaps not as ruthless as Strafford. He is much disliked except by the King. And I do not like him, either. I believed, even at the time, that he was an evil man, trying as he did to ruin a gentleman's reputation."

James preferred not to continue any conversation that could include Captain Christian because he was beginning to doubt the wisdom of his action in dismissing him, and so this attitude of Charlotte's only made him feel worse.

*

Eleanor and John were strolling along the river bank and had been so deep in conversation that it rather startled them both suddenly to realise they were further from home than ever before.

"We shall be dropping by the time we arrive back!" Eleanor declared, staring disbelievingly at the house they had come upon – at least, they had come upon the grounds which sloped almost down to the river. "This is the home of Lord Strange's father."

John nodded his head.

"Yes; he came here to retire when he gave everything over to his son."

"I wonder why he never wanted to care for the island himself?" She and John had stopped but were not yet retracing their steps. "Earl William has never been interested in his little kingdom."

"And yet he spent a small fortune in his attempts to attain it."

"Lawsuits? Yes, indeed. Ferdinando's wife fought hard for the rights of her daughters – and she won in the end."

"A good thing, too," returned John, but added that it was a pity she had been persuaded to give up the Isle of Mann. "Its rule might have been so different had it not come into the hands of the Stanleys again."

"It is a shame for that little island," she said musingly. "It is so beautiful, with wonderful scenery – the glens and hills, the beaches and the moorland scenery – it has everything except tranquillity. There is growing unrest which must be a reflection of what is going on here. Do you suppose the King will continue in this foolhardy fashion?" They had begun to walk back and she had tucked her arm into his. "Rob should be going to the inn this evening so he will bring us all the news from London."

"I do think the King will continue to flaunt the power of the Commons," replied John. "He has a problem in that he has come so far there can be no turning back without humiliation and this would never be acceptable to a man who truly believes in his own divine rights."

*

Edward and Ewan had been in London attending the funeral of a kinsman and on their way back to the island they stayed overnight at Deva Place and naturally Eleanor was eager for the latest news. She was told that the situation between King and Parliament had further deteriorated by the impeachment of the Earl of Strafford.

"Strafford?" Eleanor, who was with the two men in the drawing room, glanced swiftly at the Deemster. "It was he who was responsible for Edward's falling out of favour—" She transferred her attention to her lover. "It was Strafford who caused you to lose your office of Governor of the island. He was Wentworth at that time?"

"The same, my dear." There was a glint in Edward's eyes as he added, "I hated him for what he did, but I never thought to see him punished for his sins."

"Who was responsible for his arrest?" She was avidly eager for all the latest news while at the same time filled with anxiety at the way events were moving as a result of the King's continued obstinacy.

"It was ordered by Parliament," answered Ewan. "And the King was helpless to protect his favourite. They have said that Strafford and the Archbishop were the chief of the King's evil counsellors and it was agreed that he should be impeached for treason before the House of Lords."

"We think the King was optimistic enough to expect Strafford to put up a successful defence but the trial faltered and Charles was told to sign a bill of attainder."

"What exactly would that mean?" Eleanor could not but notice the gravity on the faces of both men and, therefore, was not surprised when Edward explained that it meant the Earl could be put to death without any legal judgement.

"That seems most unfair," protested Eleanor and glances were exchanged between the cousins. It was plain that they were remembering Sam Garrett who, in her opinion, had not been given a fair trial. "I have no sympathy for Strafford," she continued thoughtfully, "as he was barbaric in his treatment of the Scots during their rebellion, but to execute him without a fair trial..."

She was frowning darkly and looked to the men to agree with her but Ewan merely shrugged while Edward picked up his tankard and quaffed some of the ale it contained. "The King has not signed the bill of attainder, has he?"

"Not yet, but he is under great pressure. He is in real trouble now, Eleanor, because mobs were forming in the city as we left. They were gathered before the House of Lords and rumours were circulating that the Queen could be in danger. She is a devout Roman Catholic as you know, and since the death of Charles' favourite, the Duke of Buckingham, he has fallen in love with her, so it seems he will have to sign and send Strafford to his death in order to protect her."

"The people want his death, then?"

"Yes, and Laud's also."

"Our country is in a sad way." She tried to push the idea of civil war out of her mind but found it impossible. "Oh, why will not the King come to his senses!" she cried on a rare spurt of anger. "He will throw the whole country into chaos!"

"Let us hope that he will learn a lesson from what is happening and realise that tyranny can not prevail, that his ways are not what his people want. If he can only bring himself to practise a little humility then all will be saved... but otherwise..." The Deemster's voice trailed significantly and he spread his hands. Eleanor resolved to pray harder than ever before, pray that the dear Lord would turn the King's footsteps in a direction that would save him and his country from disaster.

Chapter Eleven

The gathering of men in the drawing room at Milntowne was mainly surnamed Christian but also present at this important meeting were John Teare, Captain of the Parish of Jurby whose wife was Margaret, sister to Edward and William; Ewan Curphy, a Member of the House of Keys, and several other wealthy landowners from various parts of the island, all of whom were related to the Christian Clan.

Ewan the Deemster, now aged sixty-four, presided over the meeting which had been called to discuss the demands of the Governor, a Lancashire landowner, that martial law be proclaimed in order to stem the riots which were sweeping through the island.

"I know I did right in refusing to provide soldiery to turn on our own people." Edward Christian spoke with firm conviction and every one of the others present nodded in full agreement.

It was in January of this year, 1643, that the Lord of Mann – who had now become Lord Derby – had reinstated the ex-Governor into favour by giving him military command of all the Manx forces with orders to see they were well-trained and that every able man on the island be called to service. This move was the result of the threat of an invasion of the island by the Scots who were supporting the Parliamentarians in their war against the King and which had begun in August of the previous year when King Charles, unable even in a most dire situation to listen to wise advice, left the capital and set up his standard in Nottingham.

"Governor Greenhalshe, coming over as he did from England, has scant knowledge of the sufferings that have led to this uprising," said the Deemster contemptuously. "Does he really suppose we would use this militia to subdue our own people? They have been subdued long enough, suffering under the tyranny of the Stanleys, forced by them to pay crippling tithes, to starve their children to support an already wealthy clergy." The Deemster paused a moment. "But what is our next move? Greenhalshe has threatened to send for Lord Derby unless Edward agrees to use the militia on our own people."

"Which I shall never do!"

"The people are in an ugly mood, ready for open rebellion and that is what the Governor fears." Ewan glanced at his cousin. "It could be bad for you if Derby does come over and listens to his complaints against you. Greenhalshe has never seen eye to eye with you over anything at all."

"Only because he wants the people kept under!" Edward's eyes were blazing. When he was Governor he had managed to keep the people fairly contented despite the crippling taxation inflicted by the Earl and the Church. Governor Greenhalshe had no idea how to handle the present crisis and to Edward's mind he was totally inadequate for the important post he was holding.

"Will Derby be able to come?" It was William, the Deemster's son who spoke into the silence which had fallen on the company. "Surely he is too involved over there, in the cause of the King."

"At present he is taking it easy at Lathom House," returned Ewan Curphy. "It would seem the King feels he can do very well without him."

Several others nodded. The king had allowed Lord Derby this sojourn at his home, so it certainly did appear that his services were no longer of much importance to the King.

"It would be expected that he would come over in response to his Governor's urgent request." John Teare was well aware that if the Lord did come over and set about punishing those who supported the people then he would certainly not go free. Ever since he married into the Christian family he had been a keen supporter in their aims to bring about an improvement in the lot of the island's heavily burdened inhabitants. Nor would Ewan Curphy go free – in fact, as he glanced around he saw only two who would probably escape: the Deemster because Stanley had always been afraid of him, and William, his son who was at present much in favour with the Earl, holding several offices of authority. It was not that William was content merely to remain an onlooker as yet, but that he possessed much of his father's wisdom and caution, and John suspected the Deemster had warned him to hold back, for the present, from any active involvement. But none could doubt where William's sympathies lay and when the crucial time came he would be ready with his full support. Even as a child he had worried over the plight of the poor and there had been many occasions when his father had warned him not to air his views so openly. The Earl of Derby was, after all, the Lord of Mann, he reminded his son and, therefore, all-powerful as well as being possessed of all the ruthlessness of his forebears, all their hatred of the clan whose lands they had coveted for so long.

"It is a bad business, this unrest." The Deemster seemed to be speaking to himself as he sat there, at the head of the long oak table, mechanically fingering his beard, his eyes staring into space. "And made worse owing to the Governor's requesting that Edward's militia should be used actively to suppress it."

He was thinking that the situation on the island was worsening and he saw no immediate improvement simply because the Earl was so adamant, in his own small way, as was the King over the water. His thoughts switched to the Ronaldsway property which he had inherited from his widowed sister and which the Earl had desperately wanted. Ewan had overthrown Stanley's claim – and thereby tossed another live coal on to the fire of hatred that had burned through generations of Christians and Stanleys. Astute as ever, the Deemster had sensed a warning of worse to come from the Earl who, with his English lands confiscated by the Parliamentarians, would use even more ruthless methods of taxing his subjects. And owing to this warning the Deemster had begun already to make plans for his own future. He was becoming too old for all this and had acquired properties in Cumberland... just as a safeguard. He would give Milntowne to his eldest son, John, and Ronaldsway to William. The time was rapidly approaching when he would act on the idea that had recently come to him: to settle in Cumberland and enjoy a peaceful retirement. He would still hold the office of Deemster, but eventually even that could be handed over to John.

His thoughts were interrupted by the brisk voice of his cousin, William, the Receiver-General.

"I feel we ought to make some effort to appease Greenhalshe. It is a dangerous situation otherwise, bearing in mind that the Governor is so highly thought of by the Earl." He looked troubled as he glanced around. Greenhalshe was far too close to his overlord. His word would carry more weight with him that all the Christians put together.

"His demands can not be met," from Edward whose authority over the island's soldiery was formidable. "He has already been told that in my opinion martial law is injudicious."

"But he considers his authority on the island is higher than yours," cut in Ewan, "and of course he is correct since he acts for the Lord in his absence."

"Perhaps," conceded Edward, "but his authority does not cover the military forces, and these shall never be used on our own people." His voice was firm and hard. "While ever I am in charge of the militia no Manxman is going to fire on another Manxman."

"You have to remember," mused Ewan Curphy, "that in the Earl's opinion they are not 'men'. He has several times described his subjects here as animals and at other times he has treated them as if they were inmates of a lunatic asylum. I feel sure he would never hesitate – should he come over – to crush this rebellion by force."

"He will have to relieve me of my command, then!"

The Deemster gave a bitter laugh.

"The man will do that, cousin, I can promise you." He paused a moment, the gravity of the situation occupying all his thoughts for a full minute. "He will not only launch an attack on the ordinary people but it is my prediction that he would also attack us."

"I have thought of it," put in John Teare worriedly. "If he does heed Greenhalshe's request then we are everyone of us in danger. You have to remember that the Earl is not a happy man at this time. He has been branded a traitor so could lose his life if captured; he has lost all his lands over there. He will be thinking of his wife and children, weighing up their future against his continued support of the King and what its result could be. If he came here – escaping to safety as you might say – and remained until the war is over it would suit him very well."

"Yes, I agree," from the Receiver-General. "Castle Rushen is already luxuriously equipped so his family could move in at any time, living there in peace until the time came when they could return to Lathom."

"They could return only if the Royalists win the war; otherwise Lathom will never be returned to them. Also, if the King should lose, Derby dare not return."

"It seems to me," said John Teare thoughtfully, "that the Earl will definitely come over, in order to crush this uprising. Whether or not he will stay none of us can predict. We are not sure King Charles can do without him. The Earl has already raised five thousand menatarms for the King and given him fifty thousand pounds. It is very likely the King will require his support eventually."

"But meanwhile..." The Deemster's eyes were narrowed, his voice terse. "Should he come – and I fail to see how he can ignore a call for help from his chief lieutenant on the island – it could be hell for the Manx nation."

All nodded in agreement; all were deeply troubled. Ewan Curphy uttered with a sigh,

"It is over a year since Governor Greenhalshe promised to look seriously into the many grievances, to have the Keys investigate and report to him, but the promise was never kept. If it had been, and some remedy found, then this present situation would never have come about."

Again there was a unanimous nod of agreement. The Governor had grossly neglected his duty... but it would be others who would suffer if the Lord should decide to come over to the island.

"Your denial of troops for the Governor has humiliated him," put in William thoughtfully. "He will want revenge for that."

"True," agreed Edward. "It *is* humiliating for the man acting for the Lord to have his order set at naught – but then he ought not to have given me such an order. His idea of using force is insupportable." He knew that his decision had the support of patriots throughout the island but as he glanced around at the company gathered here he saw that they were all deeply troubled as to the nature of the Governor's accusations against the head of the militia. "Greenhalshe will tell a good tale," he went on presently, "and yet if Derby had any sense he would be asking his Governor how he had allowed the situation to get out of hand in the first place."

The meeting progressed without any solution having been found. It seemed likely that the Earl would come over and as to what happened then, well, they could only wait and see.

Refreshments of wine and ale eased the gloom that had fallen over the men and soon the Deemster was inquiring about the training of the militia, wanting to know if his cousin had come up against any difficulties.

"I found the northern men sociable enough and eager to obey my orders," answered Edward with a faint smile. "They train well and seem set to become good soldiers. We shall be ready if the Scots decide to attack us."

"Well, if you train them with the zeal with which you trained your seamen, it is a wonder they have not rioted on you!"

"We understand one another," the Sergeant Major assured him mildly. "I am not such a hard taskmaster as when in my youth. Yes, the north is no trouble to me but—" He broke off and a heavy frown creased his brow. "It is no use concealing the fact that there is a great risk in training men to be soldiers, especially in these troubled times when the Manx nation is already in revolt." He paused in thought. "Men in the south are in a mutinous mood."

It was just as the meeting was about to break up that a messenger arrived in much excitement to announce that another man had been arrested for refusing to pay tithes.

"Who is it this time?" inquired the Deemster sharply.

"James Lucas, sir."

The messenger was told to leave and for a while after the door closed behind him there was silence in the room, one man glancing at another.

A month previously it had been Robert Harrison's refusal to pay tithes that had landed him in prison. But an incensed mob had freed him and he was carried to a hideaway, which act 'had put such fear into the heart of Governor Greenhalshe that he decided to yield' and so Harrison was allowed to go free.

But now another arrest.

"It is my opinion that the result will be the same." John Teare broke the silence at last. "He will be found guilty then rescued by the mob."

"I agree with your prediction." But the younger William was shaking his head as he went on to add, "This only worsens the situation, though, and, gentlemen, we have gained nothing by this meeting."

"Perhaps," mused Edward after some considerable thought, "it would be better if Derby did come over—"

"Are you so naive," cut in his cousin almost angrily, "as to be blind to your own danger should the Lord come over here?"

"At worst I would be relieved of my office," shrugged the Sergeant Major casually. "It would not be the first time he has put me to one side."

Ewan drew a breath. He saw no way by which the situation on the island could end peacefully. Greenhalshe was a blunderer. A year ago he could have listened to the complaints and done something to soothe feelings which at that time were merely ruffled. But now... The island could find itself in the throes of a full-scale revolution. But the Deemster's chief anxiety at this moment was for his cousin, Edward, whose refusal to supply the Governor with soldiery could be declared treason by a Lord whose hatred could drive him to extreme lengths. The Deemster looked around at the men seated at the table. Patriots all, but two stood out: his son and his cousin, Edward – and William, too, the Receiver-General. Three who could be in the most danger... grave danger. And himself as well, for was he not the sharpest thorn in Stanley's side? It was said often that the Lord of Mann had some kind of a brain disorder: certainly some of his actions were bereft of all reasoning. Should he come in response to the Governor's request then there was no knowing what insane form his quelling of the revolt would take.

Well, decided Ewan, I shall not be caught unawares. And his thoughts went again to the noble house in Cumberland, a mansion of over forty bedrooms, its name: Unerigg... but which, somehow in his mind's eye, seemed to be spelled: Ewanrigg.

*

Lord Derby scanned the message brought from his Governor in the Isle of Mann and his teeth gritted together. Those cursed Christians even yet again! Why had he ever entrusted Edward to have full charge of the militia! And what of Greenhalshe? It was clear that he was unable to deal with the situation – but what was he there for?

He was here at Lathom only because the King had given him leave to go home in order to attend to some pressing matters and to spend a short time with his wife and children. He had been home a mere few hours when Charlotte was taken to bed with a miscarriage and a smothering depression fell upon the Earl. Cares loomed on every aspect of his horizon. He had received no thanks from the King for all he had done; his kingdom across the water appeared to be on the verge of open revolt; his eldest son and heir, Charles, was a disappointment to him, and his wife was dangerously ill.

So much seemed to have happened since that day when he had ridden at the head of his men, a magnificent figure on a gleaming horse, the breeze fluttering his plumed headgear. A trusty Cavalier who would one day, when victory was achieved, receive honours in the form of another title and more estates to add to the lands he already owned in Lancashire and Cheshire. More tithes to collect, more wealth filling the Stanley coffers.

Yes, he had ridden to meet his King with both excitement and optimism in his heart. The grandeur of the horses and armour, the gleaming of swords, the excited clamour all around as the King's men prepared for a victorious battle which could possibly end all fear of the country being plunged into a prolonged war. Prince Rupert was there, a twenty-three-year-old professional soldier who gave confidence to all around him. Trumpets blared and the battle began and the cavalry under the charge of Rupert went into action, with the King and his two sons watching on the hilltop. Guns roared and musket-fire followed swiftly. Derby had found himself riding close to Prince Rupert, and the King's nephew laughed and said all was going well. But James had noticed some lack of discipline in what at first seemed to be a magnificent charge, for excitable youths galloped wildly away without apparently having received any orders. James remembered so well the sinking sensation in the pit of his stomach, the awful admission that this, the first encounter of the two sides, could end in disaster for the King. Chaos in the field was increased by loss of daylight as dusk came upon the scene, for this was October and the day had been dull to begin with. Carnage was all around, with mortally wounded and those dying in agony lying side by side. Horses twisted in pain, suffering torment before the writhing muscles were mercifully stilled at last. So ended the Battle of Edgehill.

It had proved to be an indecisive battle, although Prince Rupert had later told James that victory had been within their grasp but by the stupidity of a few wild, undependable amateur soldiers it had been thrown away.

There had been more successful battles but the King seemed to have too many advisers with conflicting views. James had received a small wound in the fighting and it was partly owing to this that Charles had said he could have a short sojourn at Lathom before joining him again.

And now this disturbing message calling him to the island to sort out the position there. He decided to send a message to the King informing him of the happenings and as there was still a threat of a Scots invasion of the island King Charles said yes, it would be wise to go. The readiness with which the permission was given made it all too clear that the King placed very little importance on the help given; it also confirmed the Earl's suspicion that he had many enemies and he did wonder if they had advised the King to dispense altogether with his services. He knew he was disliked by the Queen because he had married a woman with Calvinistic beliefs, and it had come to James' ear that the Queen had advised her husband not to put too much trust in James Stanley.

Well, at least he was now free to look to his own kingdom and he set off with sufficient infantry and cavalry to put down forcibly any uprising, and with the grim determination to do just that if it should prove necessary. He would teach these – animals who was their master! Yes, animals, needing to be tickled and stroked more often than kicked, but this time he was in no mood for attempting to soothe their ruffled feelings in the way he had fifteen years ago when, as a youth of only twenty he had – as he later told his wife – come to the people with kindness and in an affable mood, and he had let them know he would listen with sympathetic ears to any complaints they had to make. Not so this time, though! He would subdue the whole island once and for all, and the ringleaders would rot in the dungeons of Peel and Castle Rushen for the rest of their lives!

*

When Sir John Kingsley came along the lovely avenue of trees that lined the drive to Deva Place he was whistling a tune to himself. Supping with Eleanor was always a happy and exciting experience for him. He loved her now with the same intensity as when he first set eyes on her so many years ago. To him she had grown even more beautiful and he had come very close to worshipping her... and still he waited, sometimes wishing Edward Christian in his grave, and yet fully aware of the possibility of Eleanor devoting the rest of her own life to his memory. What love! John knew that if ever she did become his he would never be loved as the Manxman was loved. He did not really wish Edward dead. In fact, he admired him greatly for his fight to bring about an improvement in the living standards of the Manx people. In his various offices of responsibility he had approached the Lord of the Isle and although his efforts had not borne fruit he still persevered and he had told John he would do so till the end of his life.

A prim maid admitted him and he smiled at her as he handed her his cloak.

He walked into the drawing room then stopped in his tracks, his breath catching in his throat, as the smile died on his lips.

"Eleanor... whatever is the matter?"

She looked ghastly, her face ashen, her eyes sunk deep into their sockets, her hair matted in places as if she had crushed it over and over again while in the throes of some insane frenzy.

"Susanna – Edward, your son—" He strode towards her as he spoke. "My dearest, what has happened to make you like this?"

"It – it is – Edward – but not my son—" She put her face in her hands and her shoulders shook as sobs began to rack her body.

"Dear Eleanor, tell me, what has happened?" He was bending over her chair, his arms about her shoulders.

"Edward, my Edward – he is imprisoned – by that man – I hate him! I want to kill him!" A stifled scream ended the words. Sobs shook her slender body again. "He will kill my dearest love, my darling..."

John could only stand there, looking helplessly down at her, for it was plain she would not be comforted whatever he might do. Edward imprisoned. What had he done? And how come that the Earl was on the island when he should have been with the King? He had to know, and he must do something to help her. He knelt beside her chair and took one small white hand in his.

"My sweet Eleanor, tell me all – it will make you feel better; I do assure you, it will relieve, if only in some small measure, this terrible distress." Tentatively he drew her head on to his shoulder, heartened when she did not rebuff him, as he had half expected her to. "When did you hear of this, and how came the news?"

For answer she swung a hand to indicate a paper on the table. Rising, he walked over, picked it up and read the message sent to her from the Deemster. Edward and others were imprisoned in Peel Castle.

"It was brought by a seaman. You will see – see that Ewan is – to come over – to – to tell me – me – everything—"

Sobs prevented further speech altogether; she came forward in her chair, putting her head in her hands and rocking her body back and forth as one in a fit. John dropped the letter on the table and came swiftly to her.

"Do not, Eleanor – please stop. I can not bear to see you in so much grief. Let us talk about this. We know little of what has happened. It might not be as bad as you believe."

She looked up at him through her tears, her mouth trembling convulsively.

"It is as bad as it can be. I know it – feel it – here!" A tightly closed fist was pressed to her heart. "I shall die too, if that fiend has him... him... Yes," she quivered, "I shall die too."

"It merely says in Ewan's note that Edward was arrested along with many more influential men on the island, that Lord Derby went over at the request of Governor Greenhalshe to put down some rioting. And, dear Eleanor, he does say not to worry too much because the Earl knows just how far he can go."

"But he would say that for me not to worry. But Lord Derby hates all the Christians – they have had this feud for two hundred years, John, and now – now it is coming to a head."

"No," He shook his head. He had studied this feud at some length since knowing Edward Christian, and he was convinced that the final solution would come about only when a Derby came along to do the sensible thing and decide to pass an Act which would leave the lands where they belonged – in the possession of the men whose gift they were in the first place. "Lord Derby can not solve the problem of the land tenures. But we do not know if that is the issue. I rather believe it concerns Edward's helping the rebels, for he has for many years given his energies to relieving their lot."

"But he would never help the people to riot," she protested. "Edward was wild, and never law-abiding when he was young, but he has changed in recent years and all he wants from the Earl is fair dealing for everyone on the island, rich and poor alike." She had stopped crying but sobs still shook her slender frame. She looked up at him and added chokingly, "I have not told you, John, but Susanna has met a gentleman and is quite determined to marry him. As you know I had planned for her to marry into the aristocracy and that is why I sent her to London, to those relatives of Ewan's. I was so sure she would be regarded with favour by many titled gentlemen—" She spread her hands and burst into tears again. "I am undone on all sides!"

"You are not pleased with this man? You can not say he is unsuitable until you have met him—"

"He is a Puritan! And they are going – with many more Puritans – to America – to – to l–live th–there. I shall never see my daughter again. It is to be goodbye forever!"

America... My God, so far away. John swallowed thickly, frustrated by his own helplessness. This was a stricken woman at whom he was looking and he did wonder if the scars now inflicting her would ever heal. Until now there had been no ravaging of her beauty by time, but at this moment she looked very old, far older than her forty-four years. Her son was in Ireland practising law and although she was happy that her hopes for him had materialised, she had expressed sadness more than once that he was so far away from her. And now her daughter... going to a new life at the other side of the world. For a moment he knew a fierce anger against Susanna. How could she desert her mother, go so far away that it would mean they might never meet again? And yet... It was the right of every human being to choose their own partner. Eleanor would eventually understand. He only prayed that this man, when Eleanor did meet him, would satisfy her that he could make her daughter happy. His thoughts were interrupted by Eleanor's declaring she would go over to the island the day after tomorrow. With a shocked expression John quickly pointed out the impossibility of her travelling alone. Moreover, had she forgotten that Ewan would be here within the next day or two?

She bit her lip, admitting that John was right. But she was desperate to get to Edward, to see him and talk to him... to comfort him.

"I can not bear to think of him in a dungeon!" she cried. "I must get to see him!"

"My dear, calm yourself. Edward is a political prisoner and so are those with him. They will certainly not be in a dungeon, but more likely all together in one of the living apartments of the castle."

"Is that true? Political prisoners are treated differently from others?"

"From ordinary felons? Of course, dear. I thought you would know about that."

Some of the tenseness went out of her. She looked at him through her tears and said quiveringly,

"I am so glad you have told me this. It – it does make a bit of difference – easier for me to bear."

But what would happen to him in the end? And his brother, good kind William, the Receiver-General into whose home she had been welcomed as if she were an equal, given good food for herself and her son, given lessons so she could improve herself. And what of the other William, Deemster Ewan's son? No, he was obviously not a prisoner since Ewan would have said so in his letter. Besides, he was in favour with the Earl... or had he too now fallen out of favour? So many questions—

John cut into her thoughts, an unexpected sternness in his voice as he said she must make him a promise that she would not go over to the island alone.

"Yes, I shall have to make the promise because, as you say, it is quite impossible. I shall wait for Ewan and travel back with him."

John said nothing. He wondered if Eleanor had thought about Edward's wife, who would not be pleased at having her husband's long-time mistress staying on the island. But there was a possibility that she was in ignorance of Eleanor's existence seeing that Eleanor had left the island eight years before Edward was married. But John was doubtful of Ewan agreeing to take Eleanor back with him, anyway. He was a very wise man and would ponder long on any possible difficulties that could result from a visit to the island by Eleanor.

John stayed until after midnight and even then he was loath to leave her, but at least he had managed to calm her and she assured him that she would be all right. But as she accompanied him to the door she took his hand and asked him to come early in the morning.

"You are such a comfort," she confessed and actually managed a smile. "Where would I be without you?"

John swallowed something painful in his throat. A comfort to her... For so many years he had been her friend, a regular visitor when Edward was away, which was often for long periods, but not so regular a visitor when Edward was in residence at Deva Place. But strangely, he and Edward had become good friends, and John was genuinely distressed by the news of his imprisonment. He hoped all the men would be released... but he had his doubts in the light of the bitter feud that existed between the people concerned. He had long since changed his opinion of the Stanleys, having learned so much about their persecution of the Manx people, and especially he disliked the present Lord of Mann who, immediately he became the ruler, had issued the ultimatum to the landowners, ignoring completely the Act made by King James whereby all inherited lands in the Isle of Mann, and those acquired by marriage or by purchase, were to remain the property of those in possession.

A full week went by and Ewan had not arrived. Eleanor was fast giving way to nerves and it was all John could do to calm her. She wept so much and so bitterly that he became desperate to find a way of comforting her. All she desired was to go to the island and talk with Edward.

"Why does he not come as promised!" she cried. "I can not bear it! John, if you will come with me I will go over. Please come with me for you were right when you said it would not be possible for me to go alone."

Although he did not believe it was the right thing to do, he promised to think about it and let her know the following day. But later the same day a further letter arrived, brought by another of the crew of one of the Deemster's ships, and it was to say that Ewan could not come over just yet but he would see her before the trial.

When John read the letter and saw the state his loved one was in, he agreed to go over with her to the island.

"Is there an inn close by the place where we land?" he asked, getting down to practicalities.

"Yes, of course. We shall be landing in Ramsey Bay and there is a small inn a few minutes' walk away where we can stay and I can go and see Ewan on the following morning. He will take me to see Edward."

John gave a small sigh. She was plainly in a fever of excitement at the prospect of going over to the Isle of Mann, but she had given no thought whatsoever to her situation once she arrived there. He strongly suspected that the Deemster would be displeased rather than welcoming at her unexpected arrival on his doorstep. And he was not so sure that Edward would approve her action either. The man had a pride above many, John knew, and it must hurt that pride to be seen in prison by the woman he loved – that was, presupposing permission for a visit were granted, which John fervently hoped would be the case, since he hated to think what effect a refusal would have on Eleanor. And the Earl? Had she given a thought to what his reaction would be? He was almost certainly in ignorance of her existence, so there would have to be some explanation for her request to visit the ex-Governor. While pondering over all this, John overlooked one vital matter: the possibility of danger to Eleanor herself.

*

The Deemster paced the floor of his drawing room, having twice impatiently waved away a lackey who had come in to tell him something. This was a damnable situation. But he had to remain calm, he admonished himself, for this present mood was altogether alien to his innate cool and collected self-possession.

Edward and William, still in Peel Castle in spite of his repeated attempts to bring about their release. John Teare, also, their brother-in-law, along with that young hothead cousin of his who had been advising the people not to pay tithes, and had found himself in prison for his trouble. William, his youngest son, was as yet free, and Ewan had a plan to keep it that way. Yes, if William would not take his advice and leave the island, then his safety had to be ensured.

He continued to pace the floor, his brain working overtime. The whole situation in Mann was deteriorating, and he bethought himself yet again that it had been a wise and farseeing move when he had purchased Unerigg. Once he had settled this matter of his imprisoned kinsmen he would be away, establishing himself permanently in Cumberland, for the Lord of Mann was becoming more daring, his actions more positive, since at one time he would never have dared arrest and imprison a Christian. The wily Deemster's eyes narrowed. Was it the right moment to make the move that would ensure the safety of his son, that would keep him in favour with his overlord? He shook his head, puzzled that he was hesitating to use the winning card he held so confidently. It was as if some instinct warned him to hold on to it for a little while longer. But eventually the Ronaldsway property, in which William now lived, would be made over to him... on a lease for three lives. That should satisfy the greed of the Earl who had all along maintained the Deemster had acquired it illegally, that on the death of Ewan's widowed sister without children the property should have automatically become the possession of the Lord of Mann. But by the complicated 'Law of Corbes,' Ewan had been able to outwit his rival aspirant. Now, though, he would present his son with the property and see that he accepted it in a way which would appease the Earl. And by this act William's safety could be assured.

Yes, that would take care of one of his sons. He would provide for John, his eldest, by presenting him with Milntowne. Edward, his other legitimate son was already safe from any Derby persecution married a widow whose brother had left her the Westmorland property of Rosgill Hall, where Edward now lived with his wife.

His thoughts soon returned to the plight of his kinsmen, imprisoned at Peel. Much as he would have liked to get away he had no intention of deserting them. He would see Derby again and hope they could, after some inevitable fencing, come to some agreement that would set them free. But it would be tough, he admitted, vividly recalling the entry of the Earl on the island in June. That his intention had been to put terror into his subjects was soon made clear by the march across the island of his English soldiery and his boast that he had brought sufficient to subjugate the island's whole twelve thousand souls if the malcontents continued to defy the authority of his officers. The Deemster guessed at the Earl's thoughts: he confidently placed reliance on the fact that the Manx people were not basically aggressive, and, therefore, a strong show of arms would see them cowering before it. Such was the object of the march, to flaunt the Earl's goodly supply of pikes and muskets before a people who must be made to realise they were his subjects and he their overlord.

At last Ewan tugged at a bellrope to fetch the lackey and to order a tankard of ale to be brought to him.

The man appeared but before he could give the order he was told something that made his mouth gape and a spark of anger enter his eyes. But recovery was swift and he was telling the lackey to show the lady in.

"What," he almost bellowed, "is the meaning of this! What has made you come here when I wrote to say I should be coming over to Chester to see *you*!"

Pale but defiant, Eleanor let her hood fall from her hair before answering his questions.

"I had to come. You must have known I would be unable to wait and wait, without news of my Edward. I want to see him—"

"Have you come alone?" he broke in shortly. "Do you realise the danger of travelling alone?"

"I am not alone," she replied quietly then asked if she could sit down.

"Yes, of course. What do you mean, you are not alone? That maid you have would never travel on a ship."

"John was kind enough to come with me." She took off her long cloak and laid it over the back of the chair before sitting down. "Surely you must have known the effect your intelligence would have on me," she went on in the same quiet tone. "I was frantic, out of my mind with worry. To think of Edward in a dungeon nearly drove me mad."

"Edward is not in a dungeon."

"I know that now but at the time I read your letter I imagined him in one of those awful damp black holes under the castle. John assured me that Edward would at least be in a comfortable apartment."

"I doubt not that the lord of our isle would have enjoyed throwing a Christian into a dungeon," mused the Deemster, for the moment diverted. "But he knew just how far he could go with safety. But never mind that," he said impatiently. "About John, where is he now?"

"We stayed at the inn last night and he went back after escorting me here. I said you would walk me back, as I do not know what I shall be doing or how long it will take. Can I see Edward now – I mean, will you take me? I have riding clothes with me, in a bag."

He gave an impatient sigh, then a smile appeared to soften the taut features and to assure her that his spurt of anger had dissolved.

"You are a brave and beautiful lady, my dear." He touched the soft curls that had strayed on to her forehead. "My cousin has been blessed by a love which is to me beyond all understanding. Whatever lies before him now, he has had more than his fair share of happiness." His smile had faded; his voice was grave because of her change of expression. "Yes, dear, he could have much that is unpleasant lying before him. As yet there is no indication of what the exact charges will be, or even when the trial will take place. But—" He paused to take her hand. "I suspect the Earl will like to prolong his gloating, which he can do as long as these men are in prison. You must prepare yourself for a goodly delay before the trial comes up. You see, if Edward is acquitted, his imprisonment will end—"

"And Lord Derby's gloating will also end."

She bit her lip. How could she survive a long wait, with her beloved Edward languishing in prison – for no matter how comfortable his lodgings might be, he *was* in captivity. And to a man who had known the wide freedom of the oceans, this restraint must be hell itself. She looked up at him and asked again when she could visit Edward, to which he answered reluctantly,

"It might not be possible to see him—"

"Not possible!" she broke in swiftly. "As he has not yet been charged I imagine he can have unlimited visitors?"

The Deemster could not repress a smile at her naivety.

"The Earl has probably forbidden any visiting at all. He will be fully aware that plots will already be afoot to attempt a rescue, and his safeguard would be to make sure the prisoners have no contact with friends or relations. And besides all this conjecture," he continued with a sudden frown, "there is the matter of just who you are supposed to be. I am now considering the possibility that you might be able to visit but we can scarcely present you as his mistress; you must have realised that?"

She coloured slightly, admitting that she had never given it a thought.

"How like a woman," was his sardonic rejoinder. "Little thought went into anything, from what I can see. What made you so sure you would be allowed to visit him?"

"I was so – frantic," she explained on a little self-deprecating note, "that I just wanted to get up and fly to him as quickly as I could. I was going to come immediately but John pointed out the folly of such impulsiveness. However, when I received your second message saying your visit to Chester was delayed I decided to come over – and here I am."

"An embarrassment to me," he returned bluntly. "What am I to do with you? My wife is away in Lytham visiting relatives – as you know, she came from there. I suppose you had better stay here, though, both of you."

"Thank you," she breathed with such clear evidence of relief that he remarked the accommodation at the inn must leave a lot to be desired.

"It certainly could be better." She looked up at him, wondering if he fully appreciated the terrible heaviness within her heart, the anxiety of not knowing what would happen to the prisoners. She managed to voice the question which had been with her during every waking moment since the receipt of his letter. "Ewan... can – is it possible for Lord Derby to – to have these prisoners – sentenced to death?" Tears instantly filled her eyes. "If he dies, I want to die too!"

Ewan turned away, too full to speak. Hard and ruthless was a description often given to him, but it was something very different that made him the patriot that he had become. Hard and ruthless he could be where the Earl was concerned, yes, all of that! But the poor of the isle had always troubled him, the oppression of the Stanleys through the ages, the poverty. Like his cousin he had a soft core to the granite covering and it was most troublesome to him at this moment as even yet again he marvelled at the great love of this woman, a love that could make her say she would want to die if her lover lost his life.

He said at last, with total confidence as he turned once more towards her,

"Edward will never receive the death sentence. Derby would not dare to go as far as that."

"How can you say so? We all know of his deep hatred for the Christians. He has no conscience, Ewan; none of the Stanleys ever did have one. He would care nothing about justice and honour."

"Perhaps not, but weighed against that is his fear of a really serious revolt – Oh, yes, I know he has brought his English soldiery over which it would seem you have already heard about. But the man is an expert at deceit; this is a huge piece of bluff on his part, his aim being to put terror into the hearts of his subjects. But it is not possible for him to use much of the soldiery here because it would be needed elsewhere if his King should call him back to support him, which is quite likely as this war is not going well for the Royalists. So you see, my dear Eleanor, Derby knows just how far he can go with safety."

"It is a help, what you have told me. It has allayed my worst fear, that Edward might die. But now, I pray you, dear Ewan, arrange for me to see him."

"I shall try," he promised, and then, "But who are you supposed to be? Some explanation is necessary – Wait! I have it. John can be your husband. That is it! Sir John and Lady Kingsley, friends of Edward, request permission to visit him."

"No..." Eleanor was shaking her head. "We can not pose as husband and wife."

"Oh," he returned blankly, "why? What is your objection? John will readily agree, I am sure."

Eleanor fell silent. Was this the only way? She remembered that John had known the Earl when he was just a boy... it was unlikely that Lord Derby would meet Sir John and even more unlikely that he would be interested in him and his "wife" even if he did recognise him. Nor was it conceivable that they would even meet. Lord Derby was living at Castle Rushen and Edward was in Peel.

"Edward will hate it," she murmured at last. "I am sure he will."

"Nonsense. Has he ever been jealous of John?"

She said no, for the simple reason that Edward knew that he himself had all the love she would ever be able to give.

Ewan convinced her that his suggestion was the one most likely to influence Derby to permit the visit. And in fact it did succeed and the visit was arranged for the Friday afternoon, two days hence. Meanwhile Ewan ordered them both to keep to the privacy of Milntowne, for although it was over twenty years since she had lived on the island, it was just possible that she might be recognised.

She was veiled as she rode between Ewan and John across the island to Peel where the great grey stone castle reared its head in a sort of grotesque splendour as if as a reminder of its great age. She shivered with the cold even though it was a time of full summer. Some kind of renovations appeared to be in progress although there was no sign of any workmen. But the Earl's guardsmen were much in evidence, reminder of the many extra soldiers present on the island at this time. One of them had obviously been told to expect their arrival for he stepped forward, saluted the Deemster respectfully, bowed to Eleanor and indicated the way they were to go.

Edward had been warned of their coming and he was immaculately dressed in a high-waisted doublet with panes on the upper part, and a deep basque. His hair was shoulder-length and he had let grow a smudge of hair below the bottom lip. His appearance cheered her just a little but she knew she would never forget this day when she saw her loved one here, imprisoned, helpless against the power being exerted by a merciless enemy whose tyranny and greed had led to the uprising which had been responsible for this plight which Edward and the other prisoners now found themselves. How she hated the Earl! Never before could she recall having hated anyone with such a black venom. She had always been so gentle, of a sober, tranquil temperament... but now she felt she could kill the man who had put her beloved Edward here.

"My dear..." He seemed for a moment too full to speak; he just took her hands in his and stood gazing into eyes that were far too bright. Bravely she blinked back the threatening tears and a smile fluttered to her lips.

"Oh, my dearest..." She turned her head. Edward dropped her hands and gave his full attention to the men who had brought her.

"Ewan, it was good of you to arrange this – and you, my friend, I thank you for bringing Eleanor over here. How is it with you? Was the sailing smooth?"

"Very smooth," smiled John, grasping the outstretched hand with both of his. "I suspect you do not fully approve but, I beg of you, Edward, spare me the blame. I was coerced and I had the choice of accompanying Eleanor or seeing her come alone."

There was another few minutes chatting between the three men before Ewan obligingly suggested he and John wait outside. Immediately the great oaken door was closed the lovers were in each other's arms. "My dearest..." It was Eleanor's turn to find speech difficult and more difficult still the suppression of tears. "Why are you here, my love?" she cried eventually. "Ewan has explained, but what charges has the Earl against you all?"

"Trumped up ones, they are sure to be." He appeared not to be over anxious and she was heartened by his confident air. "We shall be tried by the people; they are on our side. We shall be acquitted."

"You sound so sure," she said, perplexed. "Are you not afraid?"

"Afraid!" A laugh rang out and for a moment she saw again the bold searover, the fearless pirate who thought nothing of attacking a vessel twice the size of his own. And he never once suffered a defeat... "I have never been afraid in my life and I shall not begin now. Let Derby do his worst. His ignorance of the loyalty of our Manx brethren will be brought home to him when we all walk from that courtroom free men!"

"I pray you are right, Edward, but unlike you I know a great fear – here in my heart. Hold me – comfort me. The fear hurts, Edward – actually pains me!"

"No, no, my little sweeting. Weep not, for they are wasted tears. I shall be with you long before summer leaves turn to gold. Believe me, dearest, you and I shall stroll along the river bank, hands clasped as we have done so many times before. We shall see the swallows fly and the swans turn their young away. Yes, I shall be with you in our own heaven long before the autumn leaves begin to part from their branches."

She fell silent, keeping to herself what Ewan had predicted about the Earl's delaying a long time before bringing the men to trial. He could do that; he had the power and she thought how like the King he was, using arbitrary methods to subjugate his people. The King of England was in dire trouble as a result of his despotism, for the people had risen up against him. But the Manx nation had been subdued so many times, this little country tossed from one owner to another, defeated and plundered, grasped by avaricious hands, right down through the ages, sometimes abandoned, often neglected, that the spirit of its inhabitants had well nigh been broken so that it needed men like Edward and his brother, Ewan and his sons... and more, but there were still not enough to vanquish a tyrant who could raise five thousand well-trained soldiers in the cause of his King, and who now had some of them here as a warning to those intrepid enough to continue their fight for freedom.

What would be the end of it all? Would this little emerald gem come into its own one day, perhaps in the far distant future when tyrants like Derby no longer held power... when perhaps, their line had become extinct. How she wished him dead now, this day, this moment!

Ah, wishful thinking! The time was now, in the year 1643, and many brave men were awaiting trial. This was stark reality and that it would one day be history was of no importance on this sunny summer afternoon – which would live in her memory till the day she died.

Chapter Twelve

It was a remarkably elegant apartment into which Deemster Ewan Christian was shown on a bleak November day in the year 1643. Having been in the room many times before, Ewan merely made a cursory glance around but in doing so discovered some articles of furniture, and Arras and Brussels tapestries adorning the walls which, he realised, must have been brought over when his lordship crossed to the island with his infantry and cavalry five months ago. There were some fine cabinets containing treasures of art and a large collection of Limusin enamels, all of which had obviously come from Lathom House. There had been some recent renovations, too, and the Deemster wondered if the Earl were intending to reside on the island, out of danger, until the war in England was over. Certainly Castle Rushen was a safe place to be.

The Earl greeted Ewan Christian with a smile and introduced him to Lords Niddesdaile, Carnwath and Digby, his boon companions in what appeared to be an orgy of drinking. Two other Royalists who had accompanied him from England in June were over by a window, having been looking out and when they turned Derby presented them as Sir Marmaduke Langdale and Sir William Hudleston.

Invited to sit down, the Deemster sank into a comfortable satin-cushioned chair which was to one side of the blazing coal fire, on the chimney piece above which was blazoned the arms of the Derby family.

"To what do I owe the pleasure of a visit from the chief of the clan Christian?" inquired the Earl with an edge of mocking satire to his voice. "You will drink ale with us?"

"You know why I am here," replied the Deemster coolly, ignoring the offer of ale. "I had expected that we would speak together in private."

His dark eyes wandered significantly round the company, all of whom were seated now, eyes expectant as if in anticipation of some form of unique entertainment. The Earl hesitated for a moment and then,

"Gentlemen, I beg your pardon for a short absence I am bound to make. But drink and be merry! I shall hurry my business with the good Deemster for I know which company I prefer!"

Ewan sent him a glance of contempt. The man had already drunk too much and it was no surprise when he stumbled on his way out of the room.

"I shall come straight to the point," began the Deemster before his lordship could speak. "When is this trial to be? The men have been imprisoned for well nigh on five months without charges being made against them. I demand that my kinsmen be tried within the next month."

The Earl's arrogant eyes looked him over from head to foot.

"Demand, my friend?" he echoed haughtily. "You are in no position to demand anything. I am the sovereign lord of this isle and only I can make demands." He paused and a sneer twisted his mouth. "These plaguey Manx are a trial to me, I will have you know. They are like animals as I have said so many times before - Ah, anger darkens your eyes, Ewan, but yes, your people are animals and they made up their minds to turn on my officers and although their teeth are small and ineffectual they can cause some discomfort—"

"James, stop this nonsense! You and I understand one another better than to expect either to listen to wasted words! The trial of my cousins, and others—"

"There are no others," he interrupted rudely. "Some were fined and freed weeks ago as you very well know. The rest - apart from the ringleader and his brother - were freed today."

"I see..." Freed today, leaving just two of those originally arrested, two Christians, and both having held the highest positions in the administration of the island. "So when will these two be freed?"

"Freed?" with an arrogant lift of the dark brows. "You are absurdly optimistic, my friend. I can assure you that the ex-Governor will pay with his life, and as for William... I am not sure about him yet."

"Pay with his life?" The Deemster actually laughed in the Earl's face. "The ale has dulled your senses, James. You have no charge that could bring the death sentence. He will be tried by the people and you need no telling that my cousin is held in deep respect by those whose cause he has championed all these years."

It was the Earl's turn to laugh as he said maliciously,

"I have decided he will not be tried by the people, with whom he is so popular, as you remark. No, I am by no means blind to the fact that a jury would acquit him, and so he will be tried by the Keys."

"The Keys! But you have already terrorised them. How can my cousin have a fair trial if it is to be conducted by a body of men who dare not say you nay?" Ewan was aware of a dead weight having settled in the pit of his stomach. He had underrated the Earl, had never even thought of a possibility such as this. The Keys were chosen by the Lord, and this was one of the grievances that had been festering for generations. The Keys should be chosen by the people. "You can not do this, James. Fairness will be expected of you regarding this trial."

"Then there will be some disappointments," returned the Earl sardonically. "You must take me for a fool to suppose I would leave the fate of that traitor in the hands of a mob who have been deluded into believing the ex-Governor has worked for their cause, as you are wont to term their complaints. Should I be so foolish your cousin would walk free and laugh at me."

Ewan sat silently staring into the coals. Not for anything would he betray the bleakness within him. The Earl, slouched in a heavily carved chair, his thin, jewelled hand resting on the arm, had a sneer on his lips and a gleam of triumph in his eyes. But the Deemster saw nothing of this as his brain worked furiously to invent a counter-weapon with which to attack the threat that was hanging over his cousin who, somewhere in the castle at Peel, was in all probability conversing happily with his brother in the apartment which they now shared, result of his own insistence that the Earl should allow them to be together. Chatting all oblivious of the fiendish plan thought out by a man possessed by hate and greed.

The Earl broke the silence, stating quite categorically that the Deemster and all the other relations of the ex-Governor should wisely become used to the idea of the sentence that was soon to come upon him because, being tried by the Keys, there was no possibility of his receiving anything less than the death sentence.

"Why this mad craving for his life!" demanded Ewan, outwardly calm but inflamed within at this diabolical scheming on the part of the Earl.

"Because it will be at least one pestilence that will no longer cause me trouble. Also, 'tis always safer to take a man's life than his possessions, for children will sooner forget their father than the loss of their patrimony." He stirred restlessly, evidence of his desire to go back to his friends.

"You still have not given me a date for the trial." Ewan sent him a level look. "I want a date," he added forcefully. "It is my right to receive this information."

"It is fixed for early December."

Ewan made no comment on that but after a small pause he referred to the recent attempt that had been made on the life of the Lord of Mann.

"Was that not a warning, James?" he added watching him closely. "You need no stronger proof that you are hated by your subjects on this isle."

"Did you have a hand in it?" The Earl had coloured up at the reminder and his mouth went tight.

"Had it been my work," the Deemster was swift to reply, not without a touch of humour, "a more successful result would have come of it."

"I have the name of the culprit. He will hang for it!"

"You have his name? Do I know this man?"

"Perhaps. His name is John Parsons. He is in hiding but he will be caught – and those hiding him will have their ears cut off."

John Parsons... Ewan had a good idea where he would be. An impulsive youth but certainly not actually wicked. He was working for a shoemaker in Ramsey the last time he had heard of him. The lad was probably sick with fear... Ewan had a ship sailing for Liverpool tomorrow afternoon. Parsons' was one life the Earl would *not* manage to take.

Ewan again changed the subject, asking how long the Earl was intending to stay on the island.

"The King has ordered me to remain and to build up the defences. He fears an invasion by the Scots. For King Charles the island is in a strategic position if, and when, he can get supplies from Ireland. The

Countess and our children will be living mainly at Castle Rushen but sometimes we shall have a change and live at Peel."

"I saw you had added some furnishings and other fine objects."

"There will be more to come. We want to be comfortable, and we shall be entertaining of course."

"More Royalists will follow you, I suppose?" The hint of contempt was not lost on the Earl and he asked sharply,

"Are you suggesting that these friends of mine are all cowards!"

"I am thinking how very convenient it is for them to have this island open to them, offering safety and escape from the troubles across the water."

"We shall all rally to the aid of His Majesty if called upon to do so," was the Earl's chill rejoinder. He lifted a hand to stifle a yawn but the significance of the gesture was ignored. The Deemster remained in his chair. He was wondering if the Earl would follow in the steps of his forebears, who with watchful eyes to see which side was winning, would turn coat at the opportune moment and support the winning side. But perhaps such a dexterous move was not possible in this, the case of the seventh Earl, because he had already been declared a traitor by the Parliament led by Hampden and Pym.

With a change of subject Ewan asked about the Earl's sixteen-year-old son and heir.

"It is rumoured that he is a disappointment to you, James. A wild youth who disregards your authority."

Again the Earl's cheeks flushed with angry colour. He never did put a guard on his tongue, this cursed Christian, the most troublesome of them all, yet the one he dared not arrest. With a glowering look into the face of his antagonist he replied that as Charles would soon be coming over along with his other children, the Deemster would be able to judge for himself. James was fervently hoping for an improvement in his wayward offspring, that he would have become more well-mannered and polished by the time he arrived on the shores of the kingdom over which he would one day rule.

"He is young," he added coldly, "and I expect your own sons have passed through a similar phase."

"I recall not such a phase."

"You are brave, Ewan," sneered his overlord, "but bravery will not serve in what you are still hoping to achieve."

"The saving of my cousin's life?" Faintly the Deemster smiled. "Do not be so sure, my friend."

With the shattering news that the Earl was having Edward tried by the Keys, Ewan was immediately resigned to the fact that he would never walk from the court to freedom, but he had no intention of giving up the fight for his life. The Earl was becoming dangerous, though, and much more intrepid than ever before.

And he was intending to live on the island so there was no knowing what further tyranny was in store for the Manx people. His thoughts switched to Eleanor and something akin to real pain shot through him. How was he going to tell her that the Earl wanted her lover's life?

"It is time for me to leave," he said rising from his chair. "I should think again, James, about your intention as regards my cousin's trial. The Manx nation is in an ugly mood, the situation in England having, quite naturally, affected their way of thinking. You could have a rebellion on your hands, for Edward Christian is a well-loved patriot as I have already said."

"A rebellion?" with a lifting of the straight black brows and a sneer of contempt settling on the thin, cruel mouth. "Have I not dealt successfully with the mob who defied my officers' authority?" A laugh rang through the small antechamber in which the discussion was taking place. "I very soon put them in good awe, with the minor agitators instantly thrown into jail where a sojourn in the dungeons had them begging pardon for their misbehaviour and promising to be very good in the future." The sneer returned and the Deemster's eyes sharpened with a mingling of anger and contempt. "I had them cowering in no time at all."

"No need for these reminders," Ewan snapped. "We all know of the methods you employed, since you bragged about it to your friends, affording them much diversion – Do not look so surprised that your conversations with friends leaked out. The total loyalty of his servants is something no man is fortunate enough to enjoy. That you laughed and sneered is known abroad through the island. Also that you admitted to bribing some of the officers, sending them among the people to spy and report back to you. Is such intriguing worthy of a ruler—? But what am I saying? Your King does the same; maybe you learned it all from him, James, but take care... and learn a little more: that man was never meant to be enslaved, and it requires no wise intelligence to predict that if the King loses the war he could also lose his head."

"The—! Ewan, you talk like a fool! No one would send our King to the block. Go home, my friend," he added wearily, "you bore me with such nonsensical talk!"

The Deemster shrugged his shoulders and turned to the door.

"I will bid you good day, James."

"Good day to you, Deemster Christian – oh, I almost forgot." A pause ensued and, suddenly aware that its purpose was to add significance to what was to follow, Ewan felt a sensation of chill running along his spine. "You, as one of the Deemsters, will be required to sign the ex-Governor's death warrant."

*

As Eleanor listened to what the Deemster had to say a great fear entered her heart, stifling her very breathing, rising up into her throat to choke her.

"His – his life..." Her eyes were staring, her whole body stiff. She seemed lifeless, he thought, and for a moment closed his eyes, unable to bear the sight of such agony. He had pondered long on whether or not to tell her the whole or whether merely to warn her that Edward could receive a long prison sentence. But in the end he decided to mention the Lord's desire for his life, because it were better she be prepared for the worst. "But it can not be!" she cried in a strangled voice. "He shall not kill my Edward – Ewan, you can save him—!"

"Eleanor, dear," he broke in gently, "you have not listened fully to what I have said. Edward is to be tried by the Keys, who were chosen by the Earl and are such a drivelling body of cowards that they go in terror of their lord and master. And it seemed to me at first that, should he instruct them to bring in the death sentence, they would not dare disobey him. However – no, dear Eleanor, please hear me without interruption. I began to picture the situation and came to the conclusion that the Members of the House of Keys could probably be put in fear of the people – who did not elect them, remember, but believe they should have the right to do so. An uprising is still simmering and although Derby is confident he can put it down, he will also be aware that should the King recall him he would have to go – and take his army with him, and it is only the presence of this army that is keeping the people subdued. I am sure something can be done to prevent the Earl from achieving his object. I am giving it deep, prolonged thought and can assure you that I shall find some way of saving Edward's life."

"You really believe so? You are not just saying it to – Ewan, please tell me! I must know! Will he die... !" She put tightly closed fists to her breast. "I want to die myself!" she cried, "because I can not go on..." She stopped and sent him a look of apology. "Forgive this outburst, Ewan. I am like someone possessed; I feel I am going out of my mind."

"A state, dear Eleanor, that does neither of us any good. I must admit that I hesitated about coming over and bethought myself to send a letter in preference, then saw that it was a coward's way to shirk the distress I am going through because of the heartache you are suffering. Oh, yes, I pictured this very scene, and my own helplessness to comfort you. Shall I send for John to come over?"

She shook her head.

"Not yet. I want to – to talk about Edward, to know everything and the worst that can happen to him."

She thought of the months of waiting in an agony of suspense, months that seemed to lengthen into years as she pictured Edward still confined to the apartment and the grounds surrounding the castle. Her one comfort was that Ewan had managed to persuade the Earl to allow the brothers to live together in the one apartment which had two bedrooms and a very comfortable small drawing room. She had been over twice since that first time but Ewan had suddenly perceived that she could be in danger as, if the Earl should discover her real identity, and her relationship with his ex-Governor, nothing would afford him greater satisfaction than to throw her in prison on some vague charge just so he could torture Edward with the knowledge that his mistress was also in jail. Eleanor had protested but Ewan's case was fully supported by John, who wondered that he himself had not seen the danger.

"The worst that can happen to him," said the Deemster, "is of course—"

"Do not say it!" She shook her head and tears began streaming down her face. "I shall not listen!"

"It is my firm opinion that the Keys will – when I have spread the rumour – be as afraid of Edward's supporters as of their master. I believe the verdict will be imprisonment, not death."

He saw her cringing at his voicing of the last word and wished he had not spoken it.

"What is this rumour?" she wanted to know, sending him an interrogating glance. It was a cold November day but the drawing room at Deva Place was warm and bright from the blazing fire which burned in the huge grate. Ewan had arrived half an hour ago and a meal was being prepared for him.

"It should not be difficult for me to have the rumour spread that the supporters of Edward were ready to do some injury to the Keys if they brought in a verdict—" He spread his hands. "And it is for that reason I truly believe they will have to compromise. But, Eleanor, you must resign yourself to Edward's being imprisoned for several years."

He almost said "if not for life" but refrained. It would be cruel to reveal all that was in his mind. She was suffering enough, and in any case, it could be that his cousin would be given less than a life sentence.

"I want to go across for the trial," she was saying over the meal at which both of them picked before leaving altogether. "Do not say me nay, Ewan," she added swiftly on noticing his expression. "I must be there, giving him my support. He will feel better if I am near, so please, I beg of you, make no argument with me."

But he was shaking his head and his mouth was set in a firm implacable line.

"Edward would not want it, Eleanor. I say this because I have in fact made a mention of it to him. He was most vehement that you should not be there."

"But—"

"No buts. Edward has given me a firm order to make sure you do not attend his trial. You would not deny his wishes, surely?"

Her body sagged. She wanted to be near him at this most terrible time of his whole life, wanted to give him comfort by sending her thoughts to his across and between all the people who would be present on the occasion where the hated Derby would be presiding, gloating that at last he had one of the Christians where he wanted him, standing accused of treason.

"I shall have to bow to his wishes," she murmured at last. She looked him through a mist of tears. "You will come quickly to me, though, when it is all over?"

"I promise, my dear, that you will have the result just as quickly as possible."

*

Government officers, the Deemsters and the twenty-four Keys were assembled at Castle Rushen where Captain Edward Christian, ex-Sergeant Major of the land forces of the Isle of Mann, stood charged with 'several and many most mutinous and dangerous combinations and practices, conspiracies and strange misdeameanours against the peace of our Sovereign Lord, ye King, and the Lord of this Island".

Ewan's face was pale and grave. He had set the rumour circling among the Keys, that the people, smarting under the punishments meted out to them by fines and imprisonment so recently inflicted by Derby and incensed by the refusal of the Lord to permit their hero a trial by jury, were ready to set about the Keys if their verdict was sentence of death.

Several of the Christian Clan had been busy putting fear into the twenty-four concerned and reminding them that unrest was still bubbling beneath the surface and that it required very little to have it boiling over.

And the first to be attacked would be the Keys.

Now as he sat in the courtroom the Deemster was wondering if the scheme had worked since he was unable to tell from the mask-like faces of many of the Keys. Would they dare offend the Lord by sparing the accused the sentence he in his malevolence desired with an almost insane intensity? Or would they be so in fear of him, and any reprisals, that they would obey the order which he had obviously given?

That this trial was unfair would surely go down in history, thought Ewan as he listened to the charges being read out, his cousin being accused of inciting rebellion, encouraging the people not to pay tithes, that he had attempted to frame a new form of Government by which the House of Keys would be elected by the people and not by the Lord, and many other charges were brought against him. When the indictment came to an end Ewan's dark eyes were narrowed. The sly and wily Lord of the Isle had deliberately had no mention made of the true basis of the long-standing feud: the question of land tenures. This was the real grievance, the festering sore that refused to heal, the one important issue which Edward had repeatedly brought to the fore, and it had not been included in the accusations against the ex-Governor. When the matter of Edward's having 'assumed unto himself the chief power and command of the chief fort and garrison of the island – Castle Peel, so that he might better enable himself to overthrow the government' Ewan saw his cousin give a great start – and no wonder, seeing that the Lord had himself given him command of the militia with instructions to make Peel Castle his headquarters and to train an army there. Ewan himself gasped in astonishment when Edward was charged with – according to the word of the Earl – being in process of selling the island to a foreign power, and had not the Earl made his timely appearance the ex-Governor would have 'delivered the whole Island and its People thereof to the invasion of this foreign enemy in these dangerous and distracted times.'

The Earl had told his cronies that there was much work to be done before a trial could take place, Ewan recalled, having received this piece of information from one of his servants whose friend was in the service of the Earl. So this then was the 'work' mentioned, this fabrication invented by the Earl in order to ensure his conviction.

The Deemster saw there was only one conclusion possible, and especially as the Captain, aghast at the abundance of false evidence produced by his enemy, refused to plead. He was too proud, the self-possessed sea captain, and he was taken away with his head held high.

He had been fined a thousand marks, 'to be levied on the lands tenements, goods and chattels of the said Edward Christian to the use of the Most Honourable the Lord of the Island of Mann. And his body to perpetual imprisonment..." Among those signing were Governor Greenhalshe, and Cannell, who had accepted bribes on more than one occasion from the Earl. Ewan had proof of it. And Ewan thought he had never known a worse moment than when he was compelled, because of his office as Deemster, to sign also.

It was a harsh sentence but at least Edward's life was saved, the Deemster was telling his sons when later in the day they met for supper at Milntowne.

"But life, father," protested William whose admiration for Edward was never concealed. He had often told his father that in his own fight for freedom from oppression he would use Edward's methods as an example. "Will it be life, or can there be a chance that he could be free in a few years' time?"

"Can you see Derby releasing him, now that he has a Christian penned up in prison?" John put in sceptically. "No, our kinsman will die there."

"And his brother—" Ewan frowned and set his teeth. "What has the fiend in store for him, I wonder?"

"We can only wait and see. But it was Edward's persistent bringing up of the question of the land tenures that put him so much out of favour with the Earl. William was a more passive objector."

Ewan said after a while, bringing to the fore what all had in their minds but none could bring himself to voice,

"Eleanor? I promised I would hasten to her with the result. I am going to Chester tomorrow... but I would rather cut off my hand than face this task."

Yet strangely, Eleanor took the news calmly and it occurred to Ewan at once that she had expected the death sentence so the fact that her lover was to live came as a relief. But reaction would set in once she realised she would never set eyes on him ever again, since it was unlikely the Earl would allow him visitors. And of course there would always be the danger to which she would expose herself if she went to the island.

"The Earl," she said after a long silence had stretched between them, "how did he take it – the prison sentence, I mean, when he was so determined to have Edward's life?"

"I have no knowledge of his reaction as yet. I was away early this morning to catch the boat. However, he will obviously be gnashing his teeth, and probably devising some punishment for the Keys' defiance."

"Ewan, do you feel that it really is life?" She was still calm; it was unnatural and the Deemster was sorely troubled about her. She had two maids and the footman, but he decided to call and see Sir John and ask that he come over and stay at Deva Place for a few days, if Eleanor would agree, that was.

"It is hard to predict," he replied. "Who knows what might happen? Supposing the Earl died? His son might be persuaded to release him."

"The Earl is young, only thirty-six years old." And my Edward is fifty-three, she added, but to herself. "It is most unlikely that Lord Derby will die first." A sob caught her throat but the outburst of grief which Ewan expected never materialised. "Shall I ever see him again?"

An excruciating pain shot through her head and involuntarily she put a hand to it. "That our love affair would end like this..." She lifted tear-bright eyes to his. "You know," she murmured, so softly that he only just caught the words, "I never ever thought of a time when we would be separated forever."

The Deemster said nothing. In fact, he was so choked up himself that even to attempt words would be futile. And so they sat still and quiet by the glowing fire, its flames providing the only light in the room, as the candles were not yet lighted, as it was only three o' clock in the afternoon. But it was a very dull day, with grey glowering clouds suggesting the approach of a storm, or perhaps it was going to snow. She thought: Christmas will be here in a few days' time, and this year Edward said he would come, as we had not been together at this lovely time for many a year.

"And now," she whispered, unaware she spoke her thoughts aloud, "We shall never have a Christmas with each other, not ever... in *this* world..."

Ewan pressed his lips together. Never in his whole life had emotion affected him like this. He was actually fighting to hold back the tears! He, the tough old scion of Viking stock... almost weeping!

She was staring into the fire, her small hands clasped together and resting on her knees, her body rocking back and to, almost imperceptibly. The amber-flickering silence of the cosy room seemed filled with drama as if something were being born that would haunt it forever more.

She spoke at last, turning to look at him, this noble head of the clan Christian who had almost from the beginning accepted her into the family, perhaps not quite as an equal at first, but for a long time now she had been given the status of a wife. Her children bore the name Christian and that had pleased the Deemster about whom the Earl had once declared that someone in a mood of humour had said that the Deemster did not get so many bastards for lust's sake but for policy, to make the name flourish, and the Earl had spoken with dissatisfaction of the Manx custom of giving bastards the father's name.

"I suppose I had it in my mind that we would die together."

"What...?" He frowned in puzzlement. "What are you talking about, Eleanor?"

"Ah, it was that my thoughts went back, Ewan..." She managed a little twisted smile. "I was saying that I never saw a time when we would be separated forever – as we are now. And it must have been that my mind insisted that we would die together—" She broke with a self-deprecating shake of the head. "Take no notice, Ewan, I am not of clear brain—" She brushed a hand through her hair impatiently. He wondered if she were coming close to a breakdown and it was with a feeling of relief that he let his eyes wander to the window from which, in the distance across the river, could be seen the sturdy black and white mansion – Kingsley Hall. A staunch friend, was John, patient and kind, a man with love and hope in his heart. Why did a woman like Eleanor have to love a man like Edward who, after all, had given her so little? Strange creatures, women.

He stayed at Diva Place for two days, leaving with an easy mind only because Eleanor, wise to the state she was in, had agreed to John's moving in to Deva Place for a while.

On the morning he was leaving she clung to him.

"Give my love to my dearest Edward, and the letter I have written, and tell him I will write every day of my life."

"You have put that in your letter, dear."

"Yes, but tell him also. Tell him I love him and that I shall pray constantly that the good Lord will be with him, and that the day might come when we shall be able to see each other and never to give up hope."

"Eleanor, dear, all this is in the letter." Ewan touched her cheek with his lips. "I shall tell him all the same," he promised gently. And do keep in mind that he will be in comfortable lodgings and he is free to walk in the grounds of the castle. The views are beautiful as you know."

"I fear the Earl in his anger at failing to have his life might put him in a dungeon—"

"Then fear not," he broke in roughly. "I still have a few things up my sleeve. Derby and I have sparred many times; he wins, then I win, and as he has had several wins recently it is my turn. He knows how far to go, believe me. Underneath all the princely swagger there still lurks a fear of the power of the Christians."

He was recalling the Earl's once saying that he liked not the way the Christians had made themselves chiefs in the isle, occupying all the best houses and lands, matching with the best families in marriage, and he had sneeringly added that these Christians would even have called themselves kings had they dared.

*

A shock was to meet the Deemster on his return to the island. William, his son, was at Milntowne when he entered, booted and spurred and hungry.

"Father, you will not believe it, but Derby has put it abroad that no matter what the sentence passed on Edward by the court, he has the power to overrule it. He wants our cousin's life!" William was in a fever of wrath. "That man's hatred of us knows no bounds – and by the way, another attempt was made on his life. Unfortunately it failed."

The Deemster's face was grim. He feared for this patriot son of his, the dark one as he was sometimes called. He said sternly,

"You will make me a promise, William. You will never be tempted to make a similar move?"

"Attempt to kill him? I might!"

"William, you do happen to be in his favour and I advise you to keep it that way. My God, man, you have just had proof of his insane hatred of our family! Do you want to find yourself in the same position as Edward?"

Fearlessly his son stared into his eyes.

"Something has to be done. We could have another forty years of despotic rule before us. We ought to appeal to the King."

"The King?" with a lift of his brows. "The King has more on his mind than ever before. His war is not going as well as he had hoped. No, my son, a petition to the King would only find its way on to a fire." He became thoughtful. "I believe I can deal with this latest threat... yes, I am sure I can." He looked at his son again. "I want that promise, William. If you have no thought for your own well-being then please me by thinking of your wife and children!"

The stern old man was staring directly into the very dark eyes of one of the nation's staunchest patriots, a man who, he believed, could fight to the death for a cause. Fear did not often enter into the Deemster's heart, but it did now. Perhaps he should insist on his leaving the isle, going over to Lancashire where he had lived in the early years of his marriage to Elizabeth Cockshutt. Ewan had given him some coal mines he owned in the hope that his restless son would settle down and exploit them and for a time William appeared to be content, having acquired a charming house at Nether Sparth where Elizabeth gave birth to two children. But on a sudden impulse William had brought in trustees to manage the mines and returned with his wife and children to his homeland where, installed by his father at the estate of Ronaldsway which he was now farming successfully, he made some creditable renovations to the ancient house which had originally been the dwelling of King Orry. It was a pleasant enough estate, mused the Deemster, still staring into his son's eyes, with its lands spreading around and nothing to mar the views between it and the hills to the north and east, nor was there anything to blot the landscape stretching away to   two miles distant, and it was owing to its closeness to Castle Rushen that the Earl had so badly wished to acquire the Ronaldsway estate. The Deemster moved, to pull a bellrope. His son was moving to the window, his shoulders squared, his doublet open to reveal white linen shirting beneath. Anger bottled up in congestion seemed to be consuming him. He had always admired Edward, this second cousin of his, and as a young child he would listen, spellbound, to the tales Edward would have to tell of his exploits at sea.

Edward's plight could spell danger for William, whose mood was murderous at this moment.

A lackey entered the room and an order was given for wine and refreshments to be brought.

William swung around, eyes blazing.

"Are we to bend to the tyranny? Are we to let Edward die? Yes, I am in favour with Derby at present but I am a Christian and there never can be harmony between us and the Stanleys. I do not need to tell you that, Father."

"Calm yourself, my son. Violence gains nothing in the end. I move more subtly in my little private battles with our Lord Derby. Edward shall not die, I promise you—"

"He could be dead already!"

"Not so, and you very well know it. If Edward were to die, it would be a public execution since that would be what the Earl would order, and delight in. You said just now that another attempt has been made on his life. This circumstance, William, will have cautioned him to count the cost of a thoughtless and impulsive move on his part. Trouble yourself no more about Edward. I can deal successfully with his lordship."

"If you are so sure you can save his life then why can you not get his release altogether?"

Ewan made an impatient gesture with his hands.

"Edward has been tried and sentenced to imprisonment. This I have no power to change. But he was not sentenced to die and this I have the power to uphold – that is, I can prevent the sentence being changed."

"But as I see it, Derby does have the power to overrule the court's decision. After all, he is the ruler of the island—"

"William, please trust me. As I say, *I* have the power to save our cousin's life."

*

Two days after the Deemster had left Chester Sir John Kingsley was pacing the floor of the drawing room at Deva Place.

"Surely you can wait till we can get a message to Ewan," he said with a sort of desperation in his voice. "This – premonition as you call it, could be all wrong. I am sure it is all wrong."

"John—" Eleanor halted his pacing with a hand on his arm. "I know that Edward is in grave danger. The knowledge seemed to come to me in a flash, while I was sleeping, and it woke me. I was wet through with sweat and very, very frightened. Edward and I are so close, John, that I am able to receive this message from him. Lord Derby wanted his death; Ewan told me, and when we discussed the sentence both Ewan and I agreed that the Earl would be mad with fury that Edward was not to die. But now... I am sure the Earl is going to have him killed. I must go over, must see Edward before – before..."

A flood of tears, the terrible sound of sobs, the hands outstretched imploringly... Unable to resist all these John turned and held her close and found himself saying, very much against his will,

"Stop crying, dearest Eleanor. I will go with you to the island."

*

The sea was rough, and throughout the voyage Eleanor fretted at the inevitable length of time the ship was taking. John, greatly troubled for her safety once she was on the island, was bitterly regretting his weakness in agreeing to bring her, and yet what else could he have done? She had threatened to go alone and that he would never have allowed to happen. Seeing her huddled by the rail, distressed and cold, was enough to break his heart. He went to her; she let him hold her close and he hoped his own body warmth would be transferred to hers. She shuddered now and then, but he was gratified to know that she was in fact deriving not only warmth but comfort from his closeness to her. How he loved her! She had been the love of his life for so long, while he had grown from boyhood to manhood and now he was approaching middle age.

And he was praying to the dear Lord to save the man who had stood in his way all this time.

"We will stay at the inn," she decided as the Bay of Ramsey at last came into view. "I think that Ewan would be very annoyed and he can be stern at times so that I feel sure he will angry with us both."

"Eleanor, just what are your plans once we are on the island? I have asked you several times. You have no plans, have you, other than making your way to Peel Castle. But what then? How do you gain entry – and even if you do..." He tailed off, not daring to show his impatience lest he distress her even more. "I feel we must make our way to Milntowne first, dear. It is the only way, and apart from anything else, we shall have first-hand news – you will most probably have this fear set at rest, for as I have said before, I trust not this dream of yours, and it is my belief too that the Earl will have more sense than to take Edward's life at a time when there is so much unrest on the isle."

"He is not afraid of an uprising," she returned flatly. "He has crushed the nation's spirit with a show of arms which he would not hesitate to use, so ruthless is this man."

"Then if you are not going to Milntowne what are you going to do?" he asked persistently.

She remained silent, afraid to tell him of her intention of seeing the Earl himself. That it was a wild illogical decision was the thought continually hammering in her brain. A man with such hate in his heart would never be moved by the pleading of his prisoner's mistress, and yet some spirit was forcing her; it was as if she was being led and not doing this of her own volition. The thing was: how could she get away from John? If they stayed at the inn, though, it should not be too difficult... she could slip away after they had been shown to their separate bedchambers. Would the Earl see her? It was a long way to Castle Rushen where he lived when on the island – or maybe he was at Peel? Yes, she would go to Peel where she would be close to her beloved Edward. And if her plea to the Lord was successful she would surely be allowed to visit him.

Suddenly the impossibility of the whole idea was brought home to her with stark reality as all the difficulties that had previously been thrown from her mind returned in full force. How could she walk all the way from Ramsey to Peel? And in any case, she would be missed by John within half an hour at most of leaving the inn and he would get a horse and ride immediately to Milntowne. Ewan would automatically know she was on her way to Peel; she would be caught up with along the road... She turned in John's arms and looked up at him.

"I have no idea what to do," she confessed in a breaking voice. "All I know is that I want to be with Edward – I must be with him, John, so please do something!"

It had to be Milntowne, and pray the Deemster was at home.

*

The wrath of the Deemster, who had always been so kind to her, resulted in a breakdown of nerves and a cry of protest rang through the room.

"Stop! Stop upbraiding me! I will not listen—" She pressed her hands to her ears. "Leave me alone! I want to see the Earl – he can not kill my Edward. I shall kill him first. Yes, I shall take a knife with me and if the Earl denies my pleading I shall run it through his heart!"

"Eleanor, my dear child..." John's gentle voice made no impression on her; she paced wildly about the room, glowering at Ewan and accusing him of being cruel and unfeeling and asking why he should suppose she had to seek *his* permission to come on the island. He acted at last, taking her by the shoulders and shaking her.

"Ewan," began Sir John in protest. "That is not the way."

"It is the only way," was his grim rejoinder. "As for you – I am at a total loss to understand how you could be so foolhardy as to bring her here; you must have realised the danger! Nothing would give Derby greater satisfaction, yea, and pleasure, to have this woman captive. He would certainly have something to gloat about then." His mouth was tight, his eyes glimmering with rage, his hands bruising Eleanor's shoulders. He looked down at her. "Did it never occur to you that this mad act could bring great suffering to the very man you want to help?"

"Suffering?" Her spasm of uncontrol had spent itself, helped by the Deemster's action. "What do you mean?"

He almost flung her from him in his anger and impatience.

"Have you no imagination, woman! How will he feel if you are imprisoned in a dungeon... beneath the comfortable apartment wherein he is lodged! Think, and you—" He turned on Sir John. "Did you never consider that!"

John spread his hands in a little helpless gesture.

"I have already explained, Ewan, the quandary I was in. Would you have had me let Eleanor come alone?"

"I would have had you lock her in her bedchamber till she came round to some logical thinking!" was the Deemster's scathing rejoinder, at which John merely gave a sigh and spread his hands again. Best not to argue with Ewan in this mood – and in all fairness John could not but sympathise with him because he was now in a quandary too, wondering what to do with Eleanor – he could either hide her here indefinitely or try to get her off the island again. But there was just one difficulty to that solution, because it was no solution at all, since, judging by what had already taken place, Eleanor would not be persuaded to leave until she knew definitely the fate of her lover.

"Well," sighed Ewan with relief when all was quiet again in his drawing room, "perhaps, Eleanor, you are in a fit state to listen to what I have to say."

She bit her lip, looking contrite.

"I am so sorry, dear Ewan, for all those horrid—"

"Forget it," abruptly as he held up a hand. "I in turn should have controlled my temper. As it was, none of us had any chance of talking. However, the scene is over and I can now tell you, Eleanor, that Edward will not die." Again he lifted a hand. "Do not either of you interrupt or I shall lose my temper again – and hate myself for it since I have always prided myself on possessing a well-balanced temperament. I have the means of saving my cousin's life - but please refrain from asking me to explain, as I have no intention of doing so. What transpires – and saves Edward's life – is between the Earl and me. He comes here this evening at my invitation. We shall sup together, drink wine and look to be in good cheer with one another."

"You would entertain the Earl here?"

"Eleanor," warned Sir John quietly.

"The Earl and I shall chat – quite amicably," continued the Deemster as if no interruption had occurred, "as we have several times in the past. We each have things to talk over—" His shrewd dark eyes wandered from Eleanor to John and in their depths was a very odd expression, an unreadable expression, so Eleanor wondered why she should have the idea that the Deemster was feeling most inordinately satisfied with himself. "I look forward to the pleasure of his lordship's company, and the conviviality we shall enjoy together. You know," he added finally, "the Lord of our Isle is a most accomplished conversationalist."

The Deemster rarely smiled, but a half smile came to his lips and hovered there for a moment before, becoming suddenly brisk, he suggested they take some refreshments.

*

The dining saloon at Milntowne had seen many gatherings of Christians down through the ages, but tonight there sat just one, the powerful head of the clan, and his invited guest, the powerful Lord of the Isle. Both were wily, both on guard... and each was confident that the winning move would be his. Oh, yes, both knew this apparently social occasion held some underlying significance. How could it be otherwise, with the Deemster's kin under sentence of death?

"It is a pleasure to have your company, James." Ewan produced one of his rare smiles; the Earl responded. "Supper is slightly delayed but it is cosy, is it not, in here? We shall drink to – er – friendship?" So cool the stare directed at his lordship, and equally cool his own stare. Two clever manipulators, each profoundly aware of the long-standing feud whose cause was the land tenures. Or should it rather be put down to the rapacity of the Stanleys whose acquisitions had always come easily as favours from kings or by advantageous marriages? Yes, vast wealth had been accumulated easily... until the frustration of Manx resistance to demands to give up lands held through so many generations.

The two men drank several glasses of wine before and during the meal, but neither was adversely affected; each brain was as clear as before the first sip was taken.

It was the Earl who eventually broke the cover of pretence by saying sardonically, and with all the arrogance of his breed,

"Suppose we get down to the reason why I am invited here, Ewan? The meal was most enjoyable, as was our friendly conversation, but your lord now desires that he shall be informed of what you have in mind, though I am sure I need not warn you of the futility of a plea for the traitor's life."

So smooth and confident. The Deemster smiled to himself and reached out to take a piece of marchpane from a pewter dish, a sweetmeat he rarely ate but tonight he had a sweet tooth.

"Lord Derby," he chided softly, "I never plead."

"Surely you are not contemplating a demand?"

"Not that either. Nay, I asked you here because there are several matters for our discussion." He eyed the marchpane then put it back in the dish. The desire had passed. "One matter is that of the Ronaldsway estate which as you know I inherited from my sister."

"The transfer was illegal. The property was mine by my right of the Lord, because there was no direct heir."

"The law of Corbes is legal. However, my son and I have talked of your claim, James, and we both felt sympathetic towards it." He paused to send his opponent a level look. Perception had already dawned in the Earl's dark eyes. "Yes, we agreed that perhaps you were entitled to put in a claim. And in view of our findings we both felt that William should accept the lease for three lives which you offered and which we at first refused."

The Earl gave a gust of laughter.

"A well-timed concession, friend Ewan, but it will not serve." The mood changed dramatically: the affability was gone. "I want the traitor's life and nothing you can do – I repeat, nothing – will deny me the pleasure of seeing him publicly shot on Hango Hill!" The thin lips were left slightly apart and moisture formed upon them.

"Nay, my dear Christian, you will have to think of something better than that!"

"So you do not want the lease for three lives?" The Deemster's manner had lost none of its cool confidence, and the Earl was puzzled.

"I shall have the lease eventually," returned his lordship with the same cool confidence being shown by his companion.

"Ah, well, we shall leave this in abeyance for the present—"

"Seeing that the bribe fell on deaf ears," sneered the Earl taking up the flagon and pouring himself more wine. The glass was held in his hand a while, being twisted around so as to catch the amber light from the candles set in their holders in the middle of the table. "What else have you in mind?" pressed Lord Derby putting the glass to his lips and regarding the Deemster over its rim.

"Oh, it is nothing in the way of a bribe – I dislike this word, my lord. Please do not let us use it again." Ewan's voice was curt with displeasure.

"As you wish," smiled the Earl, eyes twinkling with humour. "There is much I admire in you, Christian. But do go on. You have some other thing on your mind?"

"It is merely something that came to my ears – some time ago, as a matter of fact. Then some further evidence came more recently as a result of some inquiries – discreet inquiries, of course that I had set in motion." He waved a hand. "You have quaffed your wine quickly. Do partake of more."

"Thank you." The Earl was frowning suddenly. Ronaldsway... He wanted that estate badly. A lease for three lives being offered...

"You were saying?"

"Ah, yes. I wonder, James, how many of your subjects, including all your high officers, are in the knowledge of your having seized – quite illegally, I am assured by one of my kin who practises law – certain ecclesiastical revenues for the benefit of your personal household upkeep, both here and in England. This has gone on for some long time—" He gestured to the lackey standing by and ordered him to bring in more coal for the fire. "We all know, of course, why you abstained from appointing a bishop; you needed the bishopric funds for the filling of your own purse..." ,His eyes lingered on his adversary's face as he picked up his glass and began drinking the wine. "There are some very valuable rents attached to these various ecclesiastical establishments and it would be interesting to learn just how you use them—"

"Christian! That is enough! What is all this about? But why do I ask! Let us not talk of bribery, you say – but you are not slow in taking about threats." An ugly light had entered Ewan's eyes and the thin lips were tightly compressed. "I have said I intend to have your cousin's life, and I shall! Spread your lies and I shall have *you* charged—" He was brought to a halt by the imperative lift of the Deemster's hand.

"No feigning innocence, I pray you. It irks me, James, and wastes time. What I have accused you of can be proved." He regarded him with a direct stare. "I believe you know me well enough to be sure I have my facts correct before voicing them."

The Earl's teeth could be heard grinding together.

"Edward Christian is a traitor and the penalty is death!"

"Did you really expect him to turn his soldiery on his own people?"

"I expected loyalty, obedience to my Governor who acts in my name."

The Deemster was shaking his head from side to side.

"What a lot you have to learn about people, James. The Christians in their varied capacities as your officers over the years, have endeavoured to give you loyalty. But no Manxman is going to give the order for brother to fight brother on this isle. Am I to assume that the main grievance you have against my cousin is his flat refusal to supply Greenhalshe – who is not a Manxman, remember, but one of your cronies from Lancashire – with the means to kill and maim a people who are already living in misery?"

"You exaggerate! These people are lazy, slothful and without any ambition. If you want to eat you work; otherwise you starve."

A dangerous glint came to the Deemster's eyes. This man was not fit to live, much less rule over an island. Nothing would have afforded him greater satisfaction than to tell him what he thought about him but he had a mission to accomplish and that was his urgent priority. He was just as determined to save Edward's life as was the Earl to take it.

"I asked if your main grievance against my cousin was his refusal to supply your Governor with troops?"

"Yes," gritted the Earl. "I admit it! There would have been no need for me to go to the expense of bringing over my own private militia if that traitor had carried out his duty to me as his overlord!"

"I noticed at the trial there was no mention of the other vexed issue: that of the land tenures. I congratulate you on your stratagem," the Deemster went on tersely. "Had that question been mentioned as one of the charges Edward would immediately have had the support of every landowner in this country – and here I am including those with small holdings whose lands you also desire to seize for yourself."

The Earl's face was purple with rage. Why had not one of his forebears settled the land question once and for all? Why was it not settled by the seizure of the lands by force? He said at last,

"Just what is the point of all this? You have made it clear that you are asking for a reprieve for the ex-Governor and I have made it clear that there will be none." But there was less force in the tenor of his voice this time and this was far from going unnoticed by the observant Deemster.

"There did come to light another small matter," he began slowly, measuring each word so that it would register with the man who was now slightly the worse for the wine he had quaffed. "It came as a complete surprise – this little secret which was unearthed by one of the men I engaged in looking into your affairs." Still slowly came the words and for a moment the Earl was clearly puzzled. "I am sure you would not wish yourself the embarrassment which this added discovery would cause – on top of the matter of the seizure of the ecclesiastical benefices I have mentioned... Er, are you quite sure, James, about the Ronaldsway lease?" No answer but the Earl's face was by now twisted with fury. "The secret of this new discovery is of course safe with me. I would never gossip, but—" He looked distressed, which did not deceive his companion at all. "My servant, the one who accidentally made this discovery – but I dare say I can quiet him, for your sake... and that of your lady Countess." He paused before saying, very softly, "I see you are enlightened as to this little secret." Reaching over he poured more wine into the Earl's glass. "The Ronaldsway lease – it is a most desirable property, is it not? But you know because you have always wanted it. My son has done many improvements to it and the farmlands are most productive. But then you know what an excellent manager William is, since he has for some time managed your Abbeylands for you – the lands bestowed on the Stanleys by the late King James as a... favour?"

"Just what are you insinuating!" The Earl was put out at last and the Deemster smiled to himself within the cover of his beard. The Earl made one last attempt, though, beginning to bluster as he accused the Deemster of lying, of threatening his overlord, of attempted bribery. And finally he declared he would have him arrested on the morrow and thrown into prison.

It was a few minutes later, as he was seeing his guest to the door, that Ewan said imperturbably,

"Also, there is the question of Edward's brother, William. As you do not appear to have any charges against him – at least, none that would stand in court – I suggest you release him at once. Good night, James. Mind the ruts in the road which have deepened with the rain. I would not want your horse to stumble, so take care."

He closed the door, called for some wine and went into the drawing room where a fire glowed and the candles in their sconces sent a soothing warmth around the panelled walls. He sank into a chair when the wine came and allowed a long, contented sigh to issue from his lips, even though his stolid countenance remained unmoving.

The wine was good, given him many years ago by a young merchant adventurer. Ewan had not offered it to his guest; a lesser vintage was good enough for him.

At last he smiled to himself. It had not been even necessary actually to mention the charming house on the hill above Douglas where recently had come to live a pretty maid with her tirewoman...

His was the winning move... but then he had known that it would be. It was a pity, though, that Ronaldsway had to be the bargaining power – yes, a pity. It had been quite a victory, having originally thwarted the Earl's claim to it.

*

The Deemster was preparing for his departure from the island. He was aging rapidly, and with his innate shrewdness he had known for some years that there would be no real peace in Mann in his lifetime.

But in the end it was a reluctant decision, something he knew he must do but which could not be done without a certain amount of regret since after all the Isle of Mann was his homeland and anywhere else would be exile. He was happy with his house, though, the lovely Unerigg Hall with its forty-eight rooms and its extensive demesne lands. Here he would quietly live out the few remaining years of his life. Even though he had felt his son, William, to be safe, he had tried to persuade him to leave and take up residence at Nether Sparth, which he still owned, but he and his wife were happy farming Ronaldsway. William hated the Earl for keeping Edward in prison but he was wise enough to take advantage of his secure position, since there was nothing to be gained by antagonising the powerful overlord; on the contrary, there would be much to lose, as Derby was not hesitating to continue bringing charges against all kinds of people. Having regretted freeing William, Edward's brother, he had had him summoned before the Court of General Gaol Delivery, charged with treason. He wanted him in prison alongside his brother. But by the intervention of Ewan he was released, but six others charged with him were heavily fined for seditious activities against the Government. Derby had to be absent from the island, having rushed over to Lathom at the urgent request of his wife, for help against the siege invested by the Parliamentarians. After Prince Rupert came to the rescue he and Derby captured Bolton but were defeated at the battle of Marston Moor, which gave Cromwell control of the north of England.

"You had better go to the Isle of Mann," the King ordered Derby, "and concentrate on its defences."

The Countess and her children had already fled there for safety and were in residence at Castle Rushen. It was a disappointment to Ewan that his son refused to leave, as he saw danger for him if a rebellion should break out. However, the bargain struck over Ronaldsway had made William's position comparatively safe, for the present.

The Deemster visited Eleanor soon after he moved to Cumberland and stayed for three weeks. Her son had married an Irish heiress, Elizabeth, daughter of Sir Joseph Wattinger, and was living in a fine house on the outskirts of Dublin, where he had joined a firm of lawyers. Susanna was happy in her new country and Eleanor had recently received a letter from her telling of a happy event soon to come to her and her husband.

"To think," said Eleanor as she and Ewan strolled along the river bank, "I shall soon be a grandmother. I feel quite old."

"But you do not look old, my dear." He stopped to examine her face. It did have a few lines, and the sadness that had come into her life had taken most of the sparkle from her eyes. The full generous mouth was still rosy and tempting. Ewan wondered just how many times he had wanted to kiss it. "How old are you? I have forgotten."

"Forty-five. You know," she went on thoughtfully, "growing old is not what we want, and yet we insist on looking ahead – I mean, tomorrow always seems to promise more than we have today."

He sighed in sympathy with her meaning, but he could offer no words of hope. Edward was in prison for life and while ever the Earl of Derby lived, there could be no possibility of freedom for him. And even if the Earl did die, his son gave no promise of being any better. Still wild and defiant of his parents, he was in one scrape after another. It was unlikely that he would have any interest in his kingdom once the war was over and they were all back at Lathom House again. Of course, should the Parliamentarians win, then all the lands belonging to the Derbys would be confiscated permanently.

"You would be very lonely here but for John," he mused walking on again. "I wonder if you fully appreciate your good fortune in having such a faithful friend as he?"

"You have no idea how often I thank the dear Lord for that friendship, and John does know that I care about him."

"Care?"

"As a true friend. Where would I have been without him?"

The Deemster nodded mechanically and stopped again to watch a fishing boat ploughing its way against the flow of the river.

"The eels they want are upstream, you said?"

"That is right. I love this river, always have. When I was a little girl my mother would bring me here of an afternoon and we would make daisy chains and pick gillyflowers to put in our hair. Sometimes she would bring barley cakes and we would sit and have a feast."

Her thoughts had flown away, back in time, and as he looked down to see her expression Ewan thought: she is still just a little girl, and she always will be one.

"I am privileged to have known you," he told her unexpectedly. "You are certainly a very special person."

She coloured daintily and returned the compliment.

"And I am privileged to have you for my very good friend, Ewan. Whatever the future holds I have had a good life. You see, I often think of where I would be now if Edward had not – well – er…"

"Kidnapped you?" he put in laughing. "One day I must get you to tell me the whole story as I am sure it will be most diverting. But you were saying…?"

"There would only have been one thing for me to do. I would have been some lady's tirewoman, and if I had married it would have been to someone poor and I would have had a baby every year which would have made us even poorer."

"For goodness' sake! I can stand no more of such a depressing speech. Why waste time on something that never happened?"

"I know." She laughed and he thought: how many times has she laughed since that day, over a year ago now, when Edward was arrested? She had borne up better than he expected. Her fortitude was remarkable. He knew she derived comfort from writing and receiving letters. She and Edward wrote to one another every day and he saw to it that the letters were delivered in the quickest possible time. Rob's was a familiar face at the port of Chester as he went regularly to meet the particular ship which would be in that day. Usually it was one of the Deemster's but John Teare also owned ships which plied between England and the Isle of Mann and between the island and Dublin.

When Ewan had gone Eleanor felt lost and lonely because John had gone to London to visit a relative who had asked him to come. She was an aunt who had never married and she had recently lost her brother who was also her heir. John had always been close to her as a child for she had made her home with his mother and father for many years until, suddenly declaring she had seen nothing of her country, she had gone off, travelling to many towns and villages before finally deciding that London was the place for her. Eleanor had never before realised just how much she had come to rely on her dear friend, but perhaps one never does, she mused, until they are absent from one's reaching.

*

It was 1645 and Charles' defeat at the Battle of Naseby was news that greatly troubled the Earl of Derby. He had been carrying out the order of his King and fortifying the island against the possible invasion by the Parliamentarians. He built forts and increased the militia. He added to the cavalry, constantly drilled the infantry. Each parish was forced to supply men and also to pay them. Levies on the laity and clergy paid for the officers' salaries and other expenses. There was a great deal of military activity throughout the island and alongside it all the time the unrest continued to simmer. It did not help when Derby brought more English soldiers over and the people had to billet them out of their own pockets.

It was a beautiful summer day when the news was received that the Parliamentarians under Fairfax and Cromwell had secured a decisive victory at Naseby over the Royalists under the command of Charles and his nephew, Prince Rupert. The Earl and Countess of Derby were relaxing in the gardens of the castle when a messenger arrived, having come over on the Rushen sloop.

"What does it mean?" The Countess had been more concerned with beautifying and enlarging Derby House than with the war, which, she felt, was no longer the concern either of her or her husband. He had done his duty by taking part in several battles over there and in fortifying the Isle of Mann. The King would win, she believed, and then they would have all their lands restored to them and be able to take up residence again at Lathom House. But this defeat could mean that the King's chances of winning were perhaps delayed.

"It means," answered the Earl gravely, "that in my opinion, our King has lost the war."

Her heart jerked.

"No, it is not possible! Rupert is such a brilliant soldier the King can not lose."

A long, drawn-out sigh issued from the Earl's lips. He thought of the lands he owned and which had been confiscated but which he had been so confident of getting back once the Great Rebellion was over and peace came to his country again.

"It takes more than one brilliant soldier to win a war," he said at last. "Yes, Rupert is a professional soldier but the King has repeatedly vacillated. He could have marched on London after Edgehill but he seemed unable to make up his mind which advice he would take and the result was that his generals were unable to advise him at all in the end."

"You really think this is the end of the war?"

"Not quite. The King could continue the fight – and in fact I believe he will, but to me the war is lost."

The Countess swallowed, feeling sick inside. This place in which they lived was luxurious and pleasant; they entertained lavishly with glittering balls and masques, but Lathom was far more desirable and sumptuously furnished. They were surrounded by their own lush farmlands; they had a much larger number of servants than they had at Castle Rushen.

"Are you saying, James, that we shall never have our estates back – shall never live in our beautiful home again?"

"I do not know, Charlotte." He shook his head; the disastrous news had taken the very heart out of him. "These are sad times for us, but at least we have a comfortable home here."

He glanced around; the gardens, well-tended by several labourers, were aglow with colour. But he was thinking of Lathom and all its splendour. He also thought of the letter he had received, a few months ago, from the Lords' Committee saying that if he would turn over to them certain prominent Cavaliers to whom he was giving lodging at the castle, they would help in bringing about a reconciliation between him and Parliament. Perhaps he should have answered that letter instead of tossing it on the fire, treating it with the contempt it deserved. A reconciliation with Parliament would have meant the restoration of his lands. He had not been very clever over that, he decided with a grunt of self-disgust which brought a questioning glance from his wife. All he said was,

"But I was so sure, at the time, that the king would win and so I would have my estates back anyway..." He stopped on noticing Charlotte's expression. "I was merely thinking aloud, my dear. It is of no matter."

But it did matter. He gritted his teeth. The great wealth of the Stanleys had been accumulated solely because each one had been an opportunist, clear-sighted enough to know which side to be on at a critical moment in time.

And he had missed that moment in time...

*

The Earl of Derby's statement about the King's difficulty in making up his mind, was shown to be true during the next two years. He reached the point where he could not make his mind whether to continue fighting in England or to join his supporters in Scotland, but after major defeats he went from his Oxford headquarters in disguise and travelled north and made for the camp of the Scottish Covenanter army. Once there he was asked to sanction a full system of Presbyterian church government throughout the two countries. This he refused to promise and he was handed over to the English Parliament. From the safety of the Isle of Mann the tragedy over the water was watched with dismay by the Cavalier gathering at Castle Rushen, and with relative indifference by the rest of the island. It was a separate kingdom with its own government, its own ruler; not for the Manx people the problems of a country whose king had brought upon it years of war and hardship and was now plunging headlong into further disaster purely because of pride, of the stubborn clinging to the belief that he was God's deputy on earth and, therefore, answerable only to Him.

"What is to be the end of it?" Charlotte, Lady Derby who had put up such a gallant resistance to the siege of Lathom House, was afraid, probably for the first time in her life. "The King seems to have lost his senses altogether."

"He does," agreed the Earl with a sigh. He paused before adding slowly, "You have not heard the latest news, my dear. I received a letter yesterday from Prince Rupert..." Another pause, with his wife waiting with the deepest anxiety in her eyes for him to say what she already knew to be something she would hate to hear. "His Majesty is a prisoner of Cromwell's army."

"Oh, God! Cromwell – he will imprison him for life."

For life... The proud monarch who, after all, was the victim of his father's teaching... the proud King Charles of England imprisoned for life. Derby shook his head.

"It can not be," he told her confidently. "The King will be rescued. He has many loyal followers still. They will devise some way of freeing him."

"You had better increase even more our militia here, James," she advised. "I fear we shall be invaded and we must be ready when they come."

"I shall certainly put all my energies into it," he promised, and for the next few months he was busy training his army, and building up a navy. In England, Cromwell and Fairfax decided to attempt a reconciliation with the King, Cromwell suggesting a written constitution which without undermining the king's authority would yet meet with the agreement of his leading subjects.

"It looks promising." The Earl and his Cavaliers at the castle were almost jubilant at the news from England. They, like their noble host, had had their lands confiscated by Parliament and so this news filled them with hope.

"I have enjoyed being here, James, but to have my home and lands back in my possession will be a great relief. I am nostalgic for England."

Lord Carnwath glanced around. "I expect we all are."

The Earl and his wife exchanged glances. Yes, it was the same with them. They too were nostalgic for England.

It never entered the heads of any of them that the King would even yet again allow pride to rise above wisdom. But he did, beginning to play off his enemies one against the other, bargaining first with the Parliamentarians then with the Scots. He had escaped from Hampton Court to the Isle of Wight and from there his bargaining continued. The peace party among the Parliamentarians worked hard to force the King into an agreement as all they desired was a cessation of all hostility between their King and his country.

"Why does he continue to prevaricate?" The Earl's party of Royalists was gathered in a luxuriously furnished chamber in the castle, drinking ale around a long oaken table. "This is his chance to get back on his throne. Is the man going to throw it away!" Lord Niddlesdaile was seeing his hopes of the restoration of his lands fading rapidly. And across the water in Cumberland Deemster Ewan Christian was wishing he had not sent a large sum of money to support the King's cause.

"He is a fool," he told his son who was on a visit with his wife. "Can he not see his star is falling?"

"Well, none of this affects us in the island," was the naive interjection of William's wife. At which the shrewd eyes of the old man opened very wide.

"You think not? You imagine our island is going to be overlooked by Cromwell's army? Nay, if there is one thing on which Derby and I could ever agree, it is his continuing to build up the island's defences."

But how would the Earl and his crónies fare if the isle was invaded? It could be his fate to end up where he had put his ex-Governor.

Chapter Thirteen

The King was dead. On a bitterly cold winter day in January the Rushen sloop had ploughed its way through an icy sea to bring the news which informed the Cavaliers at the castle that the King had been put on trial by the army leaders after they had purged the House of Commons of the peace party which had vainly tried to bring about some kind of agreement with the King when he was on the Isle of Wight.

And, having been found guilty of waging war on his own people, King Charles I of England was publicly executed on the thirtieth of January in the year 1649 outside the Palace of Whitehall.

The Royalists, stunned that the sentence could have been carried out, could only stare speechlessly at the Earl, who had read out the contents of this second letter he had received.

"We are all done for!" Lord Digby managed to speak at last. All of them were thinking of their lost lands, and there was anger against the dead monarch. "Why was he so foolish? We shall never have our estates back!"

The Earl's eyes were staring into space. He had had his chance. If he had agreed to hand these men over to Parliament all his lands would have been restored to him.

And across the water at Unerigg Hall in Cumberland Ewan Christian was saying to one of his henchmen,

"I heard a rumour some time back that Lord Derby was promised the return of his English estates if he would deliver up those Royalists he has living on the island to the Parliamentarians. For once in the remarkably successful career of the Stanley family one of them lacked foresight – but I suppose it was bound to come one day that their luck would run out."

"How right you are, sir. But surely it is time they had a setback."

"I find myself seeing many more setbacks for our Lord, Walters."

"What kind, sir?"

"He could have to surrender the island." How wise it had been of him to leave, for much as he loved his native land he, unlike the Earl, had known just how to act for the good of his own interests. He had brought his wealth out with him, though he had left his lands to his sons.

"You think these Roundheads will invade the Isle of Mann?"

"It is possible."

"Well, our people can not be any worse off, for his lordship has treated them all very badly."

The Deemster nodded. His thoughts were naturally with his cousin, jailed six years ago. It seemed possible, in view of all that was happening, that Edward would one day be free. He wondered if the possibility had occurred to Eleanor and hoped it had not. He would hate to have her build up hopes that might never come to fruition.

It was not until the summer that the Earl received the formal requisition which he had been expecting. He was required by the English Parliament to surrender the island and he would receive the sum of fifteen thousand pounds as compensation for his loss.

"It has come from General Ireton," he told his friends. "He was one of the judges at the King's trial." He tossed the missive aside with a gesture of scorn. "Fifteen thousand pounds! It is an insult!"

But Charlotte studied the situation with more gravity than he and she reminded him of all the problems of the island, the unrest and resistance to paying tithes and other taxes.

"If we could also have our home and lands back – I am sure you could make this a condition – then we would be free of this place."

He looked at her coldly.

"You are suggesting I accept a paltry fifteen thousand pounds for my kingdom?"

"It has been troublesome to us from the beginning," she reminded him on a little note of persistence. "You remember I wrote to my mother to tell her of our difficulties?"

Ignoring that the Earl said harshly,

"I shall reply to this with the threat that if they send any further messages of the like I shall burn the paper and hang the bearer."

"James, you must not take a risk like that!"

"There is no risk. I have the island well armed and my navy is strong, too."

Despite his anger he made no attempt to answer General Ireton's letter immediately. He had to think about it. But at length he had it all set out in his mind, and he wrote from Castletown in mid-July, 1649.

"Sir, I received your letter with indignation and scorn, and return you this answer: That I cannot but wonder whence you should gather any hopes from me that I should, like you, prove treacherous to my sovereign, since you cannot but be sensible of my former actings in His late Majesty's service." He went on to say he intended keeping the island and this must be taken as his final answer. "And if you trouble me with any more messages on this occasion I will burn the paper and hang the bearer. From one who accounts it his chiefest glory to be His Majesty's most loyal and obedient servant, Derby."

Ireton's response to the Earl's message was to inform him that the Lordship of the Isle of Mann was now conferred upon Thomas Fairfax.

"Let him come!" laughed the Earl defiantly. "We can meet any challenge."

But months passed and all that disturbed the peace of the island was the continued complaints of the people, and one illustration of the hatred in which the Earl of Derby was held happened when he was in a rowing boat coming back to the shore after having been aboard one of his naval vessels out in the bay at Derby Haven.

"I was almost killed," he told Charlotte when he arrived home. "A shot was fired from the ship in the direction of the boat I was in. It was pretended to be a mistake—"

"A mistake," broke in his wife, frowning. "How could it be a mistake? But by the goodness of God you are safe!"

"Aye, but my friend Richard Weston was killed, also one of the men who was rowing us back to the shore. Also, Colonel Snead was badly injured."

"How terrible. But it was only one shot, you said? How could it do all that damage?"

"I do not know but an inquiry is afoot. There were many musket bullets coming from that gun."

"You are not popular," she murmured and he gave a gust of laughter.

"If I allowed that fact to bother me I should have taken your original advice and run away from the island. I have never been popular and it grieves me not. I have the militia to put down any serious rebellion and these half-witted subjects of mine have the full knowledge of it."

The response to the Earl's invitation to his Royalist friends – and which extended to his tenants and 'all other of His Majesty's loyal subjects who would like to repair to this island – was an influx which resulted in some further accommodation being required and that of Peel Castle served a good purpose. Derby had offered his friends safety, entertainment and encouragement to develop any qualities they might have which would help in the 'utter ruin' of the enemy.

But still there was no sign of an invasion by the Parliamentarians and during the tense period of waiting there came news that the late King's son, Charles II, had landed in Scotland, was crowned King of the Scots and was planning an invasion of England. He made the Earl of Derby commander of all the forces in Lancashire and Cheshire and elected him a Knight of the Garter.

"Pray our fortunes have changed," was the heartfelt comment of the Countess as she watched the preparations taking place for the departure of her husband and his army for the shores of England.

"We have a seriously difficult task, my dear. Cromwell's forces are stronger than ever before so I am informed."

He was going over on a preliminary visit to talk with the King, and then he would be back to make the final arrangements. But a month before he was due to leave on the first visit the island's shores were attacked, but the Earl's naval forces were more than adequate to deal with the situation and so the Earl went off with an easy mind. He took some soldiers with him – about three-quarters of his force but most of the Cavaliers who were living in the castles remained behind, in charge of the final preparations.

Just before he was due to depart for the port of Ramsey from where he was to sail, the Countess told him she had received a message from Lord Strange, who, after a serious misdemeanour five years ago when he was nineteen, had fled to his mother's relatives in Holland.

"He threatens to go over to England and join the Commonwealth."

She had withheld the news from her husband, not wishing to distress him at a time when he had so much on his mind already. But her resolve wavered; she felt he ought to know of this latest outrage threatened by the son who had caused them both so much trouble.

"The Commonwealth!" exploded the Earl. "Why? To upset us even yet again? My God, it was bad enough him marrying a bastard – and a whore from what was told us."

How well he remembered Charlotte sailing away in the sloop, hoping to avert the disaster. But on reaching England she was refused a passport by Parliament and was forced to return, having failed in her attempt to make their son see how unsuitable a marriage it was. At the Hague the band of Royalist refugees also endeavoured to dissuade him but it was all to no avail.

"He seems not to remember he will one day be Lord of Mann." There was a sob in Charlotte's voice. How come the good Lord had given them a son and heir like this?

"He shall never be Lord of Mann," gritted the Earl, his face purple with anger. "I shall disinherit him and leave everything to our other children! I consider it would be a stain on my blood if I were to allow Charles to inherit. Let us hope our son, Edward, will be more credit to us and add honour to our name."

Across the water in Cumberland where Ewan was entertaining Eleanor and John as his guests along with his son William and his wife, and their eldest son, George, a discussion was going on in the large and elegantly furnished drawing room in the west wing of Unerigg Hall.

It was a sunny spring day with daffodils glowing golden in every border and a spate of activity as nesting materials were being carried about, and sometimes fought over. Eleanor was sitting on a window seat where every now and then she would turn her head and become interested in the beauty provided by colour and movement.

"...so much going on over there that sometimes I wonder if there are to be drastic changes to our island?" Ewan's voice drifted to her and she turned back into the room. "It was good to hear that Lord Derby's navy gave a good account of itself."

"Yes, Father. The Earl has talent when it comes to organising anything to do with warfare."

"He has done some good things in the past few years," interposed Elizabeth. "He has paid for more young men to go to English universities and he is wanting a college built in the island."

"But he will have to leave it all now that he is to fight for King Charles the Second. When is the uprising planned for?"

"Next year – in the summer, I think."

"Then there will be no invasion of the island yet awhile, as Cromwell's army will be too busy preparing for the attack. Derby is in charge of all the Lancashire and Cheshire forces, you say?"

The Deemster winced as he moved his legs in trying to make himself more comfortable in his chair. His age was beginning to tell, and he had lately considered handing the hereditary office of Deemster over to his eldest son, John, who in fact was already deputising for him over on the island. But he sometimes had to go over himself if there happened to be something important to sign or a court to hold.

"Yes, father, he is in charge. And he has made me commander of whatever militia he leaves behind. It will not be much as already three parts of it is gone with him."

Ewan looked at his son. Steward of the Abbeylands and commander of the militia, Member of the Keys... The Earl was certainly favouring him. Commander of the militia... Edward had been in command of the militia and had been accused of using it to further his 'seditious activities'. William was still a staunch patriot... and his father was sorely troubled. He said with a frown,

"Have you not had second thoughts about moving from the isle? I have some more coal mines I can make over to you. And you do have a charming house at Nether Sparth—" He turned to Elizabeth. "You would like to go back there, I am sure?"

"Yes, I certainly would, but William is settled in the Isle of Mann and I am only his wife." A faint smile accompanied the last words and Eleanor thought: she is happy in her enslavement to her husband. I am sure I would have to rebel.

The conversation continued and although neither Eleanor nor John took much part, they were interested in what was being said.

But after a lull the Deemster looked at her and inquired gently,

"Where are your thoughts, my dear?"

Sad eyes suddenly smiled.

"I believe you know," she answered. "And do not scold me, Ewan, when I say that once his lordship is off the island I shall go over and visit my Edward."

He was shaking his head.

"Who is going to give you permission?"

"I have faith in bribery," was her defiant rejoinder. "I believe there is no one without a price."

This time the old man was nodding.

"'Twould be a great risk even though Derby will not be there to have you arrested."

"A risk, of course, but one I am willing to take."

"Your mind is really made up?" It was John who spoke, sending an anxious look in the Deemster's direction.

"It is. And I shall hope you will accompany me," she added with a smile.

William glanced at his father and then at his young son, George. The boy was sturdy and good-looking with his grandfather's calm and almost stolid personality. He said in a troubled voice,

"Please do not go, Aunt Eleanor. It is much too dangerous."

She smiled affectionately at him and said not to worry. She would be very careful and certainly had no intention of getting caught.

After a while John suggested he and Eleanor walk in the gardens, and she eagerly accepted. She loved being out of doors and spent most of her time in the gardens at Deva Place which were the envy of everyone who saw them. Not that many people did see them, but there was Alicia who visited sometimes with her husband and children, and Ewan came over periodically. Then there was Mother Tidley who came from gypsy stock but who now lived in a tiny cottage beneath a bridge in Chester. A quaint dwelling in an even quainter location. Eleanor loved going there, descending rough stone steps and entering into a narrow alley and then... the incredible view of the river with its green banks and the elegant mansions on the opposite side. The massive wall of the bridge to one side but the open length of the River Dee on the other. Eleanor and Widow Tidley had met in the most improbable circumstances when Eleanor, walking over the bridge carrying a basket of fruit she had purchased from the market, decided to stop and look down into the water, placing the basket on the stone top of the bridge. Too late she made a grab at it, then had to watch as it fell down on to the tiniest plot of ground imaginable. A bent old woman screamed abuse, waved a fist and said the next one to throw their rubbish over the bridge on to her land would be reported to the Lord of the Manor who would have that person put into the stocks.

"I am so sorry— "

"You will come down here and pick it up!"

"Yes – of course. I am really sorry—"

"And do not shout any cheek down to me! Come on, before I get me up there and drag you down. You will pick up every..." Her voice had trailed as her eyes caught sight of a rosy red apple by the wall of the house. Eleanor watched as she went about, examining the other fruit – ripe yellow plums and a fat brown pear. "Well, now, I have a mind to let you off this time. You can have your basket. Wait there while I bring it up."

Ten minutes later Eleanor was seated in a cosy room which smelled of lavender and thyme. Bunches of herbs seemed to be hanging all over the place. The warm milk that had been given her was fresh and sweet.

"I exchange herbs for everything," the old woman told her. "I get eggs from the farm – I have a long way to walk but I do not mind. I sell my herbs sometimes too. So if you want any just come. I am in in the afternoons because it is then I tend my herb garden."

"But you can not grow all these herbs on that tiny plot – In fact, there are no herbs growing there."

The wrinkled face with its grotesque nose and outthrust chin creased into a smile.

"I have some more ground—" She thumbed to a place away from the bridge. "It was not belonging to anybody so I took it." She stopped to listen. "Ah, I must leave you a minute. An ass has gone over the bridge and I want the dirt. It makes the herbs grow big."

Collecting a stick and a shovel, she went off, returning in a few minutes smelling very much of the country. Eleanor had quickly excused herself but the meeting was the start of what developed into what could almost be called a friendship. Widow Tidley maintained she could tell fortunes but Eleanor had never encouraged her because she had no belief in such powers. Eleanor had invited her to Deva Place because she realised that the woman loved gardens and she had nowhere to grow flowers herself. She was delighted and gave Will and Rob no peace as she asked all the names and all about how to grow them. She took cuttings given her and put them in pots so that her tiny dwelling was almost overflowing with them. And she even had them on the steps. She came about once a month and was always welcome. She would bring herbs and take flowers in exchange.

"Eleanor..." John's quiet voice brought her from her reveries and she looked up and smiled at him. "Where were you, dear?"

"With Widow Tidley – gardens always seem to remind me of her."

"She has an obsession about them. Pity she does not have a bit more land. From what you say hers would not even support a couple of rose trees."

The sun was beginning to set by the time they had walked around the extensive grounds; and tea was being served in the winter parlour.

"Just in time." Ewan's eyes went from Eleanor's to that of her companion. He had watched from the window as they crossed the wide sweep of green sward fronting the house. Her arm was tucked in his; they could have been made for each other... John looked so happy and contented. Ewan's thoughts switched to the island and the man who had been in Peel Castle for over six years. And he wondered what would happen if, should the island fall into Parliamentarian hands, Edward were released.

*

The Countess of Derby stood watching the fleet sailing away into the distance. James had taken nearly all the troops, the ships, and the Royalist refugees who had been living on the island at her husband's invitation. She was entrenched here at Rushen, and James had put a trusted man in charge at Peel Castle. She had been entrusted with the government of the island by James who had signed a commission to that effect. Her feelings were mixed, for while on the one hand there was the promise of victory and a restoration of the monarchy, on the other hand there could be another defeat. The island had been left almost defenceless – an easy target for Cromwell's army, should there be an attack. And what of the islanders themselves? A restless nation with many grievances and no means of crushing it should there be a rebellion. She thought of her life before her marriage – luxury and no complexities, but from the very beginning her marriage had been marred by turmoil and ferment. Had it not been for the island she and James could have lived a peaceful existence, but always there had been the island lurking in the background, with its troublesome people, its so-called patriots, its Clan Christian... And a Christian was in charge of the militia. But she liked William of Ronaldsway; they were neighbours and William and his wife had always been welcome guests at the glittering balls and masques which she had delighted in holding at her home, Castle Rushen. Yes, she was sure she could trust the Deemster's son, even if he was second cousin to that traitor shut up in Peel Castle.

The ships were just a smudge on the horizon when she turned and walked slowly back to her home. She felt alone, and very tired. She was fifty years old. Charles, her son, was twenty-four and could have been here supporting her, but instead he had joined the Commonwealth party. It was incredible, but then he had been a tribulation to her and James since the day he could walk. An unruly child who would always go his own way. It could have been so different, though. He could have been the one entrusted by the Earl to rule in his absence. She was glad he had been disinherited, he was unfit to be the ruler of a kingdom, no matter how small that kingdom was.

She had her ladies, and some good friends. But should the island be attacked she did wonder if she would have sufficient support for its defence. She straightened her back. She had withstood a siege once, and she would do so again! Her husband would be proud of her on his return.

*

The sun was bright in a clear blue sky; the sea had been smooth, the voyage uneventful. The Earl of Derby's spirits were high as he cast anchor on the north side of the River Wyre and the Manx soldiers scrambled ashore, with the gentlemen of quality, his Cavalier friends, moving more slowly and with dignified gait.

He heard the Manx soldiers muttering to one another; they had not been happy at being brought away from their island. And it was unfortunate for the Earl that on his way down to Worcester to join the King he met up with a superior force near the town of Wigan and coming off worst in the skirmish, lost many of his Manx soldiers; they scattered in all directions and he never saw them again. They were off, he surmised grimly, to find the quickest way back to their island. He sighed. Was there no loyalty in his subjects?

He went on, gathering more strength on the way as he was joined by other supporters of the new King. He and Charles met at Worcester. Their greeting was warm, their optimism high. They supped wine together at a candlelit table and Charles made promises which cheered the Earl's heart.

"There will be several manors – in addition, of course, to those that I shall restore to you. And perhaps a dukedom, my friend, as rewards for your faithful service. I know my father was not over grateful for the fine support you gave him, but he *would* listen to your enemies at Court, and I believe your closeness to the throne gave him some anxiety. But that is all done with and gone. You and I shall crush these regicides who will suffer the same fate as my poor father."

"Aye," mused the Earl shaking his head. "'Twas a sad day – But as you were saying, sire, it is all gone and we have a bright future before us."

"The good Lord will bless our campaign," responded the King devoutly.

*

Was it only a month since he had waved goodbye to his wife? The Earl of Derby, Lord of the Isle of Mann, sat with his head in his hands, confined in the Castle of Chester, and cursed himself for ever having given his support to the King. The battle of Worcester was over so quickly; his parting with the King was also swift as they both knew the danger were they captured by the victorious Cromwellian forces. Had Charles had more success than he? the Earl wondered. He hoped he would manage to escape to France where he could live out the rest of his life in peaceful exile.

"But me... what is to be my fate?"

He could not for one moment imagine that he would be condemned to death but he deeply regretted that scathing reply to Ireton's request that he give up the Isle of Mann to Parliament. To have threatened to hang a messenger was most unwise. Yes, a grave mistake that might cost him dear.

He stood up, frowning at the hardness of the bench they had provided for him. He would demand something more comfortable than that!

He rang a bell and soon another chair was brought.

"Put it by the table," he ordered and was respectfully obeyed. He had earlier requested pen and paper and now he sat down to write to his wife,

"My Dear Heart,

It is my misfortune to be a prisoner. The King is dead, or narrowly escaped in disguise. All the nobles of the party killed or taken, save a few. I escaped a great disaster at Wigan but met with worse at Worcester, being not so fortunate to meet any that would kill me, and thereby have put me out of the reach of envy and malice. I thought that to be here at Chester would mean I would see my daughters, but now I fear coming may cost me dear unless Almighty God whom I trust, helps me. But whatever comes I have peace in my breast but only the afflictive sense of your grief and that of my poor children. Colonel Duckenfield will come to the island, and to save bloodshed you must make condition for yourself, the children and our friends and servants. Duckenfield is a man of honour and will deal fairly with you if you deliver up the island to him." He stopped, pen poised, before continuing and then finally he signed himself, "Derby."

He thought of writing to his son but decided against it, for Charles could not be forgiven for what he had done. In his new Will the Earl had said that he was disinheriting his eldest son for disobedience to His Majesty and that to the grief of his parents he had joined the rebels of England and thereby brought a stain upon their blood if he were permitted to inherit.

Several days went by and his isolation became more and more oppressive.

"I mislike these visions that come before me..." Edward Christian – curse that haughty face that intruded so constantly into his mind! There had been nothing unjust in his treatment of the traitor. "I should never have made the bargain with Ewan, I should have had the ex-Governor's life."

But there was not only the estate he had coveted, there was that veiled threat made by the Deemster when he hinted at the house on the hill above Douglas. The Earl loved his wife, but she was grown fat and she was showing the seven years difference in their ages. There was nothing wrong in bedding a pretty maid now and then – and what right had the Deemster to accuse anyone? The bastards he had sired were beyond count.

Another day, another period of brooding... and the images relentless, insistent, baneful. The oppression – which the Christian "patriots" spoke of. He had *never* oppressed his subjects. He had merely collected the tithes and taxes due to him – and those ecclesiastical benefices... He had needed them! Did the people expect him to cut down on the expenses of his household? And the vexed and never-ending matter of the land tenures. He was the Lord of Mann, owner of the isle and, therefore, owner of all its lands. That absurd custom – the Tenure of the Straw whereby men believed their dwellings were their own ancient inheritances going back, the ex-Governor was wont to remind him, to long before the name of Stanley could be produced on anybody's lips. "I told him the Christians were much deceived if they believed they could pass lands to heirs or dispose of them otherwise, without my sanction!"

The rents they paid him as due to their overlord were mean and not of much value to him and if it should be the good Lord's will that he should return to his kingdom all would be changed. The Christians' day was done. No longer would they be the most powerful landowners on the isle. He would take those lands, if he had to do so by force.

Yet another day passed and although he had asked for information regarding the time set for his trial he had been told nothing.

He wrote to Charlotte again, fretting that there was no quicker way of getting letters to her. Pray the sea was calm, though he feared it would be rough at this time of the year. He had endured stormy passages himself with delays caused by the constant setting of sails and reefing them again, and in a really hard gale, the sea frequently breaking over the deck.

The day of his trial by court martial dawned grey and brought with it a terrible foreboding that lay like a weight on his heart and mind. He stood, icy cold and unmoving as the charges were read out: he had traitorously borne arms of Charles Stuart against Parliament; that he was guilty of a breach of an Act of Parliament of the twelfth of August sixteen hundred and fifty-one, prohibiting all correspondence with Charles Stuart or any of his party; that he had fortified his house at Lathom against the Parliament, and that he now held the Isle of Mann against them." He was found guilty and sentenced to death.

Although stunned, he squared his shoulders and walked from the court with his head held high. How could the Lord God allow this? he repeatedly asked himself in the hours that followed as he sat alone in the chill apartment he had been given, or paced its stone floor in a frenzy of movement which gradually but relentlessly seemed to be robbing him of hope.

But no, he must not give up so easily. He would send a petition to Parliament, and he would say he was instructing his wife to surrender the island into its hands. That should be enough to save his life.

But it was to no avail. He was to die for his loyalty to King and country.

*

"Your son, Lord Strange, to see you." The lackey whose task it was to serve the prisoner, made a little respectful bow and stood aside so that Charles and his wife, Helena, could enter the room.

It was not the Earl's wish to see his son but he knew Charlotte would want it, at this time when he was not long for this world.

"Father, I beg forgiveness," began his son, who did appear to be genuinely affected by his father's plight. And the Earl in his present situation felt he ought to forgive, but forget he could not. There had been too much heartache caused to him and his wife. Many were the tears she had shed at the actions of her eldest son. However, Lord Derby was, to his own astonishment, favourably impressed by the young woman of illegitimate birth, and he instantly resolved to write to Charlotte saying they had been misinformed about their son's wife, and she must forgive them both and be friends, for she would need their support after his death.

He spoke graciously to Helena, and said he thought she took good care of his son.

"I try, sir, but you must know that Charles has not a strong constitution."

He nodded. Charles was a seven-months child and never strong as a boy. Nor did he appear in fine health now.

"I am intending to ride quickly to London," Charles was promising as he and his wife made ready to depart. "I shall make an attempt to save your life."

"I thank you, my son, and I shall pray that the good Lord our Father will show Cromwell what is the right thing to do." But even as he spoke, the Earl was reminded of the terrible cruelty inflicted on Ireland by Cromwell and wondering what the Good Lord was doing then.

He felt more alone than ever after the departure of Charles and his wife, and again the images flooded in to torture him. Why was it that in these images he saw himself as a despot? He was a deeply religious man, a good husband and father; he was brave and loyal and honourable, a devoted patriot whose fight for the freedom of his country had brought him to this. He had been interested in the welfare of his Manx subjects so why had they disliked him, muttered against his just and kindly rule?

So many images and visions... the bargain made between the Deemster and himself and his refusal at first of the compromise offered. He told the Deemster he wanted the ex-Governor's life. And Ewan had looked him straight in the eye and predicted that he would leave a legacy of hate behind him on the island as it was, but if he took Edward's life his name would go down in history as the most inhuman ruler the island had ever known.

A legacy of hate. It hammered at his brain; he pressed clenched fists to his ears. He would not listen! But other visions drifted by and each drummed itself into his memory. There was that time when a petition was presented to him to free some parishioners of London and St Germans who had been sent to prison by the Vicars-General without being told the reason for the imprisonment. He had not considered it an important enough matter for the Lord of the Isle and instantly dismissed it from his mind. An act like that should not have caused people to hate him? In any case, the parishioners were freed quite soon afterwards.

Why had his God deserted him in this hour of need? Had he not always spent many hours in prayer? He remembered well some of the prayers, as he repeated them to God over and over again. One concerning the island he particularly remembered as he had made his children learn it too: "Heavenly Father. Assure this Country unto me and mine. Continue to us the power, profit and honour of it – and Thou, O God, shalt have all the glory."

Yes, he had promised God all the glory. What more could he want?

His thoughts would often turn to his wife, who had so gallantly protected their home at Lathom until the relief came in the form of Prince Rupert and his army. But there would be no army to protect her now – and it had come to his ears that Colonel Duckenfield was to invade the island. He had already written advising her to surrender, making conditions for all who resided at the castle: herself and the children, the servants and all others, but he was fearful that she would not receive the letters he was writing. And his thoughts would often go to his son and he would ask himself if he should make a new Will, reinstating him. But all the time a doubt would creep in as to whether Lord Strange's concern was genuine or not. Aware that he was disinherited, and that his father would soon be dead, was it feasible that Charles should try to bring about a change of heart in his father?

The Earl decided not to change his Will in favour of the son who had caused him so much trouble, who had run off and joined the rebels while his brothers and sister were confined to the Isle of Mann which was always in danger of invasion by Cromwell's army. The Earl might have forgiven Charles, but he had no faith in any real change in his son's character. It was as well, he thought, that Lord Strange, soon to be the eighth Earl of Derby, would never be the Lord of Mann.

*

The date set for the Earl of Derby's execution was October the fifteenth, just nine weeks after he had left the safety of the Isle of Mann to join his King at Worcester. Until the end he had held hopes of a reprieve, but the day arrived and he found himself praying, with the priest, and wishing it was all over.

On the scaffold he asked to see the axe. The block was not ready and as the minutes dragged by his breathing became more erratic as a sensation of dramatic suspense tortured his entire nervous system. His lips moved soundlessly, before, control breaking for a moment, he cried out in a strangled voice,

"How long, good Lord! How long!" Then he was calm and quiet. Turning to the executioner he said, "I beg you, good man, do your work well," and he gave him two pieces of gold. He pointed to his coffin. "When I am sleeping in my small chamber I shall not be troubled by the noise, nor the guards here."

He looked up to the sky and suddenly he was back in his little sea-girt kingdom and he saw it not ruled by the rebels of England, but by his son, Edward, a fine strong boy. He said in a clear and carrying voice, "The Kingdom of Mann belongs to the illustrious House of Stanley, in which, with the blessing of the Lord, it will continue while men live on earth."

Chapter Fourteen

St Thomas's Eve, and all the fires were lit and the candles flickering. Deva Place, patrician of its kind, shone in the light of a moonlit sky and a million stars. Eleanor, glowing and beautifully gowned, had her son over from Ireland, with his charming Irish wife. She had John over for the special supper she had arranged... and she had her beloved Edward, older, wiser – she hoped – and ready for a long rest among the lovely surroundings of Deva Place and its immediate environs.

But for the present she was alone by the fire, leaning back in the cushioned chair, pure contentment on her face.

So much had happened since that day she had stood and watched Colonel Duckenfield's expedition set sail from this Chester river.

He was going to invade the Isle of Mann whose noble lord had, only three days before, been executed in the square at Bolton. Rob had received the news only a day later and as he related the Earl's end in detail she had wept in pity for a man she had believed she would always hate with a black venom, a man she could at one time have killed herself.

The Earl of Derby was a victim of the times in which we live, she thought. Like the poor misguided King of England, he had lost his life because of pride and the arrogant belief in matters unimportant. But like the King he was now at rest, sleeping peacefully – not like his poor Countess who was a bereaved widow waiting to see what her ultimate fate would be. But meanwhile she was being comfortably cared for by William, Ewan's son who had been in charge of the militia and who had had to make a decision so many men had been forced to make before: to fight or to surrender. The Countess was advised by her husband to surrender but Edward, who had brought all the news, said she did not receive the Earl's letters until he was dead. William, with the wisdom which would have been shown by his father, had surrendered in order to save the Manx nation from a bloody war. They had suffered enough, he said, and handed over every fort except Peel and Rushen which he had not been able to take and hold. He was optimistic of this new rule. Knowing the character of Lord Strange, and unaware that his father had disinherited him, William Christian – the brown-haired one – decided it could not be any worse for his people to be ruled by the English Parliament than a wild and unreliable man like the new Earl of Derby. In fact, he was very sure it would be much better.

There had been much rejoicing in the great Christian family when Edward was released by Duckenfield and then he had come over to Chester where his faithful Eleanor was ready with open arms to receive him.

Eleanor glanced up from her daydreaming as her pretty daughter-in-law came into the room, daintily attired in a blue silk dress with the large classical sleeves which had recently come into fashion and which dominated the bodice which was fastened at the front with two jewelled clasps. It was an informal gown worn, Eleanor suspected, because Virginia was pregnant.

She smiled a welcome and patted the space beside her on the sofa.

"You look very lovely with those fair curls, my dear. I used to have similar hair to yours."

"It is still beautiful," returned the girl shyly.

"But there are many grey locks in it. Never mind, as you are aware, I am very happy these days, having Edward's father with me and saying he will stay for a long time."

"I like him very much – I admire bravery and he was brave."

"And perhaps too daring," sighed Eleanor. Then she said slowly, "Am I to have a grandchild with whom I can play?"

Virginia laughed.

"It must be awful to have grandchildren you have never seen."

"Sadly it is. And I do not expect ever to see them which is sadder still. But you – you are breeding?"

She smiled happily.

"We are both so delighted. Yes, dearest Mother, you will have this grandchild to play with for I have told Edward we must come over much more often because you are getting – er..."

"Older, my dear," laughed Eleanor. "It is one of the things over which we have no control. I am fifty-two years old. I feel sixteen again though, now that I have my dearest Edward back. Virginia," she added suddenly losing all her gaiety, "can you have any idea what it feels like to have your lover in prison and you believe it is for life?"

The girl shuddered visibly.

"I do not know how you managed."

"Without John I think I would have let myself go completely, and become an old bent and haggard woman not caring whether she lived or died."

"John is a wonderful gentleman. Edward has told me how long he has been in love with you."

"Do not look so sad, Virginia. John is not unhappy, just the reverse. You see, he always reminds himself that if there had been no Edward then he would never have met me in the first place."

At that moment John was talking to Edward. They had come down together from their respective bedchambers where they had been changing for supper.

"I have decided to go away," John said decisively. "You and Eleanor will not want a third person around. You have so much to make up for—" He lifted a protesting hand. "No, nothing will make me change my mind. The aunt of mine whom I have been visiting in London – well, she lives outside of London in the Kent countryside where she has a large estate recently inherited from a distant relative – desires to reside back in London. Having inherited the estate she felt she ought to move there but the house is far too large, she says, and in any case she likes the London life. She is making this property over to me as I am her sole heir anyway. I protested at first, until she threatened to give it away to the first gypsy who passed by so I am going to live there and repair the neglect which the property and land has suffered during the years when it was owned by an aged gentleman who lived the life of a hermit there."

Edward looked at him.

"Eleanor is going to be very upset at this news, John."

"Perhaps, but she will see it is for the best."

"Do you never think you would like to be married, John?"

A slow smile came to John's lips and hovered there. "I am forty-seven and still in love with Eleanor. How could I marry and make some woman unhappy? I feel too old, anyway to start a family, which I would have to do were I to marry a young female, as it is the desire of them all to have children."

It was a tearful parting but as John promised to come up often it was not as sad as it could have been.

"You see, dear, as I am not giving up Kingsley Hall I must keep an eye on it. But I have Rob as my most trusted steward so I shall not see anything wrong when I come up to visit."

"Perhaps Edward and I will come and see this property? It sounds charming."

"It is rather attractive. Yes, you will be welcome always." He bent to kiss her cheek. "You know that, dearest Eleanor. Be happy. But I know you will be. You have waited a long time to have Edward all to yourself."

"He intends to live here now – well, for ever, I expect, though he will have to go over to the island sometimes because he loves it."

"Even though it has a new Lord?"

"Fairfax sounds to be a nice gentleman. He did not want the King executed."

"Seems strange to think of the Lord of Mann being any other than a Derby."

"Yes it does. But the Derbys were never good for the island."

"It is now said that James had a mental disorder."

She nodded but made no comment. He kissed her again and was gone. It was a week later that Edward received a letter saying his brother was ill and not expected to get better.

"I shall have to go over," he told her, "but I shall be back as soon as I can."

"Give him my love." Eleanor let her thoughts switch to those days when she had been so welcome at William's home. So long ago, when she was only sixteen years old. William was younger than Edward but Edward was exceptional for his age, especially as he had spent eight years shut up, often in solitary confinement. And he would still be there, would have died there, had not the Earl of Derby made the mistake of not surrendering the isle earlier, because she felt sure the English Parliament would have allowed him to stay on there, probably as Governor.

It was a new experience for her to be so alone as she was after Edward had left. When she first came to Deva Place, she had her son, then had given him a sister. She had met John and had never been lonely since.

And now she had neither Edward nor John for company. She went into Chester and paid a visit to Widow Tidley. The pungent smell of herbs met her as usual and as usual fresh warm milk was given to her.

"You have never let me tell your fortune," the old woman said. "Most ladies like to have me tell their fortune."

"I do not believe in such things. I have told you many times."

Eleanor sipped her milk, her eyes wandering to the view to the river. Further along was the busy port, the port from which Duckenfield had sailed away to the Isle of Mann. But here the river was totally unspoiled, tranquil, serenely beautiful. "Rivers are strange..." She spoke her thoughts aloud. "They begin life as a tiny stream coming down a mountainside. They are joined by other small streams till they become bigger and bigger and they wash away the land as they make their way to the sea. They become wider and wider. Have you ever thought of that?" She looked up, amusement in her eyes. "I was sort of dreaming at first."

The old woman laughed and asked even yet again if she could tell her fortune.

"Very well." Eleanor decided to humour her. "I hope it will not be anything unpleasant."

"That is what most people are afraid of." Reaching out she took Eleanor's left hand. "You are going to live to be very old," she predicted, "and so you will see many changes."

"More changes?" Eleanor thought she had seen enough changes already, the country without a king being to her the most tragic. She had her lover back and that change in her life was the most important.

"I see you very happy for a time..."

"A time?"

"A long time, dearie. Then some sadness... Perhaps you are right in not wanting your fortune told..."

"I have said many times that I do not believe in it." Eleanor snatched her hand away, aware that her heart was beating overrate. And yet, if she was going to be happy for a long time what was she worrying about? She looked apologetic and held out her hand again. "You can tell me some more, because if I am to live to be very old then I am bound to have some unhappiness."

She was thinking that one day she must lose her beloved Edward, and from then on she could never be happy.

"I see you with a dark gentleman and you greatly like and respect him. He is brave, but... he loses his life for his country. He is a patriot and a martyr."

Eleanor stared then shook her head.

"I know of no such gentleman. The three I know who might have died for their country are all too old for any further activities."

"That may be, but I do see this..." The old woman stopped and let the hand fall again on to Eleanor's lap. "This man is not loved by you, only liked. But his death will make you sad."

"I can think of no one at all. And now perhaps, having told my fortune, you will be satisfied." Eleanor rose from the chair with a smile and reached up to unhook a bunch of thyme. "May I have this?"

"For you, everything is there."

"You can have flowers when they come out, and eggs. Rob will bring you some during the week."

*

Edward was away for a month and when he returned to Deva Place it was with the sad news that his brother was dead.

Eleanor wept and thought: He is no more, the fine man I knew and who was kind to me, but also a man who was a staunch patriot, undaunted by the threats of his overlord. His time in prison had only been ten months but he was also compelled to pay Lord Derby a large sum of money every year of his life, as a fine.

"Both gone now," she murmured chokingly, "William and Susanna. They were so kind to me." She reached for his hand. "They helped to make me what I am."

"A lady of quality." He kissed her lovingly and said, "William was in no pain, dear. His last word was something you will like to hear – it was Susanna – yes, he whispered it to me and then he closed his eyes and was gone."

Edward's voice was now choked and she put her arms around him and there was a long silence while they drifted into the past and in their closeness comforted each other.

Summer faded into autumn and autumn into winter and then it was spring again and they lived happily together with never a cross word, never a frown. For Eleanor it was bliss, happiness she had never dreamed of on that soul-shattering day when she was told her lover was to stay in prison for life. And now he was hers till one of them should die. He had no wish to live in the Isle of Mann again but he did visit from time to time and he would bring her back all the news. William, Steward of the Abbeylands, was happy on his estate in Ronaldsway. He was still the Receiver-General and he seemed to approve of the new Lord of Mann, Thomas Fairfax, who had not as yet even mentioned the matter of the land tenures. All the wealthy landowners were optimistic that the question was shelved for ever more.

But, said Edward on returning one day, the people were not too happy at the Puritans with their sour faces and objections to all kinds of pleasure meddling in the island's affairs.

"Not more unrest, surely?" Eleanor did wonder if the island would ever know peace at all. The Scots had raided Ramsey on a few occasions and the English rulers of the island had provided two ships for the protection of its shores.

"No, not unrest," he assured her. "But some discontent, I think. As far as I can see, all is to go on in the same way as when the Earl was there."

"With no improvements for the people?"

"Not that I noticed." He smiled at her and took her hand. "Let us not talk of the isle, my sweeting. We shall walk in the sunshine of the beautiful garden you have made."

"I feel I am in heaven." She came close, in the action of a young girl, and his arms came around her. "Be with me always, Edward. Never be tempted to go back to live on the island."

"I live here now, and always shall do."

They had one of the new carriages and would go for rides to Northwich or even as far as Knutsford where King Canute was supposed to have forded the river. They wandered along the banks of the Dee or spent the long summer days in their own gardens or sometimes sailed along the river in a pleasure boat. Chester was their city for shopping and also they drove in every Sunday to go to the church there.

Time sped by with news coming from their daughter periodically. Susanna had three sons now and two daughters. Edward had a son and one daughter. They came over twice a year, in the summer and late December. These visits were eagerly looked forward to by both Eleanor and Edward who would have the children enthralled with his stories of his exploits at sea. And it was then that Eleanor would live again the drama of her first meeting with the young hot-headed swashbuckling privateer and the subsequent weeks during which they were lovers and she learnt to care deeply for the man she knew would never marry her. All so long ago, and so many changes since then.

Edward went to the island again the following June, and came back to say that Ewan, now infirm, had given over the office of Deemster to his eldest son, John, and that John's son, Edward, was the other Deemster.

"We must visit Ewan," decided Eleanor on hearing this news. "He can not come to us and I am sure he would like to see us."

The Deemster's weak condition made Eleanor depressed. And when they happened to see his doctor and he said the end was not very far away she burst into tears. Another of her friends... Her daughter so far away that it was unlikely she would ever see her again; Alicia far away, too. Susanna and William dead, and now Ewan, her very dear friend who had accepted her as one of the family. Although they went back to Deva Place they left word with one of Ewan's manservants that they were to be informed of any deterioration and this message came six weeks later. They went to Cumberland and stayed for almost a month, coming home the day after the funeral.

The following year William, the Deemster's third son, was appointed to the office of Governor by Lord Fairfax.

So once again the important offices were in the hands of the Christians. But Fairfax had appointed several Commissioners to investigate various aspects of the way the island had been governed and the chief of these was James Chaloner who had been one of the King's judges, although he was not there when sentence was passed.

"William and Chaloner do not seem to be getting along at all well," was Edward's comment on the return from one of his visits. "In fact, many of our family are objecting to the way he goes on."

"Well, I hope none of them goes too far." She was thinking of the uprising that had sent so many important Manx people to prison, including Edward and William Christian. "There has been enough trouble."

"You have the two factions," explained Edward. "The Commonwealth people and those who would rather see a king on the throne of England."

"I am not troubling my head about it." Eleanor was far too happy to give thoughts to an island she would never visit again – at least, she did not think there could ever be an occasion when she would go over there, especially as she was reaching the stage in her life when travelling any distance at all was becoming too much trouble.

John had been up to see them several times since he went to reside in Kent, and on the last occasion Eleanor sensed a restlessness in him and asked what was wrong.

"You have found a charming lady?"

He smiled then, that faintly enigmatic smile which always set her wondering what he was thinking.

"No, my dear Eleanor, it is not anything like that. It is that when I compare Kingsley Hall with this other property I find myself lost in nostalgia. Wandshurst is a wonderful mansion built of sandstone and, is massive. It is too massive, not cosy like this house or mine over the river there." He looked at her and shook his head. "I shall not come back yet, though. I still have much to do by way of renovations."

"Perhaps you will like it better when these are all finished?"

"Perhaps."

He stayed away for over a year during which time Oliver Cromwell died and as his son decided he had no gift for being Lord Protector of England, he went into retirement, leaving the country without a leader.

"There are many who want a king on the throne again." Edward had been on another visit to the island, this time to attend the funeral of one of his cousins, having been sent for when it was known he was dying. "Lord Fairfax seems not to know what he wants, while his relative, Chaloner, appears to be taking on more and more responsibility." His mouth was grimly set and for some reason she could not define she knew a little access of apprehension.

"It is plain that you are unfavourably disposed towards Chaloner?"

"He is for the Commonwealth, and we are not."

"We?" she echoed again aware of that uneasiness within her.

"The Christians and all the others."

She frowned in concentration.

"But it was William Christian who surrendered to the Commonwealth invaders?"

"Only to save the island from bloodshed – but you know this already."

Eleanor made an impatient gesture with her hands.

"Surely the island is not to be divided about something that is happening over here?" She stopped rather abruptly as something in his expression registered. "Edward, is this more serious than you are telling me?"

There was a long pause before he spoke.

"It is serious, yes, Eleanor. I have advised William to leave the island and live over here. He has a substantial house and lands at Nether Sparth."

"Leave the island? William? I do not understand. You advised him to go away – what about Ronaldsway? He loves it."

"I feel he is in danger – remember that I have spent eight years in prison. I would not wish any of my kin to suffer like that. Ewan wanted William to leave but he refused, being well in favour with Derby at that time. He is not in favour now..." Another pause and then, "I know you dislike me speaking about troubles on the island, but they do exist and can not be ignored. I shall now tell you the worst: Chaloner has removed William from both his offices, those, of Governor and of Steward of the Abbeylands."

The Abbeylands... given to the Stanleys after the Reformation.

Eleanor shook her head in bewilderment. William had been Steward of the Abbey for a good many years.

"I am mystified as to the authority of Chaloner to do these things to William?"

A short hard laugh came from Edward's lips.

"It would seem that Fairfax has put the entire management of the island in the hands of Chaloner – Fairfax has not yet visited the Isle of Mann and it seems to us that, as with the Derbys, his only interest will be the collection of revenues."

There was a distinct edge of bitterness in his tone but it was the light in his eyes which brought Eleanor a sudden jerk of fear. She must never forget she was looking at one of the island's staunchest patriots, a man with a fierce love for his homeland, as proved by the frequency with which he went over there. She was no fool; she had known that his heart was hers but his loyalties belonged to the Isle of Mann.

William Christian, son of Deemster Ewan, was also one of the island's staunchest patriots and it was remembering this that made her say she did not think he would leave and live in Lancashire. She recalled that his estates there had been sequestered but were restored to him by an order of Parliament.

"Why should he leave? The danger which all you landowners were in is past. It was only the Stanleys who persecuted you and now they are gone and done with for ever."

Edward lifted an eyebrow at this.

"It may interest you to know that if a king is restored here in England, then the Derbys will be reinstated."

"Well, it will be that nice man, Edward—"

"His brother would contest that Will – yes, it has been given probate but nothing is settled. King Charles – should he come to the throne – will naturally give favour to those who supported his father."

"Lord Derby's son – Lord Strange as he was then – gave King Charles no support – on the contrary, he joined the Commonwealth."

"His father forgave him, saying he was much changed in character. The King would think of this and probably invalidate a Will made at a time when Earl James was under pressure from many sides."

"I like it not," sighed Eleanor after some thought. "If Earl Charles should ever be Lord of Mann the first thing he would do would be to seek revenge on all those who agreed to the surrender."

"So you see that William must leave the island. This trouble with Chaloner is what worries me, though, not what might come later."

From then Edward was restless the whole time; she sensed an impatience to be back on the island among his own kin, ready to support them. Would he never learn? Prison had given him many grey hairs and a frame leaner than ever. But it would take more than prison to daunt the spirit of any Christian patriot and Eleanor gradually resigned herself to his returning to his homeland should he feel his presence was necessary. But for the time being she tried to ignore his restlessness and grasp as much happiness as she could. She said one day as they walked in the gardens enjoying the late spring sunshine,

"We have grown old, Edward, and I had hoped, when you were miraculously freed, that you and I should live out our lives in peace, but there is a festering worry inside me that fills me with dejection. If only I could be sure you will not become involved an any troubles that come to the isle... But I am not sure, Edward, and I fear for you."

She looked up into the tough old face and reminded him of his age. He laughed and swept her into his arms in the way he would have done in the youthful days of his roistering.

"My sweeting, you worry that pretty head of yours far too much. The good God controls our actions and we have to do—"

"Stop, Edward! Everyone blames God! It is the most absurd thing – look where it landed the King! He always said he was guided by God. No, Edward, you are captain of your own actions..." She paused for effect. "If you join in any moves against the Lord of the Isle it will be entirely of your own volition and nothing at all to do with God."

*

At the end of July there came a messenger to Deva Place with the news from Lancashire that William was in residence at Nether Sparth and that he would pay a visit to Eleanor and Edward and stay a few days if it pleased them to accommodate him. Eleanor was delighted and their visitor arrived a week later.

But as soon as she saw him she felt a sudden sickening feeling in the pit of her stomach. He looked so grave, and sad. He soon told them the news that John and his son had been suspended from their office as Deemsters by Chaloner who had falsely accused all three of them of appropriating the Lord's funds for their own private gain. The Deemsters were confined to within half a mile of their homes even though William's son George had proved by the books kept by his father that no money had been stolen, in fact there was a handsome surplus.

"I had already come away," William said. "I managed to get off the island secretly one night – taken aboard by one of your one-time smuggler friends," he said, turning to Edward with a laugh. "Chaloner says I left illegally, without a licence from him."

"He has taken over completely?" The glint in his eye was much disliked by Eleanor who knew instinctively that Commissioner Chaloner meant trouble for the Christians. His summary dismissal of the Deemsters was something even Lord Derby had not dared do. The Christians of Milntowne held the office as hereditary and it had passed from father to son over nine generations.

"It seems like it." William, having had a long ride, looked tired and Eleanor suggested he go to his bedchamber to rest a little while and change his clothes. He nodded and, taking up the bag he had brought with him, was conducted to his room by the maid who had come in response to Eleanor's summons.

"I fear there will be much trouble over on the island." Her voice carried all the apprehension that was oppressing her but for once Edward failed to notice. She saw that his mind was away... in the isle which seemed fated to be plagued with vicissitudes till the end of time. The long term of imprisonment inflicted by a despot for nothing more than his demands for justice for his people, had made the ex-Governor a hero in their eyes, a national champion, and Eleanor felt this knowledge would not be far from his mind at this time. What would they be expecting of him? He was a fighter for rights, and she would be deceiving herself if she denied there was a possibility of his going back.

And he did go back.

"Merely to see what is going on," he assured her. "Have no fear, my love, I shall be with you for the fair on St Thomas's Day in Chester." It was early November and Edward was seventy years old.

He went in the carriage to the port and she accompanied him. She watched him board; she waved to him, almost blinded by tears.

*

The first letter she received from him was to say he had important things to attend to, but although he would not now be with her for the fair, he would be with her early in January. John frowned at the news and exclaimed impatiently,

"Surely he is not becoming involved again!"

"I very much fear so." She was devastated by the news, remembering all her recent fears. "He is seventy years old, John. Why does he want to waste what life he has left on fighting?"

"We are not sure he is fighting." Nor what he was fighting for, he added to himself.

*

Eleanor and John spent Christmas together but she felt her heart was dead. She and her lover had been together so much, had become so close. The years had sped by on golden wings, and now she was put in mind of Widow Tidley's prophecy that she would have a long period of happiness. But what now...?

John was patient and kind, and tenderly understanding.

"I hate to see you so unhappy," he said on a deep sigh. "What can I do?"

"Nothing." She shook her head and it was silver that caught the candle glow now and not gold. "I always feel selfish where you are concerned, dear John. You were my mainstay for years... and then you went away. I – we had no wish for you to do so."

"I explained. It was for the best. You and Edward deserved to have all the time together, just the two of you."

"And now we are apart again, and – and – oh, I fear I shall never see him again!" Tears shone on her lashes but she managed not to let them fall. It was all so unfair to John.

The second letter was longer, containing news which confirmed the worst of her fears.

John was still at Kingsley Hall and quite naturally he had fallen into the routine which was followed before Edward came to live at Deva Place. He watched her open the letter, saw to his dismay her face drain of all colour. He caught her as she swayed, and led her to a chair.

"He can not leave the island – by – by the order of the Commissioner and there are others, too. It seems they supported a Lieutenant Hathorne and Chaloner was imprisoned." She handed him the letter. It was the very first time she had allowed anyone else even to touch one of Edward's letters. "Read it for yourself." She put her face in her hands and wept bitterly into them. "I shall never see him again, never!"

John read the letter with growing impatience. Why had Edward run these risks? He and Eleanor were so happy here, at Deva Place, but he had to go and join his fellow patriots and attempt to put a stop to the arbitrary activities of the man who had made himself ruler in the absence of Lord Fairfax who, in John's opinion, should have shown some interest at least, in the little country that had been given to him. Chaloner had been imprisoned at Peel Castle but released on orders from Parliament. His reprisal had been to keep those responsible on the island until such time as he decided what to do with them. John turned away, unwilling that Eleanor should see his expression. It was very grave...

*

Edward Christian was back in Peel Castle, along with others who had supported the military commander who had summarily arrested the Commissioner and put him in prison at Peel. It was William who was the reluctant bearer of the news.

Eleanor, her face ashen, did in her misery think of the others concerned and asked who they were. Familiar names all... John Teare, Ewan Curphy, John Christian of Sulby, William Gawne and of course, Hathorne who had caused it all.

"How long are they to be there?" She marvelled at the steadiness of her voice when her whole body seemed to be shaking. She looked at William and was so glad he had shown the sense to move from the island for assuredly he would have joined all these others in their protest against tyranny.

It was a bright sunny day in May when the news reached her. She waited until August and then told John she was going over to the Isle of Mann.

"I sent a messenger to William, as you know," she said, "and the news from the prison was that Edward is ill and weak. I must go to him."

John made no protest, but offered to go with her.

"I am grateful for your offer, John," she said chokingly, "but it is best that you do not come this time. I will take Marie."

He knew why. This time she would be at Edward's deathbed.

*

Eleanor and Marie stayed with Edward's steward at Poyll Dhouie Manor, and with his help Eleanor was given leave to visit her lover just whenever she liked. She found him frail but undaunted and knew he would repeat it all had he his time to come over again. He was comfortably housed, and cheerful, but she was prepared for the worst.

And it was on a grey day in January 1661 that she held him close to her breast and heard him say,

"My little sweeting... kiss me. Hold me, dearest. Never leave me... I..." His voice failed but on his bloodless lips there lingered a smile. "That... glorious hair... but all grows dark. I can not see..."

"But you can feel my arms about you, my darling!" She swallowed, managing to keep her voice steady while her throat was blocked by grief. "I am with you, dear, dear Edward, holding you close to my heart."

"Ah, yes, my own wonderful lass, my little sweeting..." His voice trailed away to silence, and only then did she allow the tears to fall.

She was strangely calm as she attended his funeral at Maughold Church and there was no reaction when she arrived back at Deva Place with her sorrowing little maid. Many tears had been shed over Captain Edward Christian and she guessed there would still be more. But for the present there seemed to be no more left. She was not thinking of his death, but of the happiness in their lives, and especially during the past eight years, and she found herself comforted. Edward had gone, but all the wonderful memories remained... She was actually managing to smile when John arrived during the evening. He walked into the room after having been announced, and stood a moment, a tall, distinguished nobleman, grey-haired, and with lines fanning out from the corners of his eyes. She stretched out her hands to him and he came forward to clasp them comfortingly in his.

Chapter Fifteen

King Charles II had been crowned and the Act of Indemnity passed. This made it clear that he wanted no bloodbath in retaliation for the past eleven years; the only reprisals would be against the regicides. He was a forgiving man, he declared, and wanted only peace and happiness for his people.

And so the Countess of Derby failed in her petition to the House of Lords to bring her husband's murderers to just punishment and likewise her son failed in his efforts to have the sequestered manors restored to the House of Stanley. He persisted, in a state of angry frustration, pointing out that a bill had passed both Houses. But the ultimate decision lay with the King, and as his trusted minister, Clarendon, maintained it would be a breach of the Act of Indemnity, he was sent away having gained nothing but Lathom, and the island. Almost in ruins, and denuded of all its splendid trappings and treasures, Lathom proved a suitable place in which the young Earl could brood over his wrongs and curse the father who had lacked the foresight which could not only have saved his estates, but his life also.

Now, though, the Earl's going over to the Commonwealth was bringing its punishments. All he had left was a little isle set in a misty sea.

For the whole of the summer he remained at Lathom, swearing he would never be seen at Court again, cursing the King and his minister, Clarendon, and in this mood he suddenly saw a way to defy his King and at the same time to score a victory over the hated clan Christian. The idea came one day when he was visited by the Governor of the island, Nowell, whose seat was Read Hall, not so far away from where William Christian was living at Nether Sparth, in Lancashire.

"William Christian? Yes, he visits the island often. It is my opinion that he would like to return and take up residence again at Ronaldsway."

"And what is preventing him from doing so?"

"The fear of reprisals, I should imagine."

"By me?" The Earl raised his eyebrows. "Has he not heard of the Act of Indemnity?"

"Surely, since everyone has. But he is unsure about whether it covers the Isle of Mann."

"As far as I am concerned it does cover the isle." The Earl's eyes were narrowed, his mouth compressed. "I should let it be known on the island that the Act will protect all who were concerned in the rebellions which occurred ten years ago, and which so greatly distressed and inconvenienced my dear mother."

Dear mother... The Governor's mouth curved cynically. When the Earl was Lord Strange he had not given a care for his parents. His father had never expected that he would help his mother or do anything to make the lot of his siblings any easier. Selfish, vain, cruel, he was typical of his family and although the Governor decided he would obey the request just made, he would also warn William Christian to make sure of his safety before making any move to live permanently on the Isle of Mann.

William paid a visit to Deva Place to attend the marriage of two people for whom he had the greatest respect.

Eleanor had not really wanted to marry John, but she felt she owed it to him to make him happy, to reward him for all the long years of devotion. She could never love him with the strong passion she had felt for Edward, even till the hour of his death, but she realised that what she now felt for John was, in fact, love. Love of a very different kind, but love all the same.

She had said at first,

"I am too old for marriage, John. Let us continue as we are."

"Too old? You will never grow old, my dear. You are ageless. And as I love you – have loved you for so many years, I desire marriage now, not merely friendship." He too was old; no longer was the difference in ages important. It had diminished with the passing of the years. "You are still beautiful – my dear Eleanor, do not deny me a few years of real happiness."

She had smiled then, and realised that life without him would be grim indeed.

A few friends of them both were invited to a small party and when it was over Eleanor found herself alone with William for a few minutes, so naturally she asked about the Isle of Mann, from where he regularly received news, borne hither by his sons.

"Is it as beautiful as ever – but it must be. Mountains and glens and little rocky coves never change. The Earl does not live there, I hear. He broods over his losses and dwells on the fact that his great-grandfather could live in such a lavish style." Her voice was tinged with contempt as she added, "Anyone else would be grateful for owning a little kingdom and go over and live there and work for its improvement. It is a marvellous challenge for a man."

"For the right man, yes. The Stanleys have never done much at all to improve the island." He paused a moment. "I would like to go back, to live at Ronaldsway, but..." He tailed off with a sigh and Eleanor sent him a puzzled glance. "I must find out if the Act of Indemnity covers the island. If it does then it is safe for me to return. I have felt like an exile, Eleanor, and now I desire to be where I was born."

"Well, please, I beg of you, do make sure, William. You know what the Derbys did to your cousin; you know that your father wisely moved because he was beginning to feel unsafe. Be careful, I pray you!"

"I shall make quite sure, I promise you – and now, do take that serious look from your face. It is your wedding day and you should not be troubling yourself about me."

"I would be happier if you were staying in Lancashire."

"I have assured you, dear Eleanor, that I shall make quite sure of my safety for the Stanleys were never to be trusted. Nor can their actions be anticipated for they have unbalanced minds."

She merely nodded and he asked which house they intended to make their home.

"We both love Deva Place, but Kingsley Hall is beautiful too. Imagine, William," she mused with in her eyes a faraway look, "I have the choice of two stately homes, and once I lived..." She tailed off and turned to look at him. "You never saw the house in which I lived when on the island, did you?"

"It is pulled down, I believe. It is so far in the past, Eleanor, so very long ago."

And she had become a charming lady of quality – but the roots must have been there already and for a moment he was lost in wondering about her real background. She could have come down from the line of a king. So many people had.

He left the following day and a few weeks later she received the intelligence that he was back in the island and living at his beloved Ronaldsway. He wrote to Eleanor and John,

"We are happy again, and safe. I made absolutely sure that King Charles' Act of Indemnity applied to the island as well as England, Scotland and Ireland and all the dominions and territories, so there is nothing the Earl can do to us. The good Lord be praised."

Later in the year Edward and Virginia and their children, Ewan and Margaret, came to stay at Deva Place and the day after their arrival Virginia let slip the fact that they had all come to love Chester because of these visits and of course, Edward had spent most of his childhood there. They were seriously thinking of accepting an offer recently received by Edward to join a company of lawyers with whom he had had dealings and in consequence become friendly.

"We would like to be nearer to you, Mother," Virginia went on, "so you can see more of the children who, I know, love you dearly, and their Uncle John too."

"But this is marvellous news! Why did you not tell me before yesterday as soon as you arrived?"

"Because we have not quite made up our minds – at least, yesterday we had not. But Edward and I talked a good deal about it and – well, I believe we shall make the move." She turned her head as her husband came into the room and Eleanor happily noticed the loving glances exchanged between them. "I have let out the secret," she confessed. "I hope you are not vexed with me?"

He shook his head.

"No, of course not." He pursed his lips. "But we do have to be sure of finding a suitable home, dear. Something comparable to the one we reside in now."

At that moment John came in from the garden, bronzed and with his hair a little tousled. Without pause he said quietly,

"It might solve our problem, Eleanor, dear." He turned to the others. "You see, we argue all the time as to which house we shall settle in. At present we are here, at Deva Place, but last week we were across the river, as your mother says she cannot make up her mind. We shall be at Kingsley Hall next week." His eyes glimmered with humour and the other three were laughing. "So as you are your mother's heir..."

He left the rest unsaid but by the time the couple and their children were going home it had all been arranged. Edward had been into Chester to see his two friends who had rather luxurious offices in Watergate Street and the deed of partnership was signed. Two months later Eleanor was moving out of the lovely Tudor mansion to which Edward Christian had brought her and their son over forty years ago. Tears came, naturally, and John understandingly let her cry. But she assured him she was not unhappy. In fact, she had come to love Kingsley Hall and, she said absurdly through her tears,

"Rob will be delighted that I am to be living on the estate where he is the steward."

*

William and his wife settled happily into the routine of life at Ronaldsway. Two of their sons were living close by and life seemed to be running smoothly for them all when, without the slightest warning of danger, William was arrested, charged with treason and put into prison. All who knew him were stunned; the Earl knew of the Act of Indemnity, surely? It was owing to that that his mother, the Countess, failed in her bid to be revenged for her husband's death.

"Your crimes were not against the English king but against the Lord of Mann," he was told by the Deemster who had usurped John of Milntowne, William's brother. "The Act of Indemnity has nothing to do with this island. We are a separate nation; we do not belong to England. It is Lord Derby's intention to be revenged and you are the chief culprit."

Was this true? William's sons were asking. Was the island left out, because it was a separate kingdom with its own government?

The jury at his trial were mainly in the Earl's service and, therefore, intimidated. Moreover, they were of such humble rank and uneducated that they understood practically nothing of what was going on. The Earl remembered how his father had wanted the life of Captain Edward Christian, and had failed to achieve his desire.

"But I," he confidently told his wife, "shall succeed in *my* desire. I shall have him hanged, drawn and quartered, which is the punishment for treason."

His wife looked anxiously at him. He had never been strong; she had to watch his health and she misliked the way he would work himself up into a frenzy of hate whenever he spoke of the Christians.

"Charles, please think again about this. The excitement and the worry of it all must surely make you ill again."

"No such thing. I am well at present." He uttered a sigh, though, and then said explosively, "If the Christians – and all the other landowners – had only given up their estates to us none of this would have happened! They are stubborn fools!"

"But only fighting for what they believe is right," she returned gently. "After all, from what I have learned, the lands really do belong to them, since they have inherited them from father to son through so many generations – just as the Stanleys did."

He glowered at her, his thin mouth moving convulsively as fury consumed him.

"The Stanleys are owners of the island – the whole of it, not a few pieces of land here and there! These Christians have much more than they started with! They buy, and they marry into one another's families so as to enlarge the estates—"

"Your family did exactly the same," she broke in to remind him. "I believe all your ancestors married in order to add possessions to what they already had. Can you name even one who married without gaining a substantial dowry?"

"This is different! We are talking about my kingdom!"

"The King of England does not desire to own every piece of land throughout the country, Charles." She spoke softly, soothingly, but he rounded on her and she feared he might use her with violence, so she went away to attend to their little son, William, who was soon coming up to his third birthday. She hoped he would not be like his father, or his grandfather... or any of the vengeful Stanleys who, she thought sadly, would always be hated by the inhabitants of their island kingdom.

Her son, though, would be a very different ruler. She would teach him to be kind and tolerant, and never to covet that which belonged to others, for it was time this feud between the Stanleys and Christians was settled so that all could live happily together.

*

The charges against William Christian were read out and he listened carefully without moving a muscle of his face and all the time his eyes were narrowed but alert. Evidence of the Stanley virulence was there, the hatred of an unbalanced mind. William thought of the fate of his cousin, Edward, who had spent eight years in prison – as a result of the seventh Earl's malignity, and now his son, who seemed set to become an even worse ruler, was seeking revenge for something that had taken place ten years ago.

William's eyes strayed to where his brother, John, and his son were sitting, on a bench by the door, their faces grave as they heard Robert Norris, the Deemster who had replaced William's brother, denouncing their father as a traitor, the chief actor in the risings of 1651, the man who had deserted the Countess in her hour of need. He who had surrendered the militia and several forts to the invading army. George and Ewan had left the court when William next turned his eyes in their direction and he smiled confidently to himself. Just a few hours ago when they had visited him in prison they had made him a solemn promise that if it should appear to them that the trial could go against him, they would go to London as quickly as possible and petition the King, for, they said, this act of the Lord in seeking revenge was illegal, in total defiance of the order of the King that there should be no reprisals other than those he would take himself, which were against the ten who were directly responsible for his father's murder. The ten were hanged in January 1661 and that, declared the King, was the end of any form of retribution on the part of any who might have suffered as a result of the Civil War, and although there were many whose sense of justice was outraged, none dared defy the King... except the eighth Earl of Derby, Lord of Mann who had once before defied Charles, over the question of his marriage, which Charles said must not take place as the woman was unsuitable as a wife to the heir of Lord Derby, and a future Lord of Mann.

Eleanor, living happily at Kingsley Hall, was aghast at the news of William's arrest. It had come – as most of the news had come for many years – from Rob who, going to the inn in Chester for his pint of ale, heard about the arrest from one of the shipmen who frequently came over bringing wool and hides to be sold in England.

Her face drained of colour, Eleanor sought out her husband where he was out on the lawn, training a young puppy they had bought at the Chester Fair a few days previously.

"But this is illegal – a gross perversion of feudal power!" he exclaimed. "Is the man quite mad? I can not believe that even he with his insane hatred of the Christians would flaunt the King's authority."

"He probably believes he will escape punishment on account of his father's having died for his loyalty to Charles – yes, that is why the Earl is taking this chance. Oh, John, I fear greatly for William, and his family."

He sent for his steward who came promptly to the drawing room into which his employer and Eleanor had retired in order to have a discussion on this latest outrage of the Earl of Derby.

"Rob, did this friend of yours who brings you so much news from the Isle of Mann tell you anything else – I mean any more than you have told Mistress Eleanor?"

"He said that the ex-Receiver's brother and his nephew had come over and were riding with great haste to London to inform His Majesty of what has happened. The shipman said there was much grumbling against the Earl because he had chosen a jury who were terrified of him and so would bring in a verdict of guilty against William Christian."

"Thank you, Rob. Go again this evening – will there be a ship into Chester today?"

"Not today, sir, but there should be one tomorrow if this calm weather holds."

"Then find out all the news and let us have it quickly."

He feared for the health of his wife if this situation should worsen as it was already bringing back the trial of her lover which then, as now, was not conducted in a fair and just manner. These Derbys! He disliked to remember that his father had once been a friend of the sixth Earl, William... but he was never concerned with the administration of the kingdom that had come to him so unexpectedly, on the sudden and inexplicable death of his elder brother. John decided that William was the best of a thoroughly detestable family.

"This choosing of a jury he has put terror into," began Eleanor when the steward had left the room. "It is all so like the trial of Edward. You recall that his father put terror into the Keys who were trying Edward. And now the son is doing the same with this jury."

"Dearest," interrupted her husband taking her cold hand in his, "you did hear Rob say that George and Ewan are riding as swiftly as they can to London. The King will intervene, have no fear."

And she uttered the words which were already ringing in his brain,

"If they are in time! Surely it has occurred to you that Derby will hasten the trial—"

"But even if William is convicted Derby will have to release him again." And once more she echoed the words he had left unsaid,

"If Derby has not speedily concluded the proceedings and – and – taken William's life."

Sir John turned away, desperately wanting to reassure her, but from what he had learned of the viciousness of the Stanleys in their feud with the Christians he himself feared for the ex-Receiver's life.

Over on the island William waited in vain for the return of his brother and his nephew. It was such a long way to London and back... and although he was sure the King would intervene, he gradually became resigned to the fact that it would all be too late.

The Keys had previously been considering whether a jury was required at all, since treason was an offence for which the accused could be tried without a jury. It was decided to have him tried by jury.

*

"He has refused to plead," was the information brought to Kingsley Hall by Rob. "Such an attitude seems very strange to me."

"He is acting in exactly the same way as Edward!" exclaimed Eleanor, horrified. "He denies the right of the Court to try him."

"It is all foolishness." John made an impatient gesture with his hands. "He will be adjudged guilty."

"Poor Elizabeth..." Eleanor knew exactly what William's wife would be going through at this time for had she not been through it all herself almost twenty years ago? "I wish I could be there to comfort her."

"She has her sons – my dearest, please do not relive that agony, I beg of you! We can do nothing to help in this disaster, and if William refuses to plead he is not even trying to help himself."

She looked at him and her heart suddenly felt dead. These patriots, fierce fighters for a better deal for their fellow islanders... all going one by one... Yes, she knew instinctively that William's life would be taken since, as John had said, he would be adjudged guilty.

*

Lord Derby was playing with his son when the messenger came to inform him that some of the Keys refused to sign the report that, because the prisoner refused to plead, he was at the mercy of the Lord for his life and his possessions.

"Refused!" The Earl glowered at the Deputy-Governor who had brought the message. "Then they shall be dismissed!"

His wife's face paled. She said timidly,

"Charles, please think before you act. And you are working up your temper again and it is not good. The doctor warned—"

"Be quiet!" snarled her husband. He wanted speed! Those brothers of the traitor had left the island without his permission, gone to London to petition the King! "I want this trial speeded up, and the traitor hanged, drawn and quartered without further delay!"

Helena was terrified, had been from the first, but now she revealed her fear.

"The King forbade such action as you are taking," she quivered. "Have you the courage to defy him? He will punish you, imprison you. Please, Charles, listen to me, just for this once. I fear for you if you continue with this—"

She stopped just in time, having been going to voice the word which came so naturally to her lips: "persecution".

"Will you keep out of this, woman!" He was debating on who he could appoint in place of the Keys he intended to dismiss. These were the seven who had been supportive of the rebellion – yes, he could dismiss those but who would replace them? In a frenzy of haste he made a choice and induced them by bribery to do his bidding without any form of protest.

*

An icy wind was blowing from the sea on the January day when William Christian was brought to Hango Hill where he was to be "shot to death that thereupon his life may depart from his body."

Tall and dignified and stooping slightly, the last of the nation's three staunchest patriots turned his face to look his last on the house he had loved, Ronaldsway, and he thought: the Stanleys, father and son, have coveted this property for many years... And now the Lord of Mann could claim it, and all his other possessions. His brothers had not been speedy enough, nor had his own petition reached the King in time. He was calm, and ready to die. But he was grateful that his wife's plea that he be spared the terrible punishment inflicted on those condemned for treason had been listened to. He thought of her; they had been happy together though life had at times been hard. He was glad his father was not here to suffer grief at this killing of his son. He looked around at faces pale and drawn, at bodies shivering in their thin and worn attire... and he thought of the Lord with his fine clothes, his sumptuous castle dwelling with its abundance of warm fires. What good had any of them done, the many like his two cousins and himself, all brave, undaunted... but what had they achieved? What chance of peace had this little island when its fate was to be ruled by despots like Charles, Earl Derby and all the Derbys that would come after, tyrants whose power over their subjects was that of life and death? They could imprison, torture and kill; they were beyond any law by which they themselves could be punished simply because they were the law, their authority was unassailable. "But who knows? One day the freedom for which we fought may come."

Again his eyes strayed to the grey stone house which had been built around King Orry's Tower; ancient and historical, it had yet been cosy, the home in which most of his children had been born... in which some of them had died in infancy. Fiercely he had loved Ronaldsway and he had expected it one day to go to his eldest son. But instead Derby had gained, by a trial that was a farce from start to finish – in fact, no trial at all owing to the suborning by the Earl, the threats, the hate – Derby had gained possession of his neighbour's house and all his chattels, and he had callously left Elizabeth and their children destitute.

The crowd was silent but he saw many tears flowing. He wanted to pray but that could come later. His friends – ah, yes, almost everyone here was his friend – wanted to hear him speak. He would not disappoint them.

He began, his voice strongly carrying to the outermost edge of the mass gathered there, on this cold and dismal day, with the sea grey and sullen, the clouds above it glowering and heavy.

"As you all know, I have done much for the noble family of Derby, who are now taking my last breath." He paused to take a glance at his home, to which he had returned from exile, confident he was safe from any reprisal which Derby would have liked to have made. "No one knows better than I the power Lord Derby has over this isle. He has used that power in defiance of the King. It was the King's most gracious Act of Pardon and General Indemnity which gave me the assurance and confidence to return."

He went on to speak of the false charges brought against him and of the threats made to the jury; he said he had always been prepared to pay fair taxes, but only those. He reminded the people of many promises made by the Earl, and then were broken once the people had gone quietly back to their homes. Derby had said he would never treat them as slaves but it was as slaves that he oppressed them. He repeated what he had said before, that the Court had no authority to try him, and that the jury were terrified of their master; they dare not defy him. Again he paused as his eyes strayed even yet again to the grey stone pile of Ronaldsway. The Derbys' eyes had been on it for a long time, just as they had been on Lough Mollo, Edward's home and estate. "At this time I can not but think of the King's Pardon," he went on in the same clear and carrying voice. "I was told that there was no doubt about its extending to this isle and to all other places within His Majesty's dominions and countries." He looked all around at the sad and upturned faces. "There is now a thin veil only betwixt me and death. I request your prayers but not your tears. For I am not afraid. I say to you all that I quake not, but happily look to my peaceful place in heaven. Farewell, my friends; farewell dear isle that gave me birth, this sweet spot – my Ronaldsway where I have been happy with my beloved wife and children. Farewell to life and, friends, you will one day find that in my dying I shall have helped to win the freedom we all have so long fought for. Drop not a tear over my grave; but just remember that I die for justice. The blessing of Almighty God be with you all."

He stood a moment, then went down on his knees and prayed earnestly for a few minutes. When he rose there was a murmur;

people swayed and some closed their eyes. William asked for a piece of paper.

"White paper," he said, "and hurry, for I want this business done."

The paper brought, he held it over his heart. "The place is marked correctly; do not go astray with your aim, but be cool and steady, good soldiers, and now... fire..."

Chapter Sixteen

The Countess of Derby pressed a cold compress to her husband's head. She was troubled about his health. He was only thirty-six years old but his face was sallow and lined, his eyes sunken in their sockets and the skin loose around his mouth.

"You should try to be calmer," she pleaded. "All this excitement and working yourself into a passion is very bad for you." She recalled how it was said that his father was psychotic. And only yesterday the doctor had warned that Charles' violent bursts of temper were harmful to his health, and especially his mental health.

"I am sometimes puzzled by his ills," the doctor admitted with a shake of his head. "He could suffer a lingering illness... But perhaps I am wrong," he added in a more soothing tone as he caught the Countess's expression. But she just had to know more.

"This lingering illness, please tell me if it is to be very long and – and painful?"

"'Tis something I should have kept to myself," he returned regretfully. "Forget I said it, my lady. With the right treatment he should be better quite soon."

"This place depresses him," she sighed, glancing around at the faded wall coverings and places where valuable pictures and other works of art, having been removed, left dismal gaps as reminders of the splendour in which the mansion of Lathom House had once basked. "My husband dwells all the time on what poverty we have to endure – comparing it with the lavish lifestyle of his great-grandfather, and he is filled with bitter resentment, so he works himself up into these passions, as if he is trying to battle against fate."

"What he seems to forget," returned the old doctor dryly, "is that he is of a secondary line, and that if his great-uncle had lived to have sons then all this..." he spread his hands, "and the title, would never have been his at all."

He was thinking of the untimely death of that young man, and the symptoms which suggested poisoning.

"Yes, we do understand, but it is hard nevertheless."

Helena was thinking of this conversation as she tended her husband, and she was wondering if the doctor could have been right when he hinted at a long pining illness.

"Is that any better?" She leant away and regarded his flushed face anxiously. "Has the headache gone?"

"Certainly it has not gone!" he snapped, and his eyes took on a glittering expression. "It is caused by this act of my Deputy-Governor in commuting the punishment of that traitor! I wanted him hanged, drawn and quartered!"

Foam was gathering at the corners of his mouth but as the Countess bent to wipe it away he struck her hand and uttered a vicious curse. "Go away, woman, you vex me sorely with your fussing."

He reached for the tankard of ale she had placed on a table by his side. He was huddled in a chair close to the fire and now and then she saw him shiver. "Nowell had no right to take it on himself to show mercy and let him be shot. 'Tis too easy a death—!"

"Dearest," broke in Helena, desperately, "you are feverishly putting yourself into a passion again. I beg of you, try to keep calm. As for the mercy which Nowell showed – well, it was owing to the dreadful state William Christian's wife was in. She went to him and implored him to let her husband be shot. You ought to think of your poor father, Charles, and how your mother must have felt, knowing he was to be beheaded and there was nothing she could do. Elizabeth begged for mercy for William and I am glad that the Deputy-Governor had the heart, and the courage, to grant her wish."

"So! You are glad he had the courage to defy me! I can have him shot!"

Helena chose to ignore that wild statement; she saw that her husband was in an uncontrollable temper and all she could do was to try her best to bring him back to sanity.

"It is time for your physic," she murmured soothingly. "But first, enjoy your beer, my love."

He glowered at her and said he was taking no poison supplied by that fool of a doctor. And then he added as the thought came to him,

"You spoke of my mother's suffering. Well, you talk like the fool that you are. My father was dead a week before she knew, so how could she suffer?"

Helena left that unanswered; she was more concerned that he take his physic and she went off to get it.

To her surprise and relief he took it and for a few minutes it seemed he would calm down. But suddenly he sprang up, his mouth moving convulsively for what to her seemed an eternity before he said explosively,

"What right had Nowell to give way to Mistress Christian! It was my wish that her husband be hanged! I told him so!"

"It is all over now," she reminded him patiently, "so it matters nothing how he died, does it?"

"I wish he was still alive!" he fumed beginning to pace the floor. "It irks me that he knows no pain! There is no satisfaction within me. I wish I had kept him alive, to rot in a dungeon! Yes, in a dark wet, cold dungeon in Peel Castle!"

She said with the same quiet patience,

"As a political prisoner, he would never have been in a dungeon."

Stopping his pacing he slammed a fist on the table, causing the empty tankard to jump then clatter noisily.

"If I say he would be in a dungeon then he would be!" He glared at her, gritting his teeth. "My word is law there. I am the Lord of Mann!" He seemed about to topple and she ran to his side.

"Sit down, Charles, I do beg of you. Surely you can see how troubled I am?"

"Yes, yes..." He sank down into the chair, brushing thin white fingers through his hair. Shoulder-length and tousled, it was in complete contrast to the neatly groomed beard and moustache. He wore a high-waisted doublet and an abundance of frills and ruffles at his neck and cuffs. Helena, on the other hand, was far more soberly dressed in an indoor winter gown with the open-fronted skirt pinned at the back to form the hint of a bustle. She wore a lace cap from which tendrils of russet hair escaped. She was breeding again but decided it was not the kind of news to interest the Earl at this time so she kept her discovery to herself.

He was holding out his hand and she took it in hers. She had not thought, when she married the handsome heir to an earldom, that she would soon be his nursemaid. Perhaps she should have considered a little longer, for after all the marriage was frowned upon by so many, including King Charles the Second. "I should not get excited, as you say."

"There, that is better. You are calmer now. Forget all this trouble, dearest, now that it is all over and finished with."

But she spoke with more confidence than she felt. She had heard there were murmurings about three others who had been punished by her husband. Ewan Curphey, a Member of the House of Keys, had been imprisoned and his estates seized. Then the Captain of the Patrick Militia and John Caesar, Lieutenant of the Malew Militia... both had been sent to prison and their estates confiscated by her husband. None of these three had been given any legal trial. Charles' arbitrary stretching of his feudal power was not a good thing to her way of thinking. Men would not lie down under such treatment.

"Bring William to me." The Earl managed a smile and he took her hand in his again. "And his brother. I will entertain myself with my sons and forget all else."

Helena went away, up to her bedchamber where she stood by the window staring out over the grounds, once so immaculate, tended by an army of gardeners, but now neglected and certainly bleak and uninteresting on this January day where, in the sky, ominous clouds were shutting out most of the light. She felt depressed, unable to dismiss from her mind all the follies being committed by her husband. She knew for sure that William Christian spoke the truth when, in his speech just before he died, he spoke of the jury being prompted and also threatened. It was true; Charles had threatened the poor, illiterate people who had been chosen to try the accused. William had also stated that the "pretended court of justice was not qualified". She dared not let her husband know of her belief that the Major-General of the Militia had done what was right when he surrendered to Cromwell's invading forces. As he had said, he did it to save the Manx people from a battle which they could not possibly win, simply because the Lord of Mann had taken most of the soldiers over to England for use in support of the King. In her opinion William had committed no crime, and yet he had been executed. And this against the express wish of King Charles who, determined on clemency, had signed the Act of Indemnity. The King had asked for the prisoner to be brought to London, so that he himself could question him... but her husband maintained he did not receive this order until after William was dead. She felt sure he lied, but kept her convictions to herself, naturally. What she hoped would not happen was that William would be regarded as a martyr and proclaimed a national hero. Her husband would certainly go off into one of his mad fits of fury should a circumstance like that come to his ears.

Alas for her hopes. It was Norris who brought the news. Already ballads were being written to his memory, and on hearing this the Earl picked up a tankard of ale and flung it across the room, then screamed abuse at the unfortunate Norris who soon made his escape, vowing never to set foot in Lathom House again.

"That – that traitor – a hero! And me—" The Earl crashed his fist against his chest – "what will they say about me? That I am a murderer no doubt!" He shot up from his chair, thrusting his wife to one side as she made to calm him. "I should have imprisoned him for life – but I wanted to know he had been hanged, drawn and quartered – I was even deprived of that satisfaction by Nowell—! I shall get rid of him, throw him into gaol!"

He paced the floor, and his wife drew a long breath. It was true that the Derbys, father and son, had some kind of a brain disorder. How could it be otherwise when they acted so irrationally? What of her son, William, who would one day inherit the island? Would his rule be any different? Already his father was instilling into him a hatred of the Christian family, telling his son that they were holding on to lands which belonged to him as Lord of the Isle. She fervently hoped the feud would not be continued by William, but she sighed again and thought: it will continue, I feel it in my heart.

*

King Charles was in a quandary. Here before him, to be perused even yet again during this period of indecision, was the Petition whereby William Christian had pleaded that the Earl of Derby's proceedings against him were a violation of the Act of General Pardon and Indemnity, and he asked that his case be heard before the King himself in General Council. And Derby had sworn the King's demand for the prisoner to be brought to London reached him too late.

"Like you, sire, I am of the opinion that Derby has lied." Edward Hyde, Earl of Clarendon, a close adviser to His Majesty, was with him, having been sent for to discuss the problem facing the King.

"Yes, he has lied," agreed Charles grimly and there was an angry glint in his eyes. "He wanted revenge, and he defied my Act in order to attain it. But, Edward, we have to take into account his father's loyalty to my father and to this country. He gave his life... and here I am, desiring to punish this infamous son of his for murdering one of my subjects, while at the same time remembering the sacrifice of his father." He spread his hands in a little gesture of frustration. "What am I to do, Edward, tell me that?"

"It is indeed a troublesome problem." The Earl paused a moment in thought. It was on his advice that this scamp of a son of the seventh Earl had not been given back his sequestered lands in Lancashire and Cheshire, and now he was again called upon to give advice about the same young man. He had followed his career to some extent and he was well aware of the feud, of the Derbys' persecution of the inhabitants of the little isle in which they ruled on the lines of ruthless autocracy. He had no patience for an overlord who did nothing for the benefit of his subjects, who, from all accounts, terrorised them into submission. And if his memory served him right this one had never even been on the island's shores in the last fifteen years. But his orders were received regularly by those he had placed in power, and those orders had to be obeyed – although Nowell had not obeyed the diabolical order that William Christian be hanged, drawn and quartered. That Charles Stanley was of depraved mind the Earl had no doubt and had it been left to him he would have paid for his crime by receiving the same punishment as the man whose life he had taken. But what of the two who had decreed the violent death, Norris and Cannell? The Earl decided he would advocate some severe punishment for them, and for some others who came to mind. The sudden impatient movement of the King brought him from his reverie and he glanced up. "Were it I," he said deliberately at length, "I would send Derby to the block."

"Really, Edward!" The King sent him a frowning glance. "I have let it be known that I have wanted no vengeful punishments. I want peace for my people – and now you tell me to send Derby to the block."

"I said if it were me, Charles. But it is you and here you are, with your mind grappling with this problem. But I must remind you, sire, that Charles Stanley was very conscious – when he decided to have Christian murdered – of the fact that his father's sacrifice would carry much weight if it should happen that you were displeased with him over this business."

He leant back, taking up the wine just poured by a servant and placed on a small table at his elbow. Attired in the height of fashion, he wore a loose-fitting jacket with open sleeves, the cuffs of which were ruched up and fastened with loops of ribbon, the same ribbon being used to edge the wide petticoat breeches. His high-heeled shoes with their long narrow toes were tied with bows of ribbon. His hair, very long and thick, was parted in the centre and the King, watching him fingering one trailing lock, strongly suspected he was wearing pieces of false hair. The King smiled faintly. He had been brought one of the newly fashionable periwigs but as yet had disdained to wear it. His own hair, shoulder-length, satisfied him well enough for the present.

"I have to agree with what you say, Edward." The King's smile had faded; he was once again totally absorbed by his problem. "Stanley did have it in mind that I would consider his father's sacrifice. But nevertheless, he will have to be punished. My Act of Indemnity was not passed to be broken. Others with greater grievances have obeyed my wishes. But it seems to me that the Stanleys have always regarded themselves as kings of the island."

"True. 'Twas once they were actually crowned." Edward shook his head and a frown appeared upon his brow. "I think it was a pity the island was given back to them by your grandfather."

"Yes," nodded the King. "And if I took it from Charles it would be a fitting punishment."

"And good for the people. I am of the opinion that they must be heartily sick of these Stanleys."

"No doubt you are right, Edward, but I shall not go that far. I am informed that the two sons of the dead man are to ask me for reparation?"

"That is so. I am told that they are to present petitions for redress. You have to remember that the Earl has confiscated all of William Christian's possessions, leaving his widow a pauper and homeless, and his children robbed of their patrimony."

At this the King's mouth compressed.

"I have heard the Derbys have always coveted Ronaldsway, the home of William and his family."

The Earl nodded his head.

"It has also come to my ears, sire, that the properties of three others, now imprisoned on a similar charge as Christian, have been seized by Charles Stanley for his own use, although he has had his bribed Commissioners spread it abroad that all seizures have been for the benefit of the bishopric."

"Ha!" The King gave a short and cynical laugh. "That, my friend, is a most unlikely story!"

"These three had no legal trial."

"No—!" The King's eyes opened wide. "Is this true? I know the trial of William Christian was farcical... but to allow no trial at all. Is this true?" he queried again, a heavy frown gathering between his eyes.

"Perfectly true, Your Majesty. I have it on excellent authority."

"Then that is one conviction I need have no hesitation about! These men will not only have their estates returned but they will also be awarded damages!"

"And given their freedom, of course?"

"Certainly!" The King looked across at his friend. "We still have made no decision regarding the way I must deal with Derby. Surely you have some suggestion – other than sending him to the block," he added on a rather dry note.

"You could deprive him of some of the lands he does still possess. Also, bear in mind that his humiliation at being brought before the King in Council will be a severe punishment to a man of Charles Stanley's pride."

"And of course, the loss of all he has taken from the widow and children of his victim," supplemented the King with a grim expression on his dark countenance.

"Yes, indeed." Edward paused. "Shall you take Lathom from him?"

The King shook his head.

"That once-stately pile is a burden to him, so let us keep it that way. He has been brooding within its faded and denuded walls ever since we refused to restore the lands sequestered by Parliament. He can remain there and lick the wounds we shall soon be inflicting upon him."

"You are determined to punish him, then?"

"Have I not made that clear? Much as I appreciate his father's loyalty, I am unable to make that an excuse for the deliberate violation of my wishes. If I allowed Derby to get away with it where would I be with all the others who have wanted revenge?"

*

The Privy Council was met to hear "The Earl of Derby's case stated for the vindication of the Proceedings at Law in the Isle of Mann against William Christian." It was presided over by King Charles himself.

The King glanced around until his eyes rested on the Earl and he was remembering that young man's previous defiance when he married the illegitimate Helena de Rupa. He was also remembering that while his father was fighting for his King and country he went over to the Parliamentarians. If ever there was a traitor, mused the King, then here was one, sitting there, still arrogantly confident that the case he had so carefully prepared would steer his King's thoughts away from any punishments he might have had in mind.

"Confident he might look," whispered Clarendon at the King's elbow, "but in good health? – I see a man aging far too quickly." He grimaced. "'Tis said he flies into wild rages."

"His doctor visits him regularly – Wait, and listen to what excuses he has managed to get together."

The King's eye was now directed towards where the Earl sat, erect and outwardly cool but his skin had a sallow look and his eyelids drooped repeatedly.

"'Twould seem we have to listen to a deal of preliminaries."

Edward gave a grunt of disgust. "We know all of this."

His Majesty made no answer, but listened patiently to the information given that the Lords of Mann were formerly homagers to the Kings of Norway... It droned on and on through the reigns of Scottish and English kings and overlords until "William le Scrope held it until beheaded and then the island was given to Sir John Stanley, from whom by hereditary descent the same is come to Charles, now Earl of Derby..."

"How much more of this!" The King was now losing patience. "Does the man believe we need the entire background? If it continues I shall put a stop to it."

"I saw the scroll, sire, and I fear there is much more before the vital part is reached. We are to hear that the island was bequeathed by Act of Parliament in the reign of your grandfather—"

"Spare me! I shall peruse my own notes and you can remind me when all these absurd preliminaries are finished."

A few minutes later the King was listening again. He heard the Earl plead that he supposed the accused William Christian would have fought the invaders and not surrendered, against the wishes of his mother, the Countess Charlotte. The King spoke then.

"James, the Countess's husband, wrote to advise her to surrender. He said in a letter to her that..." he glanced down at some notes he had made "...it would be unwise to resist, especially as the enemy had command of three nations."

There was a general murmur at this and when it had died down the King continued, "It is also known that the Countess herself offered to surrender even before this letter from her husband was received. James and his Countess both had shown a desire to surrender." He turned to look directly into Lord Derby's face. "So why did you charge William Christian with unlawfully surrendering the island to the enemy? He did what he knew was best for the people of Mann... and, Charles Stanley, you knew this all the time."

His voice was stern but quiet. It drew respect from all of those present and awe now crept into the Earl of Derby's heart. The King seemed hard and inflexible in his attitude and Stanley racked his brain to find a way of reminding him of the sacrifice his father had made to the Stuarts without its seeming too obvious way of deflecting the King's growing anger. But the King was speaking again. "The Countess, in fact, had already offered the island to Colonel Duckenfield, who was in charge of the expedition which was to have attacked Mann, in exchange for her husband's life."

His eyes were piercing and his voice held an edge of condemnation which was beginning to affect Lord Derby's nerves. "What have you to say in your defence, Charles Stanley?"

Derby licked his lips and glanced wildly around. He saw only hostility on the faces of the Judges and Counsel; he saw fear on the faces of his Governor, the Deemsters and three members who had been specified by William's son, John, as 'forming the pretended Court which tried my father'. John had already been allowed to speak and had said in a clear forthright way that the murder of his father was an unjustifiably vengeful act by Lord Derby who stretched his feudal powers; that he had ignored the King's orders and that his mother, the Countess, had been in full agreement and harmony with her son's illegal conduct. The King and Council had listened sympathetically and the king had asked kindly if he had anything else to say; and John asked that all the lands and other chattels seized be restored to his family. His Majesty had nodded then but told John he could sit down so that the proceedings against the accused could continue.

"His Majesty has asked you a question." The voice of Clarendon cut into the rather tense silence which followed the king's words.

"I can only say again that William Christian took an oath to bear faith and fidelity to my father, James, Earl of Derby who had raised him to several offices of trust, and that without authority did take advantage of the absence of my father—"

"And of you," cut in one of the Council dryly. "It is stated that you stayed in England while your mother and her other children lived in great danger. It is also said that your father knew for some considerable time that he could expect no support from you if any emergency should occur. He disinherited you because you went over to the enemy against which he was fighting."

A deep silence enveloped the chamber. Derby swallowed to release the blockage of fear that had risen in his throat. This could be serious and for the very first time he was beginning to regret his vengeful act in having Christian executed. On being summoned to appear before the King in Council he had treated the matter lightly, telling his wife not to look so troubled as it was nothing serious. The King merely wanted to know what had happened. He, Charles, would soon be able to convince his King that he had done only what was right in bringing a traitor to justice. But Helena had tearfully reminded him that the King had decreed that no one except the ten regicides had to suffer any reprisal for the part they had played in the Civil War. Derby had shrugged that off... but now... He said at last,

"My mother was not in any danger. She was living in much comfort and luxury at Castle Rushen—"

"She was living there, without the support of her husband, on an island that was continually under threat of invasion by the might of Cromwell's forces."

"My father had left a navy to protect the island."

"He left the island practically defenceless," interposed Earl Clarendon. "He took the main body of the militia to support our gracious King Charles in his bid to regain the throne. No, sir, it is a falsity for you to tell us your mother was safe."

Again Lord Derby glanced around. Fear was deepening in his heart. Would he end up on the block, as his father had done? But no, the King had said over and over again that he was against reprisals. So perhaps he was safe. They were only trying to frighten him. His head came up. He was not afraid any more.

The King spoke, declaring that the Earl had made no defence at all.

"We are of the opinion that you committed a maliciously vengeful act. You must remember that we know of the age-long feud existing between the clan Christian and the Stanleys, and we know what it is all about. We are wanting some further explanation of your conduct."

He was playing for time, torn even now because he was thinking of the bravery of this man's father. He had not hesitated to come to his aid even though he must have considered the danger of defeat and of his own capture. He knew that capture meant death. And eight years before that he had unhesitatingly gone to the support of his father and had fought bravely in several battles, fought beside the gallant Prince Rupert. How then, could he punish James's son? Yet how could he let him go free? It was for the prevention of revenge that he had adopted the policy of leniency resulting in the Act of Indemnity, which all others had observed except this man here before him, the son of the man who had died while he, the man he had supported, had escaped and was now on the throne of England. He turned to Clarendon and his eyes were deeply troubled. "What must I do?" he whispered.

"He is on trial, sire. It is not entirely in your hands any more."

"But my word will carry."

"Why should he benefit by what his father did?"

"You are right, but..."

Lord Derby was asking leave to speak again and it was granted.

"The traitor – William Christian made his house at Ronaldsway the headquarters for the planning of the insurrection. He told the people that the Countess had agreed a surrender and would sell all the people for twopence or threepence a head. He besieged my mother in Castle

Rushen and she was forced by him to sign a treaty of surrender. The forces then plundered her home…"

"We have heard all this," broke in one of the Judges impatiently. "You read it out at the start of these proceedings. What we want to know is why you brought a man to trial knowing it was a flagrant violation of the King's Act of Pardon?"

"I said in my original plea, that I and everyone concerned in his trial believed the Act did not apply to the Isle of Mann."

"And why should it not apply to the Isle of Mann?"

"It was not named. It applied to England, Scotland and Ireland, and it was stated clearly, 'and to the Dominions and Territories thereto belonging.'"

"Well?" from the King who had listened intently.

"Sire, the Isle of Mann does not come under a "Dominion or Territory" of England. Therefore, William Christian could be tried by me, as Lord of Mann." An arrogant note had crept into Lord Derby's voice which brought a dangerous glint to His Majesty's eye.

"Are you trying to convince us that an inhabitant of the island can be guilty of treason against the Lord of the Isle but not against the Crown?"

"Yes, sire, I am saying that."

"Then you are wrong!"

There was a loud murmuring around the chamber. George and Ewan, William's sons, watched the Earl's face darken, and a foam was appearing at the corners of his mouth.

"He never expected this," whispered George. "The Derbys have always been so sure of themselves."

"He will be punished, but it does not bring our father back."

"No, it is very sad. But at least our mother will have her home again."

Derby, desperate now as he realised the proceedings were going against him, again stressed that the Isle of Mann was a kingdom separate from that of the Crown of England.

"It has always been governed by its own distinct laws, its own orders in matters both criminal and civil. It was not anciently a part of England – though it pays homage to it – nor has any Act of Parliament made it part of England, and so, my lords, I again plead that unless the Isle is particularly named in an Act, it is not bound by that Act."

He was watching the King's face and his spirits dropped. Was he about to hear that the island was to be seized from him? With a sort of desperation he added swiftly, "In consideration of this, Your Majesty would not take from me that which my ancestors and I have enjoyed by gift of our gracious Kings ever since the seventh year of the reign of King Henry the Fourth?"

He was feeling ill suddenly, breathless. The King considered his Act of Indemnity did cover the Isle of Mann and, therefore, the Earl of Derby had disobeyed his sovereign.

"You must realise that I am very sensitive to the promises I made on ascending the throne of England," said the King sternly to the Earl who was now slumped in his seat. "Wholesale accusations and trials could only impair the peace I am determined to create. Should I allow you to go unpunished then others would expect to be treated in the same way. Had you been any other man it would have meant a long term of imprisonment, but I do have to bear in mind the loyalty of your gallant father who gave his life in my cause. In addition to entire restitution being made to the widow and her children, you will pay certain damages to those you have deprived of their kinsman."

One of the Judges then addressed the Deemsters. The offices they had usurped from William's son and grandson would be restored and the offenders would be heavily fined and also consigned to the prison of the King's Bench. Norris and Cannell exchanged glances; both were seething because they had merely acted upon orders from the Earl. The Judge went on,

"The three members of the 'pretended' Court of Justice which illegally tried and sentenced William Christian shall also be heavily fined and imprisoned, when they can spend much time in thinking over what they have done to an innocent gentleman."

The Earl glanced their way. Three Richards: Stevenson, Colcall and Tyldesley. Men who had served him well, men easily bribed...

The next and last was the Deputy-Governor, Henry Nowell who was ordered to be committed to remain in prison until proceeded against in the cause of justice.

"To the end," continued the Judge, "the guilt of the blood which hath been unjustly spilt, may in some way be expiated, and His Majesty receive some kind of satisfaction for the untimely loss of a subject."

The King nodded in agreement of all this, then turned to look at George, William's son.

"How did your father die?"

"Bravely, sire. The Earl's soldiers desired to bind him as he stood on the spot where he was to die, looking across at the house we all loved, Ronaldsway. My father pushed the soldiers away, saying he was not afraid of their bullets for they could not deprive him of his courage."

"Well said!" applauded the King, while the Earl of Derby wiped the froth from his mouth with his lace cuff. "You have reason to be proud of your father." He was thinking of the younger children and how happy they would be to have their home restored to them and their mother. It made him feel good – yes, this had been a fine day's work. He was also in agreement with the plea of William's wife having been listened to: that her husband be not hanged, drawn and quartered, as the Earl would have liked, but that he be allowed a less painful and degrading death. He glanced at the Earl. He looked unhealthy. He would never make old bones, he decided. Turning again to George he asked, "What else about your father? Did he pray before he was shot?"

"Yes, Your Majesty, he did, and he asked the Almighty's blessing for the people of our isle. Then he asked for a piece of paper—"

"Paper?" echoed the King, puzzled. "To write upon?"

"No, Your Majesty, to hold against his heart, and so he directed the soldiers in their aim, telling them to hit this paper, and – and n–not miss..." He was suddenly choked up and murmured, "I am sorry, sire."

"It is understandable," returned Charles kindly, and he added as the idea occurred to him, "It could well be that your brave parent will be revered in the island – become a national hero, in fact." He cast a glance at Lord Derby and before he could continue Clarendon was whispering in his ear,

"He is gnashing his teeth."

"That," submitted the King smoothly, "was what I said it for, to humiliate him and to have him vex himself over the matter until the day he dies."

George said rather diffidently,

"Already, Your Majesty, people are regarding my father as a hero and a martyr."

Several heads were nodding. Derby went red in the face. How much longer had he to endure this before these proceedings were declared closed!

But he was to be further humiliated by the King's saying, his voice harshly censorious,

"We recall that you were a great trial to your parents, that you had to flee to Holland because of some serious misdemeanour you wantonly committed. Well, I now advise you to try to make amends and to live as your noble father would have wished for his son and heir. Go to your little kingdom and devote your life to the improvement of the people's lot, for I hear they are in a sorry plight. Had you been there at that crucial time when your father was away fighting for me, then none of this would have happened, since you yourself would have been in charge. An overlord is not there merely to collect taxes; he has obligations to his subjects. So take my advice and see to your duties."

Go and live on the isle! The Earl's lip curled. He could find something better to do than spend his time trying to tame those rebels! So long as the revenues kept coming in his officers could run the island for him.

*

Twilight was falling over a snow-covered landscape and already every window in Kingsley Hall was glowing. It was the eve of Christmas and Eleanor was sitting by the fire, her lace shawl drawn tightly about her shoulders.

Christmas... yet another and she was still here... with so many of her friends gone. Ah, but she was so tired! She managed, however, to produce a smile as her daughter came in carrying her very new granddaughter. A golden little lass who would have all her great-grandmother's beauty and charm, so all the family had declared two months ago when she was born, over at Kingsley Hall, where the widowed Susanna now lived, with her eldest son who had come to England with her five years ago on the death of her husband. Ned managed the estate, Rob being retired and living contentedly in the cottage which Eleanor had given to him.

Susanna bent to allow the baby to receive a kiss.

"I am about to take her across, darling, but I knew you would want to kiss her before I do so."

Eleanor kissed the rosy cheek... but she was kissing another, her lovely little daughter... So long ago.

"She is a bright child – so wide awake. But I am not wide awake. I want to sleep..."

"Are you cold, love?" asked Susanna concernedly. "You shivered."

"I am tired, Susanna, so very, very tired. Life has become a weary burden to me."

Susanna straightened up, biting her lip. Her mother was eighty-seven years old and this was by no means the first time she had spoken like this. Hiding her sudden depression Susanna said brightly,

"As you are tired, dearest, I shall keep everyone away from this room for an hour or so. It is no use my suggesting you go to your bedchamber because you are a stubborn lady. Have a quiet rest before you go up to get ready. Bertha will be up to help you dress. Wear that lovely mantua we bought for you in Chester – you know the one I mean, the one with the full skirt and pleated bodice."

"I know the one, my dear. I shall not let you down, not when you have gone to all this trouble. I shall make an entrance like a queen."

"You are a queen! Bless you. And now I must away and get this child to its nursemaid; it is coming up to her bedtime."

Her mother gave a small sigh, although she endeavoured to appear interested as she asked how many of the family Susanna had gathered together for this party, which was being held at Deva Place.

"Twenty-two! Was it not clever of me?"

"Very." Faintly her mother smiled. Yes, she loved them all, but did she really want twenty-two of them around her all at once? She frowned suddenly and said in a vague sort of way,

"Twenty-two? I had no idea... I believed it to be nineteen, and that was counting you all, including the new babe."

"Three are from the Isle of Mann. It was to be a surprise. They are John, Father's great-nephew—"

"The John Christian to whom Edward left Poyll Dhouie?" The seventh Earl had managed to seize Lough Mollo when he imprisoned his ex-Governor but by some oversight he had not confiscated Poyll Dhouie and as Eleanor had no desire that it should be left to her, it had come to the grandson of Edward's elder brother, John, who was farming it with his son, Edmond. "So he is to be here. That will be nice."

But would it? More memories revived...

"And Edmond and Margaret are coming with him."

"Ah..." Poyll Dhouie, where she had stayed on that fateful night when dear Alicia was ravished. Alicia had died more than ten years ago. "And I am still here..."

Eleanor heard the door close and she breathed a sigh of relief. She desired only to be alone, to rest – Why had her legs become so weak? Until a month ago she was able to walk along by the river each day, her faithful King Charles spaniel trotting happily by her side, but for the past three weeks she had managed only to get as far as the seat a short distance away where she would remain for an hour or so, as she had no wish that her family should become anxious about her.

A log slipped, showering the panelled room with an amber glow as stars flew up into the massive chimney. She felt cosy and warm now, in this Tudor manor to which her beloved Edward had brought her sixty-five years ago. So much had happened as the years raced by. How long was it since her lover died in her arms in that prison on St Patrick's Isle? Her mind did let her down these days, she thought irritably. Why these lapses of memory—? Wait, though, yes, it was almost twenty-six years ago.

"And I am still here... it is just as Edward said, I have lived to be very old."

So many dead; so many memories drifting back. It had been a long, tortuous journey through her life. There had been blissful periods with interludes of anguish, and at one time the beguiling temptation to lie down and die. This was when her Edward was condemned to dwell for life in that gaunt grey prison to where he had been sent by envy and hate.

But with time all passes; with the sunrise comes light. And in the end... what was it all about?

The fire was a red glow now and the room had darkened. She liked it this way and would sit here all night if she could, but there was the party... Susanna had wanted to arrange it for her birthday but she had said birthdays meant nothing to her any more. So, intent on bringing the whole family together on some occasion Susanna had arranged it for Christmas, knowing her mother could make no objections to that.

Visions drifting into her memory. Deemster Ewan, patriot and her dear friend; his son who had died so bravely, murdered because of vengeance and greed. But the perpetrator of the heinous crime was punished by a long painful illness to which he succumbed at the age of forty-four... but it was said that his son was carrying on the persecution of the Manx people.

More visions, more ghosts... Sweet Susanna who had left so many grieving hearts behind her. She would have been happy to know that Eleanor's daughter was named after her, and that now another, this two-month-old babe was to have her name. They had asked Eleanor to choose the name.

Eleanor dozed but was awakened by Rascal, her dog, jumping up on to her knee.

"You consider I have neglected you too long?" She stroked his silky fur and he licked her hand. He was old, a gift from Rob whose hobby it was to breed dogs now that he was retired. Rob had a homely wife and two fine sons and a daughter. And when John died and left her everything he owned she had made the cottage over to Rob and his wife. Kingsley Hall was unoccupied for over a year because on John's death Eleanor had been persuaded to move back to Deva Place and live with her son and Virginia. Both were dead now and Ned, their eldest son, had inherited the lovely mansion where Eleanor was still treated as if she were the mistress.

The snow was dropping more thickly now and all without was blanketed and a little depressing in spite of the twinkling lights in the house across the river. The trees looked forlorn – that tall ash wherein a thrush seemed always to be singing in the summertime, singing from dawn to dusk. What pleasure he had given her and Edward when of an evening they would sit in the arbour and be so at peace with each other and the world outside.

"Edward..." She leant back after dropping her shawl from her shoulders. It was getting far too warm in here. Her mind began once more to wander and the ghosts went drifting by again. She was with John... John who had loved her for so long. She smiled now and felt at peace because she had made him happy – oh, so happy, giving him a love so very different from that which she gave to Edward. John had died in her arms, a contented smile on his lips. How long? She was suddenly irritable again at her loss of memory. Ah, yes, it was almost seven years. She had given him eighteen years of happiness and they had grown old together. He left everything he owned to Eleanor, even the property in the south of England. This was now in the possession of Richard, one of Eleanor's grandsons to whom she gave it as a wedding present. Her mind went back for a mere second to that hovel. Little had she known at that time that she would provide so well for her children and their children. And she had even provided for the new babe.

The door opened silently and she looked around. It was Bertha with a tea tray.

"Some refreshment, Mistress Eleanor." The maid brought up a small table and the tray was placed upon it. "We decided you must have something as the party is not till two hours or more. We are all going to sing in the hall first and that is when you will make your entrance." She was young and enthusiastic, unable to believe yet in her good fortune at having been engaged as maid by the lady Susanna whom she adored... but not quite as much as she adored her mother. "I am to help you to dress, and you will be beautiful in the mantua!"

"Which is far too young for me. You all conspired. I am a very old lady..."

"Not in heart, madam. You are – now what did Thomas say? Oh, yes, that his grandmother was ageless."

"He is a flatterer, you all are. Now be off; I was dreaming and you interrupted me."

"Pleasant dreams?" The girl's eyes twinkled. She is a saucy lass! thought Eleanor, but she does bring a ray of light into a room.

Bertha left as silently as she had come. Eleanor drew thin fingers through her sparse white hair and leant back against the cushions. The fire was sending up golden flames as another log moved, and more light was added to the candleglow; and still the old lady sat there, the tea gone cold, forgotten. She felt so at peace all at once, and gave a sigh of blissful contentment. Her face in repose had a sort of gentle nobility about it, and the beauty that even deep lines and wrinkled skin could not erase. She was suddenly floating above all the struggles and sadness, the hopes and the fears. Detached from the earth, she felt herself to be suspended in a vacuum, where perfect peace was.

Into these heights a face appeared, that of a young and lusty lover, pirate, brigand, rebel, laughing at her with those vivid blue eyes. He beckoned, knowing she was ready at last. Was it the soft hissing of the sap escaping from the logs, or had she really heard the whisper: "My little sweeting..."

A lovely smile broke, but she said apologetically,

"I am not ready, dearest, not *quite*, that is. You see, I have to dress up and make an entrance, so as not to disappoint our daughter. You do understand? No, you do *not* understand? But—" She pressed a hand to her heart... not a pain exactly, but a little flutter that was taking her breath away.

Rascal lifted his head to look at her. He whined and placed a paw upon her lap.

www.ingramcontent.com/pod-product-compliance
Lightning Source LLC
Chambersburg PA
CBHW071850020726
47502CB00003B/687